ALSO BY ANNE TYLER

If Morning Ever Comes (1964)

The Tin Can Tree (1965)

A Slipping-Down Life (1970)

The Clock Winder (1972)

Celestial Navigation (1974)

Searching for Caleb (1976)

Earthly Possessions (1977)

THESE ARE BORZOI BOOKS,
PUBLISHED IN NEW YORK BY
ALFRED A. KNOPF.

MORGAN'S PASSING

Anne Tyler

MORGAN'S
PASSING

ALFRED A. KNOPF
NEW YORK 1980

THIS IS A BORZOI BOOK
PUBLISHED BY ALFRED A. KNOPF, INC.

LIBRARY OF CONGRESS CATALOGING IN PUBLICATION DATA
Tyler, Anne.   Morgan's passing.   I. Title.
PZ4.T979MO   1980   [PS3570.Y45]   813'.5'4
ISBN 0-394-50958-7   79-20272

Manufactured in the United States of America

MORGAN'S
PASSING

1967

There used to be an Easter Fair at the Presbyterian church every year. Early Saturday morning the long, gentle hill out front would be taken over by tents, painted booths, mechanical rides on lease from the Happy Days Amusement Company, and large wooden carts slowly filling up their windows with buttered popcorn. A white rabbit, six feet tall, would bow in a dignified way as he passed out jellybeans from a basket. In the afternoon there would be an egg hunt behind the Sunday School building, and the winner was given a chocolate chicken. Music floated everywhere, strung-out wisps of one song weaving into another. The air always smelled like cotton candy.

But the Baltimore climate was unpredictable. Sometimes it was really too cold for a fair. One year, when Easter fell in March, so little was growing yet that the egg hunt was a joke. The eggs lay exposed and foolish on the bald brown lawn, and children pounced on them with mittened hands. The grownups stood hunched in sweaters and scarves. They seemed to have strayed in from the wrong season. It would have been a better fair with no human beings at all—just the striped tents flapping their spring-colored scallops, the carousel playing "After the Ball," and the plaster horses prancing around riderless.

At the puppet show, in a green and white tent lit by a chilly greenish glow, Cinderella wore a strapless evening gown that made her audience shiver. She was a glove puppet with a large, round head and braids of yellow yarn. At the moment she was dancing with the Prince, who had a Dutch Boy haircut. They held each other so fondly, it was hard to remember they were really just two hands clasping each other. "You have a beautiful palace," she told him. "The floors are like mirrors! I wonder who scrubs them."

Her voice was wry and throaty, not at all puppet-like. You almost expected to see the vapor rising from her painted mouth.

The Prince said, "I have no idea, Miss . . . what was that name?"

Instead of answering, she looked down at her feet. The pause grew too long. The children shifted in their folding chairs. It became apparent that the ballroom was not a ballroom at all, but a gigantic cardboard carton with the front cut away and a gauze curtain at the rear. A child in the audience said, "I have to go to the bathroom."

"Ssh."

"Your name," said the Prince.

Why didn't she speak?

Really, the children saw, she was only a puppet. They sat back. Something had snapped. Even the parents looked confused.

Then Cinderella flopped onto her face in a very unnatural way, and a human hand emerged from her skirts and withdrew behind the scrim. The children stared. On the stage lay her dead and empty shell, with her arms flung back as if broken. "Is it over?" a child asked his mother.

"Hush. Sit still. You know that's not how it ends."

"Well, where's the rest, then? Can we go?"

"Wait. Here comes someone."

It was a grownup, but just barely. He felt his way through the bedsheet that hung at one side of the stage: a dark, thin boy in khakis and a rust-colored corduroy jacket, with a white shirt so old and well washed that all the life had gone out of it. There was something fierce about him—maybe the twist of his mouth, or the defiant way he kept his chin raised. "Ladies and gentlemen," he said, running a hand through his hair. "Boys and girls . . ."

"It's the Prince," said a child.

"Boys and girls, there's been . . . an illness. The play is over. You can get your money at the ticket booth."

He turned away, not even waiting to see how this would be taken, and fumbled at the sheet. But then he seemed struck by another thought, and he turned back to the audience. "Excuse me," he said. He ran a hand through his hair again. (No wonder it was so mussed and ropy.) "Is there a doctor in the house?" he asked.

They looked at each other—children, mostly, and most of them under five. Apparently there was no doctor. The boy gave a sudden, sharp sigh and lifted a corner of the sheet. Then someone at the rear of the tent stood up.

"I am a doctor," he said.

He was a lank, tall, bearded man in a shaggy brown suit that might have been cut from blankets, and on his head he wore a red ski cap—the pointy kind, with a pom-pom at the tip. Masses of black curls burst out from under it. His beard was so wild and black and bushy that it was hard to tell how old he was. Maybe forty? Forty-five? At any rate, older than you'd expect to see at a puppet show, and no child sat next to him to explain his being there. But he craned his head forward, smiling kindly, leading with his long, pinched nose and waiting to hear how he could help. The boy looked relieved; his face lost some of its tension.

"Come with me," he said. He lifted the sheet higher.

Stumbling over people's feet, sidling past the children who were already swarming toward the exit, the doctor made his way to the boy. He wiped his palms on his thighs and stooped under the sheet. "What seems to be the trouble here?" he asked.

"It's her," said the boy.

He meant the blond girl resting on a heap of muslin bags. She was small-boned and frail, but enormously pregnant, and she sat cradling her stomach—guarding it, looking up at the doctor out of level gray eyes. Her lips were so colorless, they were almost invisible.

"I see," said the doctor.

He dropped down beside her, hitching up his trousers at the knees, and leaned forward to set a hand on her abdomen. There was a pause. He frowned at the tent wall, weighing something in his mind. "Yes," he said finally. He sat back and studied the girl's face. "How far apart are the pains?" he asked.

"All the time," she said, in Cinderella's wry voice.

"Constantly? When did they begin?"

"About . . . an hour ago, Leon? When we were setting up for this performance."

The doctor raised his eyebrows—two black thickets.

"It would be exceedingly strange," he said, "if they were so close together this soon."

"Well, they are," the girl said matter-of-factly.

The doctor stood up, grunting a little, and dusted off his knees. "Oh, well," he said, "just to be on the safe side, I suppose you ought to check into the hospital. Where's your car parked?"

"We don't have one," the boy said.

"No car?"

The doctor looked around him, as if wondering how all their equipment had arrived—the bulky stage, the heap of little costumes, the liquor carton in the corner with a different puppet's head poking out of each cardboard compartment.

"Mr. Kenny brought us," said the boy, "in his panel truck. He's chairman of the Fund-Raising Committee."

"You'd better come with me, then," the doctor said. "I'll drive you over." He seemed fairly cheerful about it. He said, "What about the puppets? Shall we take them along?"

"No," said the boy. "What do I care about the puppets? Let's just get her to the hospital."

"Suit yourself," the doctor told him, but he cast another glance around, as if regretting a lost opportunity, before he bent to help the boy raise the girl to her feet. "What are they made of?" he asked.

"Huh?" said the boy. "Oh, just . . . things." He handed the girl her purse. "Emily makes them," he added.

"Emily?"

"This is Emily, my wife. I'm Leon Meredith."

"How do you do?" the doctor said.

"They're made of rubber balls," said Emily.

Standing, she turned out to be even slighter than she'd first appeared. She walked gracefully, leading the men out through the front of the tent, smiling at the few stray children who remained. Her draggled black skirt hung unevenly around her shins. Her thin white cardigan, dotted with specks of black lint, didn't begin to close over the bulge of her stomach.

"I take an ordinary, dimestore rubber ball," she said, "and cut a neck hole with my knife. Then I cover the ball with a nylon stocking, and I sew on eyes and a nose, paint a mouth, make hair of some kind . . ."

Her voice grew strained. The doctor glanced over at her, sharply.

"The cheapest kind of stockings are the best," she said. "They're pinker. From a distance, they look more like skin."

"Is this going to be a long walk?" Leon asked.

"No, no," said the doctor. "My car's in the main parking lot."

"Maybe we should call an ambulance."

"Really, that won't be necessary," the doctor said.

"But what if the baby comes before we get to the hospital?"

"Believe me," said the doctor, "if I thought there was the faintest chance of that, I wouldn't be doing this. I have no desire whatever to deliver a baby in a Pontiac."

"Lord, no," Leon said, and he cast a sideways look at the doctor's hands, which didn't seem quite clean. "But Emily claims it's arriving any minute."

"It is," Emily said calmly. She was walking along between them now, climbing the slope to the parking lot unassisted. She supported the weight of her baby as if it were already separate from her. Her battered leather pocketbook swung from her shoulder. In the sunlight her hair, which was bound on her head in two silvery braids, sprang up in little corkscrewed wisps like metal filings flying toward a magnet, and her skin looked chilled and thin and pale. But her eyes remained level. She didn't appear to be frightened. She met the doctor's gaze squarely. "I can feel it," she told him.

"Is this your first?"

"Yes."

"Ah, then," he said, "you see, it can't possibly come so soon. It'll be late tonight at the earliest—maybe even tomorrow. Why, you haven't been in labor more than an hour!"

"Maybe, and maybe not," said Emily.

Then she gave a sudden, surprising toss of her head; she threw the doctor a tilted look. "After all," she said, "I've had a backache since two o'clock this morning. Maybe I just didn't *know* it was labor."

Leon turned to the doctor, who seemed to hesitate a moment. "Doctor?" Leon said.

"All my patients say their babies are coming immediately," the doctor told him. "It never happens."

They had reached the flinty white gravel of the parking lot. Various people passed—some just arriving, holding down their coats against the wind; others leaving with balloons and crying children and cardboard flats of shivering tomato seedlings.

"Are you warm enough?" Leon asked Emily. "Do you want my jacket?"

"I'm fine," Emily said, although beneath her cardigan she wore only a skimpy black T-shirt, and her legs were bare and her shoes were ballet slippers, thin as paper.

"You must be freezing," Leon said.

"I'm all *right*, Leon."

"It's the adrenalin," the doctor said absently. He came to a stop and gazed off across the parking lot, stroking his beard. "I seem to have lost my car," he said.

Leon said, "Oh, God."

"No, there it is. Never mind."

His car was clearly a family man's—snub-nosed, outdated, with a frayed red hair ribbon flying from the antenna and WASH THIS! written in the dust on one fender. Inside, there were schoolbooks and dirty socks and gym bloomers and rucked-up movie magazines. The doctor knelt on the front seat and swatted at the clutter in the rear until most of it had landed on the floor. Then he said, "There you go. You two sit in back; you'll be more comfortable." He settled himself in front and started the engine, which had a whining, circular sound. Emily and Leon slid into the rear. Emily found a track shoe under her right knee, and she placed it on her lap, cupping the heel and toe in her fingers. "Now," said the doctor. "Which hospital?"

Emily and Leon looked at each other.

"City? University? Hopkins?"

"Whatever's closest," Leon said.

"But which have you reserved? Where's your doctor?"

"We haven't reserved anyplace," Emily said, "and we don't have a doctor."

"I see."

"*Anywhere*," said Leon. "Just get her there."

"Very well."

The doctor maneuvered his car out of the parking space. He shifted gears with a grinding sound. Leon said, "I guess we should have attended to this earlier."

"Yes, actually," said the doctor. He braked and looked in both directions. Then he nosed the car into the stream of traffic on Farley Street. They were traveling through a new, raw section barely within the city limits—ranch houses, tree-less lawns, another church, a shopping mall. "But I suppose you lead a footloose sort of life," the doctor said.

"Footloose?"

"Carefree. Unattached," he said. He patted all his pockets with one hand until he'd found a pack of Camels. He shook a cigarette free and lit it, which involved so much fumbling and cursing and clutching at dropped objects that it was a wonder the other drivers managed to stay clear of him. When he'd finally flicked his match out, he exhaled a great cloud of smoke and started coughing. The Pontiac wandered from lane to lane. He thumped his chest and said, "I suppose you just follow the fairs, am I correct? Just follow the festivities, stop wherever you find yourselves."

"No, what happened was—"

"But I wish we could have brought along the puppets," the doctor said. He turned onto a wider street. He was forced to slow down now, inching past furniture shops and carpet ware-houses, trailing a mammoth Mayflower van that blocked all view of what lay ahead. "Are we coming to a traffic light?" he asked. "Is it red or green? I can't see a thing. And what about their noses, the puppets' noses? How'd you make the stepmother's nose? Was it a carrot?"

"Excuse me?" Emily said. "Nose?" She didn't seem to be concentrating. "I'm sorry," she said. "There's some kind of water all over everything."

The doctor braked and looked in the rear-view mirror. His eyes met Leon's. "Can't you hurry?" Leon asked him.

"I *am* hurrying," the doctor said.

He took another puff of his cigarette, pinching it between his thumb and forefinger. The air in the car grew blue and layered. Up ahead, the Mayflower van was trying to make a left turn. It would take all day, at this rate. "Honk," Leon said. The doctor honked. Then he clamped his cigarette in his teeth and swung out into the right-hand lane, where a car coming up fast behind nearly slammed into them. Now horns were blowing everywhere. The doctor started humming. He pulled back into the left lane, set his left-turn signal blinking, and sped toward the next traffic light, which hung beside a swinging sign that read NO LEFT TURN. His cigarette had a long, trembly tube of ashes hanging from it. He tapped the ashes onto the floor, the steering wheel, his lap. "*After the ball is o-ver,*" he sang. He careened to the right again and cut across the apron of a Citgo station, took a sharp left, and emerged on the street he wanted. "*After the break of morn . . .*" Leon gripped the back of the front seat with one hand and held on to Emily with the other. Emily gazed out the side window.

"I always go to fairs, any fair in town," the doctor said. "School fairs, church fairs, Italian fairs, Ukrainian . . . I like the food. I also like the rides; I like to watch the people who run them. What would it be like, working for such an outfit? I used to take my daughters, but they're too old now, they say. 'How can that be?' I ask them. 'I'm not too old; how come you are?' My youngest is barely ten. How can she be too old?"

"The baby's here," Emily said.

"I beg your pardon?"

"The baby. I feel it."

The doctor looked in the mirror again. His eyes were more aged than the rest of him—a mournful brown, bloodshot and pouched, the skin beneath them the tarnished color of a bruise inside a banana. He opened his mouth, or appeared to. At any rate, his beard lengthened. Then it shortened again.

"Stop the car," Leon told him.

"Well . . . ah, yes, maybe so," the doctor said.

He parked beside a hydrant, in front of a tiny pizza parlor called Maria's Home-Style. Leon was chafing Emily's wrists. The doctor climbed out, scratching the curls beneath his ski cap and looking puzzled. "Excuse me," he said to Leon. Leon got out of the car. The doctor leaned in and asked, "You say you feel it?"

"I feel the head."

"Of course this is all a mistake," the doctor told Leon. "You know how long it takes the average primipara to deliver? Between ten and twelve hours. Oh, at least. And with a great deal more carrying on, believe me. There's not a chance in this world that baby could be here yet."

But as he spoke, he was sliding Emily into a horizontal position on the seat, methodically folding back her damp skirt in a series of tidy pleats. He said, "What in the name of—?" It appeared that her T-shirt was some sort of leotard; it had a crotch. He grimaced and ripped the center seam. Then he said, "She's right."

"Well, *do* something," Leon said. "What are you going to do?"

"Go buy some newspapers," the doctor told him. "Anything will be fine—*News American, Sun* . . . but fresh ones, you understand? Don't just accept what someone hands you in a diner, saying he's finished reading it . . ."

"Oh, my God. Oh, my God. I don't have change," Leon said.

The doctor started rummaging through his pockets. He pulled out his mangled pack of Camels, two lint-covered jellybeans, and a cylinder of Rolaids. "Emily," he said, "would you happen to have change for a dollar?"

Emily said something that sounded like yes, and turned her head from side to side. "Try her purse," the doctor said. They felt along the floor, among the gym clothes and soda straws. Leon brought up the purse by its strap. He plowed through it till he found a billfold, and then he raced off down the street, muttering, "Newspapers. Newspapers." It was a cheerful, jumbled street with littered sidewalks and a row of tiny shops—eating places, dry cleaners, florists. In front of one of the cafés were various newspapers in locked, windowed boxes.

The doctor stepped on his cigarette and ground it into the pavement. Then he took off his suit jacket. He rolled up his sleeves and tucked his shirt more firmly into his trousers. He bent inside the car and laid a palm on Emily's abdomen. "Breathe high in your chest," he told her. He gazed dreamily past her, humming under his breath, watching the trucks and buses rumble by through the opposite window. The cold air caused the dark hairs to bristle on his forearms.

A woman in high heels clopped down the sidewalk; she never even noticed what was going on. Then two teenaged girls approached, sharing fudge from a white paper sack. Their footsteps slowed, and the doctor heard and turned around. "You two!" he said. "Go call an ambulance. Tell them we've got a delivery on our hands."

They stared at him. Identical cubes of fudge were poised halfway to their mouths.

"Well?" he said. "Go on."

When they had rushed into Maria's Home-Style, the doctor turned back to Emily. "How're you doing?" he asked her.

She groaned.

Leon returned, out of breath, with a stack of newspapers. The doctor opened them out and started spreading them under Emily and all around her. "Now, these," he said conversationally, "will grant us some measure of antisepsis." Leon didn't seem to be listening. The doctor wrapped two newspapers around Emily's thighs. She began to blend in with the car. He hung a sports section down the back of the seat and anchored it to the window ledge with the track shoe she'd been holding all this time.

"Next," he said, "I'll need two strips of cloth, two inches wide and six inches long. Tear off your shirttail, Leon."

"I want to quit," Emily said.

"Quit?"

"I've changed my mind."

The cook came out of Maria's Home-Style. He was a large man in an apron stained with tomato sauce. For a moment he watched Leon, who was standing by the car in nothing but his jeans, shakily tugging at his shirttail. (Leon's ribs showed and his shoulder blades were as sharp as chicken wings. He was much too young for all this.) The cook reached over and took the shirt and ripped it for him. "Thanks," said Leon.

"But what's the use of it?" the cook asked.

"He wants two strips of cloth," said Leon, "two inches wide and six inches long. *I* don't know why."

The cook tore again, following instructions. He gave the shirt to Leon and passed the strips to the doctor, who hung them carefully on the inner door handle. Then the cook propped a wide, meaty hand on the car roof and bent in to nod at Emily. "Afternoon," he said.

"Hello," said Emily politely.

"How you doing?"

"Oh, just fine."

"Seems like he wants to come on and get born," the cook said, "and then he wants to go back in a ways."

"Will you get out of here?" Leon said.

The cook let this pass. "Those two girls you sent are calling the ambulance," he told the doctor. "They're using my free phone."

"Good," the doctor said. He cupped the baby's head in his hands—a dark, wet, shining bulge. "Now, Emily, bear down," he said. "Maria, press flat on her belly, just a steady, slow pressure, please."

"Soo now, soo now," the cook said, pressing. Leon crouched on the curb, gnawing a knuckle, his shirt back on but not buttoned. Behind them, a little crowd had gathered. The teenaged girls stood hushed, forgetting to dip into their fudge sack. A man was asking everyone if an ambulance had been called. An old woman was telling a younger one all about someone named Dexter, who had been a breech birth with multiple complications.

"Bear down," said the doctor.

There was a silence. Even the traffic noises seemed to have stopped.

Then the doctor stepped back, holding up a slippery, bleak lump. Something moved. There was a small, caught sound from someplace unexpected. So fast it seemed that everyone had been looking away when it happened, the lump turned into a wailing, writhing, frantic, indignant snarl of red arms and legs and spiraled telephone cord. "Oh," the crowd said, breathing again.

"It's a girl," said the doctor. He passed her to the cook. "Was a girl what you wanted?"

"Anything! Anything!" the cook said. "So long as she's healthy. Soo, baby."

"I was talking to Emily," the doctor said mildly. He had to raise his voice above the baby's, which was surprisingly loud. He bent over Emily, pressing her abdomen now with both palms. "Emily? Are you all right? Bear down again, please."

While he pressed, she couldn't get air to speak, but the instant he let up she said, "I'm fine, and I'd like my daughter."

The cook seemed reluctant to hand her over. He rocked the baby against his apron, thought a moment, and sighed. Then he gave her to the doctor. The doctor checked her breathing passages—the mashed-looking nose, the squalling cavern of a mouth. "With such a racket, how could she not be fine?" he asked, and he leaned in to lay her in Emily's arms. Emily nestled the baby's head against her shoulder, but the wailing went on, thin and passionate, with a hiccup at the end of each breath.

"What'd you do with those cloths?" the doctor asked Leon.

Leon was standing up now, so as to get a glimpse of the baby. Something kept tugging his lips into a smile that he kept trying to bat down again. "Cloths?" he said.

"Those cloths you tore, dammit. We're nowhere near done here yet."

"You hung them on the door handle," someone in the crowd said.

"Oh, yes," said the doctor.

He took one cloth, leaned in, and tied it around the baby's cord. For all the blunt, clumsy look of his fingers, he did seem to know what he was doing. *"After the ball is over,"* he sang in his beard-blurred voice. While he was knotting the second cloth, a faraway cry started up. It sounded like an extension of the baby's cry—equally thin, watery-sounding in the wind. Then it separated and grew more piercing. "The ambulance!" Leon said. "I hear the ambulance, Emily."

"Send it back," Emily said.

"They're going to take you to the hospital, honey. You're going to be all right now."

"But it's over! Do I have to go?" she asked the doctor.

"Certainly," he said. He stepped back to admire his knots, which looked something like the little cloth bows on a kite tail. "Actually," he said, "they're coming in the nick of time. I have nothing to cut the cord with."

"You could use my Swiss Army officer's knife," she told him. "It's in my purse. It's the Woodsman style, with a scissors blade."

"Remarkable," said the doctor, and he rocked on his heels, beaming down at her. His teeth seemed very large and yellow behind the tangled beard.

The siren drew closer. A spinning red light wove through the traffic, and the ambulance screeched to a halt beside the doctor's car. Two men in white leaped out. "Where is she?" one asked.

"Here we are," the doctor called.

The men flung open the back doors of the ambulance and brought a stretcher crashing to the street—a wheeled bed, too long and narrow, like a coffin, with too much chrome. Emily struggled to a sitting position. The baby stopped in mid-cry, as if shocked. "Do I have to do this?" Emily asked the doctor. And while the attendants were helping her out of the car (chairing her onto the stretcher, newspapers and all), she kept her face turned toward the doctor and waited to be rescued. "Doctor? I can't stand hospitals! Do I have to go?"

Of course," the doctor told her. He stooped for her purse and laid it on the stretcher.

"Is Leon coming too?"

"Certainly he's coming."

"Are *you?*"

"Me? Oh."

"Best if you would, Doc," the driver told him, unfolding a sheet over Emily.

"Well, if you like," the doctor said.

He closed his car door and followed the stretcher into the ambulance. There was another stretcher, empty, next to Emily's. He and Leon sat on it—both of them gingerly, just on the edge, with their knees jutting out. "Pretty fancy," the doctor said to Leon. He meant, presumably, the interior of the ambulance: the deeply carpeted floor, the gleaming tanks and gauges. When the men slammed the doors shut, there was a sudden, luxurious silence. The street noises faded, and through the tinted windows the people on the sidewalk seemed as soundless and slow-moving as creatures on the ocean floor. They slid away. A café and a pawnshop glided past. Even the siren was muffled, like something on an old-fashioned radio.

"How're you feeling?" the doctor asked Emily.

"Fine," she said. She lay still, in a tangle of loosened braids. The baby stared severely at the ceiling.

"We really appreciate all you've done," Leon told the doctor.

"It was nothing," said the doctor, turning down the corners of his mouth. He seemed displeased.

"If Emily didn't have this thing about hospitals, we'd have made our arrangements sooner, I guess. But the baby wasn't due for another couple of weeks. We just kept putting it off."

"And I suppose you were on the move so much," the doctor said.

"No, no—"

"But the style of your lives: I don't imagine you can plan very far ahead."

"You have the wrong idea about us," Emily said.

Flattened on the stretcher, with the crisp sheet covering the newspapers and her sodden skirt, Emily seemed untouched, somehow—pristine and remote, with her gaze turned inward. "You think we're some kind of transients," she said, "but we're not. We're legally married, and we live in a regular apartment with furniture. This baby was fully planned for. We're even going to have a diaper service. I've already called to set it up, and they said to let them know when she came and they'd start delivery promptly."

"I see," said the doctor, nodding. He appeared to be enjoying this. The disorderly beard flew up and down, and the pom-pom on his ski cap bobbed.

"We've planned out every detail," Emily said. "We didn't buy a crib because cribs are extraneous. We're using a cardboard box for now, with padding on the insides."

"Oh, wonderful," said the doctor, looking delighted.

"When she gets too big for the box, we'll order this aluminum youth-bed rail we happened to see in a catalog. You can fit it onto any mattress. What's the point in all that equipment—cribs and strollers and Bathinettes? Besides, the youth-bed rail will even work in hotels and other people's apartments. It travels well."

"Travels, yes," the doctor echoed, and he clamped his hands between his knees, leaning with the ambulance as it sped around a curve.

"But we're not . . . I mean, it's only that we travel to give shows sometimes. There'll be someone wanting 'Snow White' or 'Cinderella' somewhere outside the city. But we're almost always home by night. We're never *shiftless*. You have the wrong idea."

"Did I say you were shiftless?" the doctor asked. He looked over at Leon. "Did I?"

Leon shrugged.

"We've thought of everything," Emily said.

"Yes, I see you have," the doctor said gently.

Leon cleared his throat. "By the way," he said, "we haven't discussed your fee."

"Fee?"

"For your services."

"Oh, emergency services aren't charged for," the doctor said. "Don't you know that?"

"No," said Leon.

He and the doctor seemed to be trying to stare each other down. Leon lifted his chin even higher. The light caught his cheekbones. He was one of those people who appear to be continually ready to take offense—jaw fixed, shoulders tight. "I'm not accepting this for free," he said.

"Who says it's free?" the doctor asked. "I expect you to name your baby for me." He laughed—a wheeze that ruffled his beard.

"What's your name?" Emily asked him.

"Morgan," said the doctor.

There was a silence.

"*Gower* Morgan," he said.

Emily said, "Maybe we could use the initials."

"I was only joking," the doctor told her. "Didn't you know I was joking?" He fumbled for his Camels and shook one out of the pack. "It was meant to be a joke," he said.

"About the fee," said Leon.

The doctor took his cigarette from his mouth and peered at the sign on the oxygen tank. "The fact is," he said, replacing the cigarette in its pack, "I had nothing better to do today. My wife and daughters have gone to a wedding; my wife's brother is getting married again." He clutched Leon's shoulder as they turned a corner. The ambulance was rolling up a driveway now. They passed a sign reading EMERGENCY ONLY.

"My daughters are growing up," the doctor said, "doing womanly things with their mother, leaving their father out in the cold. Each one when she was born seemed so new; I had such hopes; I was so sure we'd make no mistakes. Enjoy this one while you can," he told Leon. The baby started and clutched two bits of air.

"I had sort of thought she would be a boy," Leon said.

"Oh, Leon!" said Emily, drawing the baby closer.

"Boys, well," the doctor said. "We tried for a boy for years, ourselves. But you can always hope for next time."

"We can only afford the one," said Leon.

"One? One child," the doctor said. He fell into thought. "Yes, well, why not? There's a certain . . . compactness to it. Very streamlined. Very basic," he said.

"It's a matter of money," Leon said.

The ambulance bounced to a stop. The attendants flew out their front doors and around to the back, letting in the din of a gigantic, sooty machine just outside the emergency room, and the smell of hot laundry water and auto exhausts and wilted cafeteria food. They grabbed Emily's stretcher and rushed away with it, wheels shrieking. Leon and the doctor clambered to the pavement and trotted after it.

"Do you have dimes?" the doctor shouted.

"Time for what?"

"Dimes! Money!"

"No, I'm sorry," Leon said. "Could you use a dollar bill?"

"For you, I meant!" the doctor shouted. They passed through a set of swinging doors. He lowered his voice. "Not for me; for you. For the phone. You'll want to call about the baby."

"Who would I call?" Leon asked, spreading his arms.

The doctor stopped short. "Who would he call!" he repeated to himself. He wore the open, delighted expression he'd worn in the ambulance when he'd been told about the youth-bed rail.

Then a nurse lifted Emily's sheet, clucked at the blood-soaked newspapers, and ran alongside the stretcher as it rolled down a corridor. Another nurse took Leon's elbow and led him toward a typist in a glass compartment. Everything spun into action—polished, efficient, briskly clacketing. The doctor was left behind.

In fact, he was forgotten, for the moment. When Leon and Emily next thought of him, he was nowhere to be found. He'd just melted away. Had he left any word? Leon asked Emily's nurse. The nurse had no idea whom he was talking about. Another doctor had been called in, a resident in obstetrics. He said it was a fine delivery, healthy baby. All things considered, he said, Emily should be thankful. "Yes, and Dr. Morgan is the one we should thank," Leon told him. "Besides, we hadn't settled the fee." But the resident had never heard of Dr. Morgan. And he wasn't in the phone book, either. It seemed he didn't exist.

Later on (just a few weeks later, when their daughter's birth had faded and they felt she had always been with them), they almost wondered if they had imagined the man—just conjured him up in a time of need. His hat, Emily said, had made her think of a gnome. He really could have been someone from a fairytale, she said: the baby elf, the troll, the goblin who finds children under cabbage leaves and lays them in their mothers' arms and disappears.

1968

1 You could say he was a man who had gone to pieces, or maybe he'd always been in pieces; maybe he'd arrived unassembled. Various parts of him seemed poorly joined together. His lean, hairy limbs were connected by exaggerated knobs of bone; his black-bearded jaw was as clumsily hinged as a nutcracker. Parts of his life, too, lay separate from other parts. His wife knew almost none of his friends. His children had never seen where he worked; it wasn't in a safe part of town, their mother said. Last month's hobby—the restringing of a damaged pawnshop banjo, with an eye to becoming suddenly musical at the age of forty-two—bore no resemblance to this month's hobby, which was the writing of a science-

fiction novel that would make him rich and famous. He was writing about the death of Earth. All these recent flying saucers, he proposed, belonged to beings who knew for a fact that our sun would burn out within a year and a half. They weren't just buzzing earth for the hell of it; they were ascertaining what equipment would be needed to transfer us all to another planet in a stabler, far more orderly solar system. He had written chapter one, but was having trouble with the opening sentence of chapter two.

Or look at his house: a tall brick Colonial house in north Baltimore. Even this early on a January morning, when the sun was no more than a pinkish tinge in an opaque white sky, it was clear there was something fragmented about Morgan's house. Its marble stoop was worn soft at the edges like an old bar of soap, and heavy lace curtains glimmered in the downstairs windows; but on the second floor, where his daughters slept, the curtains were made from sections of the American flag, and on the third floor, where his mother slept, they were lace again, misting the tangle of ferns that hung behind them. And if you could see inside, through the slowly thinning gray of the hallway, you would find the particles of related people's unrelated worlds: his daughters' booksacks tumbling across the hall radiator, which also served as mail rack, sweater shelf, and message bureau; his wife's League of Women Voters leaflets rubber-banded into a tower on the living-room coffee table; and his mother's ancient, snuffling dog dreaming of rabbits and twitching her paws as she slept on the cold brick hearth. There was a cribbage board under the sofa. (No one knew this. It had been lost for weeks.) There was a jigsaw puzzle, half completed, that Morgan's sister, Brindle, filled her long, morose, spinsterish days with: a view of an Alpine village in the springtime. The church steeple was assembled and so were the straight-edged border and the whole range of mountains with their purple and lavender shadows, but she would never get to the sky, surely. She would never manage all that blank, unchanging blue that joined everything else together.

In the glass-fronted bookcase by the dining-room door, rows of books slumped sideways or lay flat: Morgan's discarded manuals reflecting various spells of enthusiasm (how to restore old paintings and refinish secondhand furniture; how to cure illness with herbs; how to raise bees in his attic). Beneath them sat his wife Bonny's college yearbooks, where Bonny appeared as a freckled, exuberant girl in several different team uniforms; and under those were his daughters' tattered picture books and grade-school textbooks and Nancy Drews, and his mother's tiny, plump autograph book, whose gilded title had been eaten away by worms or mildew or maybe just plain time, so that all that remained was a faintly shining trail of baldness as if a snail had crossed the crimson velvet in a tortuous script that coincidentally spelled out *Autographs*. (And on the first, yellowed page, in a hand so steely and elegant that you'd only see it now on a wedding invitation: *Louisa dearest, Uncle Charlie is not a poet so will only write his name hereunder, Charles Brindle, Christmas Day, 1911*—that awkward little shrug of inadequacy descending through the years so clearly, though the man had been dead a quarter-century or more and even Louisa might have had trouble recollecting him.) The bottom shelf held a varnished plaque of Girl Scout knots, a nearly perfect conch shell, and a brown cardboard photo album pasted with photographs so widely spaced in time that whole generations seemed to be dashing past, impatient to get it over with. Here was Morgan's father, Samuel, a boy in knickers; and next to him stood Samuel full-grown, marrying Louisa with her bobbed hair and shiny stockings. Here was little Morgan in a badly knitted pram set; and Morgan at eleven holding his infant sister, Brindle, as if he might have preferred to drop her (and look! was that the same pram set? only slightly more puckered and with some new stain or shadow down the front). And then suddenly Morgan at twenty-four, shorter-haired than he would ever be again, raw-necked, self-conscious, beside his plump, smiling wife with their first baby in his arms. (No telling where *their* wedding photo had got to, or that

famous pram set either, for all Amy wore was a sagging
diaper.) Now they stopped for breath for a moment. Here
were fifteen solid pages of the infant Amy, every photo
snapped by Morgan in the first proud flush of fatherhood.
Amy sleeping, nursing, yawning, bathing, examining her fist.
Amy learning to sit. Amy learning to crawl. Amy learning to
walk. She was a sturdy child with her mother's sensible expression, and she appeared to be more real than anyone else
in the album. Maybe it was the slowness with which she
plodded, page by page, through the early stages of her life.
She took on extra meaning, like the frame at which a movie
is halted. (The experts lean forward; someone points to something with a long, official pointer . . .) Then the photos
speeded up again. Here was the infant Jean, then the twins
in their miniature spectacles, then Liz on her first day of
nursery school. The film changed to Kodachrome, brighter
than nature, and the setting was always the beach now—always Bethany Beach, Delaware, for where else could a man
with seven daughters find the time for his camera? To look
at the album, you would imagine that these people enjoyed
an endless stream of vacations. Bonny was eternally sun-
burned, bulging gently above and below her one-piece Lastex
swimsuit. The girls were eternally coconut-oiled and gleaming in their slender strips of bikinis, holding back handfuls of
wind-tossed hair and laughing. Always laughing. Where were
the tears and quarrels, and the elbowing for excessive amounts
of love and space and attention? What about all those colds
and tonsillectomies? Where was Molly's stammer? Or Susan's
chronic nightmares? Not here. They sat laughing without a
care in the world. At the edges of their bikinis, paler flesh
showed, the faintest line of it, the only reminder of other
seasons. And, oh yes, Morgan. One picture a year, taken
aslant and out of focus by some amateurish daughter: Morgan
in wrinkled trunks that flared around his thighs, whiskered all
over, untouched by the sun, showing off his biceps and probably grinning, but how could you tell for sure? For on his
head he wore an Allagash jungle hat from L. L. Bean, and

mosquito netting in sweeps and folds veiled his face completely.

Now the light had reached the stairwell and sent a gleam along the banister, but the carpeted steps were still in darkness and the cat slinking up them was only a shadow, her stripes invisible, her pointed face a single spear of white. She crossed the hall floorboards without a sound. She strode to the north rear bedroom and paused in the doorway and then advanced, so purposeful that you could see how every joint in her body was strung. Next to Bonny's side of the bed, she rose up on her hind legs to test the electric blanket—pat-pat along the edge of the mattress with one experienced paw, and then around to Morgan's side and pat-pat again. Morgan's side was warmer. She braced herself, tensed, and sprang onto his chest, and Morgan grunted and opened his eyes. It was just that moment of dawn when the air seems visible: flocked, like felt, gathering itself together to take on color at any second. The sheets were a shattered, craggy landscape; the upper reaches of the room were lit by a grayish haze, like the smoke that rises from bombed buildings. Morgan covered his face. "Go away," he told the cat, but the cat only purred and sent a slitted stare elsewhere, pretending not to hear. Morgan sat up. He spilled the cat onto Bonny (a nest of tangled brown hair, a bare, speckled shoulder) and hauled himself out of bed.

In the winter he slept in thermal underwear. He thought of clothes—all clothes—as costumes, and it pleased him to stagger off to the bathroom hitching up his long johns and rummaging through his beard like some character from the Klondike. He returned with his face set in a brighter, more hopeful expression, having glimpsed himself in the bathroom mirror: there were decisions to be made. He snapped on the closet light and stood deciding who to be today. Next to Bonny's wrinkled skirts and blouses the tumult of his clothes hung, tightly packed together—sailor outfits, soldier outfits, riverboat-gambler outfits. They appeared to have been salvaged from some traveling operetta. Above them were his hats, stacked six deep on the shelf. He reached for one, a navy knit skullcap, and pulled it on and looked in the full-length mirror: harpooner on a whaling ship. He took it off and tried next a gigantic, broad-brimmed leather hat that engulfed his head and shaded his eyes. Ah, back to the Klondike. He tugged a pair of crumpled brown work pants over his long underwear, and added striped suspenders to hook his thumbs through. He studied his reflection awhile. Then he went to the bureau and plowed through the bottom drawer. "Bonny?" he said.

"Hmm."

"Where are my Ragg socks?"

"Your what?"

"Those scratchy, woolly socks, for hiking."

She didn't answer. He had to pad barefoot down the stairs, grumbling to himself. "Fool socks. Fool house. Nothing where it ought to be. Nothing where you want it."

He opened the back door to let the dog out. A cold wind blew in. The tiles on the kitchen floor felt icy beneath his feet. "Fool house," he said again. He stood at the counter with an unlit cigarette clamped between his teeth and spooned coffee into the percolator.

The cabinets in this kitchen reached clear to the high ivory ceiling. They were stuffed with tarnished silver tea services and dusty stemware that no one ever used. Jammed in front of them were ketchup bottles and cereal boxes and scummy plastic salt-and-pepper sets with rice grains in the salt from last summer when everything had stuck to itself. Fool house! Something had gone wrong with it, somehow. It was so large and formal and gracious—a wedding present from Bonny's father, who had been a wealthy man. Bonny had inherited a portion of his money. When the children stepped through the attic floor, it was Bonny who dialed the plasterers, and she was always having the broken windowpanes replaced, the shutters rehung when they sagged off their hinges, the masonry put back in the chinks where the English ivy had clawed it away; but underneath, Morgan never lost the feeling that something here was slipping. If they could just clear it out and start over, he sometimes thought. Or sell it! Sell it and have done with it, buy a plainer, more straightforward place. But Bonny wouldn't hear of it—something to do with capital gains; he didn't know. It just never was the proper time, any time he brought it up.

The three smaller bedrooms, intended for a tasteful number of children, barely contained Morgan's daughters, and Brindle and Louisa shared an edgy, cramped existence on the third floor. The lawn was littered with rusty bicycles and raveling wicker furniture where Bonny's father had surely imagined civilized games of croquet. And nowadays apartment buildings were sprouting all around them, and the other houses were splitting into units and filling up with various unsortable collections of young people, and traffic was getting fierce. They seemed to be deep in the city. Well, all right. Morgan himself had been reared in the city, and had nothing against it whatsoever. Still, he kept wondering how this could have happened. As near as he could recall, he had planned on something different. He had married his wife for her money, to be frank, which was not to say he didn't love her; it was just that he'd been impressed, as well, by the definiteness that money had seemed to give her. It had hovered somewhere behind her left shoulder, cloaking her with an air of toughness and capability. She was so clear about who she was. Courting her, Morgan had specifically bought a yachting cap with an eagle on the front, and white duck trousers and a brass-buttoned blazer to wear while visiting at her family's summer cottage. He had sat outside on the terrace, securely defined at last, toying with the goblet of tropical punch that Bonny's father had insisted on mixing for him—although in fact Morgan didn't drink, *couldn't* drink, had never been able to. Drinking made him talk too much. It made him spill the beans, he felt. He was trying to stay in character.

Staying in character, he had asked her father for Bonny's

hand. Her father gave his approval; Morgan had wondered why. He was only a penniless graduate student with no foreseeable future. And he knew that he was nothing much to look at. (In those days he wore no beard, and there was something monkeyish and clumsy about his face.) When he took Bonny out somewhere, to one of her girlfriends' parties, he felt he was traveling under false pretenses. He felt he had entered someone else's life. Only Bonny belonged there—an easygoing, pleasant girl, two or three years older than Morgan, with curly brown hair worn low on her neck in a sort of ball-shaped ponytail. Later, Morgan figured out that her father must have miscalculated. When you're rich enough, he must have thought, then it doesn't matter who you marry; you'll go on the same as ever. So he had nodded his blessing and given them this house, and expected that nothing would change. Luckily for him, he died soon after the wedding. He never saw the mysterious way the house started slipping downward, or sideways, or whatever it was that it was doing. He didn't have to watch as Bonny's dirndl skirts (once so breezy, so understated) began dipping at the hems, and her blouses somehow shortened and flopped bunchily out of her waistbands.

"Your father would have sold this house long ago," Morgan often told her. "Capital gains or no capital gains, he'd say you should get a new one."

But Bonny would say, "Why? What for?" She would ask, "What's wrong with this one? Everything's been kept up. I just had the roofers in. The painters came last May."

"Yes, but—"

"What is it that bothers you? Can you name one thing that's in disrepair? Name it and I'll fix it. Every inch is in perfect shape, and the Davey tree men just fertilized the trees."

Yes, but.

He went out front for the paper. Under his bare feet the spikes of frosty grass crunched and stabbed. Everything glittered. A single rubber flip-flop skated on the ice in the birdbath. He dashed back in, hissing, and slammed the door behind him. Upstairs an alarm clock burred, as if set off by the crash. They would be swarming everywhere soon. Morgan removed the news section and the comics section, laid them on a kitchen chair, and sat on them. Then he lit his cigarette and opened to the classified ads.

LOST. *White wedding dress, size 10. No questions asked.*

He grinned around his cigarette.

Now here came Bonny, slumping in, still buttoning her housecoat, trying to keep her slippers on her feet. Her hair was uncombed and there was a crease down one side of her face. "Did it freeze?" she asked him. "Is there frost on the ground? I meant to cover the boxwoods." She lifted a curtain to peer out the window. "Oh, Lord, it froze."

"Mm?"

She opened a cupboard door and clattered something. A blackened silver ashtray arrived inside the partition of Morgan's newspaper. He tapped his cigarette on it. "Listen to this," he told her. "FOUND. *Article of jewelry, in Druid Hill Park. Caller must identify.* I would call and say it was a diamond ring."

"How come?" Bonny asked. She took a carton of eggs from the refrigerator.

"Well, chances are no one wears real pearls to the zoo, or platinum bracelets, but plenty of people wear engagement rings, right? And besides, you can be so general about a ring. Yes, I would say a ring. Absolutely."

"Maybe so," said Bonny, cracking an egg on a skillet.

"LOST. *Upper denture. Great sentimental value,*" Morgan read out. Bonny snorted. He said, "I made it up about the sentimental value."

"I never would have guessed," Bonny told him.

He could hear bare feet pounding upstairs, water running, hairdryers humming. The smell of percolating coffee filled the kitchen, along with the crisp, sharp smoke from his Camel. Oh, he was hitting his stride, all right. He had managed it, broken into another day. He spread his paper wider. "I love the classifieds," he said. "They're so full of private lives."

"Are you going to get those shoes fixed this morning?"

"Hmm? Listen to this: M.G. *All is not forgiven and never will be.*"

Bonny set a cup of coffee in front of him.

"What if that's me?" Morgan asked.

"What if what's you?"

"M.G. Morgan Gower."

"Did you do something unforgivable?"

"You can't help wondering," Morgan said, "seeing a thing like that. You can't help stopping to think."

"Oh, Morgan," Bonny said. "Why do you always take the paper so personally?"

"Because I'm reading the personals," he told her. He turned the page. "WANTED," he read. "*Geotechnical lab chief.*"

(For the past nineteen years he had supposedly been looking for a better job. Not that he expected to find it.)

"Here's one. *Experienced go-go girls.*"

"Ha."

He was employed by Bonny's family, managing one of their hardware stores. He had always been a tinkering, puttering, hardware sort of a man. Back in graduate school, his advisor had once complained because Morgan had spent a whole conference period squatting in the corner, talking over his shoulder while he worked on a leaky radiator pipe.

WANTED. *Barmaid, dog groomer, forklift operator.*

What he liked were those ads with character. (*Driver to chauffeur elderly gentleman, some knowledge of Homer desirable.*) Occasionally he would even answer one. He would even take a job for a couple of days, vanishing from the hardware store and leaving his clerk in charge. Then Bonny's Uncle Ollie would find out and come storming to Bonny, and Bonny would sigh and laugh and ask Morgan what he thought he was doing. He would say this for Bonny: she didn't get too wrought up about things. She just sloped along with him, more or less. He reached out for her, now, as she passed with a pitcher of orange juice. He crooked an arm around her hips, or tried to; she had her mind on something else. "Where's Brindle? Where's your mother?" she asked him. "I thought I heard your mother hours ago."

He laid the classified ads aside and tugged another section from beneath him: the news. But there was nothing worth reading. Plane crashes, train crashes, tenement fires . . . He flipped to the obituaries. "*Mrs. Grimm, Opera Enthusiast,*" he read aloud. "*Tilly Abbott, Thimble Collector.* Ah, Lord."

His daughters had begun to seep downstairs. They were quarreling in the hall and dropping books, and their transistor radios seemed to be playing several different songs at once. A deep, rocky drumbeat thudded beneath electric guitars.

"*Peter Jacobs, at 44,*" Morgan read. "Forty-four! What kind of age is that to die?"

"Girls!" Bonny called. "Your eggs are getting cold."

"I hate it when they won't say what did a man in," Morgan told her. "Even 'a lengthy illness'—I mean, a lengthy illness would be better than nothing. But all they have here is '*passed on unexpectedly.*'" He hunched forward to let someone sidle behind him. "Forty-four years old! Of course it was unexpected. You think it was a heart attack? Or what?"

"Morgan, I wish you wouldn't put such stock in obituaries," Bonny said.

She had to raise her voice; the girls had taken over the kitchen by now. All of them were talking at once about history quizzes, boys and more boys, motorcycles, basketball games, who had borrowed whose record album and never given it back. A singer was rumored to be dead. (Someone said she would die herself if that were true.) Amy was doing something to the toaster. The twins were mixing their health-food drink in the blender. A French book flew out of nowhere and hit Liz in the small of the back. "I can't go on living here any more," Liz said. "I don't get a moment's peace. Everybody picks on me. I'm leaving." But all she did was pour herself a cup of coffee and sit down next to Morgan. "For heaven's sake," she said to Bonny, "what's that he's got on his head?"

"Feel free to address me directly," Morgan told her. "I have the answer, as it happens. Don't be shy."

"Does he have to wear those hats of his? Even in the house he wears them. Does he have to look so peculiar?"

This was his thirteen-year-old. Once he might have been offended, but he was used to it by now. Along about age eleven or twelve, it seemed they totally changed. He had loved them when they were little. They had started out so small and plain, chubby and curly and even-tempered, toddling devotedly after Morgan, and then all at once they went on crash diets, grew thin and irritable, and shot up taller than their mother. They ironed their hair till it hung like veils. They traded their dresses for faded jeans and skimpy little T-shirts. And their taste in boyfriends was atrocious. Just atrocious. He couldn't believe some of the creatures they brought home with them. On top of all that, they stopped thinking Morgan was so wonderful. They claimed he was an embarrassment. Couldn't he shave his beard off? Cut his hair? Act his age? Dress like other fathers? Why did he smoke those unfiltered cigarettes and pluck those tobacco shreds from his tongue? Did he realize that he hummed incessantly underneath his breath, even at the dinner table, even now while they were asking him these questions?

He tried to stop humming. He briefly switched to a pipe, but the mouthpiece cracked in two when he bit it. And once he got a shorter haircut than usual and trimmed his beard so it was square and hugged the shape of his jaw. It looked artificial, they told him. It looked like a *wooden* beard, they said.

He felt he was riding something choppy and violent, fighting to keep his balance, smiling beatifically and trying not to blink.

"See that? He's barefoot," Liz said.

"Hush and pour that coffee back," Bonny told her. "You know you're not allowed to drink coffee yet."

The youngest, Kate, came in with a stack of schoolbooks. She was not quite eleven and still had Bonny's full-cheeked, cheery face. As she passed behind Morgan's chair, she plucked his hat off, kissed the back of his head, and replaced the hat.

"Sugar-pie," Morgan said.

Maybe they ought to have another baby.

With everyone settled around this table, you couldn't even bend your elbows. Morgan decided to retreat. He rose and ducked out of the room backward, like someone leaving the presence of royalty, so they wouldn't see the comics section he was hiding behind him. He padded into the living room. One of the radios was playing "Plastic Fantastic Lover" and he paused to do a little dance, barefoot on the rug. His mother watched him sternly from the couch. She was a small, hunched old lady with hair that was still jet black; it was held flat with tortoise-shell combs from which it crinkled and bucked like something powerful. She sat with her splotched, veined hands folded in her lap; she wore a drapy dress that seemed several sizes too large for her. "Why aren't you at breakfast?" Morgan asked.

"Oh, I'll just wait till all this has died down."

"But then Bonny'll be in the kitchen half the morning."

"When you get to be my age," Louisa said, "why, food is near about everything there is, and I don't intend to rush it. I want a nice, hot English muffin, split with a fork, not a knife, with butter melting amongst the crumbs, and a steaming cup of coffee laced with whipping cream. And I want it in peace. I want it in quiet."

"Bonny's going to have a fit," he said.

"Don't be silly. Bonny doesn't mind such things."

She was probably right. (Bonny was infinitely expansible, taking everything as it came. It was Morgan who felt oppressed by his mother's living here.) He sighed and settled next to her on the couch. He opened out his paper. "Isn't this a weekday?" she asked him.

"Yes," he mumbled.

She crooked a finger over the top of his paper and pulled it down so she could see his face. "Aren't you going to work?"

"By and by."

"By and *by?* It's seven-thirty, Morgan, and you don't even have your shoes on. Do you know what I've done so far today? Made my bed, watered my ferns, polished the chrome in my bathroom; and meanwhile here you sit reading the comics, and your sister's sleeping like the dead upstairs. What is this with my children? Where do they get this? By and by, you say!"

He gave up. He folded the paper and said, "All *right,* Mother."

"Have a nice day," she told him serenely.

When he left the room, she was sitting with her hands in her lap again, trustful as a child, waiting for her English muffin.

2   Wearing a pair of argyle socks that didn't go at all with his Klondike costume, and crusty leather boots to cover them up, and his olive-drab parka from Sunny's Surplus, Morgan loped along the sidewalk. His hardware store was deep in the city, too far to travel on foot, and unfortunately his car was spread all over the floor of his garage and he hadn't quite finished putting it back together. He would have to take the bus. He headed toward the transit stop, puffing on a cigarette that he held between thumb and forefinger, sending out a cloud of smoke from beneath the brim of his hat. He passed a row of houses, an apartment building, then a little stream of drugstores and newsstands and dentists' offices. Under one arm he carried a brown paper bag with his moccasins inside. They went with his Daniel Boone outfit. He'd worn them so often that the soft leather soles had broken through at the ball of the foot. When he reached the corner, he swerved in at Fresco's Shoe Repair to leave them off. He

liked the smell of Fresco's: leather and machine oil. Maybe he should have been a cobbler.

But when he entered, jingling the cowbell above the door, he found no one there—just the counter with its clutter of awls and pencils and receipt forms, the pigeonholes behind it crammed with shoes, and a cup of coffee cooling beside the skeletal black sewing machine. "Fresco?" he called.

"Yo," Fresco said from the rear.

Morgan laid his package down and went behind the counter. He pulled out a copper-toed work boot. Where would one buy such things? They really would be useful, he felt; really very practical. The cowbell jingled again. A fat woman in a fur cape came in, no doubt from one of those new apartment buildings. All down the edge of her cape, small animals' heads hung, gnashing their teeth on their own spindly tails. She set a spike-heeled evening sandal firmly on the counter. "I'd like to know what you're going to do about this," she said.

"Do?" said Morgan.

"You can see the heel has broken again. It broke right off while I was walking into the club, and you were the people who'd repaired it. I looked like an utter fool, a clod."

"Well, what can I say?" Morgan asked her. "This shoe is Italian."

"So?"

"It has hollow heels."

"It does?"

They both looked at the heel. It wasn't hollow at all.

"Oh, we see a lot of this," Morgan told her. He stamped out his cigarette and picked up the sandal. "These shoes from Italy, they come with hollow heels so drugs can be smuggled in. So naturally they're weakened. The smugglers pry the heels off, take no care whatsoever; they don't have the slightest feeling for their work. They slam the heels back any old how, sell the shoes to some unsuspecting shop . . . but of course they'll never be the same. Oh, the stories I could tell you!"

He shook his head. She looked at him narrowly; faint, scratchy lines deepened around her eyes.

"Ah, well," he said, sighing. "Friday morning, then. Name?"

"Well . . . Peterson," she said.

He scrawled it on the back of a receipt, and set it with the sandal in a cubbyhole.

After she was gone, he wrote out instructions for his moccasins: GOWER. FIX! *Can't live without them.* He put the moccasins next to the sandal, with the instructions rolled inside. Then he trotted on out of the shop, busily lighting another cigarette beneath the shelter of his hat.

On the sidewalk his mother's dog was waiting for him. She had a cocked, hopeful face and two perked ears like tepees. Morgan stopped dead. "Go home," he told her. She wagged her tail. "Go home. What do you want of me? What have I done?"

Morgan set off toward the bus stop. The dog followed, whining, but Morgan pretended not to hear. He speeded up. The whining continued. He wheeled around and stamped one foot. A man in an overcoat halted and then circled Morgan at a distance. The dog, however, merely cowered, panting and looking expectant. "Why must you drag *after* me like this?" Morgan asked. He made a rush at her, but she stood her ground. Of course he should lead her home himself, but he couldn't face it. He couldn't backtrack all that way, having started out so speedy and chipper. Instead he turned and took off at a run, holding on to his hat, pounding down the sidewalk with the dog not far behind. The dog began to lose heart. Morgan felt her lose it, though he didn't dare turn to look. He felt her falter and then stop, gazing after him and spasmodically wagging her tail. Morgan clutched his aching chest and stumbled up onto a bus. Puffing and sweating, he rummaged through his pockets for change. The other passengers darted sidelong glances and then looked away again.

They passed more stores and office buildings. They whizzed through a corner of Morgan's old neighborhood, with most of the windows boarded up and trees growing out of caved-in roofs. (It had not done well without him.) Here were the Arbeiter Mattress Factory and Madam Sheba, All Questions Answered and Love Problems Cheerfully Solved. Rowhouses slid by, each more decayed than the one before. Morgan hunkered in his seat, clutching the metal bar in front of him, gazing at the Ace of Spades Sandwich Shop and Fat Boy's Shoeshine. Now he was farther downtown than he had ever lived. He relaxed his grip on the metal bar. He sank into the lives of the scattered people sitting on their stoops: the woman in her nightgown and vinyl jacket nursing a Rolling Rock beer and breathing frost; the two men nudging each other and laughing; the small boy in a grownup's sneakers hugging a soiled white cat. A soothing kind of emptiness began to spread through him. He felt stripped and free, like the vacant windows, frameless, glassless, on the upper floors of Syrenia's Hot Pig Bar-B-Q.

3 The downtown branch of Cullen Hardware was so old and dark and filthy, so thick with smells, so narrow and creaking, that Morgan often felt he was not so much entering it as *plunging* in, head first, leaving just his bootsoles visible on the rim. There was a raised platform at the rear, underneath the rafters, for his office: a scarred oak desk, files, a maroon plush settee, and a steep black Woodstock typewriter whose ribbons he had to wind by hand. This used to be Bonny's grandfather's office. This store was Grandfather Cullen's very first establishment. Now there were branches everywhere, of course. Nearly every shopping mall within a fifty-mile radius had a Cullen Hardware. But they were all slick and modern; this was the only real one. Sometimes Bonny's Uncle Ollie would come in and threaten to close it down. "Call this a store?" he would say. "Call this a paying proposition?" He would glare around him at the bulky wooden shelves, where the Black & Decker power tools

looked foolish beside the old-fashioned bins of nails. He would scowl at the rusty window grilles, which had been twisted out of shape by several different burglars. Morgan would just smile, anxiously tugging his beard, for he knew that he tended to irk Uncle Ollie and he was better off saying nothing at all. Then Uncle Ollie would storm out again and Morgan would go back to his office, relieved, humming beneath his breath. Not that closing this branch down would have left him unemployed; for Bonny's sake, the Cullens would feel bound to find him something else. But here he had more scope. He had half a dozen projects under way in his office—lumber stacked against the stairs, a ball-peen hammer in his OUT basket. He knew of a good place to eat not far off. He had friends just a few blocks over. His one clerk, Butkins, did nearly all the work, even if he wasn't so interesting to talk to.

Once, a few years back, Morgan had had a girl clerk named Marie. She was a very young, round-faced redhead who always wore a loose gray smock to protect her clothes from the dust. Morgan started pretending she was his wife. It wasn't that he found her all that appealing; but he slowly built this scene in his mind where she and he were the owners of a small-town Ma-and-Pa hardware store. They'd been childhood sweethearts, maybe. Mentally, he aged her. He would have liked her to have white hair. He started wearing a wrinkled gray jacket and gray work trousers; he thought of himself as "Pa Hardware." The funny thing was, sometimes he could be looking right at her but daydreaming her from scratch, as if she weren't there. Then one afternoon he was standing on the ladder putting some shelves in order and she was handing him boxes of extension cords, and he happened to lean down and kiss her on the cheek. He said, "You look tired, Ma. Maybe you ought to take a little nap." The girl had gasped but said nothing. The next day she didn't show up for work, and she never came again. Her gray smock still hung in the stockroom. Occasionally, when he passed it,

Morgan felt sad all over again for the days when he had been Pa Hardware.

But now he had this Butkins, this efficient, colorless young fellow already setting out a new display of Rubbermaid products in the window. "Morning," Morgan told him. He went on up to his office. He took off his parka, hung it on the coat tree, and sat down in the cracked leather swivel chair behind his desk. Supposedly, he would be dealing with the paperwork now—typing up orders, filing invoices. Instead he opened the center drawer and pulled out his bird-feeder plans. He was building the feeder for Bonny. Next Tuesday was their anniversary. They had been married for nineteen years; good God. He unrolled the plans and studied them, running a nicotine-stained finger across the angles of various levels and compartments. The feeder hung by a post in which he would drill four suet holes—or peanut-butter holes, for Bonny claimed that suet caused cholesterol problems. Morgan smiled to himself. Bonny was a little crazy on the subject of birds, he thought. He weighted the plans flat with a stapler and a pack of drill bits, and went to find a good plank to begin on.

For most of the morning he sawed and sanded and hummed, occasionally pausing to push back his hat and wipe his face on his sleeve. His office stairs made a fine sawhorse. At the front of the store a trickle of shoppers chose their single purchases: a mousetrap, a furnace filter, a can of roach spray. Morgan hummed the "W.P.A. Blues" and chiseled a new point on his pencil.

Then Butkins went to an early lunch, leaving Morgan in charge. Morgan had to rise and dust off his knees, regretfully, and wait on a man in coveralls who wanted to buy a Hide-a-Key. "What for?" Morgan asked. "Why spend good money on a little tin box? Do you see the price on this thing?"

"Well, but last week I locked the keys inside my car, don't you know, and I was thinking how maybe I could hide an extra key beneath the—"

"Look," said Morgan. "All you do is take a piece of dental floss, waxed. Surely you have dental floss. Thread your extra key on it, double it for strength, tie it to your radiator grille and let the key hang down inside. Simple! Costs you nothing."

"Well, but this here Hide-a-Key—"

"Are you not standing in the presence of a man whose wife perpetually mislays his car keys for him?" Morgan asked.

The man glanced around him.

"*Me*, I mean. She loses all I own," Morgan said, "and I've never had a Hide-a-Key in my life."

"Well, still," the man said doggedly, "I think I'll just go on ahead with this here."

"What is it?" Morgan asked. "You don't have dental floss? Never mind! I tell you what I'll do: you come back this same time tomorrow, I'll have a piece for you from home. Free, no charge. A gift. All right? I'll bring you in a yard or two."

"For Christ's sake," said the man, "will you let me buy one cruddy Hide-a-Key?"

Morgan flung his hands up. "Of course!" he said. "Be my guest! Waste your money! Fill your life with junk!" He stabbed the cash-register keys. "A dollar twenty-nine," he said.

"It's *my* dollar twenty-nine, I'll waste it however I like," said the man, pressing the money into Morgan's palm. "Maniac."

"Junkie!"

The man rushed off, clutching his Hide-a-Key. Morgan muttered to himself and slammed the cash register shut.

When Butkins came back, Morgan was free to go to lunch. He went to the No Jive Café; he liked their pickles. All the other customers were black, though, and they wouldn't talk to him. They seemed to spend their mealtimes passing tiny wads of money to the counterman, and then mumbling and looking off sideways under lowered lids. Meanwhile Morgan slouched over his plate and chewed happily on a pickle. It really was a wonderful pickle. The garlic was so strong it almost fizzed. But you only got one to a plate, alongside your sandwich. He'd asked time and time again for an extra, but they always said no; he'd have to order another hamburger that he didn't even want.

After he finished eating, he thought he'd take a walk. He had a regular pattern of places he liked to visit. He zipped his parka and set off. The day had not warmed up much; the passers-by had pinched, teary faces. Morgan was glad of his beard. He turned up his collar and held it close and proceeded almost at a run, squinting against the wind.

First to Potter, the used-instrument dealer, but Potter had someone with him—a gawky, plain young woman trying out a violin. "Father Morgan!" Potter cried. "Miss Miller, meet Father Morgan, the street priest of Baltimore. How's it going? How're your addicts? Come in and have some tea!"

But customers here were rare, and Morgan didn't want to interrupt. "No, no," he said, holding up a hand. "I must be on my way. Blessings!" and he backed out the door.

He cut through an alley and came out on Marianna Street. An exotic woman with a torrent of black hair stood beside a hot-dog cart. Her make-up was stupendous—a coppery glaze on her skin, a flaring red slash of a mouth, and mascara so heavily applied that each eyelash seemed strung with black beads. Now that it was winter, she was wrapped in old coats and sweaters, but Morgan knew from warmer seasons that underneath she wore a red lace dress and an armload of chipped, flaking, gold-tone bracelets. "*Zosem pas!*" he called out to her.

"Well, hey!" she said. She spoke extra brightly, exaggerating her lip movements. "How you today? Get a letter from home?"

Morgan smiled humbly and looked perplexed.

"Letter!" she shouted. She wrote on her palm with an imaginary pencil. "You get a letter?"

"Ah!" said Morgan, suddenly realizing. He shook his head.

"*Pok*," he said sadly. "*Kun salomen baso*." The corners of his mouth turned down; he scuffed a boot against the wheel of her cart.

"You poor man," she said. "Well, maybe tomorrow, huh?"

"*Brankuso*," he told her. "*Zosem pas!*" and he waved and grinned and walked on.

At the corner of Marianna Street and Crosswell he hesitated. What he would really like was to turn down Crosswell —just head in that general direction. What harm could it do? He hadn't been in several weeks. He'd resisted temptation admirably. He shoved both hands in his pockets and set out.

CRAFTS UNLIMITED, the sign in the middle of the block said. It was an elderly building, four stories tall. The first-floor bay window was full of patchwork quilts, cornhusk dolls, samplers, woven goods, and puppets. The windows above it were narrower, dark and uncurtained. It was the third-floor windows that Morgan watched, from the shadow of a laundromat doorway—Emily and Leon Meredith's windows. He had learned their address with no trouble at all, just looked it up in the telephone book. He'd learned that along about now (just before the baby's nap, he supposed) one or the other of the Merediths would float up behind the window on the left and tug it open. A hand would trail out—Emily's pale hand or Leon's darker one—and there would be a still, considering moment while they pondered how to dress the baby for her outing. Morgan enjoyed that. (Bonny, with the last few children, had simply thrown whatever was closest into the stroller—a blanket, or some older child's jacket; anything would do.) He imagined that the Merediths would also sprinkle a few drops of milk on their wrists before giving their daughter a bottle, and would test the water with the tip of an elbow before lowering her into her bath—whatever was instructed, he liked to believe. Whatever the proper method was. He waited, smiling upward, with both hands buried deep in his pockets.

Had he missed them? No, here they came, out the glass

door beside the CRAFTS UNLIMITED sign. Leon carried the baby over his shoulder. (Naturally they would not have bought a carriage.) She must be nine or ten months old by now—a fat, apple-cheeked child in a thick snowsuit. Emily walked next to Leon, with her hand tucked through his arm and her face lifted and bright, talking to the baby and tripping along in her shabby trenchcoat and little black slippers. Morgan loved the way the Merediths dressed. It seemed they had decided, long ago, what clothes would be their trademark, and they never swerved from it. Leon always wore clean khaki trousers and a white shirt. Below the sleeves of his rust-colored corduroy jacket, a half-inch of immaculate white cuff emerged. And Emily wore one of three scoop-necked leotards—brown, plum, or (most often) black—with a matching wrap skirt of some limp material that flowed to mid-calf length. He had noticed such outfits in modern-dance productions on TV, and admired their fluidity. Now he saw that, worn on the street, they made fashion seem beside the point. In fact, the hemline was wrong for this year or even for this decade, he suspected, and who ever heard of such a young girl in such drab colors? But these costumes seemed to carry their own authority. She didn't look outdated at all. She looked stark, pared down. She had done away with the extras.

He enjoyed imagining their eat-in kitchen, with just two plates and two sets of silver and an earthenware bowl for the baby. He liked to think that their bathroom contained a bar of Ivory soap and three hotel towels. Well, and Leon's shaving things, of course. But nothing else. No bath oil, talcum tins, acne creams, hairdryers, children's orthodontic appliances, mingled bottles of perfume swearing at each other, dangling bras and nylons and lace-edged shower caps. He gazed longingly after the Merediths. Their two oval faces swung away, private and impenetrable. Their daughter's face was round as a coin, and stayed visible long after her parents had turned their backs on him, but she was no easier to read.

Of course, what he should have done was gallop across and catch up with them. "Remember me? Dr. Morgan. Remember? What a coincidence! I just chanced to be in the neighborhood, you see . . ." It wouldn't be difficult. He could take the baby's pulse, inquire about her DPT shots. Doctoring was so easy—a matter of mere common sense. It was almost *too* easy. He'd have more trouble sustaining the role of electrician, or one of those men who blow insulating material between the walls of houses.

Nevertheless, something stopped him. He felt awed by the Merediths—by their austerity, their certitude, their mapped and charted lives. He let them float away untouched, like people in a bubble.

4 Afternoon drifted over the store, and twilight sank into the corners. Butkins swallowed a yawn and mused at the window. Morgan invented an elaborate sort of paddlewheel device to tip squirrels off the bird feeder. He sanded each paddle carefully and fitted it into place. He felt comforted and steadied by this kind of work. It made him think of his father, a methodical man who might have been much happier as a carpenter than as an ineffectual high-school English teacher. "One thing our family has always believed in," his father used to say, "is the very best quality tools. You buy the best tools for the job: drop-forged steel, hardwood handles. And then you take good care of them. Everything in its place. Lots of naval jelly." It was the only philosophy he had ever stated outright, and Morgan clung to it now like something carved in stone. His father had killed himself during Morgan's last year of high school. Without a hint of despair or ill health (though he'd always seemed somewhat muted), he had taken a room at the Winken Blinken Motor Hotel one starry April evening and slit both wrists with a razor blade. Morgan had spent a large part of his life trying

to figure out why. All he wanted was a reason—bad debts, cancer, blackmail, an illicit love affair; nothing would have dismayed him. Anything would have been preferable to this nebulous, ambiguous trailing off. Had his father, perhaps, been wretched in his marriage? Fallen under the power of racketeers? Committed murder? He rifled his father's correspondence, stole his desk key and his cardboard file box. He mercilessly cross-examined his mother, but she seemed no wiser than Morgan, or maybe she just didn't want to talk about it. She went around silent and exhausted; she'd taken a job at Hutzler's selling gloves. Gradually, Morgan stopped asking. The possibility had begun to settle on him, lately, as imperceptibly as dust, that perhaps there'd been no reason after all. Maybe a man's interest in life could just thin to a trickle and dry up; was that it? He hated to believe it. He pushed the thought away, any time it came to him. And even now he often pored over the file box he had stolen, but he never found more than he'd found at the start: alphabetized instruction sheets for assembling bicycles, cleaning lawnmowers, and installing vacuum-cleaner belts. Repairing, replacing, maintaining. One step follows another, and if you have completed step two, then step three will surely come to you.

He sanded the paddlewheel, nodding gently. He hummed without any tune.

Butkins came up the stairs to say, "I'm going now, if that's all you need. I'll see you tomorrow."

"Eh?" said Morgan. "Is it time?" He straightened and wiped his forehead with the back of his hand. "Well, yes, surely, Butkins," he said. "So long, then."

The store fell silent and grew fuzzy with darkness. Passers-by hurried home to supper without even glancing in. Morgan got to his feet, put on his parka, and made his way up the aisle. He switched off the lights and locked the three massive, burglar-proof locks. From outside, the place looked like an antique photograph: lifeless, blurred, the knobs and bulges in its window a mystery forever. Maybe Grandfather

Cullen's ghost came here, nights, and roamed the aisles in a daze, ruminating over the rechargeable hedge clippers. Morgan turned his collar up and ran to catch the bus.

5 At supper the grownups sat bunched at one end of the table as if taking refuge from the children—Morgan in his hat, Bonny and Louisa, and Morgan's sister, Brindle, wearing a lavender bathrobe. Brindle had her mother's sallow, eagle face and hunched posture, but not her vitality. She sat idly buttering pieces of French bread, which she placed in a circle on the rim of her plate, while Louisa recounted, word for word, a cooking program she'd been watching on TV. "First he put the veal shanks endwise in a pot. Then he poured over them a sauce made of tomato paste, lemon zest, bits of celery . . . but everything was cut up ahead of time! *Naturally* it looks easy if you don't have to witness all the peeling and chopping."

Morgan reached across her for the salt.

"There's not enough real life on television," Louisa said.

"That's the whole point," Brindle told her.

"I'd like to see him try scraping the tomato paste out of that little tiny Hunt's can, too."

"Mother, you went through all this last week," Brindle said. "That's a re-run you were watching, and you made all the same objections too."

"I did not! I knew nothing about such programs last week."

"You told us every bit of it: the lemon zest, the celery . . ."

"Are you accusing me of a faulty memory?" Louisa asked.

"Ladies. Please," said Morgan. It was true there seemed to be some problem lately with his mother's memory. She had spells when she was doggedly repetitive; her mind, like an old record, appeared to stick in certain grooves. But it only made her nervous to have it brought to her attention. He scowled at Brindle, who shrugged and buttered another slice of bread.

Meanwhile his daughters ate in a separate flurry of gossip and quarrels and giggles—seven slim, blue-jeaned girls and then someone else, a little white-haired waif with rhinestone ear studs, some friend of Kate's. She sat between Kate and Amy and stared at Morgan narrowly, as if she disapproved of him. It made him nervous. He was never truly happy if he felt that even the most random passing stranger found him unlikable. He'd begun the meal in a fine mood, twirling his spaghetti theatrically on his fork and speaking in a broad Italian accent, but gradually he lost his enthusiasm. "What do you keep looking at?" he asked now. "Have we met before?"

"Sir?"

"This is Coquette," Kate told him.

"Ah. Coquette."

"Me and her are in the same class at school. We like the same boy."

Morgan frowned. "Same what?" he said.

"This boy named Jackson Eps."

"But you're only in fifth grade!"

"We liked him in fourth grade too."

"This is ridiculous," Morgan told Bonny. Bonny smiled at him; she never knew when to start worrying. "What are things coming to?" he asked his sister. "Where are we headed, here? It's all these Barbie dolls, Ken dolls, Tinkerbell make-up sets."

"*I* liked a boy in fifth grade," Brindle said.

"You did?"

"Robert Roberts."

"Oh, Lord, Brindle, not Robert Roberts again."

"Robert Roberts was in fifth grade?" Kate asked. She nudged Coquette. "Robert Roberts was Brindle's childhood sweetheart," she said.

"He was not only in fifth grade," said Brindle, "he was also in fourth, third, second . . . We used to have to share our reading-skills workbook; he was always losing his. In kindergarten we went shopping once at Bargain Billy's and he stuck a label on my cheek reading SLIGHTLY IMPERFECT. He also took me to my first school dance and my first car-date and my senior-class picnic."

Morgan sighed and tipped his chair back. Bonny helped herself to more salad.

"Then in college I broke it off," Brindle told Coquette. "I gave him back his high-school ring with the candle wax still in it to make it fit my finger—half a candle's worth, it looked like. I'd probably have drowned if I ever wore it swimming."

"Why'd you break it off?" Coquette asked her.

"I got married to someone else."

"But *why'd* you break it off? I mean, why marry someone else?"

Brindle pushed her plate away and set her elbows on the table. She said, "Well, I don't know if . . . When I talk about him, it sounds so simple, doesn't it? But see, even back in kindergarten he would sometimes act silly and sometimes bore me, and yet other times I was crazy about him, and when we grew up it got worse. Sometimes I liked him and sometimes I didn't like him, and sometimes I didn't even think of him. And sometimes he didn't like me, I knew it; we knew each other so well. It never occurred to me it would be that way with *anyone*. I mean, he was my only experience. You understand what I'm trying to say?"

Plainly, Coquette didn't understand a word. She was growing restless, glancing toward the plate of Oreos on the sideboard. But Brindle didn't see that. "What I did," she said, "was marry an older man. Man who lived next door to Mother's old house, downtown. It was a terrible mistake. He was the jealous type, possessive, always fearing I would leave him. He never gave me any money, only charge accounts and then this teeny bit of cash for the groceries every week. For seven years I charged our food at the gourmet sections of department stores—tiny cans of ham and pure-white asparagus spears and artichoke bottoms and hearts of palm, all so I could save back some of the grocery money. I would charge a dozen skeins of yarn and then return them one by one to the Knitter's Refund counter for cash. I subscribed to every cents-off, money-back offer that came along. At the end of seven years I said, 'All right, Horace, I've saved up five thousand dollars of my own. I'm leaving.' And I left."

"She had to save five thousand dollars," Morgan told the ceiling, "to catch a city bus from her house to my house. Three and a half miles—four at the most."

"I felt I'd been challenged," Brindle said.

"And it's not as if I hadn't offered to help her out, all along."

"I felt I wanted to show him, 'See there? You can't overcome me so easily; I've got more spirit than you think,'" Brindle said.

Morgan wondered if supplies of spirit were rationed. Did each person only get so much, which couldn't be replenished once it was used up? For in the four years since leaving her husband she'd stayed plopped on Morgan's third floor, seldom dressing in anything but her faded lavender bathrobe. To this day, she'd never mentioned finding a job or an apartment of her own. And when her husband died of a stroke, not six months after she'd left, she hardly seemed to care one way or the other. "Oh, well," was all she'd said, "I suppose this saves me a trip to Nero."

"Don't you mean Reno?" Morgan had asked.

"Whatever," she said.

The only time she showed any spirit, in fact, was when she was telling this story. Her eyes grew triangular; her skin had a stretched look. "I haven't had an easy time of it, you see," she said. "It all worked out so badly. And Robert Roberts, well, I hear he went and married a Gaithersburg girl. I just turn my back on him for a second and off he goes and gets married. Isn't that something? Not that I hold him to blame. I know I did it to myself. I've ruined my life, all on my own, and it's far too late to change it. I just set all the switches and did all the steering and headed straight toward ruin."

Ruin echoed off the high, sculptured ceiling. Bonny brought the cookies from the sideboard; the girls took two and three apiece as the plate went past. Morgan let his chair tip suddenly forward. He studied Brindle with a curious, alert expression on his face, but she didn't seem to notice.

6 Now he and Bonny were returning from a movie. They slogged down the glassy black pavement toward the bus stop. It was a misty, damp night, warmer than it had been all day. Neon signs blurred into rainbows, and the taillights of cars, sliding off into the fog, seemed to contract and then vanish. Bonny had her arm linked through Morgan's. She wore a wrinkled raincoat she had owned since he first met her, and crepe-soled shoes that made a luff-luffing sound. "Maybe tomorrow," she said, "you could get the car put back together."

"Yes, maybe," said Morgan absently.

"We've been riding buses all week."

Morgan was thinking about the movie. It hadn't seemed very believable to him. Everyone had been so sure of what everyone else was going to do. The hero, who was some kind of double agent, had laid all these elaborate plans that depended on some other, unknowing person appearing in a certain place or making a certain decision, and the other person always obliged. Sentries looked away at crucial moments. High officials went to dinner just when they usually went to dinner. Didn't B ever happen instead of A, in these people's lives? Morgan plodded steadily, frowning at his feet. From out of nowhere the memory came to him of the hero's manicured, well-tended hands expertly assembling a rifle from random parts smuggled through in a leather briefcase.

They reached the bus stop; they halted and peered down the street. "Watch it take all night," Bonny said good-naturedly. She removed her pleated plastic rain-scarf and shook the droplets from it.

"Bonny," Morgan said, "why don't I own a corduroy jacket?"

"You do," she told him.

"I do?"

"You have that black one with the suede lapels."

"Oh, that," he said.

"What's wrong with it?"

"I'd prefer to have rust," he said.

She looked over at him. She seemed about to speak, but then she must have changed her mind.

A bus lumbered into view, its windows lit with golden lights—an entire civilization, Morgan imagined, cruising through space. It stopped with a wheeze and let them climb on. For such a late hour, it seemed unusually crowded. There were no double seats left. Bonny settled beside a woman in a nurse's uniform, and instead of finding someplace else Morgan stood rocking above her in the aisle. "I'd like a nice rust jacket with the elbows worn," he told her.

"Well," she said dryly, "you'd have to wear down your own elbows, I expect."

"I don't know; I might find something in a secondhand store."

"Morgan, can't you stay out of secondhand stores? Some of those people have *died*, the owners of those things you buy."

"That's no reason to let a perfectly good piece of clothing go to waste."

Bonny wiped the rain off her face with a balled-up Kleenex from her pocket.

"Also," Morgan said, "I'd like a pair of khaki trousers and a really old, soft, clean white shirt."

She replaced the Kleenex in her pocket. She jolted along with the bus in silence for a moment, looking straight ahead of her. Then she said, "Who is it this time?"

"Who is what?"

"Who is it that wears those clothes?"

"No one!" he said. "What do you mean?"

"You think I'm blind? You think I haven't been through this a hundred times before?"

"I don't know what you're talking about."

Bonny shrugged and turned her gaze out the window.

They were near their own neighborhood now. Lamps glowed over the entranceways of brick houses and apartment buildings. A man in a hat was walking his beagle. A boy cupped a match and lit a girl's cigarette. In the seat behind Bonny, two women in fur coats were having a conversation. "I guess you heard the news by now," one of them told the other. "Angie's husband died."

"Died?" asked the other.

"Just up and died."

"How'd it happen?"

"Well, he finished shaving and he put on a little aftershave and he came back into the bedroom and went to sit on the bed—"

"But what was it? His heart?"

"Well, I'm *telling* you, Libby . . ."

Morgan began to have an uncomfortable thought. He became convinced that his hand, which gripped the seat in plain view of these two women, was so repulsive to them that they were babbling utter nonsense just to keep from thinking about it. He imagined that he could see through their eyes; he saw exactly how his hand appeared to them—its knuckly fingers, wiry black hairs, sawdust ingrained around the nails. He saw his whole person, in fact. What a toad he was! A hat and a beard, on legs. His eyes felt huge and hot and heavy, set in a baroque arrangement of dark pouches. "He reached for his socks," the first woman said desperately, "and commenced to unroll them. One sock was rolled inside the other, don't you know . . ." She was looking away from Morgan; she was avoiding the sight of his hand. He let go of the seat and buried both fists in his armpits. For the rest of the trip he rode unsupported, lurching violently whenever the bus stopped.

And when they reached home, where the girls were doing their lessons on the dining-room table and Brindle was laying out her Tarot cards in the kitchen, Morgan went straight up the stairs to bed. "I thought you'd like some coffee," Bonny said. She called after him, "Morgan? Don't you want a cup of coffee?"

"No, I guess not tonight," he said. "Thank you, dear," and he continued up the stairs. He went to his room, undressed to his thermal underwear, and lit a cigarette from the pack on the bureau. For the first time all day, he was bare-headed. In the mirror his forehead looked lined and vulnerable. He noticed a strand of white in his beard. White hair! "Christ," he said. Then he bent forward and looked more closely. Maybe, he thought, he could pass himself off as one of those miracles from the Soviet Union—a hundred and ten, hundred and twenty, still scaling mountains with his herd of goats. He brightened. He could cross the country on a lecture tour. At every whistle stop he'd take off his shirt and show his black-pelted chest. Reporters would ask him his secret. "Yogurt und cigarettes, comrades," he cackled to the mirror. He took a couple of prancing steps, showing off. "Never anodder sing but yogurt und Rossian cigarettes."

Feeling more cheerful, he went to the closet for his cardboard file box, which he placed on the bed. He drew intently on his Camel as he padded around, getting arranged: turning on the electric blanket, propping up his pillow, finding an ashtray. He climbed into bed and set the ashtray in his lap. There was a little coughing fit to be seen through first. He scattered ashes down his undershirt. He pinched a speck of tobacco from his tongue. "Ah, comrades," he wheezed. He opened the file box, took out the first sheet of paper, and settled back to read it.

1. *Familiarize yourself with all steps before beginning.*
2. *Have on hand the following: pliers, Phillips screwdriver . . .*

He lowered the sheet of paper and gazed at the black windowpanes. Miles away from here, he imagined, the windows on Crosswell Street were blinking out, first the left one, then the right one. The baby would stir in her sleep. Leon's hand would drop from the light switch and he would cross the cold floor to their pallet. Then all daytime sounds would stop; there would only be the sifting breaths of sleepers, motionless and dreamless on their threadbare sheets.

Morgan turned his light off too, and settled down for the night.

1 9 6 9

1 What was it that he wanted of them? He was everywhere, it seemed—an oddly shaped, persistent shadow
trailing far behind when they went for a walk, lurking in
various doorways, flattening himself around the corner of a
building. What they ought to do was simply wheel and con-
front him. "Why, Dr. Morgan!"—smiling, surprised—"how
nice to run into you!" But the situation hadn't lent itself to
that, somehow. The first time they'd seen him (or felt his
presence, really), back when Gina was a baby, they hadn't
realized who he was. Coming home from a shopping trip at
twilight, they'd been chilled by a kind of liquid darkness
flowing in and out of alleyways behind them. Emily had been
frightened. Leon had been angry, but with Emily next to him

and Gina in his arms he hadn't wanted to force anything. They had merely walked a little faster, and spoken to each other in a loud, casual tone without once mentioning what was happening. The second time, Emily had been alone. She'd left the baby with Leon and gone to buy felt for the puppets. Directly opposite their apartment building, in an arched granite doorway, a figure fell suddenly backward into the gloom of the laundromat. She hardly saw; she was calculating the yardage she would need. But that evening, as she was making a pointed hat for Rumpelstiltskin, the memory came swimming in again. She saw the figure fall once more out of sight —though he hadn't been wearing a pointed hat at all but something flat, a beret, perhaps. Still, where had she seen him before? She said, "Oh!" and laid her scissors down. "Guess who I think I saw today?" she said to Leon. "That doctor. That Dr. Morgan."

"Did you ask him why he never sent a bill?"

"No, he wasn't really . . . It wasn't a meeting, exactly. I mean, he didn't see me. Well, he saw me, but it seemed he . . . Probably," she said, "it wasn't Dr. Morgan at all. I'm sure he would have spoken."

A month or so later he followed her along Beacon Avenue. She stopped to look in the window of an infants'-wear shop and she felt someone else stop too. She turned and found a man some distance away, his back to her, gazing off down the street at nothing in particular. He might have stepped out of a jungle movie, she thought, with his safari shirt and shorts, his knee-high socks, ankle boots, and huge pith helmet. Extraneous buckles and D-rings glittered all over him—on his shoulders, his sleeves, his rear pockets. It was nobody dangerous. It was only one of those eccentric people you often see on city streets, acting out some elaborate inner vision of themselves. She walked on. At the next red light she glanced back again and here he came, hurrying toward her with a swaggering, soldierly gait to match the uniform, his eyes obscured by the helmet but his abundant beard in full view. Oh, you couldn't mistake that beard. Dr. Morgan! She took a step toward him. He looked up at her, clapped a hand on his helmet, and darted through a door reading LU-RAE'S FINE COIFFURES.

Emily felt absurd. She felt how open and glad she must look, preparing to call his name. But what had she done wrong? Why didn't he like her any more? He had seemed so taken with the two of them, back when Gina was born.

She didn't tell Leon. It would make him angry, maybe; you never knew. She decided that, anyhow, it had only been one of those unexplainable things—meaningless, not worth troubling Leon about.

So it got off on the wrong foot, you might say. There was a moment when they could have dealt with it straightforwardly, but the moment slipped past them. After several of these incidents (spaced across weeks or even months) in which one thing or another prevented them from going up to the man and greeting him naturally, it began to seem that the situation had taken a turn of its own. There was no way they could gracefully set it right now. It became apparent that he must be crazy—or, at least, obsessed in some unaccountable way. (Emily shivered to think of Gina's delivery at his hands.) Yet, as Leon pointed out, he did no harm. He never threatened them or even came within speaking distance of them; there was nothing to complain of. Really, Emily was taking this too fancifully, Leon said. The man was only something to be adjusted to, as a matter of course. He was part of the furniture of their lives, like the rowhouses looming down Crosswell Street, the dusty, spindly trees dying of exhaust fumes, and the puppets hanging in their muslin shrouds from the hooks in the back-bedroom closet.

2 Now that it was winter, business had slacked off. There had been a little burst around Christmas (holiday bazaars, parties for rich people's children), but none of the open-air fairs and circuses that kept them so busy in the sum-

mer. Emily used the time to build a new stage—a wooden one, hinged and folded for portability. She repaired the puppets and sewed more costumes for them. A few she replaced completely, which led to the usual question of what to do with the old ones. They were like dead bodies; you couldn't just dump them in the trashcan. "Use them for spare parts," Leon always said. "Save the eyes. Save that good nose." Put Red Riding Hood's grandmother's pockmarked cork-ball nose on any other puppet? It wouldn't work. It wouldn't be right. Anyway, how could she tear that face apart? She laid the grandmother in a carton alongside a worn-out Beauty from "Beauty and the Beast"—the very first puppet she'd ever made. They were on their third Beauty at the moment, a much more sophisticated version with a seamed cloth face. It wasn't the plays that wore the puppets out; it was the children coming up afterward, patting the puppets' wigs and stroking their cheeks. Beauty's skin was gray with fingerprints. Her yellow hair had a tattered, frantic look.

This whole room belonged to the puppets: the hollow back bedroom, with peeling silvery pipes shooting to the ceiling and a yellow rain stain ballooning down one wall. The window was painted shut, its panes so sooty that the sun set up an opaque white film in the afternoons. The wooden floor put splinters in Gina's knees and turned her overalls black. The china doorknob was hazy with cracks. The door hung crooked. Nights, when Emily worked late in the glow of one goose-necked lamp, the hall light that shone beneath the door was not a rod but a wedge, like a very long piece of pie.

She sat up late and repaired the witch, the all-purpose stepmother-witch that was used in so many different plays. No wonder she kept wearing out! One black button eye dangled precariously. Emily perched upon the stepladder that was the room's only furniture and tied a knot in a long tail of thread.

The puppets most in use were kept in an Almadén chablis box in the corner. They poked their heads out of the card-

board compartments: two young girls (one blonde, one bru-
nette), a prince, a green felt frog, a dwarf. The others
stayed in muslin bags in the closet, with name tags attached
to the drawstrings: *Rip Van W. Fool. Horse. King.* She liked
to change them around from time to time, assign them roles
they were not accustomed to. Rip Van Winkle, minus his
removable beard, made a fine Third Son in any of those
stories where the foolish, kind-hearted Third Son ends up
with the princess and half the kingdom. He fitted right in.
Only Emily knew he didn't belong, and it gave a kind of
edge to his performance, she felt. She ran him through his
lines herself. (Leon played the older two sons.) She put an
extra, salty twang in his voice. The real Third Son, meanwhile—more handsome, with less character—lay face-up
backstage, grinning vacantly.

Emily had never actually planned to be a puppeteer, and
even now both she and Leon thought of it as temporary work.
She had entered college as a mathematics major, on full
scholarship—the only girl her age in Taney, Virginia, who
was not either getting married the day after graduation or
taking a job at Taney Paper Products. Her father had been
killed in an auto accident when Emily was a baby; then, early
in Emily's freshman year at college, her mother died of a
heart ailment. She was going to have to manage on her own,
therefore. She hoped to teach junior high. She liked the cool
and systematic process that would turn a tangle of disarranged numbers into a single number at the end—the redis-
tributing and simplifying of equations that was the basis of
junior-high-school mathematics. But she hadn't even finished
the fall semester when she met Leon, who was a junior involved in acting. He couldn't *major* in acting (it wasn't
offered), so he was majoring in English, and barely scraping
by in all his subjects while he appeared in every play on
campus. For the first time Emily understood why they called
actors "stars." There really was something dazzling about
him whenever he walked onstage. Seen close up, he was a
stringy, long-faced, gloomy boy with eyes that drooped at

the outer corners and a mouth already beginning to be parenthesized by two crescent-shaped lines. He had a bitter look that made people uneasy. But onstage, all this came across as a sort of power and intensity. He was so concentrated. His characters were so sharply focused that all the others seemed wooden by comparison. His voice (in real life a bit low and glum) seemed to penetrate farther than the other voices. He hung on to words lovingly and rolled them out after the briefest pause, as if teasing the audience. It appeared that his lines were invented, not memorized.

Emily thought he was wonderful. She had never met anyone like him. Her own family had been so ordinary and pale; her childhood had been so unexceptional. (His had been terrible.) They began spending all their time together—nursing a single Pepsi through an afternoon in the canteen, studying in the library with their feet intertwined beneath the table. Emily was too shy to appear in any plays with him, but she was good with her hands and she signed on as a set-builder. She hammered platforms and stairsteps and balconies. She painted leafy woods on canvas flats, and then for the next play she transformed the woods into flowered wallpaper and mahogany-colored wainscoting. Meanwhile, it seemed that even this slim connection with the theatre was making her life more dramatic. There were scenes with his parents, at which she was an embarrassed observer—long tirades from his father, a Richmond banker, while his mother wiped her eyes and smiled politely into space. Evidently, the university had informed them that Leon's grades were even lower than usual. If they didn't improve, he was going to flunk out. Almost every Sunday his parents would drive all the way from Richmond just to sit in Leon's overstuffed, faded dormitory parlor asking what kind of profession he could hope for with a high F average. Emily would rather have skipped these meetings, but Leon wanted her there. At first his parents were cordial to her. Then they grew less friendly. It couldn't have been anything she'd done. Maybe it was what she *hadn't* done. She was always reserved and quiet with them. She came from old Quaker stock and tended, she'd been told, to feel a little too comfortable in the face of long silences. Sometimes she thought things were going beautifully when in fact everybody else was casting about in desperation for something to talk about. So she tried harder to be sociable. She wore lipstick and stockings when she knew they were coming, and she thought up neutral subjects ahead of time. While Leon and his father were storming at each other, she'd be running through a mental card file searching for a topic to divert them. "Our class is reading Tolstoy now," she told Leon's mother one Sunday in April. "Do you like Tolstoy?"

"Oh, yes, we have it in leather," said Mrs. Meredith, dabbing her nose with a handkerchief.

"Maybe Leon ought to take Russian literature," Emily said. "We read plays too, you know."

"Let him pass something in his *own* damn language first," his father said.

"Oh, well, this is in English."

"How would that help?" Mr. Meredith asked. "I believe his native tongue is Outer Mongolian."

Meanwhile Leon was standing at the window with his back to them. Emily felt touched by his tousled hair and his despairing posture, but at the same time she couldn't help wondering how he'd got them into this. His parents weren't really the type to make scenes. Mr. Meredith was a solid, business-like man; Mrs. Meredith was so stately and self-controlled that it was remarkable she'd foreseen the need to bring a handkerchief. Yet every week something went wrong. Leon had this way of plunging into battle unexpectedly. He was quicker to go to battle than anyone she knew. It seemed he'd make a mental leap that Emily couldn't follow, landing smack in the middle of rage when just one second before he'd been perfectly level and reasonable. He flung his parents' words back at them. He pounded his fist into his palm. It was all too high-keyed, Emily thought. She turned to Mrs. Meredith again. "Right now we're on *Anna Karenina*," she said.

"All that stuff is Communist anyhow," said Mr. Meredith.
"Is . . . what?"

"Sure, this tractor-farming, workers-unite bit, killing off
the Tsar and Anastasia . . ."

"Well, I'm not . . . I believe that came a little later."

"What is it, you're one of these college leftists?"

"No, but I don't think Tolstoy lived that long."

"Of course he did," Mr. Meredith said. "Where do you
think your friend Lenin would be if he didn't have Tolstoy?"

"Lenin?"

"Do you deny it? Look, my girl," Mr. Meredith said. He
leaned earnestly toward her, lacing his fingers together. (He
must sit this way at the bank, Emily thought, explaining to
some farmer why he couldn't have a loan on his tobacco
crop.) "The minute Lenin got his foot in the door, first
person he called on was Tolstoy. Tolstoy this, Tolstoy that
. . . Any time they wanted any propaganda written, 'Ask
Tolstoy,' he'd say. 'Ask Leo.' Why, sure! They didn't tell you
that in school?"

"But . . . I thought Tolstoy died in nineteen . . ."

"Forty," said Mr. Meredith.

"Forty?"

"I was in my senior year in college."

"Oh."

"And Stalin!" said Mr. Meredith. "Listen, *there* was a combination. Tolstoy and Stalin."

Leon turned suddenly from the window and left the room.
They heard him going up the stairs to the sleeping quarters.
Emily and Mrs. Meredith looked at each other.

"If you want my personal opinion," Mr. Meredith said,
"Tolstoy was a bit of a thorn in Stalin's side. See, he couldn't
unseat Tolstoy, the guy was sort of well known by then,
but at the same time he was too old-line. You knew he was
pretty well off, of course. Owned a large piece of land."

"That's true, he did," Emily said.

"You can see it must have been a little awkward."

"Well, yes . . ."

" 'The fact is,' Stalin says to his henchmen, 'he's an old guy. I mean, he's just a doddering old guy with a large piece of land.' "

Emily nodded, her mouth slightly open.

Leon came pounding down the stairs. He entered the parlor with a dictionary open in his hands. "*Tolstoy, Lev*," he read out, "*1828–1910.*"

There was a silence.

"Born in eighteen twenty-eight, died in nineteen—"

"All *right*," said Mr. Meredith. "But where is this getting us? Don't try to change the subject, Leon. We were talking about your grades. Your sloppy grades and this damn-fool acting business."

"I'm serious about my acting," Leon said.

"Serious! About *play*-acting?"

"You can't make me give it up; I'm twenty-one years old. I know my rights."

"Don't tell me what I can or cannot do," said Mr. Meredith. "If you refuse, I warn you, Leon: I'm withdrawing you from school. I'm not paying next year's tuition."

"Oh, Burt!" Mrs. Meredith said. "You wouldn't do that! He'd be drafted!"

"Army's the best thing that could happen to that boy," Mr. Meredith said.

"You can't!"

"Oh, can't I?"

He turned to Leon. "I'm driving home with you today," he said, "unless I have your signed and notarized statement that you will drop all extracurricular activities—plays, girlfriends . . ."

He flapped a pink, tight-skinned hand in Emily's direction.

"Not a chance," said Leon.

"Start packing, then."

"Burt!" Mrs. Meredith cried.

But Leon said, "Gladly. I'll be gone by nightfall. Not home, though—not now or ever again."

"See what you've done?" Mrs. Meredith asked her husband.

Leon walked out of the room. Through the parlor's front windows (small-paned, with rippling glass) Emily saw his angular figure repeatedly dislocating itself, jarring apart and drawing back together as he strode across the quadrangle. She was left with Leon's parents, who seemed slapped into silence. She had the feeling that she was one of them, that she would spend the rest of her days in heavily draped parlors— a little dry stick of a person. "Excuse me," she said, rising. She crossed the room, stepped out the door, and closed it gently behind her. Then she started running after Leon.

She found him at the fountain in front of the library, idly throwing pebbles into the water. When she came up beside him, out of breath, and touched his arm, he wouldn't even glance at her. In the sunlight his face had a warm olive glow that she found beautiful. His eyes, which were long and heavy-lidded, seemed full of plots. She believed she would never again know anyone so decisive. Even his physical outline seemed to stand out more sharply than other people's. "Leon?" she said. "What will you do?"

"I'll go to New York," he said, as if he'd been planning this for months.

She had always dreamed of seeing New York. She tightened her hand on his arm. But he didn't invite her along.

To escape his parents, in case they came hunting him, they walked to a dark little Italian restaurant near the campus. Leon went on talking about New York: he might get something in summer stock, he said, or, with luck, a bit part Off-Broadway. Always he said "I," not "we." She began to despair. She wished she could find some flaw in his face, which seemed to give off a light of its own in the gloom of the restaurant. "Do me a favor," he told her. "Go to my room and pack my things, just a few necessities. I'm worried Mom and Dad will be waiting for me there."

"All right," she said.

"And bring my checkbook from the top dresser drawer. I'm going to need that money."

"Leon, I have eighty-seven dollars."

"Keep it."

"It's left over from the spending money Aunt Mercer gave me. I won't have any use for it."

"Will you please stop *fussing?*" Then he said, "Sorry."

"That's all right."

They walked back to campus, and while he waited beside the fountain, she went to his dorm. His parents weren't in the parlor. The two armchairs they had sat in were empty; the upholstery sighed as it rose by degrees, erasing the dents they had left.

She climbed the stairs to the sleeping quarters, where she'd rarely been before. Girls were allowed here, but they didn't often come; there was something uncouth about the place. A couple of boys were tossing a softball in the corridor. They paused grudgingly as she edged by, and the instant she had passed, she heard the slap of the ball again just behind her. She knocked at the door of 241. Leon's roommate said, "Yeah."

"It's Emily Cathcart. Can I come in and get some things for Leon?"

"Sure."

He was seated at his desk, tilted back, apparently doing nothing but shooting paper clips with a rubber band. (How would she ever love another boy after Leon left?) The paper clips kept hitting a bulletin board and then pinging into the metal wastebasket underneath it. "I'll need to find his suitcase," Emily said.

"Under that bed."

She dragged it out. It was covered with dust.

"Meredith leaving us?" he asked.

"He's going to New York. Don't tell his parents."

"New York, eh?" said the roommate, without much interest.

From the closet by Leon's bed Emily started taking the clothes she'd seen him wear most often—white shirts, khaki trousers, a corduroy jacket she knew he was fond of. Everything smelled of him, starchy and clean. She was pleased by the length of his trousers, in which she herself would be lost.

"You going with him?" the roommate said.

"I don't think he wants me to."

Another paper clip snapped against the bulletin board.

"I would if he asked me, but he hasn't," Emily said.

"Oh, well, you've got exams coming up. Got to get your A's and A-pluses."

"I'd go without a thought," she said.

"The man wants to travel light, I guess."

"Is this his bureau?"

He nodded and let his chair thud forward. "You don't think your picture'd be on *my* bureau," he said. "No offense, of course."

She glanced at the picture—her Christmas present to Leon. It stood behind an alarm clock, still in the deckle-edged cardboard folder supplied by the studio. The person it showed only faintly resembled her, she hoped. Emily hated being made to feel conscious of her physical appearance. She walked around most of the time peering out of the eye holes of her body without giving it much thought, and she found it an unpleasant shock to be pressed onto a piano bench with her head held at an unnatural angle, forced to reflect upon her too light skin and her pale lashes that had a way of disappearing in photographs. "Smile," the photographer had told her. "This is not a firing squad, you know." She had given a quick, nervous smile and felt how artificially her lips stretched across her teeth. When the man ducked behind his camera, she'd wiped the smile off instantly. Her face emerged sober and peering, netted by worry, the mouth slightly pursed like her spinster aunt's.

She didn't pack the photo. And when she got back to Leon at the fountain, she was lugging not only his suitcase but hers as well.

"I don't care what you say," she told him. She started calling this at some distance from him, she was so anxious to get it said. She was puffing and tottering between the two suitcases. "I'm coming with you. You can't leave me here!"

"Emily?"

"I think we ought to get married. Living in sin would be inconvenient," she said, "but if that's what you prefer, then I'd do that too. And if you tell me not to come, I'll come anyway. You don't own New York! So save your breath. I'll ride on the bus one seat behind you. I'll tell the taxi driver, 'Follow that cab!' I'll tell the hotel clerk, 'Give me the room next to his room, please.' "

Leon laughed. She saw she'd won him. She set down the suitcases and stood facing him, not smiling herself. In fact, what she'd won him with was a deliberate, calculated spunkiness that she really did not possess, and she was alarmed to find him so easily taken in. Or maybe he wasn't taken in at all, but knew that this was what the audience expected: that when some girl chases you down with her suitcase and behaves outrageously, you're to laugh and throw your hands up and surrender. Laughter was not his best expression. She had never seen him look so disjointed, so uneven. There was something asymmetrical about his face. "Emily," he said, "what am I going to do with you?"

"I don't know," she told him.

Already she was beginning to worry about that herself.

By evening they were on a Greyhound bus to New York City. By the next afternoon they were settled (it felt more like camping out) in a furnished room with a sink in one corner and a toilet down the hall. They were married Thursday, which was as soon as the law permitted. She'd seen more ceremony, Emily thought, when she got her driver's license. Marriage didn't cause as much of a jolt in her life as she'd expected.

Emily found a job as a waitress in a Polish restaurant. Leon—just for the moment—cleaned a theatre after shows. In the early evenings he hung out at various coffee-houses listening to actors and poets give readings. He took Emily along, whenever she didn't have to work. "Aren't they terrible?" he would ask her. "*I* can do better than that." Emily thought so too. Once they heard a monologue that was so inept that she and Leon got up and walked out, and the actor stopped halfway through a line to say, "Hey, you! Don't forget to leave some money in the cup." Emily would have done it—she'd do anything to avoid a scene—but Leon got angry. She felt him draw in his breath; he seemed to grow bigger. By now she knew how far his anger could take him. She lifted her hand to form the shape of his elbow, but she didn't actually touch him. You should never touch Leon when his temper was up. Then he let go of his breath again and allowed her to lead him away, with the actor still shouting after them.

It turned into a very hot summer, full of rainstorms and muggy black clouds. The heat in their room was like something alive. And they were continually on the brink of having no money whatsoever. Emily had never realized how much money mattered. She felt she had to breathe shallowly, conserve her energy, walk in a held-in, unobtrusive way as she sidled between people who were richer. She and Leon began to fight about how to spend what they did have. He was more extravagant—wasteful, she said. He said she was stingy.

In July, Emily had a scare and thought she might be pregnant. She felt trapped and horrified; she didn't dare tell Leon. So when she found she wasn't pregnant after all, she couldn't share her relief with him, either. She kept that experience in her mind. She kept examining it, trying to make sense of it. What kind of marriage was it if you couldn't tell your husband a thing like that? But he would have flown into a rage, and then sunk in on himself like over-risen bread. It was *her* idea, marrying, he'd say; and *she* was the one always harping on what they couldn't afford. She pictured the scene so clearly that she almost believed it had happened. She held it against him. Her eyes filled with tears sometimes as she recalled how badly he'd behaved. But he hadn't! He had never been given a chance! (he would say). She went on blaming him anyhow. She visited a family-planning clinic and she told them that her husband would kill her if she ever got pregnant. Of course she meant it figuratively, but she could tell from the way the social worker looked at her that in this neighborhood you couldn't always be sure of that. The social worker glanced at Emily's arms and asked her if she had any other problems. Emily wanted to talk about her separateness, about how she'd kept her pregnancy scare a secret from her own husband, but she knew that wasn't a serious enough problem. In this neighborhood, women were getting murdered. (She felt how frivolous she must seem to the social worker; she was wearing her leotard and wrap skirt from Modern Dance I.) Women were getting mugged in this neighborhood, or beaten up by their husbands. Emily's husband would never lay a finger on her. She was certain of that. She rested in a circle of immunity, she felt.

She herself was not an angry kind of person. The most she could manage was a little spark of delayed resentment, every now and then, when something had happened earlier that she really should have objected to if she'd only realized. Maybe if she'd had a temper herself, she would have known what string would pull Leon back down into calm. As it was, she just had to stand by. She had to remind herself: "He might hurt other people, but he's never laid a finger on me." This gave her a little flicker of pleasure. "He's crazy sometimes," she told the social worker, "but he's never harmed a hair of my head." Then she smoothed her skirt and looked down at her white, bloodless hands.

In August, Leon met up with four actors who were forming an improvisational group called Off the Cuff. One of them had a van; they were planning to travel down the eastern seaboard. ("New York is too hard to break into," the girl named Paula said.) Leon joined them. From the start he was their very best member, Emily thought—otherwise they might not have let him in, with his deadwood wife who froze in public and would only take up space in the van. "I can build sets, at least," Emily told them, but it seemed they never used sets. They acted on a bare stage. They planned to get up in front of a nightclub audience and request ideas that they could extemporize upon. The very thought terrified Emily, but Leon said it was the finest training he could hope to have. He practiced with them at the apartment of Barry May, the boy who owned the van. There was no way they could truly rehearse, of course, but at least they could practice working together, sending signals, feeding each other lines that propelled them toward some sort of ending. They were planning on comedy; you could not, they said, hope for much else in a nightclub. They built their comedy upon situations that made Emily anxious—lost luggage, a dentist gone berserk—and while she watched she wore a small, quirked frown that never really left her, even when she laughed. In fact it was terrible to lose your luggage. (She'd once had it actually happen. She'd lain awake all one night before it was recovered.) And it was much too easy to imagine your dentist going berserk. She chewed on a knuckle, observing how Leon took over the stage with his wide, crisp gestures, his swinging stride that came from the hip. In one skit he was Paula's husband. In another he was her fiancé. He kissed her on the lips. It was only acting, but who knows: sometimes you act like a certain person long enough, you become that person. Wasn't it possible?

They started on tour in September. They left New York in the van with all their worldly goods piled on top, including Emily's and Leon's two fat suitcases and the fluted silver coffeepot that Aunt Mercer had sent for a wedding gift. They went first to Philadelphia, where Barry knew a boy whose uncle owned a bar. For three nights they played out their skits in front of an audience that did not stop talking once, and they had to cull their ideas from Emily, whom they'd fed a few suggestions and planted on a barstool just in case. Then they moved on to Haightsville, south of Philadelphia. They thought they had a connection there, but that fell through, and they ended up in a tavern called the Bridle Club that was decorated to look like a stable. Emily had the impression that most of the customers were married to other people waiting at home. It was a middle-aged crowd—squat men in business suits, women with sprayed and gilded hair and dresses that looked one size too small. These people, too, talked among themselves throughout the skits, but they did offer a few ideas. A man wanted a scene in which a teenager announced to her parents that she was quitting school to become an exotic dancer. A woman proposed that a couple have a quarrel about the wife's attempts to introduce a few gourmet foods to her husband. Both of these suggestions, when they were made, caused a little ripple of amusement through the room, and the group turned them into fairly funny skits; but Emily kept imagining that they might be true. The man did have the seedy, desolate look of a failed father; the woman was so frantically gay that she could very well have just escaped from a stodgy husband. What the audience was doing was handing over its pain, Emily felt. Even the laughter seemed painful, issuing from these men with their red, bunchy faces and the women bearing up bravely beneath their towering burdens of hair. For the third skit, a man sitting with three other men proposed the following: a wife develops the notion that her husband, a purely social drinker who can take it or leave it and quit whenever he wants to, supposing he ever did want to, is in fact an alcoholic. "Pretend like this woman gets more and more out of line," he said. "Pretend like she goes around watering the Jack Daniel's, calling up the doctor and the AA people. When he asks for a drink, she brings him ginger ale with a spoonful of McCormick's brandy extract stirred in. When he wants to go out for a friendly night with his buddies, she says—"

"Please!" said Barry, holding up a hand. "Leave something for us!"

Then everyone laughed, except Emily.

They were appearing at the Bridle Club for three nights, but the second night Emily didn't go. She walked around town instead, until almost ten o'clock, looking into the darkened windows of Kresge and Lynne's Dress Shoppe and Knitter's World. Periodically, carloads of teenagers shot by, hooting at her, but Emily ignored them. She felt so much older than they were, she was surprised she wasn't invisible to them.

In the drugstore, which was the only place still open, she bought a zippered cosmetic kit for traveling, completely fitted with plastic jars and bottles and a tiny tube of Pepsodent. She and Leon were almost penniless at this point. They were having to sleep apart—Emily and the two other women at the Y, the men in the van. The last thing they could afford was a $4.98 cosmetic kit. Emily rushed back to her room, feeling guilty and pleased. She started rearranging her belongings—carefully pouring hand lotion into one of the bottles, fitting her silver hairbrush into a vinyl loop. But she really didn't wear much make-up; the zippered bag took more room than her few cosmetics had taken on their own. It was a mistake. She couldn't even get her money back; she'd used the bottles. She began to feel sick. She went through her suitcase throwing things out—her white school blouses, her jeans, every bit of underwear. (If she wore only leotards, she wouldn't need underwear.) When she was done, all that remained in her suitcase were two extra wrap skirts, two extra leotards, a nightgown, and the cosmetic bag. The small cardboard wastebasket next to her bed was overflowing with filmy, crumpled, shoddy non-essentials.

Their third appearance at the Bridle Club was canceled in favor of the owner's cousin's girlfriend, a torch singer. "I didn't know there still were such things," Leon told Emily. He looked depressed. He said he wasn't sure this experience was as valuable as he'd once believed. But Barry May, who was more or less the leader of the group, refused to give up. He wanted to try Baltimore, which was full of bars, he said. Besides, one of the other members, Victor Apple, had a mother living in Baltimore, and they ought to be able to get a free place to stay.

Emily knew as soon as they arrived that Baltimore would not work out. Although they drove through miles and miles of it (Victor managed to get them lost), the city continued to strike her as narrow and confining: all those gloomy row-houses, some no wider than a single room; those alleys choked with discarded tires and bottles and bedsprings; those useless-looking, hopeless men slumped on their stoops. But she took to Victor's mother immediately. Mrs. Apple was a tall, cheerful, striding woman with clipped gray hair and a leathery face. She owned a shop called Crafts Unlimited, as well as the building that housed it, and various craftsmen filled her apartments, some paying only token rent until they could get on their feet. She gave the acting group a third-floor apartment, unfurnished and shabby but clean. It was split by a dark hall, with a living room and a bedroom on one side and a kitchen and a second bedroom on the other side. At the end of the hall was an antique bathroom, against whose window, long ago, the adjoining building had been constructed. You could stand at that window and see nothing but a sheet of old, spongy bricks. For some reason Emily found this comforting. It was the only view she had felt sure of lately.

It seemed to her now that adjusting to new places used up pieces of a person. Large chunks of her had been broken off and left behind in New York, in Philadelphia, in Haightsville —anyplace she had painstakingly set out her mother's silver-backed comb and brush on someone else's peeling bureau and contrived a pretense of familiarity with someone else's flaking walls and high, cracked ceiling. She followed Mrs. Apple everywhere; she couldn't help herself. She dusted the carvings and the handmade furniture down in the shop and she learned how to work the cash register. She waited on customers during busy periods—not for pay, but for the sunny smell of new wood and freshly woven fabrics, and the brisk, offhand friendliness of Mrs. Apple.

Emily and Leon slept in the front bedroom, in two sleeping bags. Victor spread his tangle of blankets in a corner of the living room. Barry and Paula and Janice slept in the back bedroom, three across. (Emily had given up trying to figure that out.) In the daytime Barry went looking for jobs while the others stayed home and played cards. They no longer practiced their skits or even mentioned them; but sometimes, watching them play poker, Emily had the feeling that to these people everything was a skit. When they lost, they groaned and tore their hair. When they won, they leaped up, flinging their cards to the ceiling, and trumpeted, "Ta-taa!" and took a bow. Their vowels were broader than most people's, and they italicized so much. You had to talk like that yourself sometimes, just to be heard above the din. Emily found herself changing. She heard herself coming down hard on her words, drawing them out. She caught sight of herself in a mirror once, unexpectedly—her small, dry face as wan as a ghost's, but one arm flung out grandly as if she were standing cloaked and hatted in the center of some stage. She stopped in mid-sentence and folded up again.

The bars in Baltimore were not the kind to want plays going on. They were *drinking* bars, Barry said, and this was a drinking city. At one place he would have had to step over a flat-out body, either unconscious or dead, in the doorway; but he hadn't seen much point, he said, in applying there. A week passed, and then two weeks. They were living on a cheap brand of water-packed tuna, and Mrs. Apple had stopped inviting them so frequently to supper. Their greasepaint box somehow fell apart. Tubes of ghastly pink flesh-tone, like fat sticks of chalk, rolled into corners and stayed there, sending out their flowery old-lady smell. Janice and Paula stopped speaking to each other, and Janice moved her sleeping bag to the kitchen.

Then Barry found a job, but only for himself. A friend of a friend was putting on his own play. Emily wasn't there when he announced it. She'd been helping out at Crafts Unlimited. All she knew was that when she got back, there was Barry packing his knapsack. A swelling was rising on his lower lip, and Leon was gone. The others sat on the floor, watching Barry roll up his jeans with shaky hands. "That husband of yours is insane," he told Emily. Even his voice shook.

Emily said, "What happened?" and the others all started

talking at once. It wasn't Barry's fault, they said; you have to watch out for number one in this world; what did Leon expect? Emily never did sort out the particulars, but she grasped the main idea. She was surprised at how little it bothered her. There was something satisfying about the damage done to Barry's lip. The skin had split where the swelling was highest; she was reminded of an overripe plum. "Oh, well," she said, "I suppose it's for the best."

"Mark my words," Barry told her, "you're living with a dangerous man. I don't know why you're not scared of him."

"Oh, he would never harm *me*," Emily said. She couldn't think why Barry was taking this so seriously. Didn't it often happen in these people's lives—drama, extravagant gestures? She removed some hairpins from her hair and pinned her braids higher on her head. The others watched her. She felt graceful and light-hearted.

Janice and Paula went back to New York; Janice planned to accept an old marriage proposal. "I just hope the offer's still open," she said. Emily had no idea what Paula was going to do, and she didn't care, either. She was tired of living in a group. She got on fine with them, right to the end, and she said goodbye to them politely enough, but underneath she felt chafed by every word they uttered.

That left Victor. Victor wasn't so bad. He was only seventeen, and he seemed even younger. He was a slight, stooped, timid boy with a frail tickle of a mustache that Emily longed to shave off. Once the others were gone, he moved his blankets to the rear bedroom. He showed up for meals looking shy and hopeful. It was a little like having a son, Emily thought.

By now they were completely out of money, so Emily started work as a paid assistant at Crafts Unlimited. Leon found a part-time job at Texaco, pumping gas. Victor just borrowed from Mrs. Apple. Mrs. Apple lent him the money, but gave out lectures with it. She wanted him to go back to school, or at least take the high-school-equivalency test. She threatened to send him to live with his father, whom Emily had always assumed to be dead. After these lectures Victor would slink around the apartment kicking baseboards. Emily commiserated with him, but she did think Mrs. Apple had a point. She couldn't understand how things had gone this far, even; everyone seemed to be living lives without shape, without backbone. "When you think of it," she told Victor, "it's amazing your mother ever let you go to New York in the first place. Really, she's a very . . . surprising woman."

"Sure, to you," said Victor. "Other people's mothers always look so nice. Up close, they're strict and grabby and they don't have a sense of humor."

Then Mrs. Apple came to Emily with an idea. (She probably felt that if she came to Victor, he'd turn it down automatically.) If they were so set on acting, she said, why not act at children's birthday parties? They could put an ad in the paper, get a telephone, borrow her Singer sewing machine to stitch a few costumes together. Mothers could call and order "Red Riding Hood" or "Rapunzel." (Emily would make a lovely Rapunzel, with her long blond hair.) They would gladly pay a good fee, she was certain, since birthday parties were such a trial.

Emily passed the idea on because it sounded like something she could manage. She would not, at least, freeze up onstage in front of a few small children. Victor was immediately willing, but Leon looked doubtful. "Just the three of us?" he asked.

"We could change costumes a lot. And there are always people around here, if we're really stuck for more characters."

"We could use my mother for a witch," Victor said.

"Well, I don't know," Leon said. "I wouldn't even call that acting, if you want to know the truth."

"Oh, Leon."

She dropped the subject for the next few days. She watched him weighing it in his mind. He came back from the Texaco station with his hands black, smearing black on the doorknobs and the switchplates. Even after he washed, black stayed in the creases of his skin and rimmed his fingernails. Sitting on the kitchen counter waiting for his tuna, he spread his hands on his knees and studied them, and then he turned them over and studied them again. Finally he said, "These children's plays, I suppose they'd do for a stopgap."

Emily said nothing.

He said, "It wouldn't hurt to give it a try, just so we don't get stuck in it."

Now, all this time Emily and Victor had been laying their plans, they'd been so sure he would change his mind. They'd already ordered a phone for the kitchen. It arrived the day after Leon gave in. They placed an ad in the papers and they made a large yellow poster to hang in Crafts Unlimited. *Rapunzel, Cinderella, Red Riding Hood*, the poster read. *Or . . . you name it.* ("Just so it doesn't take a cast of thousands," Leon said.)

Then they sat back and waited. Nothing happened.

On the sixth day a woman phoned to ask if they gave puppet shows. "I don't need a play; I need a puppet show," she said. "My daughter's just wild about puppets. She doesn't like plays at all."

"Well, I'm sorry—" Emily said.

"Last year I had Peter's Puppets come and she loved them, and all they charged was thirty-two dollars, but now I hear they've moved to—"

"Thirty-two dollars?" Emily asked.

"Four dollars a child, for seven guests and Melissa. I felt that was reasonable; don't you?"

"It's more than reasonable," Emily said. "For a puppet show we get five per child."

"Goodness," the woman said. "Well, I suppose we could uninvite the MacIntosh children."

In the two weeks before the party Emily borrowed Mrs. Apple's sewing machine and put together a Beauty, two sisters, a father, and a Beast, who was really just a fake fur mitten with eyes. She chose "Beauty and the Beast" because it was her favorite fairytale. Victor said he liked it too. Leon didn't seem to care. Plainly, as far as he was concerned, this was just another version of the Texaco job. He hardly noticed when Emily came prancing up to him with her hand transformed into Beauty.

She cut a stage from a cardboard box, and bought gauzy black cloth for the scrim. She and Victor clowned together, putting on doll-like voices to match the puppets' round faces. They had the two sisters sing duets and waltz on the kitchen windowsill. Leon just looked grim. He had figured out that most of their fee had already been spent on materials. "This is not going to make us rich," he said.

"But think of next time," Emily said, "when we'll already be equipped."

"Oh, Emily, let's not have a next time."

On the day of the party—a rainy winter afternoon—they loaded everything into Victor's mother's car and drove north to Mrs. Tibbett's stucco house in Homeland. Mrs. Tibbett led them through the living room to a large, cold clubroom, where Leon and Victor arranged the cardboard stage on a Ping-Pong table. Meanwhile Emily unpacked the puppets. Then she and Victor set the two sister puppets to whispering and snickering, trying to get Leon to join in. He was supposed to work the Beast, which he'd never even fitted on his hand; and he'd had to be told the plot during the drive over. He claimed the only fairytale he knew was "Cinderella." Now he ignored the puppets and paced restlessly up and down, sometimes pausing to lift a curtain and peer out into the garden. It was because of his parents, Emily thought. This house resembled his parents' house, which Emily had once visited during semester break. The living room had that same stiff, icy quality, with the pale rugs that no one seemed to have walked on and the empty vases, the ticking silence, the satin striped chairs, where obviously no children were ever allowed to sit. Mrs. Tibbett, even, was a little like Mrs. Meredith—so gracious and honeyed, her hair streaked, her mouth tight, with something unhappy beneath her voice if Leon would only hear it. Emily reached out to pat his arm, but then stopped herself and curled her fingers in.

The doorbell rang—a whole melody. "It's a goddamned cathedral," Leon muttered. The first guests arrived, and Melissa Tibbett, a thin-faced, homely child in blue velvet, went to greet them. These children were all five years old or just turning six, Mrs. Tibbett had said. They were young enough to come too early, with their party clothes already sliding toward ruin, but old enough, at least, not to cling tearfully to the birthday presents they'd brought. Emily supervised the opening of the presents. Mrs. Tibbett had vanished, and the two men seemed to think that dealing with the children was Emily's job. She learned the names that mattered—the troublemaker (Lisa) and the shy one who hid in corners (Jennifer). Then she settled them in front of the puppet show.

Victor was the father. Emily was each of the daughters in turn. Concealed behind the scrim, she didn't feel much stage fright. "What do you want me to bring you, daughter?" Victor squeaked.

"Bring me a casket of pearls, Father," Emily piped in a tiny voice.

Leon rolled his eyes toward the ceiling.

"What do you want me to bring *you*, Beauty?"

"Only a rose, Father. One perfect rose."

She could see the outlines of the children through the scrim. They were listening, but they were fidgety underneath, she thought. It made her nervous. She felt things were on the verge of falling into pieces. During the father's long scene alone in the palace, she saw Mrs. Tibbett's fluttery silhouette enter and stand watching. What a shame; she'd come during the dull part. "Oh. A table has been laid for me, with lovely foods," the father said. "And look: a fine gold bed with satin sheets. I wonder to whom this belongs." Mrs. Tibbett shifted her weight to the other foot.

Then the Beast arrived. Emily expected him to roar, but instead he spoke in a deep, chortling growl that took her by surprise. "Who's gobbled up all my food?" he asked plaintively. "Who's been sleeping in my bed?" (Oh, Lord, she hoped he hadn't confused this with "Goldilocks.") "My lovely bed, with the satin sheets to keep my hairdo smooth!" he groaned.

The children laughed.

An audience. She saw him realize. She saw the Beast raise his shaggy head and look toward the children. Their outlines were still now and their faces were craned forward. "Do *you* know who?" he asked them.

"Him!" they cried, pointing.

"What's that you say?"

"The father! Him!"

The Beast turned slowly. "Oho!" he said, and the father puppet shrank back, as if blown by the Beast's hot breath.

After the show the maid passed cake and punch around, but most of the children were too busy with the puppets to eat. Emily taught them how to work the Beast's mouth, and she had Beauty sing "Happy Birthday" to Melissa. Mrs. Tibbett said, "Oh, this was so much better than last year's 'Punch and Judy.'"

"We never do 'Punch and Judy,'" Leon said gravely. "It's too grotesque. We stick to fairytales."

"Just one thing puzzles me," said Mrs. Tibbett.

"What's that?"

"Well, the Beast. He never changed to a prince."

Leon glanced over at Emily.

"Prince?" Emily said.

"You had her living happily ever after with the Beast. But *that's* not how it is; he changes; she says she loves him and he changes to a prince."

"Oh," Emily said. It all came back to her now. She couldn't think how she'd forgotten. "Well . . ." she said.

"But I guess that would take too many puppets."

"No," Emily said, "it's just that we use a more authentic version."

"Oh, I see," Mrs. Tibbett said.

3 By spring they were putting on puppet shows once or twice a week, first for friends of Mrs. Tibbett's and then for friends of those friends. (In Baltimore, apparently, word of mouth was what counted most.) They made enough money so they could start paying Mrs. Apple rent, and Leon quit his Texaco job. Emily went on working at Crafts Unlimited just because she enjoyed it, but she earned almost as much now from the extra puppets that she sold there. And gradually they began to be invited to school fairs and church fund-raisers. Emily had to sit up all one night, hastily sewing little Biblical costumes. A private school invited them to give a show on dental hygiene. "Dental hygiene?" Emily asked Leon. "What is there to say?" But Leon invented a character named Murky Mouth, a wicked little soul who stuffed on sweets, ran water over his toothbrush to deceive his mother, and played jump-rope with his dental floss. Eventually, of course, he came to a bad end, but the children loved him. Two more schools sent invitations the following week, and a fashionable pedodontist gave them fifty dollars to put on a Saturday-morning show for twenty backsliding patients and their mothers, who (Emily heard later) had to pay twenty-five dollars per couple to attend.

It was mostly Leon's doing, their success. He still grumbled any time they had a show, but the fact was that from the start he knew exactly what was needed: dignified, eccentric little characters (no more squeaky voices) and plenty of audience participation. His heroes were always dropping things and wondering where they were, so that the children went wild trying to tell them; always overlooking the obvious and having to have it explained. Emily, on the other hand, cared more for the puppets themselves. She liked the designing and the sewing and the scrabbling for stray parts. She loved the moment when a puppet seemed to come to life —usually just after she'd sewed the eyes on. Once made, a puppet had his own distinct personality, she found. It couldn't be altered or submerged, and it couldn't be duplicated. If he was irreparably damaged—or stolen, which sometimes happened—she could only make a new one to fill his role; she couldn't make the same one over again.

That was ridiculous, Leon said.

She imagined the world split in two: makers and doers. She was a maker and Leon was a doer. She sat home and put together puppets and Leon sprang onstage with them, all flair and action. It was only a matter of circumstance that she also had to be the voices for the heroines.

Victor was neither maker nor doer, or he was both, or somewhere in between, or . . . What was the matter with Victor? First he grew so quiet, and paused before answering anything she said, as if having to reel his mind in from more important matters. He moped around the apartment; he stared at Emily sadly while he stroked his wisp of a mustache. When Emily asked him what his trouble was, he told her he'd been born in the wrong year. "How can that be?" she asked him. She supposed he'd taken up some kind of astrology. "What difference does the year make?"

"It doesn't bother you?"

"Why should it bother me?"

He nodded, swallowing.

That night at supper he put down his plate of baked beans and stood up and said, "There's something I have to say."

They still had no furniture, and he'd been eating on the windowsill. He stood in front of the window, framed by an orange sunset so they had to squint at him from their places on the floor. He laced his fingers together and bent them back so the knuckles cracked. "I have never been a sneaky person," he said. "Leon, I'd like to announce that I'm in love with Emily."

Leon said, "Huh?"

"I won't beat around the bush: I think you're wrong for her. You're such a grouch. You're always so angry and she's so . . . un-angry. You think her puppets are nothing, a chore, something forced on you till you get to your real thing, acting. But if you're an actor, why don't you act? You think there's no theatre groups in this city? I know why: you had a fight with that guy Bronson, Branson, what's-his-name, when you went to try out. You've had a fight with everyone around. You can't try out for the Chekhov play because Barry May's in that and he'll tell all the others what you're like. But still you say you're an actor and you're so disadvantaged, so held back, wasting your talents here when there's other things you could be doing. *What* other things?"

Leon had stopped chewing. Emily felt her chest tightening up. Victor was smaller than Leon, and so young and meek he would never hit back. She imagined him cowering against the window, shielding his head with his arms, but she didn't know how to step in and stop this.

"I realize I'm not as old as Emily," Victor said, "but I could take much better care of her. I would treat her better; I'd appreciate her; I'd sit admiring her all day long, if you want to know. We'd live a real life, not like this, with her ducked over her sewing machine and you off brooding in some corner, paying her no attention, holding some grudge that no one can guess at . . . Well, I'll say it right out: I want to take Emily away with me."

Leon turned and looked at Emily. She saw that he wasn't angry at all. He was relaxed and amused, smiling a tolerant, kindly smile. "Well, Emily?" he said. "Do you want to go away with Victor?"

She felt suddenly flattened.

"Thank you, Victor," she said, pressing her palms together. "It's nice of you, but I'm fine as I am, thank you."

"Oh," said Victor.

"I appreciate the thought."

"Well," Victor said, "I didn't want to sneak around about it."

Then he sat back down on the windowsill and picked up his plate of beans.

The next morning he was gone—Victor and his tangle of blankets and his canvas backpack and his cardboard carton of LP records. He hadn't even said goodbye to Mrs. Apple. Well, it was a relief, in a way. How could they act natural after that? And she and Leon did need to be on their own. They were a married couple; it began to seem that they really were married. She was starting to think about a baby. Leon didn't want one, but in time he would come around. They could use Victor's room for a workshop now, and then for the baby later on. It was lucky Victor had left, in fact.

But she hated how his woodsy, brown boy-smell hung in the empty room for days after he had gone.

Several times in Emily's life, similar things had happened. Men had seemed to affix themselves to her—but not to her personally, she thought. What they liked was their idea of her. She remembered a boy in her logic class who used to write her notes asking if she would take down her hair for him. Her hair: a bunch of dead cells that had nothing to do with her. "Think of it as longer, thinner fingernails," she had written back coolly. She disliked being seen from outside that way—as someone with blond hair, someone with an old-fashioned face. Once, in New York, a man had started eating every day at the restaurant where she worked, and any time she so much as passed his table he would tell her about his ex-wife, who had also worn braids on top of her head. It was a continuing story: Emily would bring his rolls and he would say, "On our second date we went to the zoo." She'd refill his coffee cup and he would say, "I'm pretty certain she loved me to begin with." After a couple of weeks he went away, but Emily couldn't forget the ex-wife. She was Emily's other self; they would have understood each other, but she had slipped off and left Emily to take the blame. Now, with Victor, Emily wondered who he'd had in mind. Not Emily, she was sure—poking around in her linty old clothes, hunting up noses for her puppets. It must have been someone else who looked like Emily but had the capacity for a greater number of people in her life. Poor Victor! It was a pity, Emily thought. She was surprised at how much she missed him. She could not imagine loving anyone but Leon, but when she'd put a puppet together and longed for someone to try him out on, she thought of Victor and their squeaky-voiced duets. She remembered Beauty's sisters clowning around at that first birthday party while Leon paced the floor.

It wasn't so easy to clown around with Leon.

4 She dressed Gina in a T-shirt, pink corduroy overalls, and a snowsuit. She buckled her little red shoes on her feet. Gina was impatient to get going. "Can we swing on the swings?" she asked.

"Not today, honey."

"But I want to swing on the swings."

"Maybe tomorrow."

"*Why* can't we swing on the swings?"

She was almost two now. Terrible Two's: they had minds all their own. But that could be said of Gina at any age. Somehow, this one small child kept both of her parents continually occupied and teetering on the edge of exhaustion. They must be doing something wrong. It didn't look so hard for other people.

Emily put a coat on and tied a scarf over her hair. It was February, a damp, cold day. Even the apartment was cold. She poked her head into the kitchen to say goodbye to Leon. He was sitting at the chipped enamel table they'd bought from Goodwill, reading the *Village Voice*. "Leon?" she said. "I'm taking Gina for a walk."

"You want me to come along?"

"Oh, no, I'll be back soon."

He nodded and returned to his paper. Emily led Gina out the door. They went down the creaking stairway, past the side entrance of Crafts Unlimited, through the glass door at the front of the building. She checked the laundromat across the street. No one was there. She hoisted Gina into her arms and set off toward Beacon Avenue. Gina kept struggling to get down; she liked to go places under her own steam. (It took her all day.) By now she was so heavy that it was difficult to hold on to her. Emily went faster than she'd intended to, pulled forward by Gina's tilted weight. Her slippers made a rustling, patting sound.

They arrived at the E-Z Cafeteria five minutes early, but Leon's mother was already waiting, seated alertly at the foremost table with her hands crossed over her purse. When she saw Emily (when she saw Gina, really), she seemed to open like a flower. Her face lifted, her hands uncrossed themselves, and the feathers on her hat stirred. "Ah!" she cried. She rose and brushed her cheek against Emily's. "I wasn't sure you'd come," she told Emily. "I didn't know if you'd want to bring her out in this weather."

"Oh, she's out in any weather," Emily said.

Mrs. Meredith settled Gina in the high chair she'd already wheeled up. "Was she cold?" she crooned. "Did her little face get frozen?" She unwrapped her like a package, and patted Gina's thick, dark hair. "Oh, exactly like Leon's hair," she said. (She always did.) "Will you look at how she's grown? Just in this one month she's grown so that I never would have known her. Though of course I'd know her anywhere," she said, contradicting herself. Gina gazed at her reflectively. She was always quieter in her grandmother's presence.

The E-Z Cafeteria was not Mrs. Meredith's style, but it was one place they could manage Gina. They could wheel her down the food line instead of waiting for their order to arrive, and they could leave without delay any time she got restless. It had taken them a while to figure this out. They'd started off at the Elmwood—Mrs. Meredith's suggestion, a place near Towson, to which Emily had had to travel by bus. It was the only Baltimore restaurant Mrs. Meredith knew of. And, to be fair, she'd had no idea she was inviting a baby to lunch as well.

What had happened was, when Emily got married she had naturally informed her Great-Aunt Mercer, back in Taney. Aunt Mercer had not been very pleased, but she'd made the best of it. On her thick, silver-rimmed stationery, which smelled as if she'd kept it in her basement for the last ten years, she wrote to ask Emily who this young Meredith might be. *What's his daddy's name? Would I be likely to know any of his people? He isn't one of those* Nashville *Merediths, is he?* And once she had her answers, of course she felt duty-bound to write his parents a get-acquainted note. Next Leon received a letter from his mother, sent direct to his New York address: *Mr. Leon Meredith.* No mention of Emily. He threw it away unopened. "Oh, Leon!" Emily said. It was true she wasn't comfortable with his parents, but you couldn't just discard your only relatives. Leon said, "I told you that was a mistake, writing your aunt. I said it would be." And the letter stayed in the wastebasket.

They moved to Baltimore, but the letters followed, for all his mother had to do was ask Aunt Mercer for his new address. And Leon went on throwing the letters away. Maybe eventually he'd have opened one (this couldn't last forever, could it?), but then the Merediths did something unforgivable. They gave his forwarding address to his draft board.

It wasn't malicious, Emily was certain, but Leon thought it was. "That's my parents for you," he said. "They'd rather have me dead in the jungle than alive and happy without them." He went on cursing them even after he failed the physical. One leg was found to be an inch and a half shorter than the other, the result of a broken thighbone in his childhood. No one had ever noticed it before. He returned with a painful limp and said, "I'm free, but I won't forget what they tried to do to me." And he continued throwing their letters away.

If Emily's name had been on the envelopes too, she'd have opened them. She was pregnant by then and wishing for her mother. Aunt Mercer was no use—with her dim, steely handwriting: *The crocuses are late this year and the rodents have been at my galanthus bulbs*—and Mrs. Apple was sympathetic but had no recollection of childbirth. ("Perhaps I was put to sleep," she said. "Do they give anesthesia for such things? I may have been asleep the whole nine months, in fact.") Emily dreamed that Mrs. Meredith would suddenly arrive in person, miraculously plumper and more motherly, and she'd fold Emily into her lap and let her be a daughter again. But she never did.

Then, three months after Gina's birth, there it was: *Mrs. Leon Meredith.* Emily marveled at how long it had taken. She smuggled the letter into the bathroom and locked the door behind her to read it. *I know it must be you who's keeping our boy from us. I saw from the start you were a cold little person. But he is our only child. Think how we must feel.*

Emily was stunned. She couldn't believe that anyone would be so unfair. Her eyes blurred and the sheet of bricks shimmered in the window.

Why are you saying these things? she wrote back. *I have nothing to do with any of this and I don't understand it. It's between you and Leon.*

His mother said, *It seems you must have taken offense at something. Please, could we start over? Could we meet at the Elmwood this Wednesday at noon?*

Emily didn't want to meet her. She felt like ripping the letter to shreds. She looked at Gina, who lay crowing in her cardboard box, and she tried to imagine anything Gina could do—marrying, mismarrying, committing murder—that would sever her from Emily's life as Leon had severed himself from his parents'. There was nothing. She just wouldn't allow it. Gina was the whole point; even what Emily felt for Leon seemed pallid by comparison. She smoothed the letter

on her lap and saw Mrs. Meredith's tense, powdery face, with
the eyebrows plucked as thin as two arched wires and the
lids beneath them always a little puffed, as if she were on the
edge of tears.

There were certain rules, Emily had been taught. She would
have to go just this once.

Mrs. Meredith came by taxi, all the way from Richmond.
Evidently, she didn't drive, and had simply hired a cab for
the day. The driver sat at the next table, spreading pâté on
a cracker and reading *Male* magazine. Mrs. Meredith waited
behind a foggy martini glass. Her back was very straight.
Then Emily entered with Gina riding the way she liked to
in those days—hanging over Emily's forearm, with her bottom propped against Emily's hip, frowning darkly at her own
bare toes. "Oh!" Mrs. Meredith cried out, and one hand flew
to her throat, knocking the martini glass into her lap.

Now that she thought back, Emily felt she really should
have prepared Mrs. Meredith. It was too theatrical—bursting
in with an unannounced grandchild. It was more like something Leon would have done. She seemed to have caught
some of Leon's qualities. He seemed to have caught some of
hers. (He seldom spoke of moving on any more.) She was
reminded of those parking-lot accidents where one car's
fender grazes another's. It had always puzzled her that on each
fender, some of the other car's paint appeared. You'd think
the paint would only be on one car, not both. It was as if they
had traded colors.

She tried to tell Leon about the lunch, once it had taken
place. She led into it gradually. "Your mother's been writing
me now, you know," she said.

But Leon said, "Emily, I don't want to hear about it and I
don't want you to have anything to do with it. Is that clear?"

"All right, Leon," Emily said.

And, oddly enough, even Mrs. Meredith seemed content
to let things be. It seemed she only wanted the connection;
just who made the connection didn't matter so much. She

liked to hear from Emily what Leon was up to. Did he help to care for Gina? "He walks her at night, and he baby-sits while I'm working in the shop," Emily told her, "but he can't yet bring himself to change a diaper."

"Exactly like Burt was," Mrs. Meredith said. "Oh, exactly!" But she never tried to press any closer than that. Maybe she found things easier as they were. She often retreated into stories about Leon's childhood, when he had been someone she could understand. "He was a beautiful baby," she said. "All the nurses told me so. Prettiest baby they'd ever seen! They couldn't believe their eyes!" Somehow, everything she said had a way of slipping out of her control. "Even the doctors stopped by to take a look. This one man, a heart surgeon, he came straight from an operation just to get a glimpse of him. 'Mrs. Meredith,' he said, 'I never saw a baby so beautiful in my life. Yes, sir, we're going to hear more of that young man. He's going to amount to something someday!' He called his wife on the telephone; I heard him in the hall. 'You ought to see this baby we've got here! Ought to see this baby!' " Next, Emily thought, there'd be a star beaming over the delivery room. She began to understand why Leon got so edgy around his mother. Mrs. Meredith's rouged face, gazing brightly at a boy no one else could see, seemed deliberately shuttered and obstinate.

In fact, she made Emily feel edgy as well, and Emily never enjoyed these lunches, or came any closer to liking Mrs. Meredith. Telling her a piece of news—or even speaking to Gina in Mrs. Meredith's presence—Emily heard her own voice take on a fulsome tone that wasn't hers at all. She felt that nothing she could say would ever live up to Mrs. Meredith's expectations. But what could she do? The very day after their lunch at the Elmwood, Mrs. Meredith started driving lessons. In a month she had her license and a brand-new Buick, and she drove the entire distance from Richmond to Baltimore although, she said, she was scared to death of multi-lane highways and disliked going over thirty miles per hour. When she telephoned Emily from a corner booth, breathlessly announcing, "I did it! I'm here to take you to lunch," could Emily just say, "No, thank you," and hang up?

They settled into a schedule: the first Wednesday of every month. Emily never told Leon about it. She knew that eventually, Gina would tell. Now that Gina could talk, it was only a matter of time. "When me and Grandma was eating . . ." she'd say, and Leon would say, "You and *who?*" and then all hell would break loose. Till then, Emily went dutifully to lunch, frowning slightly with concentration.

One time Mr. Meredith came too. He seemed baffled by the baby. He let his wife do all the talking, while he stared around at the dingy old men slurping soup in the E-Z Cafeteria. "So where's this son of mine?" he asked finally.

"He's . . . very busy at home," Emily said.

"Would you believe he was once the size of this little tyke?" he asked, jutting his chin at Gina. "I could carry him in the palm of my hand. Now we're not on speaking terms."

"Burt," said Mrs. Meredith.

"He was always quick to throw things away."

Later, when it was time to go, he asked Emily if she had all her equipment.

"Equipment?" Emily said.

"Equipment. You know."

Maybe he was asking if she were sane, marrying his son.

But then he said, "Crib, playpen, high chair, carriage . . ."

"Oh. We don't need all that," Emily said. "She sleeps in a cardboard box. It's perfectly comfortable."

"I'll send her a crib," Mr. Meredith said.

"No, Mr. Meredith, please don't do that."

"I'll send her one tomorrow. Imagine! A cardboard box!" he said, and he went away shaking his head and looking pleased, as if *his* expectations, at least, had every one been fulfilled.

The crib arrived: white, spooled, with an eyelet canopy. She'd never heard of such nonsense. Two delivery men came puffing up the stairs with it and leaned it, unassembled, against the wall in the hallway. She reached a finger inside a plastic bag and touched an eyelet ruffle. Then Leon walked in, tossing from hand to hand the cabbage she'd asked him to get at the market. "What's all this?" he asked.

"Your parents sent it," she said.

He took a step backward from the crib.

"Leon," she said. "While we're on the subject, I ought to tell you something."

He said, "I don't want to hear, I don't want to know, and I want this monstrosity gone by the time I get back."

Then he turned and left, still carrying the cabbage.

Emily thought it over. She mashed a banana for Gina's supper and fed it to her, absently taking a few bites herself. She looked out the kitchen doorway and into the hall, where the crib stood slanting elegantly. At that time Gina was six months old, and outgrowing her cardboard box. She slept more often with her parents, still munching drowsily on Emily's breast. It would be nice to have a safe container to keep her in, Emily thought. She scraped banana off Gina's chin and stuffed it back into her mouth. She looked at the crib again.

When Leon came back, the crib was still there, but he didn't mention it. Maybe he'd been doing some thinking himself. The following day Emily started assembling it. She would join two pieces and then leave it a while, as if it were only something to fiddle with—a crossword puzzle, a hoop of needlework. Then she'd come back and tighten a bolt; then she'd leaf through the paper. In a few days she had a completed crib. It seemed silly to leave it obstructing the hall, so she wheeled it into their bedroom. The effect was dazzling. All that white made the rest of the room seem drab. Their mattress on the floor had a lumpy, beaten look.

She went back to the hall for Gina and carried her into the bedroom and set her in the crib. Gina stared all around her at the eyelet ruffles, the decals, the bars. What a shock, she seemed to be saying. How did this imprisonment come about?

It came about inch by inch. These things just wear you down.

5   This child had changed their lives past recognition, more than they had dreamed possible. You would think that someone so small could simply be fitted into a few spare crannies and the world could go on as usual, but it wasn't like that at all. From the start, she seemed to consume them. Even as a tiny infant she was aggressively sociable and noisy and enthusiastic, an insomniac who seldom took naps and struggled continually toward a vertical position. They would lay her down on her stomach for the night and instantly her head would bob up again, weaving and unsteady, her eyes so wide that her forehead seemed corrugated. She loved to be talked to, sung to, tossed in the air. As she grew older, she fell in love with Red Riding Hood's wolf and they had to give him up to her. If she slept at all, she slept with the wolf against her cheek and she dreamily twisted his red felt tongue. Periodically the tongue fell off and then she would go to pieces—crying and clinging to Emily till Emily sewed it back on. And she hated to be left. Hannah Miles, across the hall, was glad to baby-sit, but any time Emily and Leon went out, Gina wept as if her heart would break and Emily would have to stay. Or Leon would make her leave anyway, really insist, and she would go, but her thoughts remained with Gina, and all through the movie or whatever she would fidget, buttoning and unbuttoning her coat, not hearing a word. Then Leon would be angry with her and they'd have a fight and the outing would be wasted, but later when they returned, Gina would be wide awake and smiling, at eleven or twelve at night, reading books with Hannah and hardly noticing they were back.

They never asked, of course, whether she was worth it. They centered their lives on her. They could marvel forever at the small, chilly point of her nose, or her fat-ringed fingers or precisely cut mouth. When finally she fell asleep, the absence of all that fierce energy made the apartment feel desolate. Emily would drift through the rooms not knowing what to do next, though she'd wanted to do so much all day and never had a chance to begin. She wondered how they'd managed to produce such a child. She herself had always been so subdued and so anxious to please; Leon had Gina's fire but none of her joyous good nature. Where did she get that? She was a changeling. She had arrived with someone else's qualities. She was the gnome's baby, not theirs.

He stood in the laundromat doorway with his hat pulled low and he sank back into the darkness as they passed. Sometimes the hat was pointed, sometimes flat, sometimes broad-brimmed. Sometimes it seemed he had aged, was slackening, falling apart as certain people suddenly do; he was seen in gold-rimmed spectacles and his beard was cut to such a stubble that he might merely have neglected shaving himself. Then later he would reappear miraculously young again, the spectacles gone, the beard in full bloom. On occasion he was not gnomish at all but just a rather beakish, distinguished gentleman in suits so tidy you had the impression someone else had dressed him. On other occasions he could have stepped into a puppet show and not been out of place. He had a gait they would know anywhere, that seemed to belong to someone much younger—a reckless, bent-kneed, lunging gait, half running, landing on the balls of his feet. But once he was seen plodding out of a secondhand-clothing store with the resigned deliberation of a middle-aged man, and he had let his hair grow unsuitably long so it straggled in an unkempt and pathetic way over the back of his collar. At Christmas, Leon thought he saw him at a puppet show all the way over near Washington; but maybe it was just someone like him, he said. Then later he told Emily he'd been stupid—not for thinking it was he (the man was everywhere, after all), but for imagining there could be anyone else, anyplace, at any time, the faintest bit like Morgan.

1971

1 Morgan's oldest daughter was getting married. It seemed he had to find this out by degrees; nobody actually told him. All he knew was that over a period of months one young man began visiting more and more often, till soon a place was set for him automatically at suppertime and he was consulted along with the rest of the family when Bonny wanted to know what color to paint the dining room. His name was Jim. He had the flat, beige face of a department-store mannequin, and he seemed overly fond of crew-necked sweaters. And Morgan couldn't think of a thing to say to him. All he had to do was look at this fellow and a peculiar kind of lassitude

would seep through him. Suddenly he would be struck by how very little there was in this world that was worth the effort of speech, the entanglements of grammar and pronunciation and sufficient volume of voice.

Then Amy started beginning every sentence with "we." *We* think this and *we* hope that. And finally: when we're earning a little more money; when we find a good apartment; when we have children of our own. This just crept in, so to speak. No announcements were made. One Sunday afternoon Bonny asked Morgan if he thought the back yard was too small for the reception. "Reception?" Morgan said.

"And it's not just the size; it's the weather," Bonny said. "What if it rains? You know how the weather can be in April."

"But this is already March," Morgan said.

"We'll all sit down this evening," said Bonny, "and come to some decision."

So Morgan went to his closet and chose an appropriate costume: a pinstriped suit he'd laid claim to after Bonny's father died. It stood out too far at the shoulders, maybe, but he thought it might have been what Mr. Cullen was wearing when Morgan asked him for permission to marry Bonny. And certainly he'd been wearing his onyx cufflinks. Morgan found the cufflinks in the back of a drawer, and he spent some time struggling to slip them through the slick, starched cuffs of his only French-cuffed shirt.

But when the four of them sat down for their discussion, no one consulted Morgan in any way whatsoever. All they talked about was food. Was it worthwhile calling in a caterer, or should they prepare the food themselves? Amy thought a caterer would be simplest. Jim, however, preferred that things be homemade. Morgan wondered how he could say that, having eaten so many suppers here. Bonny wasn't much of a cook. She leaned heavily on sherry—several glugs of it in any dish that she felt needed more zip. Everything they ate, almost, tasted like New York State cocktail sherry.

Morgan sat in the rocking chair and plucked out his beard,

strand by strand. If he got up right now and left, he told himself, they might not even notice. He reflected on a long-
standing grievance: there was one of Bonny's pregnancies that
she'd forgotten to inform him about. It was the time she'd
been expecting Liz, or maybe Molly. Bonny always said he
was mistaken; of course she'd told him, she recalled it clearly.
But Morgan knew better. He suspected, even, that she'd neglected to tell him on purpose: he tended to get annoyed by
her slapdash attitude toward various birth-control methods.
To his certain knowledge, the very first inkling he'd had of
that pregnancy was when Bonny arrived in the kitchen one
morning wearing the baggy blue chambray shirt she habitually used as a maternity smock. He was positive he would
have remembered if she'd mentioned it to him.

"Amy will start down the stairs," Bonny said. Evidently,
they were planning the actual ceremony now. "Her father
will meet her at the bottom and walk her to the center of
the living room."

"Daddy, promise me you won't wear one of your hats,"
Amy said.

Morgan rocked in his chair and plucked on, thinking of the
tall black father-of-the-bride top hat he would purchase for
the occasion. He knew just where he could find one: Tuxedo
Tom's Discount Formal Wear. He began to feel slightly
happier.

But later, when Jim and Amy had gone out, he sank into a
spell of sadness. He thought of what a sunny child Amy had
been when she was small. She'd had large, exaggerated curls
swooping upward at each ear, so that she seemed to be wearing a Dutch cap. That Dutch-capped child, he thought, was
whom he really mourned—not the present Amy, twenty-one
years old, efficient secretary for a life-insurance company. He
recalled how he had once worried over her safety. He'd been
a much more anxious parent than Bonny. "You know," he
told Bonny, "I used to be so certain that one of the children
would die. Or all of them, even—I could picture that. I was
so afraid they'd be hit by cars, or kidnapped, or stricken with

polio. I'd warn them to look both ways, not to run with scissors, never to play with ropes or knives or sharp sticks. 'Relax,' you'd say. Remember? But now look: it's as if they died after all. Those funny little roly-poly toddlers, Amy in her OshKosh overalls—they're dead, aren't they? They did die. I was right all along. It's just that it happened more slowly than I'd foreseen."

"Now, dear, this is just an ordinary life development," Bonny told him.

He looked at her. She was seated at the kitchen table, working on the guest list for the wedding. On the wall above her was something like a hat rack—a row of short wooden arms. When you pressed a pearl pushbutton anywhere in this house, there was a clunk from the kitchen gong and one of the wooden arms would fly up, alerting a non-existent servant. Beneath each arm a yellowed label identified the room that had rung—or (in the case of bedrooms) the person. *Mr. Armand. Mrs. Armand. Miss Caroline. Master Keith.* Studying these labels, Morgan had the feeling that a younger, finer family lived alongside his, gliding through the hallways, calling for tea and hot-water bottles. Evenings, the mother sat by the fire in a white peignoir and read to her children, one on either side of her. A boy, a girl; how tidy. At dinner they discussed great books, and on Sunday they dressed up and went to church. *They* never quarreled. *They* never lost things or forgot things. They rang and waited serenely. They gazed beyond the Gowers with the placid, rapt expressions of theatregoers ignoring some petty disturbance in the row ahead.

"I'd like to invite Aunt Polly," Bonny said, "but that means Uncle Darwin, too, and he's so deaf and difficult."

She was peering through black-framed, no-nonsense glasses, which she'd just started wearing for reading. Morgan said, "So did *you* die, when you think of it."

"Me?"

"Where's that girl I used to take out walking? I used to

hold on to your arm, high up, and you would look off elsewhere and get pink, but you wouldn't pull away."

Bonny added a name to her list. She said, "Walking? I don't
remember that. I thought we always drove."

He slid his fingers down the inside of her upper arm,
where the skin was silkiest. The back of his hand brushed the
weight of one breast. She didn't seem to notice. She said,
"Luckily, Jim doesn't have many relatives."

"She must be marrying him out of desperation."

Then she did look up. She said, "Couldn't you still love the
girls anyhow? You don't stop loving people just because they
change size."

"Of course I love them."

"Not the same way," she said. "It seems you get fixed on
this one appearance of a person; I mean, this single idea you
have." She clicked her ballpoint pen. "And anyway, why
leap ahead so? They haven't *all* grown up. Molly and Kate
are still in high school."

"No, no, they're gone, for all intents and purposes," Morgan said. "Out every evening, off somewhere, up to something . . . they're gone, all right." He brightened. "Aha!" he
said. "Alone at last, my dollink!" But it called for too much
effort. He drifted over to the stove, depressed, and lit a
cigarette on a burner. "House feels so damn big, we need a
ride-'em vacuum cleaner."

"You always did want more closet space," Bonny told him.

"They've dumped their hamsters on us and gone away."

"Morgan. There were nine of us at dinner tonight, counting your mother and Brindle. When I was a little girl, any
time there were nine at table we had to send downtown for
Mattie Ida to come help serve."

"What we ought to do is move," Morgan said. "We could
get a house in the country, maybe, live off the land." He pictured himself in sabots and a rough blue peasant smock. The
house would be a one-room cabin with a huge stone fireplace,
a braided rug, and a daybed covered in some hand-woven

fabric. Unbidden, Amy in her Dutch-cap curls bounced in the center of the daybed. He winced. "I'll take an early retirement," he said. "Forty-five feels older than I'd thought it would. I'll retire and we'll have some time to ourselves. Won't that be nice?"

"Now, don't go off on one of your crazy schemes," Bonny told him. "You'd die of boredom, retiring. You'd feel useless."

"Useless?" Morgan said. He frowned.

But Bonny was on the track of something new, thoughtfully tapping her pen against her teeth. She said, "Morgan, in this day and age, do you believe the bride's mother would still give the bride a little talk?"

"Hmm?"

"What I want to know is, am I expected to give Amy a talk about sex or am I not?"

"Bonny, do you have to call it *sex?*"

"What else would I call it?"

"Well . . ."

"I mean, sex is what it is, isn't it?"

"Yes, but, I don't know . . ."

"I mean, what would *you* say? Is it sex, or isn't it?"

"Bonny, will you just stop *hammering* at me?"

"Anyhow," she said, returning to her list, "in this day and age, I bet she'd laugh in my face."

Morgan rubbed his forehead with two fingers. Really, it occurred to him, if Bonny had been more serious, more responsible, none of this upheaval would be happening. Or at least it wouldn't be happening quite so soon. It seemed to him that she had let the children slip through her fingers in some sort of sloppy, casual, cheerful style that was uniquely hers. He recalled that once, while chaperoning Kate's sixth-grade class on a field trip to Washington, she'd lost all eight of her charges in the Smithsonian Institution. They'd been found among showcases full of savages, copying down the recipe for shrunken heads. At the school's annual mother-daughter picnic, where everyone else brought potato salad and lemonade, Bonny brought a sack of Big Macs and a thermos of chablis. Yes, and she had such a disastrous effect upon machinery; she had only to settle behind the steering wheel and instantly the car fell apart. Warning lights would blink, steam would issue from the radiator, the muffler would drop off, and hubcaps would roll in every direction and clang along the gutters and slither down storm drains. She'd make one simple right turn and the turn signal would never work again. No wonder he spent half his weekends on his back in the garage! And she'd passed all this on to the girls too. The first driving lesson he gave Amy, the left front window had slid down inside the door and could not be retrieved. For that he'd had to go to the dealer.

And then there was his sister, who hadn't been out of that bathrobe of hers since Christmas. It hung on her like old orchid petals, wilted, striated, heavy-smelling. And his mother's memory was failing more than ever now, though she flew into a fury if anyone hinted as much. At supper, proving her sharpness, she'd recite whole portions of "Hiawatha" or the *Rubáiyát.* "Come, fill the Cup . . . !" she'd start up out of nowhere, slamming a fork against her glass, and Brindle would say, "Oh, Jesus, not again," and all the others would groan and fall into their separate, disorderly factions around the table.

Useless? Living this life of his was such hard work that even if he retired tomorrow, he had no hope of feeling useless.

2 Amy stood at the top of the stairs, wearing white and carrying roses. The hall window behind her lit her long, filmy skirt. At the bottom of the stairs Morgan waited with his hand on the newel post. He wore his new top hat and a pure-black suit from Second Chance. (There'd been a little fuss about the hat, but he'd held his ground.) He had trimmed his beard. Gold-rimmed spectacles (window glass) perched on his nose. He felt like Abraham Lincoln.

One of Morgan's failings was that formal, official proceed-

ings—weddings, funerals—never truly affected him. They
just didn't seem to penetrate. He'd lain awake half of last
night mourning his daughter, but the fact was that now, with
the ceremony about to begin, all that was on his mind was
Amy's roses. He had distinctly heard the wedding-dress lady
tell her to carry them low, at arm's length—*too* low, even,
she said, because if Amy were nervous at all she'd tend to
lift them higher. And now, before the music had even started,
Amy had her bouquet at breast level. This didn't trouble
Morgan (he couldn't see that it made the slightest difference), but he wondered why nervousness should cause people
to raise their arms. Was it something to do with protecting the
heart? Morgan experimented. He clasped his hands first low,
then high. He didn't find the one any more comforting than
the other. With his hands folded just beneath his beard, he
tried a dipping rhythmic processional, humming to himself
as he sashayed across the hall. "*Daddy*," Amy hissed. Morgan
dropped his hands and hurried back to the newel post.

Kate set the needle on the record. The wedding march
began in mid-note. In the living room the guests grew suddenly
still; all Morgan heard was the creaking of their rented chairs.
He smiled steadily up at Amy, his spectacles catching the
light and flashing two white circles across her face. With her
hand trailing down the banister, weightless as a leaf, Amy set
a pointed satin slipper in the center of each step. Her skirt
caused a clinking sound among the brass rods that anchored
the Persian carpet. Yesterday morning Bonny had taken a
red Magic Marker and colored in the bare spots in the carpet. Then she'd used a brown Magic Marker for the rips in
the leather armchair. (Sometimes Morgan felt he was living
in one of those crayoned paper houses that the twins used to
make.) Amy reached the hallway and took his arm. She was
trembling slightly. He guided her into the living room and
down the makeshift aisle.

On this same stringy rug he had walked her for hours
when she was just newborn. He had nestled her head on his

shoulder and paced the length of the rug and back, growl-
ing lullabies. The memory didn't stir him. It was just there,
just another, lower layer in this room that was full of layers. He led her up to Bonny's minister, a man he disliked.
(He disliked all ministers.) Amy dropped his arm and took a
place next to what's-his-name, Jim. Morgan stepped back and
stood with his feet planted apart, his hands joined behind him.
He rocked a little to the lullaby in his head.

"Who gives this woman to be married?" the minister said.
From the way the question rang in the silence, Morgan suspected it might have been asked once before without his
noticing. He seemed to have missed part of the service. "Her
mother and I do," he said. It would have been more accurate
to say, "Her mother does." He turned and found his seat
next to Bonny, who was looking beautiful and calm in a blue
dress with a wide scoop neckline that kept slipping off one or
the other of her shoulders. She laid a hand on top of his.
Morgan noticed a gray thread of cobweb dangling from the
ceiling.

Jim put a ring on Amy's finger. Amy put a ring on Jim's
finger. They kissed. Morgan thought of a plan: he would go
live with them in their new apartment. They didn't know a
thing, not a thing. No doubt they'd have broken all their
kitchen machines within a week and their household accounts
would be a shambles, and then along would come Morgan to
repair and advise. He would go as an old man, one of those
really bereft old men with no teeth, no job, no wife, no
family. In some small area he would act helpless, so that Amy
would feel a need to care for him. He would arrive, perhaps,
without buttons on his shirt, and would ask her to sew them
on for him. He had no idea how to do it himself, he would
tell her. Actually, Morgan was very good at sewing on buttons. Actually, he not only sewed on his own buttons but also
Bonny's and the girls', and patched their jeans and altered
their hemlines, since Bonny wasn't much of a seamstress. Actually, Amy was aware of this. She was also aware that he was

not a toothless old man and that he did have a wife and family. The trouble with fathering children was, they got to know you so well. You couldn't make the faintest little realignment of the facts around them. They kept staring levelly into your eyes, eternally watchful and critical, forever prepared to pass judgment. They could point to so many places where you had gone permanently, irretrievably wrong.

3   There'd been a compromise on the food. Bonny had ordered several trays from the deli, and then Morgan had picked up some cheese and some crackers which the girls had put together this morning. He'd been upset to discover that there was apparently no discount outlet for gourmet cheeses. "Do you know what these things *cost?*" he asked the groom's father, who had a hand poised over a cracker spread with something blue-veined. Then he wandered across the yard to check on the Camembert. It was surrounded by three young children—possibly Jim's nephews. "This one smells like a stable," the smallest was saying.

"It smells like a gerbil cage."

"It smells like the . . . elephant house at the zoo!"

The weather had turned out fine, after all. It was a warm, yellow-green day, and daffodils were blooming near the garage. A smiling brown maid, on loan from Uncle Ollie, bore a tray of drinks through the crowd, picking her way carefully around the muddy patches where the spring reseeding had not yet taken hold. The bride stood sipping champagne and listening to an elderly gentleman whom Morgan had never seen before. His other daughters—oddly plain in their dress-up clothes—passed around sandwiches and little things on toothpicks, and his mother was telling the groom's mother why she lived on the third floor. "I started out on the second floor," she said, "but moved on account of the goat."

"I see," said Mrs. Murphy, patting her pearls.

"This goat was housebroken, naturally, but the drawback was that I am the only person in this family who reads *Time* magazine. In fact, I have a subscription. And as coincidence would have it, the goat had only been trained on *Time* magazine. I mean, he would only . . . I mean, if the necessity arose, the only place he was willing to . . . was on a *Time* magazine spread on the floor. He recognized that red border, I suppose. And so you see if I were to lay my magazine aside even for a second, why, along this animal would come and just . . . would up and . . . would . . ."

"He'd pee all over it," Morgan said. "Tough luck if she wasn't through reading it."

"*Oh*, yes," Mrs. Murphy said. She took a sip from her glass.

At Morgan's elbow, in a splintered wicker chair, an unknown man sat facing in the other direction. Maybe he was from the groom's side. He had a bald spot at the back of his head; fragile wisps of hair were drawn across it. He raised a drink to his lips. Morgan saw his weighty signet ring. "Billy?" Morgan said. He went around to the front of the chair. Good God, it was Billy, Bonny's brother.

"Nice wedding, Morgan," Billy said. "I've been to a lot, you know—mostly my own. I'm an expert on weddings." He laughed. His voice was matter-of-fact, but to Morgan it was the misplaced, eerie matter-of-factness sometimes encountered in dreams. How could this be Billy? What had happened here? Morgan had last seen Billy not a month ago. He said, "Billy, from the back of your head I didn't know you."

"Really?" Billy said, unperturbed. "Well, how about from the front?"

From the front he was the same as ever—boyish-looking, with a high, round forehead and dazzling blue eyes. But no, if you met him on the street somewhere, wouldn't he be just another half-bald businessman? Only someone who'd known him as long as Morgan had could find the bones in his slackening face. Morgan stood blinking at him. Billy seemed first middle-aged and anonymous; then he was Bonny's high-living baby brother; then he was middle-aged again—like one of those trick pictures that alter back and forth as you shift your position. "Well?" Billy said.

"Have some champagne, why don't you?" Morgan asked him.

"No, thanks, I'll stick to scotch."

"Have some cheese, then. It's very expensive."

"Good old Morgan," Billy said, toasting him. "Good old, cheap old Morgan, right?"

Morgan wandered away again. He looked for someone else to talk to, but none of the guests seemed his type. They were all so genteel and well modulated, sipping their champagne, the ladies placing their high heels carefully to avoid sinking through the sod. In fact, who here was a friend of Morgan's? He stopped and looked around him. Nobody was. They were Bonny's friends, or Amy's, or the groom's. A twin flew by—Susan, in chiffon. Her flushed, earnest face and steamy spectacles reminded him that his daughters, at least, bore some connection to him. "Sue!" he cried.

But she flung back, "I'm not Sue, I'm Carol."

Of course she was. He hadn't made that mistake in years. He walked on, shaking his head. Under the dogwood tree, three uncles in gray suits were holding what appeared to be a committee meeting. "No, I've been letting my cellar go, these days," one of them was saying. "Been drinking what I have on hand. To put it bluntly, I'm seventy-four years old. This June I'll be seventy-five. A while back I was pricing a case of wine and they recommended that I age it eight years. 'Good enough,' I started to say. Then I thought, 'Well, no.' It was the strangest feeling. It was the oddest moment. I said, 'No, I suppose it's not for me. Thanks anyway.' "

At a gap in the hedge, Morgan slipped through. He found himself on the sidewalk, next to the brisk, noisy street, on a normal Saturday afternoon. His car was parked alongside the curb. He opened the door and climbed in. For a while he just sat there, rubbing his damp palms on the knees of his trousers. But the sun through the glass was baking him, and finally he rolled down a window, dug through his pockets for the keys, and started the engine.

These were his closest friends: Potter the musical-instrument man, the hot-dog lady, the Greek tavern-keeper on Broadway, and Kazari the rug merchant. None of them would do. For one reason or another, there wasn't a single person he could tell, "My oldest daughter's getting married. Could I sit here with you and smoke a cigarette?"

He floated farther and farther downtown, as if descending through darkening levels of water. All's Fair Pawnshop, Billiards, Waterbeds, Beer, First House of Jesus, SOUL BROTHER DO NOT BURN. Flowers were blooming in unlikely places—around a city trashcan and in the tiny, parched weed-patch beneath a rowhouse window. He turned a corner where a man sat on the curb flicking out the blade of his knife, slamming it shut with the heel of his hand, and flicking it out again. He traveled on. He passed Meller Street, then Merger Street. He turned down Crosswell. He parked and switched the engine off and sat looking at Crafts Unlimited.

It was months since he'd been here. The shopwindow was filled with Easter items now—hand-decorated eggs and stuffed rabbits, a patchwork quilt like an early spring garden. The Merediths' windows were empty, as always; you couldn't tell a thing from them. Maybe they'd moved. (They could move in a taxi, with one suitcase, after ten minutes' preparation.) He slid out of the car and walked toward the shop. He climbed the steps, pushed through the glass door, and gazed up the narrow staircase. But he didn't have what it took to continue. (What would he say? How would he explain himself?) Instead, he turned left, through a second glass door and into the crafts shop. It smelled of raw wood. A gray-haired, square-boned woman in a calico smock was arranging hand-carved animals on a table. "Hello," she said, and then she glanced up and gave him a startled look. It was the top hat, he supposed. He wished he'd worn something more appropriate. And why were there no other customers? He was all alone, conspicuous, in a roomful of quilted silence.

Then he saw the puppets. "Ah, so!" he said. "Ze poppets!"
Surprisingly, he seemed to have developed an accent—from
what country, he couldn't say. "Zese poppets are for buying?"
he asked.

"Why, yes," the woman said.

They lay on a center table: Pinocchio, a princess, a dwarf,
an old lady, all far more intricate than the first ones he'd seen.
Their heads were no longer round, simple, rubber-ball heads
but were constructed of some padded cloth, with tiny stitches
making wrinkles and bulges. The old-lady puppet, in particular, had a face so furrowed that he couldn't help running
his finger across it. "Wonderful!" he said, still in his accent.

"They're sewn by a girl named Emily Meredith," the
woman told him. "A remarkable craftsman, really."

Morgan nodded. He felt a mixture of jealousy and happiness. "Yes, yes," he wanted to say, "don't I know her very
well? Don't I know both of them? Who are you, to speak of
them?" But also he wanted to hear how this woman saw
them, what the rest of the world had to say about them. He
waited, still holding the puppet. The woman turned back to
her animals.

"Perhaps I see her workroom," he said.

"Pardon?"

"She leeve nearby, yes?"

"Why, yes, she lives just upstairs, but I'm not sure she—"

"Zis means a great deal to me," Morgan said.

Across from him, on the other side of the table, stood a
blond wooden cabinet filled with weaving. Its doors were
wavery glass, and they reflected a shortened and distorted
view of Morgan—a squat, bearded man in a top hat. Toulouse-
Lautrec. Of course! He adjusted the hat, smiling. Everything
black turned transparent, in the glass. He wore a column of
rainbow-colored weaving on his head and a spade of weaving
on his chin. "You see, I also am artiste," he told the woman.
Definitely, his accent was a French one.

She said, "Oh?"

"I am solitary man. I know no other artistes."

"But I don't think you understand," she said. "Emily and her husband, they just give puppet shows to children, mainly. They only sell puppets when they have a few extras. They're not exactly—"

"Steel," he said, "I like to meet zem. I like you to introduce me. You know so many people! I see zat. A friend to ze artistes. What your name is, please?"

"Well . . . Mrs. Apple," she said. She thought a moment. "Oh, all right. I don't suppose they would mind." She called to someone at the rear, "Hannah, will you watch for customers?" Then she turned to lead Morgan out the side door.

He followed her up the staircase. There was a smell of fried onions and disinfectant. Mrs. Apple's hips looked very broad from this angle. She became, by extension, someone fascinating: she must speak to the Merediths every day, know intimately their schedules and their habits, water their plants when they went on tour. He restrained the urge to set a friendly palm on her backside. She glanced at him over her shoulder, and he gave her a reassuring smile.

At the top of the stairs she turned to the right and knocked on a tall oak door. "Emily?" she called.

But when the door opened, it was Leon who stood there. He was holding a newspaper. When he saw Morgan, he drew the paper sharply to his chest. "Dr. Morgan!" he said.

Mrs. Apple said, "Doctor?"

She looked at Morgan and then at Leon. "Why," she said, "is this the doctor you told me about? The one who delivered Gina?"

Leon nodded.

"But I thought you were an artist!" Mrs. Apple said. "You said you were an artist!"

Morgan hung his head. He shuffled his feet. "I was embarrassed about my hat," he said. "I've just recently come from a wedding; I know I look ridiculous. I said I was an artist so you wouldn't laugh at me."

"Oh, you poor man," Mrs. Apple said. Then she did laugh. "You and your 'zis and zat.' Your 'zese and zose.' "

He risked a glance at Leon. Leon wasn't laughing. He was glaring at Morgan, and he kept the newspaper clamped to his chest as if guarding secrets.

"I do want to see your workroom," Morgan told him. "I may buy a large number of puppets."

"We don't have a large number," Leon said.

"Oh, come on, Leon," Mrs. Apple said. "Why not show him? What's the harm?" She nudged Morgan in the side. "You and your 'artistes.' Your 'poppets.'" She started laughing again. Her eyes grew rays of wrinkles at the corners.

Leon stood scowling at Mrs. Apple. Then, "Well," he said ungraciously, and he stepped back and turned to lead them down the hall.

Morgan peered swiftly into the room on his right—a flash of sunken sofa and a half-empty bookcase. On his left was the kitchen; he had an impression of cold, gleaming whiteness. The next door on the left led to the workroom. There was no real furniture at all—just a sewing machine beneath the window, and a stubby aluminum stepladder on which Emily sat snipping paper. Her black skirt drooped around her, nearly obscuring the ladder. The braids on top of her head picked up light from somewhere and glinted like flying sparks. "Emily," Leon said.

She looked up. Then she jumped off the stepladder and hid whatever she was doing behind her back. "What do *you* want?" she asked Morgan.

"Why, Emily. Goodness," Mrs. Apple said. "This is Dr. Morgan. Don't you recognize him? He's come to buy some puppets. A large *number* of puppets, Emily."

"Buy them downstairs," said Emily, white-faced.

You would think she had something against him.

Morgan tried not to feel hurt. He smiled at her. He said, "I like to see the process of things. Actually."

"There's no process going on here."

He stroked his beard.

Mrs. Apple said, "But . . . Emily? Show him the shadow puppets." She told Morgan, "She's trying something new,

Doctor: shadow puppets, out of paper. See?" She crossed to the sewing machine and took something from one of its drawers. It was the silhouette of a knight in armor, attached to a slender rod. "You notice he's hinged at the joints," she said. "You work him behind a screen. He casts a shadow on the screen. Isn't that clever?"

"Yes, certainly," said Morgan. He looked around the room. He wondered what Emily sat on while she worked at the sewing machine. The stepladder, maybe? Even in his fondest fantasies he had not imagined such starkness. He was fascinated. "And will you be using shadow puppets in your shows now?" he asked Emily.

"Yes," she said shortly.

"No," Leon said.

There was a pause. Mrs. Apple gave a little laugh.

"With shadow puppets," Leon said, "it's all how they're hinged, nothing more. How Emily caused their joints to swing when she made them."

"So?" Emily said.

"You just scoot them along the ledge behind the screen, and their joints fall into place. There's nothing to *do*, even less to do than there is with the old kind of puppets."

"So?"

They stared at each other.

Morgan cleared his throat.

"Is that your child I'm hearing?" he asked.

Of course it was. She was singing something in a small, cracked voice, off in some other room. But nobody answered him. He poked his head out into the hall. Then he crossed the hall and went into the bedroom. There was a mattress in one corner and a bureau in another, and a narrow cot along one wall. A child sat on the cot, fitting Tinker Toys together. She sang, ". . . *how to get to Sesame Street* . . ." When she saw Morgan, she stopped.

Morgan said, "Hello there."

She looked at him doubtfully.

He heard the Merediths coming, and he said quickly,

"Would you like my hat?" He tore his hat from his head and set it on hers, tilting it back so it wouldn't engulf her completely.

From the doorway, Emily said, "Gina! Take that off. You never try another person's hat on."

"It's my hat," Gina said. "He gave it to me."

"Take it off," Leon said.

"No."

She had a round face and a pointed chin; she had to keep her chin raised so the hat wouldn't slide down over her eyes. This made her look proud and challenging. In fact, she resembled Leon, Morgan thought. When Emily tried to lift the hat from her head, Gina fought her hands away. "It's *my* hat. It's mine."

Morgan said, "Surely. It's a gift."

Emily stopped struggling, but she continued to stand between Morgan and the child, shielding her. Her eyes were pale and cold. She had her arms folded tightly, and Leon stood firm beside her.

Mrs. Apple said, "Dr. Morgan?" She arrived breathless, and handed him another shadow puppet. This one was a king. He might have stepped out of a stained-glass window; red and blue transparent paper covered the pierced design in his robe. Lit behind a screen, he would cast jewel-like colored shadows. "Isn't he marvelous?" Mrs. Apple said. "It's art! You could hang it on the wall."

"That's true, I could," Morgan said. He stroked the colored paper with a thumb. Something about the precision of the design made him feel sad and deprived. His gaze slid off the king and away, landing finally on the bureau. Its top was nearly bare. There were no bottles or safety pins or ticket stubs; just a single framed photo of Leon and Emily holding hands in front of this building. Gina rode on Leon's shoulders. Her plump little calves bracketed his neck. All three of them were smiling squintly into the sunlight. Morgan stepped closer and bent over the photo, pinching his lower lip between his thumb and index finger. The king hung forgotten in his left hand. Bemused, he peered into a drawer that was partway open. Then he opened it further and studied its contents: three white shirts and a box of Kleenex. "Dr. Morgan!" Emily said sharply.

"Yes, yes."

He followed the others out of the room, laying a hand on Gina's head as he passed. Her hair was so soft, it seemed to cling to his fingers for several seconds afterward.

Back in the workroom, he said, "What do you do with Gina while you're giving your puppet shows?"

Emily turned away, refusing to answer, but Leon said, "We take her along."

"And? Does she help with the productions?"

"Oh, no. She's just barely turned four."

"She knows the ropes, though," Morgan suggested. "She was raised backstage, after all. She knows to stay quiet while a play is going on."

"Gina?" Leon said. He laughed. "Gina's never been quiet a full minute in her life. We have to keep hushing her all through the show, and if it's a birthday party, it's worse. She cries when someone else gets to blow out the candles. She hates it when Emily pays attention to other children."

"Oh, you ought to see one of their shows," said Mrs. Apple. She slid the king out of Morgan's hand. Without noticing, he'd rucked up one corner of the colored paper. "They're getting so well known! They've been all the way to Washington. And a man who runs an entertainment company wanted to just take them over, make them part of his troupe, like professionals. What did you ever tell that man, Leon? Did you ever answer his letter?"

"I threw it away," Leon said.

"Threw it away!"

"It was some kind of Bible group. Gospel singers and things."

"But—threw it away! You could at least have answered it."

"And off in some poky town," Leon said. "Tinville, Tindale . . ."

"I doubt you *ever* answer letters," Morgan said. He felt suddenly pleased and excited.

Leon said, "Oh, well . . ."

"Really, what's the point? Why complicate your lives? You go downstairs to clear out the mailbox every now and then, and you glance at what's there and toss it all in the wastebasket and come back empty-handed."

"Well, sometimes," Leon said.

"When?" Emily asked him. Then she turned to Morgan and said, "We're not who you believe we are."

"Eh?"

"We're not who you imagine."

"Come look at Rip Van Winkle," Mrs. Apple said.

"We live like anyone else. We manage fine. We like to be left alone," said Emily. "Let me show you to the door."

"Oh, but Emily!" Mrs. Apple said. "He hasn't seen all the puppets!"

"He's seen enough."

"He wanted to buy a large number!"

"No, no, that's all right . . . I really must be going," Morgan said. "Thank you anyhow."

Emily spun through the door, a swirl of black skirt, and he followed her. They went down the hallway single-file—Emily, Morgan, Leon. Mrs. Apple stayed behind, no doubt looking around at the puppets in bewilderment. "Maybe some other time?" she called after him.

"Yes, maybe so . . ."

He skidded on a Tinker Toy and said, "Oh, excuse me," and lurched against the wall. He clapped a hand to his head. "I'd better go home and change," he said.

"Change?" Leon asked.

"Yes, I . . . need another hat."

His voice was echoing now; they'd reached the stairs. But instead of starting down, he looked at the door across the landing. "Who lives there?" he asked.

"Joe and Hannah Miles," said Leon, but Emily said, "No one."

"Miles? Are they craftsmen also?"

"We'll see you to the street," Emily told him. She pushed forward, edging him toward the stairs, and when he took his first step down, she followed so closely that he felt hounded. "I don't understand you," she said. (He should have known. She would not veil anything; she was as uncurtained as her windows.) "What do you want of us? What are you after? Why did you trail us all those months and lurk in doorways and peer around corners?"

"Oh? You noticed?" Morgan said. He staggered with embarrassment and grabbed the banister.

"You could have come straight up and said hello, like ordinary people."

"Yes, but I was so . . . I'd built up this idea of you. I almost preferred watching, don't you see. My own household is impossible. Very confusing, very tedious," he said. He stopped, halfway down the last flight of stairs. "Oh, *you* think it's all so romantic, I suppose," he said. "Big-city doctor! Saving lives. But mostly it's a treadmill. I work too far downtown; I attract a low class of patient. Twice I've had my office robbed by addicts looking for drugs, and one of those times I was present. They tied my secretary to her chair with a raincoat belt and they made me go through all my desk drawers. It was unnerving. There I was, tumbling out sample packs of decongestants, sinus tablets, pediatric nosedrops . . . I'm not a brave man. I gave them all I had. I tell you this to show you what sort of existence I lead, Emily, Leon . . ."

He was out of breath. He felt a white space inside his head, as if he were standing at an unaccustomed altitude. "Just hear what happened last summer," he said. "I had this patient who'd been stabbed. Stabbed in front of a Fells Point bar, something to do with a woman. They brought him in and woke me in the dead of night. That's the kind of practice I have—such fine patients. And no answering service, no condominium in Ocean City where I can vanish over the weekend . . . Anyhow. He had a long, shallow cut all down the left side, from the ribcage to the hipbone, fortunately clear of the heart. I laid him on the table in my office and stitched him up right then and there. Took me an hour and a quarter —a tiresome job, as you might imagine. Then just as I'm knotting the last stitch, wham! The door bursts open. In comes the man who stabbed him. Pulls out a knife and rips him down the *right* side, ribcage to hipbone. Back to the needle and thread. Another hour and a quarter."

Leon gave a sudden snort of laughter, but Emily just nudged Morgan forward. Morgan resumed his descent, leaning heavily on the banister like someone old and rheumatic. He said, "They come to me with headaches, colds, black eyes . . . self-healing things. A man who does sedentary work —a taxi driver, say—will spend the weekend moving furniture and then call me out of bed on a Sunday night. 'Doc, I got the most terrible backache. Do you think it could be a disk? A fusion? Will I need an operation?' For this I went to medical school!"

"Here," said Emily. They had reached the front door. She pushed it open for him and held out her hand. "Goodbye," she told him. Leon grinned anxiously behind her, as if trying to ease the insult. Morgan took her hand and was startled by its lightness and its dryness.

"You don't want to be friends at all, do you?" he said.

"No," Emily told him.

"Ah," he said. "And why would that be?"

"I don't like how you try to get into our lives. I hate it! I don't like being pried into."

"Emily," Leon said.

"No, no," Morgan told him. "It's quite all right. I understand." He looked away, toward his dusty, sagging car. He had no feelings whatsoever. It seemed he'd been emptied. "Maybe you could meet my wife," he said with an effort. "Would you like to meet Bonny? Have I told you about her? Or you might like my children. I have very nice children, very normal, very ordinary; they seem *determined* to be ordinary . . . Two are in high school. One's grown, really, a secretary; and four others are in college, here and there. Most of the year, they're gone. We hardly hear from them. But that's the way it is, right? Every parent says that. You can see that I'm a family man. Does that help? No, I guess it doesn't." It seemed he was still holding Emily's hand. He dropped it. "The oldest girl's getting married," he said. "I'm not a doctor. I work in a hardware store."

Emily said, "What?"

"I manage Cullen Hardware."

"But . . . you delivered our baby!" she said.

"Ah, well," he told her, "I haven't witnessed three of my daughters' births for nothing." He patted all his pockets, hunting cigarettes, but when he found a pack, he just stood holding it and looking into their stunned faces. "That stabbing business, well, I read it in the paper," he said. "I presented myself untruthfully. I do that often, in fact. I often find myself giving a false impression. It's not something I intend, you understand. It almost seems that other people conspire with me, push me into it. That day you called for a doctor in the house: no one else came forward. There was this long, long silence. And it seemed like such a simple thing—offer some reassurance, drive you to the hospital. I had no inkling I'd actually have to deliver a baby. Events just . . . rolled me forward, so to speak."

He wished they would say something. All they did was stare at him. Meanwhile a girl in an old-fashioned dress climbed the front steps and said, "Hello, Emily, Leon," but they didn't even glance at her, or move aside when she slipped past them and through the open door.

"Please. It's not entirely my fault," he said. "Why are people so willing to believe me? Just tell me that. And this is what's depressing: they'll believe me all the quicker if I tell them something disillusioning. I might say, for instance, that being a movie star is not what it's cracked up to be. I'll say the lights are so hot that my make-up runs, and there's forever this pinkish-gray stain around the inside of my collar that my wife despairs of. Clorox has no effect on it; not even Wisk does, though she's partially solved the problem by prevention. What she does, you see, is rub my collar with a bar of white bath soap before I put a shirt on. Yes, that seems to work out fairly well, I'll say."

"This is crazy," Leon told him.

"Yes," said Morgan.

"You must be crazy!"

But Emily said, "Well, I don't know. I see what he means, in a way."

Both men turned to stare at her. Leon said, "You do?"

"He just . . . has to get out of his life, sometimes," she said.

Then Morgan gave a long, shaky sigh and sank down on the stoop. "My oldest daughter's getting married," he said. "Could I sit here with you and smoke a cigarette?"

1973

1 The newspaper said, *Crafts Revival in Baltimore? Festival Begins June 2.* There was a picture of Henry Prescott, ankle-deep in wood chips, carving one of his decoys. There was a picture of Leon Meredith holding up a puppet, with his wife beside him and his daughter at his feet. He was a grim, handsome, angular man, and his mouth was sharply creviced at the corners. He was not a young boy any more. It took a photo to make Emily see that. She placed the paper on the kitchen table, pushing away several breakfast dishes, and leaned over it on both elbows to study it more closely. The porous texture of the newsprint gave Leon a dramatic look—all hollows and steep planes. Next to him, Emily

seemed almost featureless. Even Gina failed to show how special she was.

"The whole idea," Leon was quoted as saying, "is improvisation. We take it moment by moment. We adapt as we go along. I'm talking about the plays, you understand—not the puppets. The puppets are my wife's doing. She makes them according to a fixed pattern. *They're* not improvised."

This was true, in a way, and yet it wasn't. Emily did have a homemade brown-paper pattern for the puppets' outlines, but the outlines were the least of it. What was important was the faces, the dips and hills of their expressions, which tended to develop unexpected twists of their own no matter how closely she guided the fabric through the sewing machine. Yes, definitely, the puppets were improvised too. She wished she'd spoken up when that reporter was interviewing them—said something to defend herself.

"The heads are padded," Leon said, "and stiffened with some kind of sizing. My wife mixes the sizing. She has her own recipe, her own way of doing things. I'm allowed to help with the props sometimes, but my wife insists on making the puppets totally by herself."

Emily folded the paper and laid it aside. She went down the hall to the back room. It was Gina's room now. The sewing machine and the muslin bags had been moved to the room Leon and Emily shared; Gina's belongings had multiplied too far to be contained in one small corner. Her unmade bed was laden with stuffed animals, books, and clothes. In the rocking chair by the window sat a Snoopy dog bigger than Gina. Grandma and Grandpa Meredith had brought it for her sixth birthday. Emily felt it was ridiculous to give a child something that size—not to mention the cost. What could they have been thinking of? "Oh, well," Leon had told her, "that's just how they are, I guess. *You* know how they are."

Gina was under the bed. She emerged, frowsy-haired, with a sneaker in her hand. "Aren't you ready yet?" Emily asked her. "It's time to go."

"I was looking for my shoe."

Emily took the sneaker from her and loosened a knot in the lace. "Now, Gina, listen," she said. "We've got a play to give out in the county today, and we're leaving before you get back. When kindergarten's over, you walk home with the Berger girls and wait in the shop till we come. Mrs. Apple says she'll keep an eye on you."

"Why can't I stay home and go with you?"

"Summer will be here soon enough," Emily told her. "You'll be home all the time, come summer."

She slipped the sneaker on Gina's foot and tied it. Gina's socks were already creased and soiled and falling down her ankles. Her blouse had egg on the front. Emily had known children like Gina when she was a child herself. They had a kind of extravagant squalor; there was something lush about the tumbled appearance of their clothing. She had always assumed their mothers were to blame, but now she knew better. Not half an hour ago Gina had been neat as a pin; Emily had made certain of it. She plucked a dust ball from Gina's hair, which was rich and thick-stranded like Leon's. "Come along," she told her. "You'll be late."

She slung her purse on her shoulder and they left the apartment, clicking the latch very gently because Leon was still asleep. They walked down the stairs, where everyone's breakfast smells hung in the air—bacon, burned butter, the Conways' kippered herrings. They passed the door of the shop, which was still dark, and stepped out into the street. It was a warm, sunny morning. The city looked freshly washed, with gold-lit buildings rising through a haze in the distance, women in spring dresses sweeping their stoops, green ivy flooding through the windows of an abandoned rowhouse. Gina hung on to Emily's hand and skipped and sang:

> *Miss Lucy had a baby,*
> *She called it Tiny Tim,*
> *She put it in the bathtub*
> *To see if it could swim . . .*

Emily said good morning to Mrs. Ellery, who was shaking out her dust mop, and to the ancient blind man whose daughter, or granddaughter it must have been, set him on his stoop every fair day with a grayish quilt wrapped around his legs. "Nice weather," Emily called, and the old man nodded, turning his sealed-looking eyelids toward the sun like a plant in the window. She stopped on the second corner to wait for the Berger girls. Helena Berger shooed them out the door—two little freckled redheads in plaid dresses. They ran ahead with Gina, and at the next intersection Emily had to call, "Stop! Wait!" She hurried up, out of breath, while they lurched and teetered on the edge of the curb. She held out her hands, and the younger Berger girl took one and Gina took the other. The Berger child was all bones; Emily felt a rush of love for Gina's warm, chubby fingers, which were slightly sticky in the creases. She waded across the street, embroiled in children, and turned them loose on the other side. They scattered ahead again, skipping disjointedly.

> *Miss Lucy called the doctor,*
> *Miss Lucy called the nurse,*
> *Miss Lucy called the lady*
> *With the alligator purse . . .*

Emily sensed a presence nearby, the shape of someone familiar, and she turned and found Morgan Gower loping along beside her. He tipped his battered green Army helmet and smiled. "Morgan," she said. "How come you're out so early?"

"I couldn't sleep past five o'clock this morning," he said. "There's too much excitement at the house."

At Morgan's house there was always too much excitement. She'd never been there, but she pictured a bulging, seething box of a place—the roof straining off, the side seams splitting. "What is it this time?" she asked him.

"It's Brindle. My sister. Her sweetheart came back."

Emily hadn't known his sister had a sweetheart. She shaded

her eyes and called, "Children! Wait for me!" Then she said, "Did Kate get out of her leg cast yet?"

"Who?" he asked. "Oh, yes. Yes, that's all . . . but see, at seven or so last night, just at the end of supper, the doorbell rang and Bonny said, 'Brindle, go see who that is, will you?' since Brindle was nearest the door, so Brindle went and then . . ."

They'd reached the intersection. Emily held out her hands and the children swarmed around her, knocking Morgan backward a pace. When she'd crossed to the other side and turned to look for him, he was picking up his helmet from the gutter. He polished it with his sleeve, sadly, and set it on his head. It matched his splotchy camouflage jacket and his crumpled olive-drab jungle pants. He was always dressing for catastrophes that were unlikely to occur, she thought. "These are guaranteed, certified, snake-proof boots," he said now. He stopped to hold up one green foot. "I bought them at Sunny's Surplus."

"They're very nice," she said. "Children! Slow down, please."

"How come you have those other two girls?" Morgan asked. "I don't remember seeing them before."

"I'm trading off with their mother. She's walking Gina home today so that I can do a show."

"Well, it all seems so disorganized," Morgan said. "I come to you people for peace and quiet and I find this disorganization. Look at Gina: she hasn't even said hello to me."

"Oh, she will; you know she loves to see you. It's only that she's with friends."

"I prefer it when you both come and Gina walks between you, just the one of her. Where's Leon? Why isn't he here?"

"He's sleeping. He was out late last night, trying for a part in a play."

"It's too disorganized," Morgan said glumly. He stopped and peered down the front of his jacket. Then he reached inside and brought up a pack of cigarettes. "So Brindle goes to the door," he said, "and nothing more happens. There's nothing but silence. Well, we thought she might have faded off somewhere. Forgot where she was headed. Lost her way or something. You know Brindle. Or at least, you know *about* her: always in that bathrobe, moping. 'How was your day?' you ask, and she says, 'Day?' She acts surprised to hear there's been one. 'Go see where she's got to,' Bonny tells me. 'She's *your* sister; see what she's up to.' So I push away from the table and go to find her and there she is in the entrance hall being kissed by a total stranger. It's one of those long, deep, wrap-around kisses, like in the movies. I was uncertain what to do about it. It seemed rude to interrupt, but if I turned and left they'd no doubt hear the floorboards creak, so I just stood there flossing my teeth and the two of them went on kissing. Heavy-set man with slicked-down hair. Brindle in her bathrobe. Finally I ask, 'Was there something you wanted?' Then they pulled apart and Brindle said, 'It's Robert Roberts, my childhood sweetheart. Don't you know him?' "

"Children!" Emily called. They'd reached another intersection. She ran ahead to take their hands. Morgan followed, muttering something. "Known him all his life, of course" was what it sounded like. "Knew him when he was a *bit* of a thing, coming to play roll-a-bat with Brindle in the alley. Called her 'Idiot. Dumbhead. Moron,' in that fond, insulting way that childhood sweethearts have . . ."

The school loomed up, a gloomy building surrounded by cracked concrete, teeming with shabby children. Emily bent to kiss Gina goodbye. "Have a good day, honey," she said, and Morgan said, "How about old Morgan? No kiss for Uncle Morgan?"

He bent over, and Gina threw her arms around his neck and kissed his cheek. "Come by after school and help me again with my yo-yo," she said.

"All right, sugar-pie."

"You promise?"

"Absolutely. Have I ever let you down?"

When she ran off, he stood watching after her, smiling and

tapping cigarette ashes across the toes of his boots. "Ah, yes. Ah, yes," he said. "What a darling, eh? I wish she'd stay this size forever."

"I hate that school," Emily said.

"Why! What could be wrong with it?"

"It's so crowded; classes are so big, and I doubt I'll ever feel safe letting her walk here alone. I'd like to send her someplace private. Leon's parents have offered to pay, but I don't know. I'd have to think how to bring it up with Leon."

"No, no, leave her here. Don't forsake your principles," Morgan said. He took her elbow and turned her toward home. "I never thought you'd send your daughter to a private school."

"Why not? What principles?" Emily asked. "You sent yours to private schools."

"That was Bonny's doing," Morgan told her. "She has this money. We never see it, never buy anything inspiring with it, but it's there, all right, for things that don't show—new slate roof tiles and the children's education. Her money is so well behaved! I would have preferred a public school, myself. Why, surely. You don't want to cart her off to some faraway place, all these complicated carpools—"

"Dad Meredith happened to mention it while Leon was out of the room," Emily said. "On purpose, I guess. He must be hoping I'll wear Leon down, so when the subject comes up again Leon will be used to it. But I haven't said a word, because Leon's so proud about money. And you know what a temper he has."

"Temper?" Morgan said.

"He might just explode."

"Oh, I can't picture that."

"He's always had this angry streak."

"I can't picture that at all," Morgan said.

He stopped and looked around him. "I would offer to take you for a drive," he said, "just to celebrate the return of Robert Roberts, don't you know. I'm much too keyed up to work today. But, unfortunately, my car's been stolen."

"Oh, that's terrible," Emily said. "When did it happen?"

"Just now," he told her.

"Now? This morning?"

"This instant," he said. He pointed to an empty place at the curb, beside a mailbox. "I parked it here, where I thought you might be passing. Now it's disappeared."

Emily's mouth dropped open.

"There, there, I'm not upset," he said. "As you would say: what's a car, after all?" He spread his arms, smiling. "It's only an encumbrance. Only another burden. Right? I'm better off without it."

Emily didn't know how he could talk that way. A car was very important. She and Leon had been saving for one for years. "You ought to call the police immediately," she told him. "Come back with me and use our telephone. Time really matters."

"There'd be no point," he said. "I've never had much faith in policemen." He took her elbow again to lead her on. The grip of his tense, warm fingers reminded her of Gina. "Last summer," he said, "while we were driving to the beach, a state trooper flagged us down and asked us for a lift. He said his patrol car had been stolen. Can you imagine? He got in the rear with Molly and Kate and my mother . . . those big, shiny boots, gun in a holster . . . he leaned over the front seat and saw Bonny, saw her eating an apple core. 'You want to watch it with those seeds,' he told her. He said, 'My cousin Donna used to love appleseeds. Best part of the apple, she claimed. One year me and my brother saved up all our seeds in a Baby Ben alarm-clock box and gave them to her for Christmas. She was thrilled. She ate them every one, and by evening she was dead. Here's where I get off,' he said; so I stopped the car and out he climbed and that was the last we saw of him. It seemed he'd only popped in to bring us this message, you know? And then departed. I said to Bonny, I told her, 'Think of it, the lives of ordinary citizens in the hands of a man like that. Walking around with a gun,' I said.

'No doubt loaded, no doubt cocked, or whatever it is you do with a gun.' "

"Yes, but . . ." Emily said.

She was about to tell him that surely the next policeman wouldn't be so peculiar. But then she wondered. Some people, it appeared, attract the peculiar all their lives. "Well, anyway," she said, "it wouldn't hurt just to give the police a phone call."

"Maybe not, maybe not," Morgan said. He was reading a chipped and peeling sign: EUNOLA'S RESTAURANT. "Is this place any good?" he asked.

"I've never tried it."

"Lived right here in the neighborhood and never tried Eunola's?"

"It's a matter of money."

"Let's go in and have some coffee," Morgan said.

"I thought you had to open your store."

"Oh, Butkins will do that. He's happier without me, to tell the truth. I get in the way." He pulled open the door and shepherded Emily in ahead of him. There were four small tables and a counter where a row of men in hard hats sat drinking their coffee under a veil of cigarette smoke. "Sit," Morgan said, guiding her to a table. He settled opposite her. "Do you know what this means, this Robert Roberts business? Do you see the implications? Why, it's wonderful! First the years go by and Brindle stays in her bathrobe, moping, scuffing about in her slippers, wondering when the next meal is. 'Fix it yourself, if you're hungry,' I've told her, but she says, 'Well,' she says, 'I don't know where anything's kept, the food and utensils and such.' Understand, this is a house she's been living in since nineteen . . . was it sixty-four? Or maybe sixty-five, she moved in. Kate was already in school, I remember. Sue had started her piccolo lessons . . . Then here comes Robert Roberts! Here he comes, out of the blue. He says his wife is dead now. And anyhow, he says, his heart was always with Brindle. I can't imagine why. She's very plain to look at and she's not at all good-natured. But his heart was always with her, he says. And he was the very person she's been telling us about at the dinner table, every night of our lives. Why, our children knew Robert Roberts's name before they knew their own! They knew all his favorite board games and his batting average. And here he comes, with an armload of roses, the most colossal heap of roses; the whole entrance hall took on that rainy, dressed-up smell that roses have . . . and asking her to marry him! Isn't life . . . symmetrical? I'd really underestimated it."

A waitress stood over them, tapping her pencil. Emily cleared her throat and said, "I'll have coffee, please."

"Me too," said Morgan. "Yes, it was quite a night. The two of them sat up till dawn, discussing their plans. I kept them company. They want to get married in June, they say."

"You certainly have a lot of weddings in your family," Emily told him.

"Oh, not really," he said. He reached across the table for her purse, opened it, and peered inside. "There was Amy's, of course, and then Jean's, but I don't count Carol's; she got divorced before she'd finished writing her thank-you notes." He turned the purse upside down and shook it. Emily's wallet fell out, followed by a key ring. He shook the purse again, but it was empty. "Look at that!" he said. "You're so orderly."

Emily retrieved her belongings and put them back in her purse. Morgan watched, with his head cocked. "I too am orderly," he told her.

"You are?"

"Well, at least I have an interest in order. I mean, order has always intrigued me. When I was a child, I thought order might come when my voice changed. Then I thought, no, maybe when I'm educated. At one point I thought I would be orderly if I could just once sleep with a woman."

He took a napkin from the dispenser and unfolded it and smoothed it across his knees.

Emily said, "Well?"

"Well, what?"

"Did sleeping with a woman make you orderly?"

"How can you ask?" he said. He sighed.

Their coffee arrived, and he seized the sugarbowl and started spooning out sugar. Four teaspoons, five . . . he stirred after each spoonful, and dripped coffee on the tabletop and into the bowl. Caramel-colored beads grew up across the surface of the sugar. Emily looked at them and then at Morgan. Morgan bared his teeth at her encouragingly. She looked away again.

Why put up with him? He was really so strange that sometimes, out in public, she felt an urge to walk several paces ahead so that no one would guess they were acquainted. Or when the three of them were together, she'd make a point of taking Leon's arm. But it was funny how he grew on a person. He added something; she couldn't say just what. He made things look more interesting than they really were. Sometimes he accompanied the Merediths when they went to put on a puppet show, and from the squirrel-like attention he gave to all they did she would understand, suddenly, how very exotic this occupation was—itinerant puppeteers! Well, not itinerant, exactly, but still . . . and she'd look at Leon and realize what a flair he had, with his deep, dark eyes and swift movements. She herself would feel not quite so colorless; she would notice that Gina, who sometimes struck her as a little blowzy, was just like one of those cherubic children on a nineteenth-century chocolate box.

"Leon's picture was in the paper," she told Morgan now.

"Eh?"

She leaned forward. She saw that this must be why she'd agreed to stop for coffee. "There was an article," she said, "in the morning paper, all about our puppets."

"Oh, I missed it," he said. "I left the house too early."

"They had a picture of the three of us, but really it was Leon's article," she said.

Morgan lit a cigarette and tipped his chair back, studying her.

"He talked about the puppets, how they're . . . oh, not improvised. How they're cut from a pattern." She folded her hands and examined her knuckles. "He meant something by that. It's hard to explain. If I tell you what it meant, you'll think I'm imagining things."

"You probably are," Morgan said.

"And last night, this play he went to try for . . . what he used to do in the old days was, he'd memorize a part for tryouts. He wouldn't just go and read it, like other people. He had this very quick memory. It always made an impression. So yesterday afternoon he started to learn the part he wanted, and it turned out he couldn't do it. He'd memorize one line and go on to the next, but when he put the two together he found he'd forgotten the first one and he'd have to begin all over again. It kept happening. It was eerie. *I* knew the lines, finally, just from hearing them; but he still didn't. And he blamed me for it. He didn't say so outright, but he did. I know."

"You're imagining things," Morgan said.

"It's true that he's changed since he met me," Emily said.

Morgan rocked on his chair legs, smoking and frowning. He said, "Did I ever tell you I was married once before?"

"What? No, I don't think so. And now he's so friendly with his parents. Well, of course he can say that's all my doing; I used to be the only one who spoke to them. But now it seems . . . well, truthfully, they visit a little too much. He gets on with them a little too well."

"I married during my senior year in college," Morgan said. "Her name was Letitia. We eloped and never told a soul. But as soon as we got married, we lost interest in each other. It was the funniest thing. We took up with different crowds; Letitia became involved in an antique-music group and went off to New York over Christmas vacation . . . we drifted apart, as they say. We went our separate ways."

Emily couldn't see why he was telling her this. She made an effort and sat straighter in her chair. "Is that right?" she said. "So you got a divorce?"

"Well, no."

"What happened, then?"

"Nothing happened," Morgan said. "We just went our ways. No one knew about the elopement, after all."

Emily thought back over what he'd told her. She said, "But then you'd be a bigamist."

"Technically speaking, I suppose I am," Morgan said cheerfully.

"But that's illegal!"

"Well, yes, I guess it is, in a way."

She stared at him.

"But it's really very natural," he told her. "It's quite fitting, when you stop to consider. Aren't we all sitting on stacks of past events? And not every level is neatly finished off, right? Sometimes a lower level bleeds into an upper level. Isn't that so?"

"Honestly," Emily said. "What has this got to do with anything?" She reached for her purse and stood up. Morgan stood too and came lunging around to pull her chair back, but she was too quick for him. She didn't even wait for him to pay the cashier. She walked on out the door and left him at the register, and he had to run to catch up with her.

"Emily?" he said.

"I have to be getting home now."

"But I seem to have strayed from my point. All your talk of bigamy, legalities, you made me forget what I wanted to say."

"Half the time, Morgan," Emily said, "I believe you're telling out-and-out lies. I believe you just told me one. You did, didn't you? Did you? Or not?"

"See, Emily," Morgan said, "of course he's changed. Everybody does; everyone goes bobbing along, in and out of inlets, snagging on pilings, skating down rapids . . . Well, I mustn't get carried away. But, Emily, you're still close. You haven't parted directions. You're still very much alike."

"Alike!" said Emily. She stopped in front of a newsstand. "How can you say that? We're totally different. We come fom totally different backgrounds. Even our religions are different."

"Really?" said Morgan. "What religion is Leon?"

"Oh, Presbyterian, Methodist . . ." She started walking again. "We're nothing at all alike."

"To me you are," Morgan said. "And you get along so well."

"Ha," said Emily bitterly.

"You have the happiest marriage I know of, Emily. I love your marriage!"

"Well, I can't think why," Emily said.

But she let herself fall into step with him.

They passed a woman painting her front door a bright green. "Apple green, my favorite color!" Morgan called, and the woman laughed and bowed like someone on a stage. They passed an open window where Fats Domino sang "I'm Walkin'," and Morgan spread his arms and started dancing. The fact that he had a cigarette clamped in his teeth made it look difficult and precarious; he reminded Emily of those Russians who dance with a glass of vodka on their heads. She stood to one side, awkwardly swinging her purse and smiling. Then Morgan stopped and took his cigarette from his mouth. "Why, look at that," he said. He was staring at something just behind her. She turned, but it was nothing—a car parked next to a mailbox.

"My car!" he said.

"Your what?"

"It's my car!"

"Are you sure?"

But that was a silly question; even Emily was sure. (And why would he claim such a ruined object, otherwise?) Morgan rushed around it, breathing rapid puffs of smoke. "See?" he said. "There's Lizzie's tennis racket, my turban, my sailor suit that I was bringing home from . . . See that Nehi bottle? It's been rolling up and down the back window ledge for the past six months. Or," he said, pausing, "is it possible that someone else might have a car just like this?"

"Really, Morgan," Emily said. "Of course it's yours. Go call the police."

"What for? Why not just steal it back?"

"Well, you want the thief arrested, don't you?"

"Yes," he said, "but meanwhile it's parked in a No Parking zone and I might be given a ticket."

"When it wasn't you that parked it there?"

"You never can tell, in this world," he said. "I promised Bonny I wouldn't run up more traffic fines." He was trying all the doors, but they were locked. He walked around to the front of the car and settled on his haunches before the grille. "I don't suppose you have your Swiss Army knife with you," he said.

"My what? No."

He plucked at a string that was looped through the grille. Then he set his face close and started gnawing at the string. The woman who'd been painting lowered her brush and turned to watch. "I don't understand what you're after," Emily said.

"The key," Morgan said. Something clinked to the ground. He groped beneath the car for it.

"Over to your right," Emily told him. "Closer to the wheel."

Morgan stretched out on his stomach, with his legs trailing behind him. (The soles of his snake-proof boots were as deeply ridged as snow tires.) He reached farther under the car. "Got it," he said. A little three-wheeled mail truck the size of a golf cart bounced up and stopped. "Help!" Morgan shouted, and he raised his head. She heard his helmet clang against the underside of the bumper. "I'm hit!" he said.

"Morgan?"

"I'm run over! It's my leg!"

A mailman descended from the truck, whistling, and started toward the mailbox. Emily grabbed his sleeve and said, "Move."

"Huh?"

"Move the truck! You've run a man over."

"Sheesh," said the mailman. "Don't he see the No Parking sign?"

"Move that truck this instant, I tell you!"

"All right, all right," the mailman said. He turned back to his truck, glancing down at Morgan on the way. Morgan showed him a face that seemed all teeth.

"Hurry," said Emily, wringing a handful of skirt.

Meanwhile the woman with the paintbrush arrived, dripping apple green. "Oh, that poor, poor man," she said. Emily knelt next to Morgan. She had a sick weight on the floor of her stomach. But at least there was no blood. Morgan's leg, pinned at the shin beneath the toy tire, looked flattened but still in one piece. He was breathing raggedly. Emily laid a hand on his back. "Are you in pain?" she asked him.

"Not as much as you might expect."

"He's going to move the truck."

"Of all the damn-fool, ridiculous—"

"Never mind, it could happen to anyone," Emily said, patting his back.

"I was talking about the mailman."

"Oh."

The mailman released his brake. The truck gave a grinding sound and inched backward. "Oof!" said Morgan. He rolled free. He sat up and inspected his leg. A dusty, wedge-shaped mark ran down the green fabric.

"Is it broken?" Emily asked him.

"I don't know."

"Rip his pants," the woman with the paintbrush suggested.

"Not the pants!" said Morgan. "They're World War Two."

Emily started folding up the cuff, working gingerly, tensed for what she might have to see. By now, two old ladies with shopping bags had joined them, and the mailman was telling them, "I could report him for illegal parking, if I was that bad of a guy."

"There's nothing here," Emily said. She was inspecting Morgan's pale, hairy shin. "Can you wiggle your toes?"

"Yes."

"Can you stand?"

He attempted it, with an arm around Emily for support. He was heavier than he looked, hard-muscled, warm, and he gave off the harsh gray smell of someone who'd been smoking for a very long time. "Yes," he said, "I can stand."

"Maybe he just ran over your trousers."

He drew back from her. "That's not true at all," he said.

"But there's no blood, the bone's not broken . . ."

"I felt it. I felt the pressure, a pinch, so to speak, at one side of my calf. You think I don't know when I'm hit? Not all hurts show up from outside. You can't just stand outside and pass judgment on whether I've been injured or not. You think I don't know when a U.S. Government mail truck pins me flat to the pavement?"

"Jesus," said the mailman.

The two old ladies went on their way, and the woman returned to her painting. The mailman unlocked the mailbox. Morgan held up a hand; something glittered. "But at least I've got the key," he told Emily.

"Oh, yes. The key."

He opened the door on the passenger side. "Quick. Jump in," he said.

"Me?"

"Jump in the car. What if the thief comes? All this racket, this hullabaloo . . ."

He waited till she'd climbed in, and then he closed the door and came around to the driver's side. "I've had too much excitement lately," he told her. "I don't know why things can't go a little more smoothly." He settled himself with a grunt and leaned forward to fit the key in the ignition. "Now look," he said. "Another difficulty."

The key wouldn't go. A second key was already there, and a dangling leather case. "What are these?" he asked Emily.

"They must have been locked in the car," she said.

"I'm always amazed," Morgan said, "by how incompetent your average criminal is."

"But maybe the car wasn't stolen at all," Emily told him.
"How could that be?"

"Maybe you just *thought* you parked in that other block."

"No, no," he said impatiently. "That would be ridiculous."
He started the motor, veered out around the mail truck, and
headed up the street. It sounded as if he were in the wrong
gear. "Come back with me and meet Bonny," he said.

"Oh, Leon will be wondering where I am. And anyway,
don't you have to go to work?"

"I can't work today; I only had an hour of sleep last night.
It was Brindle, this business with Brindle. Have you ever
heard of such a thing? Robert Roberts, after all these years!"

Emily hoped he wouldn't start on Robert Roberts again.
She felt exhausted. It seemed to her that those few blocks
from Gina's school had taken hours, days; she'd expended
years' worth of energy on them. The sight of Morgan beside
her (humming "I'm Walkin' " and tapping the steering wheel,
fresh as a daisy, without a care in the world) made her head
ache.

But then her apartment building approached. Crafts Unlimited was just opening, and its fluorescent lights were fluttering on and off as if unable to gather strength. The windows
above it were dark. You could imagine that the building was
nothing but an empty shell. Morgan sailed past, still humming.
Emily didn't try to stop him.

2 Emily and Leon had given a good deal of thought to
Morgan's wife—to what she must be like, considering
the amount of time he spent away from her. He was always
dropping in on the Merediths for a visit, mentioning other
places he'd just come from and still others where he was
heading afterward. Was he ever home at all, in fact? Even
weekends? For on Saturdays he engaged in his own unique
style of shopping. He would travel to the depths of Baltimore
and return with unlikely items: dented canned goods, or

knobby packages wrapped in brown paper and tied all around with string in a dozen clumsy knots. (You would think they hadn't heard of bagging yet, where Morgan shopped.) Sundays he went to fairs and festivals. At events where Emily and Leon took their puppets, they might even run into him purely by chance. They'd look through the scrim at the seated audience—no more than a long, low hillock—and find him standing at the rear, this sudden jutting peak topped by some outlandish hat, always alone, always brooding over something and puffing on a cigarette. (But when they came out afterward to take their bows, he'd be beaming mightily and clapping like a proud parent.) Winters, when the fairs died down, he'd go to church bazaars and grade-school fund-raisers. No occasion was too small for him. He was never too busy to stop and contemplate the appliquéd felt Christmas-tree skirts or the Styrofoam snowmen with sequin eyes. So who was this Bonny, whom he was so eager to leave? Maybe she nagged him, Leon said. Maybe she was one of those tight, crimped ladies holding court alone in her careful living room, among the polished figurines that Morgan mustn't touch and the crystal ashtrays he mustn't flick his ashes into. But Emily didn't think so. Putting together all that Morgan said (his rush of accidents and disasters, his admiration of the Merediths' stripped apartment), she imagined Bonny as a slattern, in a zip-front housedress and a headful of pincurls. She wasn't surprised when Morgan parked his car in front of a well-kept brick Colonial house—after all, she'd known there was money, and slate tiles for the roof—but she blinked when she stepped out and found a brown-haired woman in a neat skirt and blouse weeding petunias along the front walk. Well, maybe it was the sister. But Morgan said, "Bonny?"

Bonny straightened and wiped her forehead with the back of her wrist. There were a few faint smile lines around her eyes. Her lipstick was a chipped, cracked, glossless red. She looked cheerful but noncommittal; she seemed to be waiting for Morgan to explain himself.

"Bonny, this is Emily Meredith," Morgan said.

Bonny went on waiting.

"Emily and her husband run a puppet show," Morgan said.

"Oh, really?"

It hadn't occurred to Emily that Bonny wouldn't have heard of her. (She had heard of Bonny, after all.) She felt a little hurt. She held out her hand and said, "How do you do, Mrs. Gower."

Bonny shook her hand. She said, "Well, are . . . you here to see Morgan? Or what?"

"She's here to see *you*," Morgan told her.

"Me?"

Morgan said, "What happened was, my car was stolen, but then I stole it back, by and by, but still there was so much excitement, what with Robert Roberts and all . . ."

"You mean, you asked her to come inside the house?"

"Oh!" Emily said. "Well, of course I don't want to interrupt your work."

"It's all right," Bonny said. "Why don't you roll down your pants leg, Morgan?" She turned to lead them up the walk.

"But, Mrs. Gower—"

"Stay, stay," Morgan urged, from a bent position. He flattened his cuff around his ankle. "She's just surprised. You've come this far; stay!"

Emily followed Bonny up the steps. She felt she had no choice, although she would rather have been anywhere else. They passed a clay pot in which herbs were growing—chives and maybe marjoram or thyme. Emily looked at them wistfully. Under other conditions, she thought, Bonny might very well have been someone she was fond of, but they'd got started wrong. It was Morgan's fault. He was so thoughtless and abrupt. She felt irritated by his dishpan-shaped helmet, bounding along beside her. "Notice Bonny's roses," he said. It could have been a hint—a clue to Bonny's soft spot—but Bonny said, without turning, "How can she? They're not blooming yet."

The three of them entered the hall. On the radiator were

a stack of library books with scummy plastic covers, a
watering can, and a box of Triscuits. Emily had to watch
her step through a little turmoil of shoes and sneakers, and by
then they'd reached the living room. "Look!" Morgan said,
pouncing on a vase. "This is what Amy made at camp, the
summer she was ten."

"It's very pretty," Emily said. It was lopsided, and a crack
ran down from the rim.

"I wish you could meet her, but she lives in Roland Park
now. You can meet Mother and Brindle, though."

"Brindle's out shopping for a wedding ring," Bonny said.

"A ring! Yes, I've told Emily all about that. And see,
here's Molly's picture on the mantel. Isn't she beautiful? It's
from her school play; they say she has a talent for acting. I
can't imagine where she got it. There's never been an actor
in our family. What do you think of her? Bonny, don't we
still have Jeannie's wedding album?"

There was something feverish about him, Emily thought.
He darted around the room, rummaging through various
overloaded shelves. Emily and Bonny stood in the doorway
watching him. Once they happened to glance at each other,
but when Emily saw Bonny's expression—oddly hooded—
she looked away again. "Please," she told Morgan, "I ought
to be going. I'll just catch a bus and go, please."

"But you haven't met my mother!" he said, stopping short.
"And I wanted Bonny to get to know you; I wanted you
two to . . . Bonny, Emily was in the paper today."

"Was she?" Bonny said.

"Where's the paper? Did you throw it out?"

"I think it's in the kitchen."

"Come to the kitchen. Let's all go! Let's all have some
coffee," he said. He raced away. Bonny straightened from
the door frame to follow him, and Emily trailed behind. She
wished she could just vanish. She thought of ducking out
soundlessly, slipping away before they noticed. She dodged
a mobile of homemade paper sailing ships and stepped into
the kitchen.

The counters in the kitchen were stacked with dirty dishes, and several animals' feeding bowls cluttered the floor. One wall was shingled with yellow cartoons and news clippings and hockey schedules, recipes, calendars, photographs, telephone numbers on torn corners of paper, dental appointment cards, invitations—even someone's high-school diploma. Emily felt surrounded, flooded. Over by the back door Morgan was plowing through a stack of newspapers. "Where is it? Where is it? Did it come?" he asked. "Aha!" He held up a paper. He laid it flat on the floor, licked his thumb, and started turning pages. "News . . . editorials . . . crafts revival in Baltimore!"

Peering over his shoulder, Emily saw Leon's sober face. He seemed to be staring at her out of another world. "Bonny, here's Leon. Emily's husband," Morgan said. "And here's her daughter, Gina. See?"

"Very nice," said Bonny, setting out coffee cups.

"You know," Morgan said thoughtfully, "I once looked a little like Leon."

Bonny glanced at the photo. "Like that man there? Never," she said. "You're two totally different types."

"Well, yes," he said, "but there's something about the eyes, maybe; I don't know. Or something around the mouth. Or maybe it's the forehead. I don't know."

He stood up, abandoning the paper, and pulled out a chair from the table. "Sit down, sit down," he told Emily. He took a seat opposite, as if demonstrating, and fixed her with an urgent, focused look till she sat too. She felt trapped. The dishes on the counters towered so far above her that she imagined they might teeter and topple, swamping her. A typewriter stood in a puddle of orange juice on the table, with a sheet of paper in the carriage. . . . *resolution was passed by a show of hands*, she read, *and Matilda Grayson requested that* . . . Bonny placed a carton of cream in front of her and a crumpled sack of Pantry Pride sugar.

"Were you working on something special?" asked Emily, motioning toward the typewriter.

"Yes," Bonny said. She handed Emily a cup of coffee and sat down next to her.

"Um . . . what do you do for a living, Mrs. Gower?"

"I'm Morgan's wife for a living."

"Oh, I see."

"Yes," Bonny said, "but do you see that it's a full-time job? It keeps me busy every minute, I tell you. Oh, from outside he seems so comic and light-hearted, such a character, so quaint, but imagine dealing with him. I mean, the details of it, the coping, stuck at home while he's off somewhere, wondering who he thinks he is now. Do you suppose we couldn't all act like that? Go swooping around in a velvet cape with a red satin lining and a feathered hat? That part's the easy part. Imagine being his wife, finding a cleaner who does ostrich plumes. Keeping his dinner warm. Imagine waiting dinner while he's out with one of his cronies that I have never met—Salvation Army bums or astrologists or whatever other awestruck, smitten people he digs up."

Emily set her cup down.

"You think I don't appreciate him. You wonder why he married me," Bonny said.

"No, no," said Emily. She looked across at Morgan, who seemed unperturbed. He was tipping contentedly in his chair, like a child who is confident he's the center of attention, and puffing on a cigarette. Twisted ropes of smoke hung around his head.

"Emily," Bonny said.

Emily turned to her.

"Emily, Morgan is the manager of a hardware store."

Emily waited, but that was the end of it. Bonny seemed to be expecting her to speak. "Yes," Emily said, after a minute.

"Cullen Hardware," Bonny said.

"She knows that, Bonny," Morgan said.

"She does?"

Bonny stared at him. Then she asked Emily, "You don't think he's a . . . rabbi or a Greek shipping magnate?"

"No," Emily said.

She decided not to mention how they'd met.

Bonny pressed her fingers to her lips. There were freckles, Emily saw, dusting the back of her hand. After all, she was a pleasant woman; she gave a little laugh. "You must think I've lost my mind," she said. "Crazy Bonny, right? Morgan's crazy wife, Bonny."

"Oh, no."

"It's just that I worried you might have been . . . misled. Morgan's such a, well, prankster, in a way."

"Yes, I know about that."

"You do?" Bonny said.

She glanced over at Morgan. Morgan smiled seraphically and blew out a whoosh of smoke.

"But I think he's trying to give it up," said Emily.

"Oh, I hope so!" Bonny said. "Why! It takes so much ingenuity to manage some of that foolishness . . . think what he could accomplish if he used that brain for sensible things! If he straightened out. If he decided to go straight."

"Not much," said Morgan cheerfully.

"What, dear?"

"There's not much I could accomplish. What do you imagine I'd be doing instead?"

"Oh, why . . . just *attending* to things. I mean, attending to where you belong." She turned to Emily. "There's nothing wrong with a hardware store. Is there? My family's always done well in hardware; it's nothing to be sneezed at. But Uncle Ollie says Morgan's heart's not in it. What's the good of a store, he says, where you have to positively wrest the merchandise from the manager? Assuming you can find the manager. I tell Uncle Ollie, 'Oh, leave him alone. Cullen Hardware is not the be-all and end-all,' I tell him, but it's true that Morgan could get more narrowed in. He doesn't know how to say no. He never refuses to be swept along."

"Mostly it's muscles," Morgan said.

This must have been something he'd told her before; Bonny

rolled her eyes at Emily. Morgan turned to Emily and repeated it. "It's a matter of muscles," he said.

"I don't understand."

"A matter of following where they lead me. Have you
ever gone out to the kitchen, say, and then forgotten what
for? You stand in the kitchen and try to remember. Then
your wrist makes a little twisting motion. Oh, yes! you say.
That twist is what you'd do to turn a faucet on. You must
have come for water! I just trust my muscles, you see, to
tell me what I'm here for. To drop me into my true activity
one day. I let them lead me."

"He lets them lead him into saying he's a glassblower,"
Bonny said, "and a tugboat captain for the Curtis Bay Tow-
ing Company, and a Mohawk Indian high-rise worker. And
that's just what I happen to hear; heaven knows what more
there is." Her lips twitched, as if she were hiding some
amusement. "You're walking down the street with him and
this total stranger asks him when the International Brother-
hood of Magicians is meeting next. You're listening to a
politician's speech and suddenly you notice Morgan on the
platform, sitting beside a senator's wife with a carnation in
his buttonhole. You're waiting for your crabs at Lexington
Market and who's behind the counter but Morgan in a rubber
apron, telling the other customers where he caught such
fine oysters. It seems he has this boat that was handed down
from an uncle on his mother's side, a little bateau with no
engine—"

"Engines disturb the beds," said Morgan. "And I don't like
mechanical tonging rigs, either. What was good enough for
my uncle on my mother's side is good enough for me, I say."

Bonny smiled at him and shook her head. "You step out
for two minutes to buy milk, leaving him safe home in his
pajamas, and coming back you pass him on the corner in a
satin cap and purple satin shirt, telling four little boys the
secret that made him the only undefeated jockey in the history of Pimlico. A jockey, six feet tall! Why do they all

believe him? He never used a crop, you see, but only whispered in the horse's ear. He whispered something that *sounded* like a crop. What was the word?"

"Scintillate," Morgan said.

"Oh, yes," said Bonny. She laughed.

Morgan trotted in his chair, holding imaginary reins. "Scintillate, scintillate," he whispered, and Bonny laughed harder and wiped her eyes.

"He's impossible," she told Emily. "He's just . . . impossible to predict, you see."

"I can imagine he must be," Emily said politely.

She was beginning to like Bonny (her pink, merry face, and the helpless way she sank back in her chair), but she thought less of Morgan. It had never occurred to her that he knew exactly how people saw him, and that he enjoyed their astonishment and perhaps even courted it. She frowned at him. Morgan pulled his nose reflectively.

"She's right," he said. "I make things difficult. But I plan to change. Hear that, Bonny?"

"Oh, do you, now?" Bonny said. She stood up to raise the kitchen window. "I don't know what to make of my garden," she said, looking out at the yard. "I was certain I'd planted vegetables someplace, but it seems to be coming up all flowers."

"I mean it," Morgan said. He told Emily, "She doesn't believe me. Bonny, don't you see what's here in front of you? Here's Emily Meredith; I brought her home. I brought her to our house. I told her and Leon, both, exactly who I was. I told about you and the girls. They know about Amy's new baby and the time Kate smashed the car."

"Is that right?" Bonny asked Emily.

Emily nodded.

"Well, I can't think what for," Bonny said. "I can't think why he bored you with all that."

"I'm combining my worlds!" Morgan said, and he raised his coffee cup to Bonny.

But Bonny said, "There's a catch to it somewhere. There's something missing. I don't understand what he wants."

Emily didn't understand either. She shook her head; Bonny shook hers. In fact, it seemed that Bonny and Emily were the old friends and Morgan was the newcomer. He sat slightly apart, perched under his helmet like an elf under a mushroom, turning his face from one to the other while the women watched, narrow-eyed, to see what he was up to.

1975

1 Even when Morgan fell asleep, he didn't truly lose consciousness. Part of him slept while the rest of him stayed alert and jittery, counting things—thumbtacks, mattress buttons, flowers on a daughter's dress, holes in a pegboard display of electrical fittings. A plumber came in and ordered some pipes: six elbows and a dozen nipples. "Certainly," said Morgan, but he couldn't help laughing. Then he was competing in a singing contest. He was singing a song from the fifties called "Moments to Remember." He knew the words, but was unable to pronounce them properly. *The ballroom prize we almost won* came out *the barroom brawl we almost won.* His partner was not a good dancer anyway, and in fact they were nowhere close to winning. Why! His partner was Laura Lee Keller, the very first girl he had ever loved—someone he had lost track of long, long before the days of "Moments to Remember." After the prom, he and Laura Lee had driven to the beach with half the senior class and lain kissing on a blanket by the ocean. Still, even now, even after all these years, the sound of the ocean reminded him of possibilities unfolding: everything new and untried yet, just around the corner. He opened his eyes and heard the ocean just a few blocks distant, the very same ocean he'd lain beside with Laura Lee, but he himself was middle-aged and irritable and so was Laura Lee, he supposed, wherever she was; and his mouth had a scorched taste from smoking too much the night before.

It was six o'clock in the morning in Bethany Beach, Delaware, in the buckling tarpaper cottage they rented from Uncle Ollie every July. Tongue-and-groove walls, painted a dingy blue too long ago, rose high above the swaybacked bed. A tattered yellow shade rustled in the window. (Where else but near the ocean would you see this kind of window—the cheap aluminum frame stippled by salt air, the bellying screen as soft and sleazy as some synthetic fabric? Where else would the screen doors and porches have those diagonal wooden insets at the corners, so that no right angles appeared to exist within earshot of the Atlantic?) The room was full of cast-offs: a looming wardrobe faced with a flecked, metallic mirror; a bow-fronted bureau topped with a mended dresser scarf (every one of the drawers stuck, and several of the cut-glass knobs were missing); a pink shag rug as thin and wrinkled as a bathmat; and a piecrust table beside the bed with a cracked brown plastic clock radio on the doily at its center. Morgan sat up and switched on the radio. He had just missed the Six O'Clock Sermonette; Guy and Ralna were singing "What a Friend We Have in Jesus." Next to him, Bonny stirred and said, "Morgan? What on earth . . . ?"

He lowered the volume a little. He inched out of bed, took a sombrero from the wardrobe, and put it on without looking in the mirror. Barefoot, in his underpants, he slogged down the hall to the kitchen. Already the air was so warm and heavy that he felt used up.

The cottage had four bedrooms, but only three were occupied. His mother slept in the second and Kate, their last remaining child, in the third. It used to be that the place was overflowing. The girls would share beds and couches; Brindle roomed with Louisa; various daughters' boyfriends lined up in sleeping bags out on the porch. Morgan had complained of the confusion at the time, but now he missed it. He wondered what point there was in coming any more. Kate was hardly present—she was eighteen years old now, busy with her own affairs, forever off visiting friends in the ugly new condominium south of town. As for Louisa, the trip seemed to shake her memory loose; she was even more dislocated than usual. Only Bonny appeared to enjoy herself. She padded along the shoreline with a bucket, hunting shells. The bridge of her nose developed a permanent pink, peeling patch. Sometimes she sat at the edge of the breakers and dabbled like a child, with her legs in a V—a rash of red on top, pale underneath. Then Morgan would pace the sand just behind her with his thumbs hooked in the waistband of his trunks, braving the sun and the sticky spray, for he was never comfortable when a member of his family was in the water. He considered swimming (like sailing, like skiing) to be unnatural, a rich person's contrivance to fill up empty hours. Although he could swim himself (a taut, silent breast stroke, with his mouth tightly closed, not wetting so much as the tip of his beard), he would never swim just for pleasure. And he would surely never swim in the ocean. His distrust of the ocean was logical and intelligent, he felt. He kept sensibly away from the edge, wearing stout shoes and woolen socks at all times. He only listened to the breakers, and plummeted into a deep, slow trance where once again he lay with Laura Lee Keller on a blanket beneath the stars.

It was too hot for coffee, but he'd get a headache if he tried to do without it. He made instant, using water straight from the tap. Beneath the taste of Maxwell House and sugar he caught the thick, dark taste of beach water, but he drank it anyway, from a jellyglass painted with clowns. Then he rinsed the glass. Then he took Bonny's purse from the kitchen table and put it in the freezing compartment of the refrigerator. (Another folly of rich people was their belief that in resort towns, crime does not exist. Morgan knew better. He sensed danger all around, and would have felt more secure in the heart of Baltimore.)

He went back to the bedroom and found Bonny sitting against her pillow. "What are you up so early for?" she asked him. "And why was the radio on?"

"I wanted to hear the news," he said.

It wasn't true; he never felt the news had anything to do with him. What he'd wanted was to drown out the sound of the ocean. This was Tuesday. They'd been here three days. There were eleven days remaining. He sighed and sat on the edge of the bed to pull his socks on. "I'll bring breakfast from the bakery," he told Bonny. "Anything you want while I'm in town?"

"The bakery's not open yet."

"I'll go and wait. I'll buy a paper. It's too quiet here."

"Well, bring some of those bow-tie things with cherries, then . . ." She yawned and ruffled her hair. A pillow mark ran down her left cheek. "Lucky you," she said. "You fell asleep right away, last night."

"I had a terrible sleep."

"You fell asleep instantly."

"But the whole night long I dreamed," Morgan said, "and woke, and checked the clock. I can't remember now what I dreamed. A man in a tailcoat stepped out of the wardrobe. I think this house is haunted, Bonny."

"You say that every year," Bonny told him.

"Well, it's haunted every year." He pulled a striped T-shirt over his head. When he emerged, he said, "All these wakeful nights, peculiar thoughts . . . the most I hope for, from a vacation, is a chance to rest up once it's over."

"Today's the day my brother comes," Bonny said, climbing out of bed.

Morgan zipped his hiking shorts, which were new and full of pockets and flaps that he hadn't yet explored. Attached to one pocket was a metal clasp. It was probably meant for a compass. "I don't suppose you brought along a compass," he told Bonny.

"Compass?"

He glanced at her. She was standing before the wardrobe in a short, plain nightgown that he happened to be fond of. He was even fond of the grapy veins in her calves, and her rumpled knees. He considered slipping up to kiss the pulse in her throat, but then he felt laden by the heat and the waves and the tongue-and-groove walls. "Ah, God. I have to do something about this *life* of mine," he said.

"What about it?" she asked, sliding a blouse off a hanger.

"It's come to nothing. It's come to nothing."

She looked over at him, and parted her lips as if about to ask a question. But then he said, "Bow-tie pastries, right? With cherries."

He was gone before she could ask whatever it was she had planned.

2 With one hand under his mother's elbow, he steered her along the boardwalk. It was nearly noon, and she wore a great black cartwheel of a hat to guard against sunburn. Her striped terry beach robe was long-sleeved and ankle-length, and it concealed not a bathing suit but an ordinary street dress, for she could no more swim than fly, she always said. Her face was pale and pursed, even in this heat, and her fingertips were cold when she touched his arm. She touched his arm to tell him to stop for a second. She wanted to look at a house that was under construction. "What an unusual shape," she said.

"It's called an A-frame," Morgan said.

"Why, it's practically all garret."

Morgan summoned his thoughts together. At moments like this, when Louisa seemed fully in touch with her surroundings, he always made an effort to have a real conversation with her. "The cost," he said, "is considerably lower than for other houses, I believe."

"Yes, I should think so," she said. She patted his arm again, and they walked on. She said, "Let's see now. How long have we been here?"

"Three days, Mother."

"Eleven more to go," she said.

"Yes."

She said, "Heavens."

"Maybe our family wasn't cut out for vacations," Morgan said.

"Maybe not."

"It must be the work ethic," he said.

"Well, I don't know what *that* is. It's more like we vacation all year round on our own."

"How can you say that?" Morgan asked. "What about my hardware store?"

She didn't answer.

"We're city people," Morgan said. "We have our city patterns, things to keep us busy . . . It's dangerous, lolling around like this. It's never good just to loll around and think. Why, you and Father never vacationed in your lives. Did you?"

"I don't recall," she said.

She would not remember anything about his father, ever. Sometimes Morgan wondered if her failing memory for recent events might stem from her failing memory of her husband; selective forgetfulness was an impossibility, maybe. Having chosen to forget in one area, she had to forget in all others as well. He felt a sudden urge to jolt her. He wanted to ask: am I aging in the same direction my father did? have I journeyed too far away from him? am I too near? what do I have to go on, here? I'm traveling blind; I'm older now than my own father ever lived to be. Instead, he asked, "Didn't you and he go to Ocean City once?"

"I really wouldn't know," she said primly.

"Jesus! You're so *stubborn!*" he shouted, slapping his thigh. His mother remained unmoved, but two girls walking ahead in bikinis looked over their shoulders at him. "Do you ever think how I must feel?" he asked his mother. "Sometimes I feel I've just been *plunked* here. I have no one from the old days; I'm just a foreigner on my own. You can't count Brindle; she's so much younger, and anyway so wrapped up in that husband of hers . . ."

"But there's always me," his mother said, picking her way around a toddler with a bucket.

"Yes," he said, "but often you sort of . . . vacate, Mother; you're not really there at all."

He had hurt her feelings. He was glad of it only for an instant; then he felt deeply remorseful. His mother raised her head high and looked off toward someone's A-frame cottage, where beach towels flapped on the balcony railing. "Why!" she said. "Wasn't that speedy."

"What was, Mother dear?"

"They've finished construction on the A-frame," she said. "It seems like no time at all." And she jutted her chin at him with a triumphant, bitter glare.

"So it does, dear heart," he said.

3   Morgan went out to get a pizza for their supper and returned to find that Bonny's brother had arrived. He'd brought his new wife, Priscilla, a pretty girl with short, straight blond hair caught back in a silver barrette. They had been married only a few weeks. They wore similar crisp, new-looking white slacks and pastel shirts, like honeymooners. Morgan hadn't even met Priscilla up till now—or people seemed to assume he hadn't, for Billy introduced her and she

shook Morgan's hand formally. Bonny said, "Priscilla went to Roland Park Country School with the Semple-Pearce girls, Morgan."

"Oh, yes,"Morgan said, but the truth of the matter was, he could have sworn that Billy had been married to Priscilla once before. He seemed to remember her. He thought she might even have visited this cottage. But she acted as if everything were new to her. "What a sweet place," she said. "What a lot of . . . character," and she walked around the living room fingering the seashell ashtrays like a stranger, and peering at the photograph of Uncle Ollie's 1934 lacrosse team, and reading all the titles on the *Reader's Digest* book condensations. Morgan was cagy; he went along with it. Then as soon as possible he cornered Bonny, who had taken the pizza out to the kitchen.

"Bonny," he whispered, "isn't that girl an ex-wife of his?"

"No, dear, she's his present wife."

"But didn't Billy marry her another time, earlier?"

"What are you talking about?"

"I know he did," he said. "He married her and brought her here; it was the same time of year."

Bonny straightened up from the oven. She looked hot; the hair around her temples was damp. She said, "Morgan, I am not in the mood for any of your jabs at my brother."

"Jabs? What jabs?"

"Just because he may have a fondness for one particular type of girl—" Bonny said.

"I'm not talking *types*, Bonny. I mean this. He brought her here several years ago and she had that little dog Kelty, Kilty, . . . why deny it? There's nothing wrong with marrying her twice. Lots of people go back, retrace, try to get it right the second time around. Why cover it up?"

She only sighed and returned to the living room. Morgan followed her. He found Billy and Priscilla on the wicker couch, talking with Morgan's mother. Billy looked old and foolish in his vivid clothes, with his bald pink skull, his pale hair straggling behind his ears. He had hold of one of Priscilla's hands and was stroking it, like something trapped, in his lap. Priscilla was pretending the hand did not belong to her. She leaned forward earnestly, listening to Louisa discuss the drive to Bethany. "I took along a thermos of Lipton tea," Louisa said, "and two nice, juicy nectarines, and a box of arrowroot biscuits that Bonny sometimes buys for my digestion." Priscilla nodded, her face alight with interest and enthusiasm. She was very young. She couldn't possibly have been married several years ago; several years ago she would still have been a schoolgirl in a royal-blue Roland Park Country School jumper. Morgan felt confused. He sat down in a rocking chair.

Louisa said, "Traffic was held up on the Bridge, so we stopped and I got out and sat in the grass by the side of the road. There was a little boy there, just a tot, and I shared one of my nectarines with him and he gave me a nice speckle pear."

"*Seckel* pear," Morgan murmured. He could not bear to have her laughed at.

"A speckle pear, this one was. I finished half of it and put the other half in a Baggie. Then we got back in the car and drove across the Bridge, but in Delaware we stopped again where the Kiwanis Club was barbecuing chickens and I had half a chicken, a Tab, and a sack of potato chips. They were out of bread-and-butter pickles. At Farmer John's Vegetable Stand . . ."

Priscilla's purse was one of those button-on things with a wooden handle. Bermuda bags, he believed they were called. You could button on an infinity of different covers to match different outfits. He would bet that her suitcase was full of covers—seersucker pink, yachting blue . . . he lost his train of thought. He wondered what had possessed him to leave his camera at home, hanging by its leather strap in the downstairs closet. For the first time in twenty years he would not have pictures of their vacation. On the other hand, what was the use of such pictures? They were only the same, year after year. Same waves, same sunburns, same determined smiles . . .

"After we reached Bethany, I started feeling a little peckish, so I walked to the market with Kate and picked out a watermelon. It was a wonderful melon, really fat and thumpy-sounding, and once we got it back to the cottage all we had to do was touch a knife point to it and it crackled all the way open. But it had no taste. Can you believe it? Had no taste whatsoever. Such a lovely color and not a scrap of taste. I just don't understand that," Morgan's mother said.

Morgan suddenly remembered another of last night's dreams. He'd been standing on a lawn beside a beautiful, graceful woman he'd never seen before. She led him toward a child's swing hanging from a tree limb. They settled on it— the woman sitting, Morgan standing, enclosing her with his feet. They started swinging over a cliff. Tiny yellow flowers dotted a field far below them. Morgan knew that when they were swinging high enough, they would leap. He would die. He wasn't upset about it. Then the woman tipped her head back against him, and he felt the length of her between his legs—the curve of her ribcage, the satiny coolness of her clothing. He was like a boy again, trembling. He saw that as long as he felt this way, he wanted to go on living, and all at once he was afraid of the leap. He woke abruptly, with his heart beating so hard that his whole body seemed to vibrate.

4   In the past few years Morgan had become a letter-writer. He couldn't have said exactly why. It just seemed, sometimes, that he grew restless and ill-contained; he couldn't sit still; there was something he wanted to tell someone, but he couldn't think what it was and he had no particular person in mind. Then he would sit down and write letters —although even that was not quite it; it was only second best. At work, he used his Woodstock typewriter, which produced an uneven, sooty print that danced all over the page. He plodded away with two index fingers, stopping after every word or so to pry up the A key, which wouldn't spring back

on its own. At home, he wrote with a leaky fountain pen whose cartridge he refilled with a plastic hypodermic needle. (He'd salvaged the needle from an emergency-room wastebasket during one of the children's accidents. Buying cartridges already filled was an extravagance, he felt.) He wrote all his daughters, even those still living in Baltimore. He wrote the traveling salesmen who came to the store, and his friends Kazari and the Greek tavern-keeper. Because he did not often have anything to say, he gave advice, as a rule. *It has come to my attention that your company's plant-sprayer bottles work exceedingly well for dousing fireplace logs at bedtime. Simply fill the bottle with water, adjust the nozzle to setting 4 . . .*

Or:

Dear Amy,

I notice that you appear to be experiencing some difficulty with household clutter.

Understand that I'm not blaming you for this, your mother has the same problem. But as I've been telling her for years, there is a solution.

Simply take a cardboard box, carry it through the rooms, load into it everyone's toys and dirty clothes and such, and hide it all in a closet. If people ask for some missing object, you'll be able to tell them where it is. If they don't ask (now, here is the important part), if a week goes by and they don't notice the object is gone, then you can be sure it's non-essential, and you throw it away. You would be surprised at how many things are non-essential. Throw everything away, all of it! Simplify! Don't hesitate!

All my love, sweetheart,

Daddy

That night, after the others had gone to bed, Morgan sat at the kitchen table and wrote a postcard to Potter, the musical-instrument man. . . . *weather has been fair and warm, a high in the 80's all three days . . . must thank the good Lord for in Rehoboth I hear they had 1¾ inches of rainfall in 47 minutes . . . Yours in Christ, Gower Morgan, S.J.* He wrote Todd, his three-year-old grandson, a fine, masculine letter: *The new pickup is doing well and the baggage space comes in handy, believe me. Was able to take our entire set of Encyclopedia Britannica to the beach. Now have 15,010 miles on the odometer with the fuel cost per mile being 2.1¢ and total operating costs per mile being 4.76¢. If you assume a 30% depreciation each year . . .*

He addressed the letter to Todd and laid it on top of Potter's postcard. He sat there blankly for a moment. Then he reached for another sheet of paper. *Dear Emily, Leon, and Gina*, he wrote. *Have been having pleasant weather and temperatures in the 80's . . .*

But it never helped to write the same things over. He crossed the sentence out and wrote, *Why not come Friday for the weekend? Simply take the Bay Bridge and continue to Wye Mills, switching there to Highway 404 and then to Highway 18 . . .*

5   Late Thursday morning Brindle showed up. No one had expected her. Morgan was on the front porch, slouching in a painted rocker and leafing through a volume of the encyclopedia. He happened to glance toward the street and there, just coming to a halt, was the little red sports car that Robert Roberts had given Brindle on their wedding day. Brindle yanked the emergency brake and got out, streaming tears. Her head was swathed in the white chiffon scarf she always slept in to calm her hair down, and she wore some kind of oversized, ankle-length white coat. In fact, she reminded Morgan of an early automobile driver. "Oh, I like that very much," he told her as she climbed the porch steps. "The veil, the duster . . ."

"It's not a duster, it's a bathrobe," Brindle said. She blew her nose in a soggy-looking Kleenex. Crying had turned her soft and full, almost pretty. Her eyelids were shiny and her sallow skin had a faint pink glow. She sank into the chair next to Morgan's and folded her Kleenex to a dry spot. "I got it last week at Stewart's," she said. "Sixteen forty-nine, marked down from thirty-two ninety-eight."

"Half-price; not bad at all," said Morgan. "Here, dear, have a cigarette."

"I don't smoke," she told him.

"Have one, sweetheart. It'll do you good."

He extended the pack and shook it invitingly, but she only blotted her eyes. "I can't stand it any more," she said. "I must have been out of my mind, marrying that . . . tree, that boulder; all he does is sit there mourning. I can't stand it."

"Have a Rolaid. Have a coughdrop. Have some Wrigley's spearmint gum," Morgan said. He tore through his pockets.

"He keeps my graduation photo on the television set. Half the time that he pretends he's watching TV, he's really watching my photo. I see him clicking his eyes back in focus when I walk into the room. When he thinks I'm busy with something else, he'll go over to the photo and pick it up and study it. Then he'll shake his head and set it down again."

Her face fell apart and she started sobbing. Morgan gazed off toward the street. He wasn't exactly humming, but he went, "Mm-mm, mm-mm," from time to time, and drummed his fingers on his open book. A little boy rode by on a bicycle, tinkling a bell. Two ladies in skirted swimsuits carried a basketful of laundry between them.

"Of course, every situation has its difficult moments," Morgan said. He cleared his throat.

Then Bonny came out on the porch. "Brindle!" she said. "What are you doing here?"

"Bonny, I just can't stand it any more," Brindle said.

She reached out her arms, and Bonny came over to hug her and tell her, "There now, Brindle, never mind." (She always knew better than Morgan what to say.) "Never you mind, now, Brindle."

"It's getting so I'm jealous of my own self," Brindle said, muffled. "I'm jealous of my photograph, and the silver-plated

ID bracelet I gave him when I was thirteen. He never takes that bracelet off. He sleeps with it; he bathes with it. 'Let it *go*,' I feel like saying. 'Can't you ever forget her?' He sits in that TV room staring at my photo . . . there's times I've even seen tears in his eyes. I say, 'Robert, talk to me, please,' and he says, 'Yes, yes, in a minute.' "

Bonny smoothed a lashing of Brindle's hair back under the white scarf. Morgan said, "Oh, but surely this will pass."

"It will never pass," said Brindle, sitting up and glaring at him. "If it hasn't passed in two years, how can you think it ever will? I tell you, there's nothing worse than two people with the same daydream getting together, finally. This morning I woke up and found he hadn't come to bed. I went down to the TV room and there he was, sound asleep with my photo in the crook of his arm. So I picked up my keys from the counter and left. I didn't even bother dressing. Oh, I was like someone half-crazy, demented. I drove all the way to your house and parked and got out before I remembered you were in Bethany. Do you know that idiot paper-boy is still delivering your papers? They were everywhere, clear across the lawn. Sunday's was so old and yellow, you'd think it was urine-stained—and maybe it was. Listen, Morgan, if you're burglarized while you're gone, you have every right to sue that paper-boy. You remember what I said. It's an open invitation to any passing criminal."

"But things started off so well," Morgan said. "I had so much hope when Robert Roberts first came calling. Ringing the doorbell, bringing you roses—"

"What roses? He never brought roses."

"Of course he did."

"No, he didn't."

"I *remember* he did."

"Morgan, please," said Bonny. "Can't you let this be?"

"Oh, very well. But sweeping you into his arms . . . remember?"

"It was all an act," said Brindle.

"An act?"

"If he'd been halfway truthful," she said, "he'd have swept my *graduation* photo into his arms. And kissed it on the lips. And given it a sports car."

Her chin crumpled in again, and she pressed the damp knot of Kleenex to her mouth. Bonny gazed over Brindle's head at Morgan, as if expecting him to take some action. But what action would that be? He had never felt very close to Brindle; he had never understood her, although of course he loved her. They were so far apart in age that they were hardly brother and sister. At the time of her birth he already had his school life, and his street life, and his friends. And their father's death had not drawn them together but had merely shown how separate they were. They had mourned in such different ways, Brindle clinging fiercely to her mother while Morgan trudged, withdrawn and stubborn, through the outside world. You could almost say that they had mourned entirely different people.

He sat forward slowly, and scratched the crown of his sombrero. "You know," he said, "I was certain he brought roses."

"He never brought roses," Brindle said.

"I could swear he did: red ones. Armloads."

"You made those roses up," said Brindle. She tucked the Kleenex into her bathrobe pocket.

"What a pity," Morgan said sadly. "That was the part I liked best of all."

6   For lunch he made spaghetti, which was Brindle's favorite dish. He put on his short-order-cook's clothes—a dirty white apron and a sailor cap—and took over the kitchen, while Bonny and Brindle sat at the table drinking coffee. "Spaghetti à la Morgan!" he said, brandishing a sheaf of noodles. The women merely stared at him, blank-faced, with their minds on something else. "I had hints from the very beginning," said Brindle, "but I wouldn't let myself see

them. You know how it is. Almost the first thing he said to me, that first day he showed up, was . . . he pulled back from me and took both my hands and stared at me and, 'I can't understand it,' he said. 'I don't know why I've kept thinking of you. It's not as if you're a beauty, or ever were,' he said. 'Also I'm getting older,' I told him, 'and my dentist says my teeth are growing more crooked every year.' Oh, I never held anything back from him. I never tried to be what I wasn't."

Bonny clicked her tongue. "He doesn't properly appreciate you," she said. "He's one of those people who's got to see from a distance before he knows how to feel about it—from the past or out of other people's eyes or in a frame kind of thing like a book or a photo. You did right to leave him, Brindle."

Morgan felt a little itch of anxiety starting in his temples. "But she didn't *leave* him; she's just taking a little holiday from him," he told Bonny.

Bonny and Brindle gazed into space. Probably they hadn't even heard what he said.

Last spring Bonny's old college roommate had divorced her husband of twenty-seven years. And of course there were those wives of Billy's (every one of whom had left him, some without so much as a note) and Morgan's own daughter Carol, who just one week after her wedding had returned, in very good spirits, to settle back into the apartment she'd been sharing with her twin sister. Also, Morgan knew for a fact that two of Bonny's closest friends were considering separations, and one had actually spoken with a lawyer. He worried that it was contagious. He feared that Bonny might catch the illness; or it was more like catching a piece of news, catching *on*; she would come to her senses and leave him. She would take with her . . . what? Something specific hung just at the edge of his mind. She would take with her the combination to a lock, it felt like—a secret he needed to know that Bonny knew all along without trying. When Bonny came back from lunch with a friend, Morgan was always quick to

point out the friend's faults and ulterior motives. "She's dis-
contented by nature; any fool can see that. How that poor
lunk of a husband ever fell for her . . . Don't believe a word
she tells you," he would say. Oh, it was women friends you
had to watch out for, not men at all but women.

He rattled a spatula on a frying pan, trying to claim
Bonny's attention. He did a little short-order-cook's dance.
"Cackles on a raft for Number Four!" he called. "BLT, hold
the mayo!"

Bonny and Brindle gave him identical flat, bemused stares,
unblinking, like cats.

"Bonny, I don't see any garlic cloves," he said, switching
tactics.

"Use dehydrated."

"Dehydrated! Dried-out garlic chips? Unthinkable."

"No one will know the difference."

"I wish you'd learn to make grocery lists," he said. "You
want to get organized, Bonny. Keep a list on the door of the
fridge and write down whatever item you finish off."

Bonny ran her fingers through her hair. She made it look
like some kind of weaving—searching out a strand, lacing it
into other strands behind her ear.

"Here's what we'll do," he told her. "Next week, when we
get back to Baltimore, I'm going to take a pad of paper to the
supermarket. I'm going to map out all the aisles. Aisle one:
olives, pickles, mustard. Aisle two: coffee, tea . . . nothing
will be omitted. Then you can get it Xeroxed two hundred
and sixty times."

Her fingers paused. "How many?"

"Five times fifty-two. Five years' worth."

She looked into his face.

"After five years I'll make you a new one," Morgan said.
"Things may have changed in the store by then."

"Yes, they very well may have," Bonny said.

She threw Brindle a quick, tucked glance, and they smiled
at each other. It was a smile so sunny and bland, and so obviously collusive, that all of Morgan's uneasiness returned. It

occurred to him that often they must discuss him behind his back. "Oh, you know Morgan," they must say, rolling their eyes. "You know how he is."

"Well, anyway," he said, "all I intended was . . . See, if we check items off on this list, shopping would be so simple. Everything would go the way it ought to. Don't you agree?"

"Yes, yes."

"Should I be the one to get it Xeroxed?"

"No, dear, I'll do it," Bonny said. Then she sighed and laughed, in that way she had, and drank the last of her coffee. "For now," she told Brindle, "let's you and me go into town and buy the garlic."

"Never mind; I'll use dehydrated," Morgan said hastily.

But she said, "Oh, the walk will do us good. We'll take your mother, too." She rose and looked under a stack of magazines. Then she looked in the oven, and finally in the refrigerator. She took out her purse and kissed Morgan. "Anything else you want?" she asked him.

"You could get cream."

"We have cream."

"Yes, but with more people coming tomorrow, and they might be as early as breakfast time—"

"Who might?"

"The Merediths."

"Merediths?"

"At least, I *think* they might," he said. "I just dropped them this note, you see, because Brindle wasn't here and I hadn't known Billy was staying through the weekend. I'd thought there'd be enough room. And there will be. Why, of course there will be! Where'd we put those sleeping bags?"

"Morgan, I wish you would check with me before you do these things," Bonny said.

"But you like them! You always say you like them."

"Like who?" Brindle asked. "Who're we talking about, here?"

Bonny said, "Oh, the . . . you remember them, Brindle: the Merediths. You've seen them at the house, several times. Leon and Emily Meredith. Well, certainly I like them. I'm very fond of both of them, you know that, but still—"

"*I* found them a little dry, personally," Brindle said. "Her, at least. No, I don't think she'd be a barrel of fun at the beach."

"Oh, Emily's not dry at all, just—"

"And anyhow," Morgan told Brindle, "I don't remember asking what you thought. For that matter, I don't remember asking you to Bethany, so you're in a fine position to criticize my guest list."

"Now, Morgan," Bonny said.

"Oh, well," said Brindle, "they won't come. Don't worry, Bonny. Emily won't like sand. She won't like mess. She won't want to go into that messy, sticky ocean. I know the type; they can't come to the banquet," she said.

Then she set out with Bonny, so cheered by her own perceptiveness that her face looked peaky and alight with pleasure, and Robert Roberts might never have existed.

7 But they did come. They arrived the next day in mid-morning, driving the little black VW that Leon had picked up secondhand. Morgan was not quite adjusted yet to the thought of their owning a car. (Though if it had to happen, he supposed that this tiny, bell-shaped machine was the most appropriate. And black; that was a nice touch. Yes, and, after all, what was wrong with itinerants possessing some form of transportation? Maybe they should buy a trailer, as well.) Morgan stood in the yard, rocking from heel to toe, watching as they parked. Emily got out first, and pulled the front seat forward for Gina. Emily had the wrong kind of shoes on—Docksiders. Morgan could hardly believe his eyes. With her black leotard and her flowing black skirt, there was something almost shocking about those cloddy, stiff brown loafers with the white rubber soles. And Gina, when she emerged, wore the squinty, grudging expression of someone

yanked from sleep. Leon's face had a clenched look and there was a shaving cut in the cleft of his chin, plastered with a tiny square of toilet paper. No, they were definitely not at their best. It seemed Morgan had only to leave town and they fell apart, rushed ahead without him, tossed aside all their old charm, and invested in unsuitable clothing. (Leon's new polo shirt was electric blue, almost painful to the sight.) Still, Morgan stepped forward, putting on a smile of welcome. "Why! How nice to see you," he said, and he kissed Emily's cheek. Then he hugged Gina and shook hands with Leon. "Have a good trip? Much traffic? Bad on the Bridge?" he asked. Leon muttered something about senior-citizen drivers and jerked the trunk lid open.

"It was an easy trip, but I don't know what the scenery was like because Leon drove so fast it blurred together," Emily said.

"Emily thinks I'm speeding if she can't read all the small print on every billboard," Leon said, "every road sign and circus poster. If she can't count all the fruit in all the fruit stands."

"Well, I didn't notice that patrolman disagreeing with me."

"The fellow's speedometer was way off base," Leon said, "and I'm going to tell them so when it comes to court." He took out a small suitcase and slammed the trunk lid shut. "These people just have a quota to fill. They'll pick up any-one, if they haven't passed out enough tickets that day."

"Ah, well," Morgan said soothingly. "You got here safely; that's what's important." He took the suitcase from Leon. It weighed more than he'd expected. "Come on in the house," he said. "Bonny! The Merediths are here!"

He led them up the front steps and into the living room. The house's smell—mildew and kerosene—struck him for the first time as unfriendly. He noticed that the cushions in the rattan chairs were flat as pancakes, soggy-looking, and the rattan itself was coming loose in spirals from the arms. Maybe this hadn't been such a good idea. Emily and Leon stared around uncertainly. Gina slouched near the door and peeled a thumbnail. This was her summer to thin out, it seemed. Her halter top sagged pathetically around her flat little chest. Morgan felt he was suddenly viewing everyone, himself included, in terms of geometry: an ill-assorted collection of knobs and bulges parked in meaningless locations. Then Emily said, "I brought a camera."

"Eh?" said Morgan. "Oh, a camera!"

"Just a Kodak."

"But that's wonderful!" he said. "I left mine at home this year. Oh, it's wonderful that you thought of it!" And just then Bonny emerged from the kitchen, smiling, wiping her palms on her skirt. He saw that things would be fine after all. (Life was full of these damp little moments of gloom that came and went; they meant nothing.) He beamed and watched as Bonny hugged everyone. Behind her came his mother, also smiling. "Mother," he said, "you remember the Merediths."

"Of course," she said. She held out a hand, first to Leon and then to Emily. "You brought me that fruitcake last Christmas," she told Emily.

"Oh, yes."

"It had the most marvelous glaze on the top."

"Why, thank you," Emily said.

"And did your husband ever recover from his stroke?"

"Excuse me?"

Morgan saw in a flash what must have happened. His mother had Emily confused with Natalie Czernov, a next-door neighbor from Morgan's childhood. Mrs. Czernov had also made fruitcake at Christmas. He was so fascinated by this slippage in time (as if the fruitcake were a kind of key that opened several doors at once, from several levels of history) that he forgot to come to Emily's rescue. Emily said, "This is my husband right here, Mrs. Gower."

"Oh, good, he's better, then," Louisa said.

Emily looked at Morgan.

"Maybe I should show you where you're staying," he said.

He picked up their suitcase again and led them down the hall to Kate's room. The bed had been freshly made and there was a sleeping bag on the floor for Gina. "The bathroom is next door," he said. "There are towels above the sink. If you need anything else . . ."

"I'm sure we'll be fine," Emily said. She opened the suitcase. Morgan glimpsed several new-looking squares of folded clothing. Leon, meanwhile, crossed the room abruptly and looked out the window. (All he would see was a row of dented trashcans.) Then he moved on to the picture that hung over the bed: a dim blue sea, flat as glass, on which rode a boat made of real shells. "We shouldn't have come," he said, peering at a clamshell sail.

"Oh, Leon, we need a rest," Emily told him.

"We have to give a puppet show on Monday morning. That means either we fight the Sunday traffic on the Bridge, or we go back at crack of dawn on Monday, driving like hell to meet the schedule, and Lord help us if we have a flat or any little tie-up on the way."

"It's nice to get out of the city," Emily told Morgan. She removed a camera from the suitcase and closed the lid again. "Leon thought we couldn't take the time, but I said, 'Leon, I'm tired. I want to go. I'm tired of puppets.'"

"She's tired of puppets," Leon said. "Whose idea were they, I'd like to know? Whose were they in the first place? I'm only doing what you said to, Emily. You're the one who started this."

"Well, there's no good reason we can't leave them for a weekend, Leon."

"She thinks we can just leave whenever we like," Leon told Morgan.

Morgan passed a hand across his forehead. He said, "Please. I'm sure this will all work out. Don't you want to come see the ocean now?"

Neither Leon nor Emily answered him. They stood facing each other across the bed, their backs very straight, as if braced for something serious. They didn't even seem to notice when Morgan left the room.

8 No, it hadn't been such a good idea to ask them here. The weekend passed so slowly, it didn't so much pass as *chafe* along. It ground to a stop and started up again. It rasped on Morgan's nerves. Actually, this was not entirely the Merediths' fault. It was more the fault of Brindle, who faded into tears a dozen times a day; or Bonny, who overdid her sunbathing and developed a fever and chills; or Kate, who was arrested in Ocean City on charges of possessing half an ounce of marijuana. But Morgan blamed the Merediths anyhow. He couldn't help but feel that Leon's sulkiness had cast some kind of evil spell, and he was irritated by the way Emily hung around Bonny all the time. (Who had befriended Emily first, after all? Who had first discovered her?) She had changed; just wearing different shoes on her feet had somehow altered her. He began to avoid her. He devoted himself to Gina—a sad, sprouty child at an awkward age, just the age to tear at his heart. He made her a kite from a Hefty bag, and she thanked him earnestly, but when he looked into her face he saw that she was really watching her parents, who were arguing in low voices at the other end of the porch.

He began reflecting on Joshua Bennett, a new neighbor back in Baltimore. This Bennett was an antique dealer. (Now, *there* was an occupation.) He looked like Henry the Eighth and he lived a gentlemanly life—eating small, expensive suppers, then reading leatherbound history books while twirling a snifter of brandy. Early last spring, when Bennett first moved in, Morgan had paid a call on him and found him in a maroon velvet smoking jacket with quilted satin lapels. (Where would one go to buy a smoking jacket?) Bennett had somehow received the impression that Morgan had descended from an ancient Baltimore shipping family and owned an atticful of antique bronzes, and he had been most cordial

—offering Morgan some of his brandy and an ivory-tipped cigar. Morgan wondered if Bennett would have accepted an invitation to the beach. He began plotting his return to Baltimore: the friendship he would strike up, the conversations they would have. He could hardly wait to get back.

Meanwhile the weekend dragged on.

Kate had disgraced the family, Bonny said. Now she was on the police files, marked for life. Bonny seemed to take this very seriously. (Her sunburn gave her a hectic, intense look.) Because the cottage had no telephone, the Ocean City police had had to call the Bethany police and have them notify the Gowers. Naturally, therefore, the news would be everywhere now. Saturday, at breakfast, Bonny laid a blazing hand on Louisa's arm and asked Kate, "How do you think your grandma feels? Her late husband's name, which up till now has been unbesmirched." Morgan had never heard her use the word "unbesmirched" before, and he wasn't even sure that it existed. He took some time thinking it over. Louisa, meanwhile, went on calmly spooning grapefruit. "What do you say, Mother?" Bonny asked her.

Louisa peered out of her sunken eyes and said, "Well, I don't know what all the fuss is about. We used to give little babies marijuana any old time. It soothed their teething."

"No, no, Mother, that was belladonna," Bonny said.

Kate merely looked bored. Brindle blew her nose. The Merediths sat in a row and watched, like members of a jury.

And on the beach—where the ocean curled and flattened beneath a deep blue bowl of sky, and gulls floated overhead as slow as sails—this group was a motley scramble of blankets, thermoses, sandy towels, an umbrella that bared half its spokes every time the wind flapped past, a squawking radio, and scattered leaves of newspaper. Kate, who had been grounded for the rest of her vacation, flipped angrily through *Seventeen*. Bonny sweated and shivered in layers of protective garments. The white zinc oxide on her nose and lower lip, along with her huge black sunglasses, gave her the look of some insect creature from a science-fiction movie. Gina dug a hole in the sand and climbed into it. Billy and Priscilla made a spectacle of themselves, lying too close together on their blanket.

And Emily, in an unbecoming pale blue swimsuit that exposed her thin, limp legs, took pictures that were going to turn out poorly, but she would not yield her camera to Morgan. She worried that he would snap *her*, she said. Morgan swore he wouldn't. (She was already pasted in his mind as he would like her to be forever—wearing her liquid black skirt and ballet slippers. He would surely not choose to record this other self she had become.) "All I want to do," he told her, "is photograph some groups. Some action, don't you see." He couldn't bear her finicky delays, the stylized poses she insisted on. Morgan himself was a photographer of great speed and dash; he caught people in clumps, in mid-motion, mid-laugh. Emily picked her way across the sand to one person at a time, stopping every step or so to shake her white feet fastidiously, and then she would take an eternity getting things just right, squinting through the camera, squinting at the sky—as if there were anything that could be done, any adjustments at all to aid a Kodak Instamatic. "Be still, now," she would tell her subject, but then she'd wait so long that whoever it was grew strained and artificial-looking, and more than once Morgan cried, "Just *take* it, dammit!" Then Emily lowered her camera and turned, eyes widening, lips parting, and had to begin all over again.

Sunday afternoon the Merediths had a quarrel about when they were going home. Emily wanted to wait till Monday, but Leon wanted to leave that evening. "Lord, yes," Morgan longed to say. "Go!"—not only to the Merediths but to everyone. They could abandon him on the beach. Fall would come and he'd be buried under drifting threads of sand and a few brown leaves blown seaward. He pictured how calm he would grow, at last. The breakers would act for him, tumbling about while he lay still. He would finally have a chance to sort himself out. It was *people* who disarranged his life— Louisa in her striped beach robe like a hawk-nosed Bedouin, Brindle in an old stretched swimsuit of Bonny's that fell in vacant folds around her hunched body. He sat beneath the umbrella in his sombrero and trunks and his shoes with woolen socks. His bare chest felt itchy and sticky. He chewed a match and listened to the Merediths quarrel.

Leon said that if they left Monday, they might very well miss their show. Emily said it was only a puppet show. Leon asked how she could say *only*. Wasn't it what she'd set her heart on, dragged him into, held his nose to—damn puppets with their silly grins—all these years? She said she had never held his nose to anything and, anyway, it was Leon's business what he did with his life. She had certainly not forced him into this, she said. Then Leon jumped to his feet and went striding southward, toward town. Morgan watched after him, idly observing that Leon had developed a roll of padded flesh above the waistband of his trunks. He was a solid, weighty man now, and came down hard on his heels. Flocks of slender girls parted to let him pass. He pushed on through them, not giving them a glance.

Possibly, Billy and Priscilla were quarreling too, for they sat apart from each other and Billy drew deep circles in the sand between his feet. The women melted closer together; the men remained on the outskirts, each alone, stiff-necked. The women's soft voices wove in with the rush of the ocean. "Look at the birds," Emily told Gina. "Look how they circle. Look how they're hunting for fish."

"Or maybe they're just cooling off their underwings," Louisa said.

Bonny, gazing at the horizon from behind her dark glasses, spoke in a tranquil, faraway voice. "It was here on this beach," she said, "that I first knew I was a grownup. I had thought of myself as a girl for so long—years after I was married. I was twenty-nine, pregnant with the twins. I'd brought Amy and Jeannie to the beach to play. I saw the lifeguard look over at me and then at some spot beyond me, and I realized he hadn't really seen me at all. His mind told him, 'Lady. Children. Sand toys,' and he passed on. Oh, it's not as if I were ever the kind that boys would whistle at. It's not as if I were used to hordes of men admiring me, even back when I was in my teens. But at least, you see, I had once been up for consideration, and now I wasn't. I was reclassified. I felt so sad. I felt I'd had something taken away from me that I was so certain of, I hadn't even noticed I had it. I didn't know it would happen to me too, just like to anyone else."

Morgan noticed someone walking toward them: a man in a business suit that was made of some dull gray hammered-metal fabric. Everyone he passed stared after him for a moment. He ruffled their faces like a wind, and then they turned away again. It was Robert Roberts. Morgan said, "Brindle." Brindle seemed to comprehend everything, just from the sound of her name. She hunched tighter on her blanket and hugged her knees and frowned, not looking. It was up to Morgan. He rose and spat his match out. "Why, Robert Roberts!" he said, and offered his hand, too soon. Robert had some distance to travel yet. He came lurching up the slope a little untidily, in order not to keep Morgan waiting. His palm was damp. His face glistened. He was a man without visible edges or angles, and his thin brown hair was parted close to the center and plastered down. It appeared that he was sinking into the sand. There was sand across the creases of his shoes, and more sand filling his trouser cuffs. He gripped Morgan's hand like a drowning man and stared fixedly into his eyes—but that was his salesman's training, no doubt. "It's Bob," he said, panting.

"Beg pardon?"

"I'm Bob. You always call me Robert Roberts, like a joke."

"I do?"

"I came for Brindle."

Morgan turned to Brindle. She hugged her knees harder and rocked, staring out to sea.

"It's the same thing all over, isn't it?" Robert said to Morgan. "It's the same old story. Once again she leaves me."

"Ah, well . . . have a seat, Robert, Bob. Don't be such a stranger."

Robert ignored him. "Brindle," he said, "I woke up Thursday morning and you were gone. I thought maybe you were just miffed about something, but it's been four days now and you never came back. Brindle, are we going round and round like this all our lives? We're together, you leave me, we're together, you leave me?"

"You do still have my photograph," Brindle told the ocean.

"What's that supposed to mean?"

Brindle got to her feet. She brushed sand off the seat of her bathing suit; she adjusted a strap. Then she went up to Robert Roberts and set her face so close to his that he drew back. "Look," she said, tapping her yellow cheekbone. "This is *me*. I am Brindle Gower Teague Roberts. All that string of names."

"Yes, Brindle, of course," Robert said.

"You say that so easily! But since you and I were children, I've been married and widowed. I married old Horace Teague next door and moved into his rowhouse; I bought little cans of ham in the gourmet sections of department stores—"

"You've told me all that, Brindle."

"I am not the girl in the photograph."

She was not. The skin below her eyes was the same damaged color as Morgan's. The dimple in one cheek had become a dry crack—something Morgan had never noticed. She was thirty-eight years old. Morgan stroked his beard.

"Brindle, what is it you're saying?" Robert Roberts asked. "Are you saying you don't love me any more?"

In the little group of women (all gazing politely in other directions) there was the softest rustle, like a laugh or a sigh. Robert looked over at them. Then he turned to Morgan. "What is she saying?" he asked.

"I don't know," said Morgan.

Louisa said, "If they marry, I hope I won't be sent to live with them."

"They *are* married, Mother dear," Morgan told her.

"You have no idea how hard it is," Louisa said, "not knowing where you'll be shipped to next."

"Mother, have we ever shipped you anywhere? Ever in all your life?"

"Haven't you?" she asked. She considered, retreating into the hood of her beach robe. "Well, somehow it feels like you have, at least," she said. "No, I prefer to stay on with you. Bonny, you won't let him send me off to Brindle's, will you? Morgan's difficult to live with but . . . eventful, I suppose you'd say."

"Oh, yes," said Bonny dryly.

"Promise?"

"Mother," said Morgan. "They're married. They're already married, and no one's shipped you anywhere. Tell her, Brindle. Tell her, Robert, Bob . . ."

But Robert faced the sea, not listening. His hair blew up stiffly, in spikes, which made him look desperate. While the others watched, he bent to dust the sand from his trousers. He pulled his shirtcuffs a proper length below the sleeves of his coat. Then he started walking toward the water.

He circled a child with a shovel and he stepped over a moat and a crenellated wall. But his powers of observation seemed to weaken as he drew nearer the sea, and he stumbled into a shallow basin that three little boys were digging. He climbed out again, ignoring their cries. Now his trouser legs were dark and sugary-looking. He accidentally crushed a paper cup beneath his heel. He reached the surf and kept going. A young man, lifting a screaming girl in the air and preparing to dunk her, suddenly set her down and stood gaping. Robert was knee-deep in seething white water. He was waist-deep. When the breakers curled back for a new assault, he was seen to be clothed in heavy, dragging vestments that looked almost Biblical.

Up until now, no one had moved. They might have been little specks of bathers on a postcard. But then Brindle screamed, "Stop him!" and all the women clambered to their feet. The lifeguard stood on his high wooden chair, with a whistle raised halfway to his mouth. Billy barreled past. Morgan hadn't even heard him get up. Morgan threw his sombrero into Bonny's lap and followed, but the lifeguard was faster than both of them. By the time Billy and Morgan hit the water, the lifeguard was in to waist level, heaving his orange torpedo at Robert. Robert brushed it away and plunged on.

A breaker crashed around Morgan's knees, colder than he had expected. He hated the feeling of wet woolen socks. However, he kept going. What he had in mind was not so much rescuing Robert as defeating him. No, Robert would never get away with this; he couldn't escape so easily; it must not be allowed. Morgan swarmed in the water, his limbs wandering off in several directions. A surprised-looking woman lifted both flaps of her bathing cap and stared. The lifeguard took a stranglehold on Robert from behind, and Robert (who so far had not even got his hair wet) flailed and fell backward. He was engulfed by a wave and came up coughing, still in the lifeguard's grasp. The lifeguard hauled him in. Morgan followed with his arms out level, his head lunging forward intently. The lifeguard dragged Robert up on the sand and dumped him there, like a bundle of wet laundry. He prodded Robert with one long, bronzed foot. "Oh, me," Morgan said wearily, and he sat down beside Robert and looked at his ruined shoes. Billy sank next to him, out of breath. Robert went on coughing and shrugging off the people who crowded around. "Stand back, stand back," the lifeguard said. He asked Morgan, "What was he, drunk?"

"I wouldn't have the faintest idea," Morgan said.

"Well, I got to make a report on this."

"Really, that won't be necessary," Morgan said, rising. "I'm from the Bureau."

"The what?"

"Parks and Safety," Morgan said. "What's your name, son? Of course I plan to mention this to the board."

"Well, Hendrix," the lifeguard said. "Danny Hendrix, with an x."

"Good work, Hendrix," Morgan said. He briskly shook the

lifeguard's hand. The lifeguard stood around a minute, scratching his head, and then he went down to the water to watch his orange torpedo float out to sea.

They propped Robert up and draped him across their shoulders—one arm circling Morgan's neck, one arm circling Billy's. Robert seemed uninjured, but he was heavy and lethargic and his shoes dragged behind him. "*Come* on, fellow," Billy said cheerfully. He looked pleased; perhaps he was reminded of his fraternity days, which he'd once told Morgan were the happiest of his life. Morgan himself stayed silent. He wished he had a cigarette.

They hauled Robert past the blanket, where the women were packing their belongings. Brindle was smoothing out towels and folding them. She would not look at Robert. Morgan felt proud of her. Let Robert see whom he was dealing with here! Let him see how they could handle it—all of them together. For this was no mere marital quarrel, no romantic tiff. No, plainly what had happened was a comment upon their whole family—on the disarray of their family life. Robert had been standing right beside this blanket, had he not, listening to Louisa forget where she was in time, Morgan arguing with her, all the others grouping into battle squads . . . and then he'd made his break, escaped. The scoundrel. He'd insulted every one of them, each and every one. Morgan felt a flash of anger. Pretending to be concerned about Hendrix, he stopped without warning and ducked away from Robert's arm and turned toward the ocean. Robert tilted and nearly fell. Morgan shaded his eyes. Hendrix was sending signals to the lifeguard on the next beach. Morgan could not read signal flags, but he could easily imagine the conversation that was taking place. WHAT WAS PROBLEM, the neighbor would ask, and Hendrix would answer, MIXUP CHAOS MUDDLE . . .

Kate was watching too. (No doubt she found Hendrix handsome.) Morgan said, "Can you tell what he's saying?"

She shrugged. "It's just the clear sign," she said.

"The what?"

"You know—all clear, everything in order."

"Little does he know," Morgan said.

9 Bonny told Morgan they were running out of beds. Were the Merediths leaving tonight or tomorrow morning? she asked him. This conversation took place in the kitchen, late in the afternoon, while Bonny was emptying ice-cube trays into a pitcher. Above the crackle and clink of ice, she whispered that it would certainly solve a great deal if the Merediths left before bedtime. Then she could put Brindle and Robert in their room. But Morgan didn't think Brindle would want to share a room with Robert anyhow. "Let it be, Bonny," he said. "Send Robert out on the porch with a sleeping bag."

"But, Morgan, they're married."

"The man's a lunatic. She's better off without him."

"You're the one who was against her leaving him," Bonny said. "Now, just because he walks into the surf a ways—"

"With all his clothes on. With his suit on. Making us look like some kind of institutional outing, a laughingstock . . ."

"Nobody laughed," Bonny said.

"It's a mark of how badly this vacation is going," Morgan said, "that, lately, I've been wondering how the hardware store is doing."

"He was just showing her he cared," said Bonny.

"I've half a mind to call Butkins in the morning and see if he's restocked those leaf bags yet. With fall coming on—"

"What are you talking about? It's July."

Morgan pulled at his nose.

"Go ask Emily what they've decided," Bonny said.

"You want me to tell them to leave?"

"No, no, just ask. If they're staying on, we'll work out something else."

"Maybe *we* could leave," he said hopefully. "The others could stay and we could go."

Bonny gave him a look.

He wandered into the living room, where his mother and Priscilla were playing Scrabble. Kate was painting her fingernails at a little rattan table. The smell of nail polish filled the room—a piercing, city smell that Morgan liked. He would have preferred to settle here, but he said, "Anyone seen Emily?"

"She's out front," Priscilla told him.

He went to the porch, letting the rickety screen door slam shut behind him. Emily was taking pictures again. She photographed Gina, who was lining up a row of oyster shells on the railing. She photographed Robert, who sat stiff and humiliated in a rocker, wearing borrowed clothes—Billy's wedding-white slacks and candy-striped shirt. Then she photographed Morgan. Morgan had to stand still for a long, long moment while Emily squinted through the camera at him. He did his best not to show his irritation. At least, he was glad to see, Emily had got out of that swimsuit. She wore her black outfit and no shoes at all. She was her old, graceful, fairy-dancer self. As soon as Morgan heard the shutter click, he said, "Now I'll snap one of you, since you're looking so fine and pretty." He came down the front steps and took the camera from her hands. She put up no resistance, for once. She seemed tired. Even when he drew away and aimed the camera at her, she didn't smooth her hair or lighten her expression.

He snapped the picture and handed the camera back to her. "Ah . . . Bonny was just wondering," he said. "Should we count on having you three for the night?"

"I don't know," she said. She rolled the film forward with a little zipping sound. "I'll have to talk to Leon," she said finally.

"Oh? Where *is* Leon?"

"He never came back from his walk. I was planning to go into town and look for him."

"I'll come with you," Morgan said. "Gina? You want to take a walk?"

"I'm busy," Gina said, laying out another row of shells.

"Robert?"

"I'm waiting for Brindle."

Morgan and Emily started down the street. It was narrow and patchily surfaced; they could walk in the center of it without much fear of traffic. They passed a woman hanging out beach towels and a little girl blowing soap bubbles on her steps. The houses were so close together that it almost seemed the two of them were proceeding through a series of rooms—hearing Neil Diamond on the radio and then an oboe concerto, catching a whiff of coffee and frying crabcakes, watching a man and a boy sort out their fishing tackle on a green porch glider. Emily said, "He'll have a mighty long wait."

"Who will?" Morgan asked.

"Robert Roberts. Brindle's gone back to Baltimore."

"She has?"

"Billy drove her to the bus in Ocean City."

"But her car's parked right out front!"

"She doesn't want it any more, she said."

"Oh," said Morgan. He thought that over. "So it's my house she's gone to, is it?"

"I didn't ask," Emily said.

"It serves him right," said Morgan. "Yes, I was on his side till now, the way he rang our doorbell, bringing roses . . . but, oh, this ocean business. No. People imagine they can hold you with such things. They cause themselves some damage and assume that we'll accept responsibility. But they underestimate us. They fail to realize. No, Brindle will never forgive him for that."

Emily said nothing. He glanced down at her and found her drawn and pale, walking alongside him with her camera held tight in one bluish hand. How had she managed to avoid a sunburn? She'd been out on the beach as long as the others. He wiped his sweaty forehead on his sleeve. "Well," he said, "I suppose you must find us very tiring. Right?"

"I've had a wonderful time," she told him.

"Eh?"

"I've had a wonderful time."

"Yes, well, that's sweet of you, but . . . never mind, I know this wasn't what you're used to. There's no economy to our life. Don't think I haven't noticed that."

"It was wonderful. It was a real vacation," Emily said. "As soon as we got your letter, I was so excited—I went out and bought us all new clothes. It's been years since I've been to the beach. Not since high school."

"Ah, yes, high school," Morgan said, sighing.

"He never thinks we can spare the time. He'd rather stay at home. We either give our shows or stay home. Sometimes I think he's doing it for spite—he's saying, 'You wanted to marry and settle, didn't you? Well, here we are, and we're never going anywhere again.' It's funny: I hoped I'd grow more like him—more, oh, active—but it seems instead he's more like me. We just sit home. I sit in that room with that sewing machine; I feel like someone in a story, some drudge. I feel like the miller's daughter, left to spin gold out of straw. Visiting here was just what we needed—so much going on, so many things happening—"

"Oh, dear, oh, dear," Morgan said. He felt very uncomfortable, and had forgotten to bring his cigarettes. They passed a man smoking on his front steps and Morgan drew a chestful of sharp gray air from him. "Doesn't the sun set differently here," he said, "so long and level; the light's so flat, somehow—" He walked faster. Emily kept up. They turned east and passed the first of a string of shops.

"He puts me in such a position," she said. "He always makes it seem that everything was my idea, that I'm the one who organized our lives this way, but I'm not. I mean, if he just *sat*, what was I to do? Tell me that!"

Morgan said, "I honestly don't believe I can last another day in this place."

"In Bethany?" Emily asked. She looked around her. "But it's beautiful," she said.

"It smells of dead fish."

"Why, Morgan."

They passed a gift-shop window hung with yellow nets and filled with spiky, varnished conch shells from Florida and pewter sand dollars, seahorses locked in Lucite paperweights, racks of pierced earrings shaped like starfish and dolphins. They climbed a set of weathered wooden stairs, and on the way up the ramp to the boardwalk Morgan glanced into the dark plate glass of the Holiday House restaurant. "Oh! My God," he said.

Emily turned to him.

"Look!" he said, feeling his cheeks, peering into the glass. "I'm so old! I'm so ruined! I seem to have . . . fallen apart."

She laughed.

"Well, I don't see anything funny," he told her.

"Morgan, don't worry. You're fine. It's always like that, if you haven't braced your face first."

"Yes, but now my face *is* braced," he said. "And look! Still!"

She stopped laughing and put on a sympathetic expression. But, of course, he couldn't expect her to understand. Her skin seemed filmed with gold; the metal filings of her hair glinted in the sunlight. She started walking again and after a moment he followed, still testing different parts of his face with his fingertips.

"I thought he'd be right around here somewhere," Emily said, gazing up and down the boardwalk.

"Maybe he stopped at a café."

"Oh, he'd never do that on his own."

This interested him. "Why not?" he asked. "What would he have against it?"

She didn't answer. She set her hands on the boardwalk railing and looked out at the ocean. It was five o'clock at least, maybe later, and only one or two swimmers remained. A single white Styrofoam raft skated away on the surf. Couples strolled along the edge, dressed in clean, dry clothing that gave them the lovingly tended look of small children awakened from naps. There were flattened squares of sand where families had been camped on blankets, and abandoned drip-castles and bucket-shaped towers. But no Leon. "Maybe he's back at the cottage," Morgan said. "Emily?"

She was crying. Tears rolled singly down her cheeks while she faced straight ahead, wide-eyed. "Why, Emily," Morgan said. He wished Bonny were here. He put an arm around Emily, clumsily, and said what he supposed Bonny might say. "There, now. Never mind," he told her, and when she turned toward him, he folded her in to him and said, "Never you mind, Emily." Her hair smelled like fresh linen that had hung to dry in the sun all day. The camera, which she clutched to her chest, made a boxy shape between them, but elsewhere she was soft and boneless, surprisingly slight; there was nothing to her. He was startled by a sudden ache that made him tighten his arms and pull her hard against him. His head grew light. She made some sound, a kind of gasp, and tore away. "Emily, wait!" he said. It was difficult to get his breath. He said, "Emily, let me explain," but she had already backed off, and Morgan was left reeling and hot-faced with shame, and before he could straighten out this new catastrophe, he looked down and saw Leon passing below them, absorbed in the evening paper.

10 They lost their good weather on Monday and didn't see the sun again till Thursday, and by then it was too late; everyone remaining in the cottage was annoyed with everyone else. Billy and Priscilla left early, in a huff—Priscilla driving Brindle's car. Louisa quarreled with Kate about some blueberry muffins, and Bonny told Morgan that he'd have to take Louisa in the pickup, going home. She certainly couldn't travel with the two of them together. But Morgan didn't want to take her. He looked forward to making the trip alone, with an extra-early start and no stops along the way. Then as soon as he reached home, he figured, he would pay a call on Joshua Bennett, the antique dealer. And maybe afterward he'd wander on downtown, just to see what he'd

missed. No, there wasn't any room for Louisa in his plans. So Saturday morning, while the others were still packing, he threw his encyclopedia into the truckbed. "Goodbye, everybody," he said, and he left. Traveling down their little street, before he turned onto the highway, he could look in the rear-view mirror and see Kate chasing after him, and Bonny descending the porch steps calling something, and Louisa shading her eyes in the door. In this family, you could never have a simple leavetaking. There were always threads and tangles trailing.

He drove slightly over the speed limit, once even swerving to the shoulder of the road to bypass a line of cars. He had only a few minutes' wait at the Kent Narrows and none at all on the Bridge. Skimming across the Bridge, he felt he was soaring. He reached the city limits at eleven, and was home by eleven-twenty—long before Bonny and the others.

The yard was overgrown, littered with rolled newspapers. The house was cool and musty-smelling behind its drawn shades, and there was a mountain of mail in the hall beneath the mail slot. In the dining room Brindle sat playing solitaire. Coffee stains yellowed the front of her bathrobe. She trilled her fingers absently when he walked in, and then she laid a jack of diamonds on a queen of spades. "Pardon my not bringing in the papers," she said, "but I didn't want to go outside because Robert Roberts was parked in front of the house for most of the week."

"Persisting, is he?" Morgan said. He sat down next to her to sort the mail.

"I couldn't even go for milk, or to buy a loaf of bread, so I managed on what was here. Sardines and corned-beef hash, mainly. I feel like someone on a submarine; I have this craving for lettuce. But it wasn't so bad. I didn't really mind. It made me think of back when we were kids, when we were poor. Morgan," she said, pausing with a ten of clubs in midair, "weren't we happier, in some ways, when we were up against it?"

"As far as I'm concerned, we're still up against it," Morgan said.

There was a dainty blue envelope from Priscilla that must contain a thank-you note. It made him tired to think of it. He passed on to a thicker one that looked more promising, and ripped it open. Inside was a sheaf of photographs, wrapped in a letter. He checked the signature: Emily. Now what? *Dear Morgan and Bonny,* she wrote, in a neat, italic hand that struck him as stunted. *Thank you again for a lovely vacation. I hope we did not put you to too much trouble. Toward the end we were so rushed, getting off in time to beat the dark, that I didn't feel we properly said goodbye. But it was so nice of you to have us and we all had such a . . .*

Morgan grimaced and turned to the photos. He flipped through them idly. Then he sat straighter and went through them again. He laid one on the dining-room table and another one beside it, and another. Bonny, Robert, Brindle, Kate . . .

Each person sat alone, suspended in an amber light that surely did not exist in Bethany Beach, Delaware. Bonny folded her arms across her stomach and smiled a radiant smile. Robert Roberts shone like a honeymooner in his borrowed shirt, and Brindle's skin had the mellow glow of a priceless painting. Kate with her stubborn pout was as sultry and mysterious as a piece of exotic fruit. Morgan's sombrero, pushed back, was a halo, and the white streaks in his beard gave him the depth and texture of something carved. Well, it was only the film. It was cut-rate film, or out of date, or underexposed.

But each person gazed out so steadily, with such trust, such concentration. Emily herself, marble-pale in folds of black, met his scrutiny with eyes so clear that he imagined he could see through them and behind them; he could see what she must see, how his world must look to her. A buoyant little bubble of hope began to rise in him. Over and over, he sorted through the pictures, rearranging them, aligning them, dropping them, smiling widely and sighing and laughing, ignoring his sister's astonished stare: a man in love.

1976

1   When spring came, Emily started walking. She walked all spring and summer, down alleyways, across tattered rags of parks, through stores that smelled of pickles and garlic. She went in the front doors and out the back, emerging on some unknown street full of delivery trucks, stacked wooden crates, construction workers with pneumatic drills tearing up the pavement. Her ballet slippers, nearly soundless, tripped along in time to the music in her head. She liked songs about leaving, about women who packed up and left, and men who woke to find their beds unexpectedly empty. *If you miss the train I'm on, you will know that I am gone . . .* She slipped between two children sharing popcorn from a

bag. *One of these mornings, it won't be long, you'll call my name and I'll be gone* . . . She brushed against an old lady with a shopping bag full of bottles, did not apologize, kept going. *I know you, rider, going to miss me when I'm* . . . Gone, gone, gone: her slippers thumped it out. She had a spiky step to begin with, but every day, all over again, she softened; she would slow down bit by bit, and wilt, and grow calm. She would think of how Leon's jacket hung across that broad, subtle curve between his shoulder blades. How complete his words sounded—more certain than other people's, spoken in an even voice that carried some special weight. How he always kept his mouth closed, not tightly clamped but relaxed and gentle, giving her, for some reason, an impression of secrets working within him.

She sighed and turned home, after all.

Often, on these walks, she was followed by Morgan Gower —a wide leather hat and a tumult of beard, loping along behind her. If she paused till he caught up, he'd make a nuisance of himself. He had entered some new stage, developed a new fixation. It was harmless, really, but annoying. He might declare himself to her anywhere—fling out his arms in the middle of the Broadway Fish Market, beam down at her, full of joy. "Last night I dreamed you went to bed with me." She would click her tongue and walk away. She would march on out and down the block, cut through an alley past a grinding garbage truck, and he would follow, but he kept his distance. His hat rounded corners like a flying saucer, level and spinning, the rest of him sauntering beneath. Glancing back, she had to laugh. Then she turned away again, but he'd already noticed; she heard him laugh too. Didn't he realize she had problems on her mind? She was overhung by thoughts of Leon, like someone traveling under a cloud. First marching, then drifting, she paced out the knots and snarls of life with Leon. Love was not a comedy. But here came Morgan, laughing. She gave in and stopped once more and waited. He arrived beside her and pointed at the neon

sign that swung above their heads. "Look! *LaTrella's Rooms.
Weekly! Daily!* Let's just nip upstairs."

"Really, Morgan."

And even in front of Leon—what did Morgan imagine he
was doing? In front of glowering, dark Leon, he said, "Emily,
fetch your toothbrush. We're eloping." When there was
music, anywhere—a car radio passing on the street—he would
seize her by the waist and dance. He danced continually,
nowadays. It seemed his feet could not keep quiet. She had
never known him to act so silly.

Fortunately, Leon didn't take him seriously.

"You'd be getting more than you bargained for," he said
to Morgan.

Still, she said, "Morgan, I wish you wouldn't joke like that
in front of Leon. What must he think?"

"What should he think? I'm stealing you away," Morgan
said, and he circled the kitchen, where Emily happened to
be washing dishes, and threw open all the cupboards. "Which
things are you bringing with you? These plates? This bowl?
This two-quart vinyl orange-juice pitcher?"

She rested her soapy hands on the sink and watched him.
"Morgan," she said. "Don't you ever get self-conscious?"

"Well," he said.

He closed a cupboard door. He stroked his beard.

"That's a very interesting question," he said. "I'm glad you
asked me that. The fact is . . . ah, yes, I do."

She blinked. "You do?"

"The fact is," he said, "with you: well, yes, I do."

He stood before her, smiling. There was something clumsy
about him that made her see, suddenly, what he must have
been like as a boy—one of those bumbling boys who can't
think what to talk about with girls; or who talk too much,
perhaps, out of nervousness—compulsively relating the entire
plots of movies or explaining how the internal-combustion
engine works. It was a shock; she had never pictured him that
way. And anyhow, she was probably wrong, for an instant

later he was back to the Morgan she had always known: a gray-streaked, twinkling clown of a man, swinging into a soft-shoe dance across her kitchen floor.

At least he could make her laugh.

2 She walked through summer and into fall. She did other things too, of course—gave puppet shows, sewed costumes, cooked, helped Gina with her homework. But at night, when she closed her eyes, she saw a maze of streets and traffic, the way compulsive chess-players see chessboards in their dreams. She was revisited by the smallest details of her walks—by the clank of a foot on a manhole cover, the spark of mica in concrete, and the Bicentennial fire hydrants sticking out their stunted arms like so many defective babies. She opened her eyes, sat up, rearranged her pillow. "What's the trouble?" Leon would ask.

There were any number of answers she could give, all true. She said, sometimes, that she thought their marriage had something badly wrong with it, something out of step, she couldn't say just what. Maybe so, said Leon, but what did she want him to do about it? He did not believe, he said, that there was anything in the world that would make her really happy. Unless, perhaps, she could bring the whole solar system into line exactly her way, not a planet disobeying. What was it that she expected of him? he would ask. She was silent.

Or sometimes she said that she worried about Gina. It didn't seem right for a nine-year-old to act so serious, she said. It broke her heart to see her so unswervingly alert to their moods, watching from a distance, smoothing over quarrels. But Leon said Gina was growing up, that was all. Naturally, he said. Let her be, he said.

Also, Emily said, their puppet shows never went well any more. Running through every play was some kind of dislocation—characters stepping on each other's speeches, unsynchronized, ragged, or missing cues and gawking stupidly.

Fairytales fell into fragments, every line a splinter. When Cinderella danced with the Prince, their cloth bodies clung together, but the hands inside them shrank away. Emily believed that the audience could guess this. She was certain of it. Leon said that was ridiculous. They were making more money than they ever had before; they had to turn down invitations. Things were going wonderfully, Leon said.

In her sleep, she dreamed she walked a revolving pavement like a merry-go-round, and she was still tired when she woke.

Often, when she had some work that could be done by hand, she'd spend her mornings down in Crafts Unlimited. She'd perch on a stool behind the counter and listen to Mrs. Apple while she sewed. Mrs. Apple knew hundreds of craftsmen, all their irregular, colorful lives, and she could talk on and on about them in her cheery way, stringing together people Emily had never heard of. Emily relaxed, expanded, watched well-dressed grandmothers buying her puppets. Once Mrs. Apple's son Victor came to visit. He was living in D.C. now and had driven over unannounced. He'd gained a good deal of weight and shaved off his mustache. His wife, a pretty woman with flossy blond hair, carried their small son in her arms. "Well, well, well," Victor said to Emily, and he hooked his thumbs into the tiny pockets of his vest. "I see you're still making puppets."

She felt she had to defend herself. "Yes," she said, "but they're much different now. They're a whole different process."

Getting off her stool, though, going to a table to show him a king with a gnarled face, she was conscious of how dreary she must seem to him—still in the same building, the same occupation, wearing the same kind of clothes. Her braids, she felt suddenly, might as well have solidified on her head. She wished she had not let Morgan Gower persuade her to go back to ballet slippers. She wished she had Gina here—all the change that anyone could ask for. Victor bounced slightly on the balls of his feet, examining the king. Melissa, Emily thought suddenly. Melissa Tibbett—that was the name of the birthday child at their very first show, when Victor had been the doll-voiced father wondering what to bring back from his travels. Melissa must be in her teens by now—sixteen years old, at least; long past puppets. Emily set the king back on the table and smoothed his velvet robe.

"How about Leon?" Victor asked. "Is he doing any acting?"

"Oh, well, not so very much. No, not so much at the moment," she said.

He nodded. She hated the understanding way he looked into her eyes.

That afternoon she pulled a cardboard box from the closet and unpacked her marionettes. She'd been experimenting with marionettes for several years. She liked the challenge: they were harder to work. She had figured out her own arrangement of strings, suspended from a single cross of Popsicle sticks. There were two strings for the hands, two more for the knees, and one each for the head and the lower back. (At fairs she'd seen double and triple crosses, like biplanes, and half a dozen additional strings, but none of it seemed essential.) She took a Red Riding Hood, her most successful effort, and went into the living room. Leon was on the couch, reading the afternoon paper. Gina was writing a book report. "Look," Emily said.

Leon glanced up. Then he said, "Oh, Emily, not those marionettes again."

"But look: see how easy?"

She pranced Red Riding Hood across the floor, up the couch, into Gina's lap. Gina giggled. Then Red Riding Hood skipped away, swinging a small yellow basket that snapped cleverly over her arm. "What do you think?" Emily asked Leon.

"Very nice, but not for us," Leon said. "Emily, our old puppets can do that, and more besides. They can set the basket down and pick it up again. They don't have all those strings in the way."

"Oh, it's just like with my shadow puppets. You won't try anything new," she said. "I'm tired of the old ones."

"So?" he asked her. "You can't just switch the universe around, any time you're tired of it."

She packed the marionettes in their box. She went for a walk, though she ought to be starting supper. At the corner of Crosswell and Hartley she paused for a traffic light and Morgan Gower came up beside her. He was wearing a tall black suit, a high-collared shirt, and a bowler hat so ancient it looked rusty. He bowed and tipped his hat. She laughed. A grin spread behind his beard, but he seemed to guess her mood and he didn't speak. In fact, when the light turned green he dropped back again, though she was conscious of his presence—keeping a measured distance behind, humming a little tune and watching over her.

3   In October, Emily's second cousin Claire called to say that her great-aunt had died in her sleep. She'd donated her remains to the cause of medical science, Claire said (just like Aunt Mercer; she would put it in just those words), but still there'd be a service at the Meetinghouse. Emily thought she ought to attend it. She hadn't seen Aunt Mercer in twelve years—not since before her marriage. They had only exchanged Christmas cards, with polite, fond notes beneath the signatures. Going now, of course, was pointless; but even so, Emily canceled a puppet show and left Gina with Leon and took the Volkswagen south.

She was nervous about making the four-hour trip alone, but as soon as she'd merged on the interstate she felt wonderful. It seemed that the air here was thinner and lighter. She was even pleased by all the traffic she encountered—so many people skimming along! No doubt they were out here day and night, endlessly circling the planet, and now at last she had joined them. She smiled at every driver she passed. She was fascinated by the private, cluttered worlds she glimpsed—maps and stuffed animals on window ledges; a passenger sleeping, open-mouthed; a pair of children combing out their dog.

She turned off the interstate and traveled smaller and smaller roads, winding through rich farm country and then poor country, passing unpainted shacks bristling with TV antennas, their yards full of trucks on blocks and the hulls of cars, then speeding through coppery woodlands laced with underbrush and discarded furniture. She reached Taney in the early afternoon. The town was still so small that several of the men hunkering before the Shell station were familiar to her—not even any older, it seemed; just painted there, dreamily holding their hand-rolled cigarettes. (Their names swam back to her: Shufords and Grindstaffs and Haithcocks. She'd had them stored in her memory all these years without knowing it.) Autumn leaves scuttled down Main Street. She turned up Erin Street and parked in front of the squat little house that she and her mother had shared with Aunt Mercer.

The yard was shadowed by great old trees. No real grass grew there—just patchy bits of plantain in the caked orange dirt, weeds trailing out of a concrete urn, and a leaf-littered boxwood hedge giving off its dusky, pungent smell. Where were Aunt Mercer's flowerbeds? She would generally have something blooming, even this late in the year. Emily climbed the front-porch steps and paused, uncertain whether to knock or to walk on in. Then the door swung open and Claire said, "Emily, honey!"

She hadn't changed. She was plump and kind-faced, with little gray curls in a pom-pom over her forehead and another pom-pom at the back of her neck. She wore a stiff, wide, navy-blue dress that barely bent to accommodate her, and heavy black shoes with open toes. "Honey, don't just stand there. Where's your little family?"

"I left them home," Emily said.

"Left them! Came all this way by yourself? Oh, and we were counting on seeing your sweet daughter . . ."

Emily couldn't imagine Gina in this house. It wouldn't

work; the two wouldn't meet in her mind. She followed
Claire through the hall, with its smell of old newspapers, and
into the parlor. The furniture was dark and ungainly. It so
completely filled the room that Emily almost failed to notice
the two people sitting on the puffy brown sofa—Claire's
husband, Claude, and Aunt Junie, Claire's mother, the moun-
tainous old woman who also lived here. Neither one was a
blood relation, but Emily bent to kiss their cheeks. She'd last
seen them when she came home after her mother's death,
and they'd been sitting on this very sofa. They might have
remained here ever since—abandoned, sagging, like large
cloth dolls. When Claude reached up to pat her shoulder,
the rest of him stayed sunk in the cushions; his arm seemed
disproportionately long and distant from his body. Aunt Junie
said, "Oh, Emily, look at you, so grown up . . ."

Emily sat on the sofa between them. Claire settled in a
rocker. "Did you eat?" she asked Emily. "You want to wash
up? Have a Coke? Some buttermilk?"

"I'm fine," Emily said. She felt *sinfully* fine, larger and
stronger and less needy than all three of them put together.
She folded her hands across her purse. There was a silence.
"It's good to be back," she said.

"Wouldn't Aunt Mercer be pleased?" asked Claire.

There was a little bustle of motion; they'd found their
subject. "Oh, wouldn't she just love to see you sitting here,"
Aunt Junie said.

"I wish she could have known," said Claire. "I wish you
could have come before she passed."

"But it was painless," Claude said.

"Oh, yes. It's the way she'd have wanted to go."

"If she had to go, well, that's the way."

Claire said, "All those troubles with her joints, Emily; you
never saw. Arthritis swolled her up so, she got extra knobs
and knuckles. Times she had a job just fixing her meals, but
you know how she was: she wouldn't give in. Times she
couldn't button her buttons or dial on the telephone, and
Mama with that elbow of hers . . . I would say, 'Aunt Mercer,

let me come over and stay a while,' but she said, 'No,' said, 'I can do it.' She just had to do it her way. She always liked to feed that cat of hers herself, said it wouldn't eat from anyone else, which was only what she liked to believe; and she was bound and determined to write her own letters. At Christmas—remember, Emily? How she always wrote you, long-hand? And sent a little something for the baby. And Easter, why, that was her day to have us all over, and do every bit herself. Polished the silver, set the table . . . but she had to see to it some time ahead, in case the arthritis, you know . . . I stopped by on Good Friday and there was the cloth on the table and the very best china laid out. I said, 'Aunt Mercer, what's all this in aid of?' 'I just want to be sure it's ready,' she said, 'for your mama can't manage a thing with that el-bow and I do like to get organized.' See, she would never even mention her arthritis. Doctor had to tell us what was what; said, 'She is in more pain than she lets on.' She hated to put us out, never cared to lean on others. In some ways, it was best that she was taken when she was."

"Oh, it was all for the best," Aunt Junie said.

Claude said, "It was a mercy."

"I should have come before," Emily said. "I never knew. She never mentioned it in her letters."

"Yes, well, that was how she was."

"But she'd be proud that you came now," Aunt Junie said.

"And you'll want to go through her things, surely—so many of her nice things that I know she would want you to keep," Claire said.

"I don't have room in the car," said Emily. But suddenly she felt she would like this whole house—the wallpaper pat-terned with wasp-waisted baskets of flowers, the carpet al-ways rubbed the wrong way, the china high-heeled slipper filled with chalky china roses. She imagined moving in. She pictured resuming her life where she'd left off, drinking her morning cocoa from the celery-green glass mug she'd found in a cereal box when she was eight. And when Claire said, "But her jade bar pin, Emily, *that* wouldn't need any space," she instantly pictured the bar pin, streaked with a kind of wood grain and twined at one end with blackened gold leaves. She was amazed at how much was still lodged in her mind. Like the Shufords, the Grindstaffs, and the Haithcocks, Aunt Mercer's house lived on in Emily, every warped shingle and small-paned window, whether she took it out to examine it or not. She would let the bar pin go to Aunt Junie, who wore such things, but in a sense she would continue owning it forever, and she might catch an accidental glimpse of it, barely noticed, some moment while waking or falling asleep fifty years from now.

"I don't have room even for that," she said.

Then she spread her hands and looked down at them—the parched white backs of them, the gold wedding ring as thin as wire.

At four o'clock they got to their feet and prepared to walk over to the Meetinghouse. Everyone seemed to have a great many coats and scarves, although it was a warm day. They helped each other, like handicapped people. Claire smoothed Claude's collar for him and straightened his lapels. "Don't you have a wrap, dear?" Aunt Junie asked Emily. "Your . . . what is that . . . skirt and top; it's so thin. Won't you borrow a sweater? You don't want to take a chill." But Emily shook her head.

Walking up Erin Street, they did meet a few young people, wearing boot-cut jeans and those velvet blazers that were popular in Baltimore too. This town was not so isolated as Emily had imagined. But the Meetinghouse—the only Friends Meeting in Taney County—was as small and poor as ever, a gray frame cubicle huddled in the back yard of the Savior Baptist Church; and everyone approaching it was old. They mumbled and clung to each other's arms, climbing the front steps. Emily hoped to see the friends she'd gone to First Day School with—never more than three or four of them in the best of times—but they must have moved away. There was no one under fifty. She took her seat on a straight-backed bench, between Aunt Junie and Claude. She looked around the little room and counted fourteen people. The fifteenth entered and closed the door behind him. A hush fell like the hush on a boat when the engine is cut off and the sails are raised.

In this quiet Emily had grown up—not a total silence but a ticking, breathing quiet, with the occasional sound of cloth rubbing cloth, little stirrings, throats cleared, people rustling coughdrop packets or fumbling through their purses. She expected nothing from it. (She had never been religious.) She wondered, for the hundredth time, what that dusty red glass was on the ledge above the east window. It was nearly overflowing with something that looked like wax. Maybe it was a candle. She always came to that conclusion. (But first she thought of something brewing—a culture, yogurt, dough, something concocting itself out of nothing.) She tried to name all the states in the Union. There were four beginning with A, two with C . . . but the M's were hard; there were so many: Montana, Missouri, Mississippi . . .

An old man with cottony hair rose and stood leaning on his cane. "Mercer Dulaney," he said, "once walked two and one-half miles in rheumatism weather to feed my dogs while I was off visiting my sister in Fairfax County. I reckon now I'll take that cat of hers and tend it, if it don't get on too bad with my dogs."

He sat down, groped for a handkerchief, and wiped his lips. "Ah, ah," he said. It made her think of Morgan Gower; he sometimes said that. She was surprised to remember her other life—its speed, its modernness, the great rush of noisy people she knew. She thought of Morgan hurtling down the street behind her; her daughter (daughter!) hailing a city bus; Leon tossing coins on the bureau before he undressed. She remembered the first time she ever saw Leon. He had walked in the door of the library reading room, wearing that corduroy jacket of his. He had stood there looking around him, hunting someone, and had not found whoever it was and turned to go; but in turning, he caught sight of Emily and paused and looked at her again, and then frowned and went on out. She had not actually been introduced to him for another week. But now it seemed to her that at his entrance—swinging through the library door, carrying a single book in his hand (his fingers fine-textured and brown, his shirtcuffs so perfectly white)—her life had suddenly been set in motion. Everything had started up, as if complicated wheels and gears had finally connected, and had raced along in a blur from then on. It was only now, in this slowed-down room, that she had a chance to examine what had happened. Why! Her mother had died! Her mother, and she'd never truly mourned her. She thought of the last time they'd spoken, on the long-distance phone in the dormitory lobby. ("It's raining here," her mother had said. "But I don't want to waste our three minutes on the weather. Did you get that skirt I mailed you? But I don't want to waste this time on clothes, my goodness . . .") She thought about her dormitory room with its two narrow iron bedsteads and the stuffed white unicorn on her pillow. She had once collected unicorns; she'd loved them. What had happened to her unicorn collection? Her roommate must have got it, or Goodwill had come, or it had simply been discarded. And think what else was gone: her favorite books she'd brought with her to college, her diary, her locket with her only picture of her father in it—a young man, laughing. She ached for all of them. She felt they had just this minute been ripped away from her. She thought of Aunt Mercer with her long-chinned, sharp, witty face, her pale, etched mouth always fighting back a smile. It was such a loss; she was so lost without Aunt Mercer.

"When she and I were girls," Aunt Junie said, dragging herself to her feet, plunking her purse in Emily's lap, "we used to walk to school together. We were the only two girls from the Meeting and we kept to ourselves. Little did I guess I would be marrying her brother, in those days! I thought he was just a pest. We had these plans for leaving here, getting clean away. We were going to join the gypsies. In those days there were gypsies everywhere. Mercer sent off for a book on how to read the cards, but we couldn't make head nor tail of it. Oh, but I still have the cards someplace, and the string puppets from when we planned to put on shows in a painted wagon, and the elocution book from when we wanted to take up acting . . . and of course we had thoughts of becoming reporters. Lady news reporters. But it never came to anything. What if we'd known then how it would turn out? What if someone had told us what we'd *really* do —grow old in Taney, Virginia, and die?"

She sat down then, and retrieved her purse from Emily, and closed her eyes and went back to waiting.

4 That evening they had supper at Claire's—casseroles brought over by other members of the Meeting, fruit pies with people's last names adhesive-taped to the tins. No one ate much. Claude chewed a toothpick and watched a small TV on the kitchen counter. He was an educated man, a dentist, but there was something raw-boned and countrified about him, Emily thought, when he gave his startled barks of laughter at a re-run of "The Brady Bunch." Claire toyed with a piece of pie. Aunt Junie studied her plate and chewed the inside of her lip. Later, when the dishes were done, they moved to the larger TV in the living room. At nine o'clock Aunt Junie said she was tired, and Emily helped her next door to Aunt Mercer's, where both of them planned to sleep.

"I suppose we'll have to sell this place," Aunt Junie said, moving laboriously along the sidewalk. "There isn't much point in keeping up two houses now."

"But where will you live, Aunt Junie?"

"Oh, I'd move in with Claire and Claude," she said.

Emily thought of something dark, like an eye, contracting and getting darker. There once had been three houses, long ago when Emily's father was still alive.

Aunt Junie shuffled ahead of Emily through the front door. A lamp glowed in the hall, casting a circle of yellow light. "You ought to pick out what you want here," Aunt Junie said. "Why, some of it's antiques. Pick out what you'd like to take home."

She leaned on Emily's arm, and they made their way to the living room. Emily turned a light on. Furniture sprang into view, each piece with its sharp shadow—a drop-leaf table with its rear leaf raised against the wall; a wing chair; a desk with slender, curved legs that used to remind Emily of a skinny lady in high-heeled shoes. She could have taken all of this, heaven knows. Offered, in general terms, a desk or a sofa, she would have said, "Oh, thank you. Our apartment does seem bare." A little itch of greed might have started up, in fact. But when she stood in this room and saw the actual objects, she didn't want them. They were too solid, too thickly coated by past events, maybe; she couldn't explain it. She said, "Aunt Junie, sell it. You could surely find some use for the money."

"Take something small, at least," Aunt Junie said. "Emily, honey, you're our only young person. You and your little daughter: you're all we've got to pass things on to."

Emily pictured Gina reading in the wing chair, twining a curl at her temple the way she always did when she was absorbed. (Was she in bed yet? Had she brushed her teeth? Did Leon know she still liked a nightlight, even if she wouldn't say so?) She missed Gina's watchful eyes and her delicate, colorless, chipped-looking mouth—Aunt Mercer's mouth. Emily had never realized. She stopped dead, struck by the thought.

Meanwhile, Aunt Junie traveled around the room, holding her crippled arm with her good hand. "This china slipper, maybe. Or these little brass monkeys: hear no evil, see no evil . . ."

"Aunt Junie, really, we don't lead that kind of life," Emily told her.

"What kind of life? What kind of life must it take just to put a few brass monkeys on your coffee table?"

"We don't *have* a coffee table," Emily said, smiling.

"Take Mercer's, then."

"No. Please."

"Or jewelry, a watch, a brooch. Pin her bar pin on your collar."

"I don't have a collar, either," Emily said. "I only wear these leotards, and they're made of something knit; they can't be pinned."

Aunt Junie turned and looked at her. She said, "Oh, Emily, your mother sent you off so nice. She read up in *Mademoiselle* and made you all those clothes for college. She was worried you'd be dressed wrong. No one *else* in your class went away to school, none of those Baptists, those Haithcocks and Biddixes. She wanted you to go off nice and show them all, come back educated, settle down, marry someone good to you like my Claire did; see my Claire? And she fixed you that sweet paisley dress with the little white collar and cuffs. Now, *that* you could pin a brooch on. She said you could wear it to Meeting. You said, 'Mama, I do not intend to go to Meeting there and all I want is blue jeans. I'm getting out,' you said, 'I'm going to *join*, get to be part of some big group, not going to be different ever again.' What a funny little thing you were! But of course she paid you no mind, and rightly so, as you can see; quite rightly so. Now, I don't know what you call this: leotard? Is that it? Well, I'm sure it's all very stylish in Baltimore, but Emily, honey, it can't hold a candle to that paisley dress your mother made."

"That paisley dress is gone," Emily said. "It's twelve years old. It's cleaning windows now."

Aunt Junie turned her face away. She looked stony and blind with hurt. She groped through the furniture—chair, desk, another chair—and reached the sofa and lowered herself into it.

"But of course I wore it," Emily said, lying.

She pictured it still hanging in her dormitory closet, a ghost passed on to each new freshman class. ("This dress belonged to Miss Emily Cathcart, who vanished one Sunday in April and was never seen again. College authorities are still dragging

Sophomore Pond. Her spirit is said to haunt the fountain in front of the library.")

She sat down beside Aunt Junie. She touched her arm and said, "I'm sorry."

"Oh, what for?" Aunt Junie asked brightly.

"If you like, I'll take the bar pin. Or something little, anything, or—I know what: the marionettes."

"The—?"

"String puppets is what you called them. Didn't you say you'd kept them?"

"Yes," said Aunt Junie, without interest. "Someplace or other, I guess."

"I'll take one home with me."

"Yes, I recollect now you said you give some kind of children's parties," Aunt Junie said. She adjusted her paralyzed arm beneath the shelf of her bosom. "It's been a tiring day," she said.

"You want me to help you to bed?"

"No, no, you run along. I can manage."

Emily kissed her on the cheek. Aunt Junie didn't seem to notice.

In the room that Emily and her mother had once shared —such an intertwined, unprivate life that even now she didn't feel truly alone here—she untied her skirt and stepped out of her shoes. Her own younger face, formless, smiled from a silver frame on the bureau. She switched off the light, folded back the spread, and climbed into bed. The sheets were so cold they felt damp. She hugged herself and clenched her chattering teeth and watched the same old squares of moonlight on the floor. Aunt Julie, meanwhile, seemed to be moving around in some other part of the house. Drawers slid open, latches clicked. Emily thought she heard the rafters creak in the attic. Oh, this leaden, lumbering world of old people! She slid away into a patchwork kind of sleep. Her mother seemed to be rearranging the bedroom. "Let's see, now, if the chair were here, the table here, if we were to put the bed beneath the window . . ." Emily sat up once to pull the spread back over her shoulders for warmth. An owl was hooting in the trees. This time when she slept, it was like plummeting into someplace bottomless.

She woke and found the room filled with a pearly gray, pre-dawn light. She got up, staggering slightly, and reached for her skirt and tied it around her. She put on her shoes and went out to the hall, which was darker. From Aunt Junie's room a snoring noise came. Oh, Lord, they would probably all sleep for hours yet. She felt her way to the living room to find her purse, where she'd stashed a comb and toothbrush. It was on the coffee table. Something knobby poked from it. She turned the lamp on, blinked, and lifted out an ancient female marionette in a calico dress.

The head and hands were plaster, crudely colored. She had a large, faded mouth and two dim circles of rouge. Her black thread hair was in braids. Her tangled strings were tied to a single-cross control bar, just like the one that Emily had invented. Or maybe (it began to seem) she had not invented it after all, but had remembered it from her childhood. Though she couldn't recall ever having been shown this little creature. Maybe it was something that was passed in the dark through the generations—the very thought of giving puppet shows, even. And here she imagined she'd come so far, lived such a different existence! She saw her Red Riding Hood scene in a whole new light now, as something crippled. She held the marionette by its snarl of strings. The blue eyes stared at her flatly. The plaster hands—one finger chipped— were suspended in a gracious, stiff position.

Out in the kitchen a clock ticked with a muffled sound, as if buried. There was barely enough room to walk between chairs and occasional tables. Everything was so stuffed and smothering. She set the marionette on the sofa and picked up her purse and left the room. Fresh air, she thought, might clear her head. She opened the door and stepped out on the porch, where instantly the cold pierced all she wore. But still the stuffy feeling didn't leave her. She descended the steps.

She went out to the street and stood shivering and looking at the car—Leon's car, compact and gleaming. After a moment she opened the door and slid inside and took a deep breath of its leathery smell. Then she found her keys in her purse. Then she switched the engine on, but not the headlights, and slipped away.

In Baltimore it was a crowded, clamorous morning in the middle of the week, with the sun flashing off a sea of metal and everyone honking and darting in and out of lanes. Emily turned down Crosswell Street and parked somewhere, anywhere, she didn't know. She flew from the car and ran inside the building and up the stairs, and then couldn't find the proper key and was jingling her way through a ring of them when Leon opened the door. He stood there looking down at her, holding a book in one hand, and she threw her arms around him and pressed her face to his chest. "Emily, love," he said. "Emily, is something wrong?" She only shook her head, and hung on tight.

5   Almost daily she had letters from Morgan, whether or not he came in person. *Dear Emily, Am enclosing this Sears ad, you really need a pipe wrench and Sears are better than any Cullen Hardware sells* . . . For he had taken over the care of their apartment, moving in on the disrepair that lurked in all its corners; he clanked blithely among the mysteries beneath the kitchen sink. *Dear Emily, Came across a hint last night that just might solve that trouble with your toaster. Simply cut a piece of heavy paper, say a matchbook cover, 1" x 1"* . . .

He was the Merediths' own personal consumer advocate, composing disgusted notes to Radio Shack on his tinny, old-fashioned typewriter, storming into auto-repair shops—solving whatever little discontent Emily mentioned in passing. She began to rely on him. Sometimes she said, "Oh, I really shouldn't ask you to do this—" but he would say, "Why not?

Who would you rather ask instead? Ah, don't hurt my feelings, Emily."

Once she had a problem with her tape recorder, the portable recorder she'd bought to use in their shows. Morgan didn't happen to be around, and while Emily fiddled with the buttons she caught herself wondering, irritably, where *was* he? How could he leave her alone like this, to cope without him when he'd led her to depend on him? She grabbed up the recorder and ran the several blocks to Cullen Hardware. She arrived breathless; she slapped the recorder on the counter between Morgan and a customer. "Listen," she said, jabbing a button. In blew the trumpet for "The Brementown Musicians"—but blurred and bleary, with some kind of vibration in the speaker. The customer stepped back, looking startled. Morgan sat on his high wooden stool and nodded thoughtfully. "It's driving me crazy!" Emily told him, switching it off. "And if you think it sounds bad now, you ought to hear it when the volume's up, in the middle of a show. You can't tell if it's a trumpet or a foghorn."

Morgan went to a revolving rack for a paintbrush, and he came back and took the recorder onto his lap and slowly, tenderly, brushed the plastic grooves that encased the speaker. Grains of something white flew out. "Sugar, perhaps. Or sand," he said. "Hmm." He pressed the button and listened again. The trumpet sound was clear and pure. He gave the machine back to Emily and returned to adding up the customer's purchases.

Like a household elf, he left behind him miraculously mended electrical cords, smooth-gliding windows, dripless faucets, and toilet tanks hung with clever arrangements of coat-hanger wire to keep the water from running. "It must be wonderful," Emily told Bonny, "to have him with you all the time, fixing things," but Bonny just looked blank and said, "Who, Morgan?"

Well, Bonny had her mind on other matters. She was helping one of her daughters through a difficult pregnancy. The baby was due in February but kept threatening to arrive now, in early November; the daughter had come home to lie flat on her back for the next three months. It was all Bonny could talk about. "When she sits up just a little, to straighten a pillow," she said, "I have this picture of the baby falling, just tumbling out of her like a penny out of a piggy-bank, you know? I say, 'Lizzie, honey, lie down this instant, please.' It's turning around my view of things. I used to think of pregnancy as getting something ready, growing something to finish it; now all I think of is holding something back that is going to come regardless. And Morgan! Well, you know Morgan. Always off somewhere, he really has no comprehension . . . At night he comes home and reads her stories from the operas. He's taken up an interest in the opera, has he told you? Such a crazy man . . . 'Don Giovanni encounters a statue and invites it home to supper,' he reads. 'Sounds like something *you* would do,' I tell him. He reads on. I believe he thinks that Liz is still a child, in need of bedtime stories; or maybe he just likes an excuse to read them himself—but for day-to-day things! For bringing trays to her and emptying bedpans!"

Emily nodded gravely. She sympathized with Bonny: he must be exasperating to live with. But, after all, it wasn't Emily who had to live with him.

She recalled how odd he'd seemed when they first knew him—his hats and costumes, his pedantic, elderly style of speech. Now he seemed . . . not ordinary, exactly, but understandable. She was beginning to want to believe his assumption that events don't necessarily have a reason behind them. Last month she and Leon were sitting with him in Eunola's Restaurant when Morgan glanced out the window and said, "How funny, there's Lamont. I thought he was dead." He didn't act very surprised. "That happens more and more often," he said cheerfully. "I often think I see, for instance, my mother's father, Grandfather Brindle, walking down the street, and he's been dead for forty years. I tell myself he might not really have died at all—just got tired of his old existence and left to start a new one without us. Who's to say it couldn't happen? Someplace there may be a whole little settlement—even a town, perhaps—full of people who supposedly died but really didn't. Have you thought of that?"

Then Leon gave a tired hiss, the way he did when Emily said something silly. Well, why shouldn't there be such a town? What was so impossible about it? Emily sat straighter, and looked guiltily into her lap. "The world is a peculiar place," Morgan said. "Tottery old ladies, people you wouldn't trust to navigate a grocery cart, are heading two-ton cars in your direction at speeds of seventy miles per hour. Our lives depend on total strangers. So much lacks logic, or a proper sequence."

"Jesus," said Leon.

But Emily felt encouraged; everything looked brighter. (This was shortly after she'd come back from Taney. Morgan's kind of spaciousness sounded wonderful to her.) She smiled at him. He smiled back. He was wearing a furry Russian hat, now that the weather had turned. It sat on his head like a bear cub. He leaned across the table to Leon and told him, "Often I fall into despair. You may find that funny. I seem to be one of those people whose gloominess is comical. But to me it's very serious. I think, in ten thousand years, what will all this amount to? Our planet will have vanished by then. What's the point? I think, and I board the wrong bus. But when I'm happy, it's for no clearer reason. I imagine that I'm being very witty, I have everyone on my side, but probably that's not the case at all."

Leon let out his breath and watched the waitress refilling their cups.

"Oh, I'm annoying you," Morgan said.

"No, you're not," Emily told him.

"Somehow, it appears I am. Leon? Am I annoying you?"

"Not at all," Leon said grimly.

"I tend to think," Morgan said, "that nothing real has ever happened to me, but when I look back I see that I'm wrong. My father died, I married, my wife and I raised seven human beings. My daughters had the usual number of accidents and tragedies; they grew up and married and gave birth, and some divorced. My sister has undergone *two* divorces, or terminations of marriage, at least, and my mother is aging and her memory isn't what it ought to be . . . but somehow it's as if this were all a story, just something that happened to somebody else. It's as if I'm watching from outside, mildly curious, thinking, So this is what kind of life it is, eh? You would suppose it wasn't really mine. You would suppose I'd planned on having other chances—second and third tries, the best two out of three. I can't seem to take it all seriously."

"Well, I for one have work to do," Leon said, rising.

But Emily told Morgan, "I know what you mean."

I *wish* I knew, was what she should have said.

His manners were atrocious (she often thought); he smoked too much and suffered from a chronic cough that would surely be the death of him, ate too many sweets (and exposed a garble of black fillings whenever he opened his mouth), scattered ashes down his front, chewed his cuticles, picked his teeth, meddled with his beard, fidgeted, paced, scratched his stomach, hummed distractingly whenever it was someone else's turn to speak; he was not a temperate person. He wore rich men's hand-me-downs, stained and crumpled and poorly kept, and over them an olive-drab, bunchy nylon parka, its hood trimmed with something matted that might be monkey fur. He smelled permanently of stale tobacco. When he wore glasses, they were so fingerprinted and greasy you couldn't read his eyes. He was excitable and unpredictable, sometimes nearly manic, and while it was kind of him to manage their affairs, the fact was that he could often become . . . well, presumptuous was the word—pushy, managerial, bending the Merediths to his conception of them, which was not remotely rooted in reality, taking too much for granted, assuming what he should not have assumed. He talked too much and too erratically, or grew stuffy and bored them with lengthy accounts of human-interest items from the paper, grandchildren's clever remarks, and *Consumer Reports* ratings; while at moments when he should have been sociable—when the Merediths had other guests, at their Halloween party, for instance—he would as likely as not clam up completely and stand around in some corner with his hands jammed deep in his pockets and a glum expression on his face. And *his* parties! Well, the less said, the better. Combining garbage men with philosophy professors, seating small children next to priests with hearing aids . . .

But once, passing a bookstore, Emily happened to notice a blown-up photo of the first successful powered flight, and the sight of Wilbur Wright poised on the sand at Kitty Hawk —capped and suited, strangely stylish, suspended forever in that tense, elated, ready position—reminded her for some reason of Morgan, and she suddenly felt that she had never given him full credit. And another time, when she switched on a cassette tape to see if it were the music for "Hansel and Gretel," she found that Morgan must have been playing with it, for his gruff, bearded voice leaped forth, disguised in a German accent. "Nu? Vhere is de button?" he said, and then she heard a Japanese "Ah so!" and two clicks, where he must have pressed the button off and on again. "Tum, te-tum," he said, singing tunelessly, rustling cellophane. There was the sound of a match being struck. He blew a long puff of air. "Naughty boy, Pinocchio!" he said in a chirping voice. "I see you've been untruthful again. Your nose has grown seven inches!" Then he gave his smoker's laugh, breathy and wheezing, "Heh, heh," descending into a cough. But Emily didn't laugh with him. She listened intently, with her forehead creased. She bent very close to the machine, unsmiling, trying to figure him out.

6 She and Leon were invited to the Percy School's Thanksgiving Festival, where they'd never been before. She wasn't sure what show they should put on. "Rapunzel"? "Thumbelina"? Late one afternoon, just a few days before the Festival, she took Rapunzel from her muslin bag and propped

her on the kitchen table. Rapunzel had not been used for a while and had an unkempt, neglected look. Her long, long braids had grown frazzled. "I suppose I should make her another wig," Emily told Gina. Gina was doing her homework; all she said was, "Mmm."

But then Leon came in and said, "Rapunzel? What's she doing here?"

"I thought we'd take her to the Festival."

"Last night you said we'd do 'Sleeping Beauty.' "

"I did?"

"I suggested 'Sleeping Beauty' and you said that would be fine."

"How could I have?" Emily asked. "We can't give 'Sleeping Beauty.' There are thirteen fairies. Not even counting the king, the queen, the princess . . ."

"I said, 'Emily, why not let's do something different for a change?' and you said, 'All right, Leon—' "

"But never 'Sleeping Beauty,' " Emily said.

"I said, 'How about "Sleeping Beauty"?' and you said, 'All right, Leon.' "

He was making it up. Except that Leon never made things up. There was no way Emily could have held that conversation, not even half asleep. Why, if you counted the old woman at the spinning wheel, Prince Charming . . . It was out of the question. They couldn't begin to handle a cast of that size. She considered the possibility that he had discussed the subject with someone else, mistakenly. They always seemed to miss connections these days. They started every morning so courteous, so hopeful, but deteriorated rapidly and ended up, at night, sleeping with their backs to each other on the outermost edges of the bed.

She noticed that two vertical grooves had started to appear in Leon's cheeks. They were not so much lines as hollows, such as you would see in a man who habitually kept his jaw set too far forward.

Then he said, "How about taking Gina? *She* could work some of the fairies."

"But it's on Wednesday afternoon," Emily said. "Gina would still be in school."

"Oh, I don't mind missing school," Gina said.

Emily suspected she was only trying to keep peace. Gina loved school. "Well, *I* mind," Emily told her.

"Oh, Mama."

"And thirteen fairies! Even if we owned that many, how would just one more pair of hands help run them all?"

"We could bring them on a few at a time, maybe," Leon said.

Emily started pacing around the table. Gina and Leon watched her. Gina chewed a pencil and swung her feet, but Leon stayed motionless. Then Emily wheeled on him and said, "Are you doing this on purpose?"

"I beg your pardon?"

"I mean, is this supposed to prove something, Leon? Are you just trying to show me I'm . . . oh, set in my ways? You want me to say I refuse to give a play with eighteen puppets in it, and my daughter playing hooky, and that will mean I'm rigid, narrow-minded?"

"All I know is, I said, 'How about "Sleeping Beauty," Emily—' "

"You never did."

Leon closed his mouth, shrugged, and walked out of the room. Emily looked over at Gina, who was watching, but Gina abruptly stopped chewing her pencil and buried herself in her homework.

Then Emily took her coat from the hook in the hall and left the apartment, jabbing her arms into her sleeves as she stalked down the stairs. It was late enough so the smell of different suppers had begun to fill the stairwell: cabbage, green peppers, oil—stifling smells. Crafts Unlimited was already dark and dead-looking. She slammed out into the street. Twilight had drained the color from the buildings. An old woman paused on the corner to set down all her bundles and rearrange them. Emily swerved around her, keeping her fists knotted in her coat pockets. She crossed against a red light and walked very fast.

He was impossible. There was no hope for either of them. She had locked herself in permanently with someone she couldn't bear.

She passed a boy and girl who were standing in the center of the sidewalk, holding hands, the girl pivoting on her heels and giving the boy a shy smile. It was heartbreaking. She would have stopped to set them straight, but of course they wouldn't believe her; they imagined they were going to do everything differently. She met a child, some friend of Gina's. "Hello, Mrs. Meredith." "Hello, um, Polly," she said—motherly, matronly, indistinguishable from any other woman.

Sometimes she thought the trouble was, she and Leon were too well acquainted. The most innocent remark could call up such a string of associations, so many past slights and insults never quite settled or forgotten, merely smoothed over. They could no longer have a single uncomplicated feeling about each other.

Then she heard footsteps behind her. They kept coming. She slowed, and the corners of her mouth started turning up without her say-so, but when she looked back it was no one she knew—a man on his way to someplace in a hurry. He kept his face buried in his collar. She let him pass her. Then she looked back again. But no matter how long she stood watching, the sidewalk was empty.

She took a right on Meller Street and walked with more purpose. She crossed another street and turned left. Now there was a stream of people bundled up, intent, rushing home to supper. It occurred to her that Cullen Hardware might be closed by now. She slowed, frowning. But no, its windows were still lit with that faded light that always seemed filmed by dust. She pushed through the door. Butkins was bent over a sheet of paper at the counter. "Has Morgan gone home?" she asked him.

Butkins straightened and passed a hand across his high forehead. "Oh. Mrs. Meredith," he said. (He was so determinedly formal, though she'd known him for years.) "No, he's up in his office," he said.

She headed down an aisle of snow shovels and sidewalk salt, and climbed the steps at the rear. Every board whined beneath her feet. On the landing, Morgan's office seemed un- usually still—no sawing, hammering, drilling, no flurry of wood chips. Morgan was lying on the maroon plush sofa. He was hatless, for once, and wore a satin-lapeled smoking jacket that very nearly matched the sofa. His hair looked flat and thin. His face was a pale glimmer in the dusk. "Mor- gan? Are you sick?" Emily asked.

"I have a cold," he said.

"Oh, just a cold," she said, relieved. She took off her coat and laid it on the desk.

"Just a cold! How can you say that?" he asked her. His energy seemed to be returning. He sat up, indignant. "Do you have any idea how I feel? My head is like a beachball. This morning I had a temperature of ninety-nine point nine, and last night it was a hundred and one. I lay awake all night, and had fever dreams."

"You can't do both," Emily said. "Lie awake, and dream as well."

"Why not?" he asked her.

He always had to throw his whole self into things—even into illness. His office looked like a hospital room. A Merck Manual lay open on the filing cabinet, and his desk was a jum- ble of medicines and cloudy drinking glasses. On the floor beside the couch were a bottle of cough syrup, a sticky tea- spoon, and a cardboard box spilling papers. She bent to pick up one of the papers. It was a photograph of the oldest, homeliest washing machine she'd ever laid eyes on, the kind with a wringer attached. *Model 504A*, she read, *can easily be connected to any existing* . . . She replaced the paper and sat down in the swivel chair at the desk. Morgan sneezed.

"Maybe you ought to be home in bed," she told him.

"I can't rest at home. It's a madhouse there. Liz is still flat

on her back trying to hang on to that baby. She gets the
wicker breakfast tray; I end up with the tin meat platter.
And people have already started arriving for Thanksgiving."

Butkins called something. Morgan said, "Eh?"

"I'll be going now, Mr. Gower."

"He ought to know I can't hear a thing with this cold,"
Morgan told Emily.

"He says he's going," Emily said. "Do you want me to help
lock up?"

"Oh, thank you. It's true that I'm not myself."

But he went on sitting there, blotting his nose with a handkerchief. Emily heard the front door shutting behind Butkins.

"When Butkins leaves the store," Morgan said, "I sometimes
wonder if he dematerializes. Ever thought of that?"

She smiled. He watched her soberly, not smiling himself.
"What's wrong?" he asked.

"What? Nothing," Emily said.

"The tip of your nose is white."

"It's nothing."

"Don't lie to me," he said. "I've known you nine years.
When the tip of your nose is white, something's wrong. It's
Leon, I suppose."

"He thinks I'm narrow-minded," Emily said.

Morgan sneezed again.

"He thinks I'm rigid, but *he's* the one. He never tries out
for plays now, and that gospel-troupe man is still after us but
Leon won't even talk to him. I'm getting claustrophobic. I
can't drive after dark any more because the space is too small
—you know, the lighted space the car travels in. I think I
must be going crazy from irritation, just from little petty
nameless irritations. Then he says that I'm the one who's narrow."

Morgan shook a cigarette from an unfamiliar green pack.
"See? We'd better elope," he said.

"Do you think you ought to be smoking?"

"Oh, these are all right. They're menthol."

He lit up and started coughing. He stumbled to his feet, as

if reaching for more air, and wandered around the office, coughing and thumping his chest. Between gasps, he said, "Emily, you know I'm always here for you."

"You want some Robitussin, Morgan?"

He shook his head, gave a final cough, and settled on his desk top. Medicine bottles clinked all around him. Emily wheeled her chair back slightly to allow him more room. His socks, she saw, were translucent black silk, and he wore pointy black patent-leather slippers that reminded her of Fred Astaire. He was sitting on her coat, rumpling it, but she decided not to point that out.

"I know you must find me laughable," he told her.

"Oh, well, I wouldn't say *laughable*, really—"

"But I'm serious," he said. "Let's stop fooling, Emily. I love you."

He slid off his desk, disentangling himself with difficulty from her coat, which had somehow twisted itself around one of his legs. Emily stood up. (What did he have in mind?) He was, after all, a grown man, real, lean-bodied. The hunger with which he drew on his cigarette caused her to step behind her chair. But he went on past her. He was only pacing. He walked to the railing, looked over the darkened store below him, and walked back.

"Of course," he said, "I don't intend any harm to your marriage. I admire your marriage very much. I mean, in a sense, I love Leon as well, and Gina; the unit as a whole, in fact . . . Who *is* it I love? But you, Emily . . ."

He flicked his ashes onto the floor. "I am fifty-one years old," he said. "You're, what, twenty-nine or thirty. I could easily be your father. What a joke, eh? I must look ridiculous."

Instead he looked sad and kind, and also exhausted. Emily took a step in his direction. He circled her, musing. "I think of you as an illness," he said. "Something recurrent, like malaria. I push the thought of you down, you see. Whole weeks go by . . . I imagine that I'm somehow deeper when I manage to overcome it. I feel stronger and wiser. I take some pleasure, then, in doing what I'm supposed to do. I carry the garbage out; I arrive at work on time . . ."

She touched his arm. He dodged her and went on pacing, head lowered, puffing clouds of smoke.

"I persuade myself," he said, "that there is some virtue in the trivial, the commonplace. Ha! What a notion. I think of those things on TV, those man-in-the-street things where the ordinary triumphs. They stop some ordinary person and ask if he can sing a song, recite a poem . . . they stop a motorcycle gang. I've seen this! Black-leather motorcycle gang and ask, 'Can you sing all the words to "Some Enchanted Evening"?' And up these fellows start, dead serious, trying hard—I mean, fellows you would never expect had *heard* of 'Some Enchanted Evening.' They stand there with their arms around each other, switchblades poking out of their pockets, brass knuckles in their blue jeans, earnestly, sweetly singing . . ."

He'd forgotten all about her. He was off on this track of his own, tearing back and forth across his office. Emily sat down on the couch and looked around her. There was a bulletin board on the wall above the filing cabinet, and it was covered with clippings and miscellaneous objects. An Adlai Stevenson button, a frowsy red feather, a snapshot of a bride, a blue silk rose . . . She imagined Morgan rushing in with them, the spoils of some mysterious, private war, and tacking them up, and chortling, and rushing out again. She was struck, all at once, by his separateness. He was absolutely unrelated to her. She would never really understand the smallest part of him.

"They stop this fat old lady," he was saying. "A mess! A disaster. Gray and puffy like some failed pastry, and layers of clothes that seem to have melted together. 'Can you sing "June Is Bustin' Out All Over"?' they ask, and she says, 'Certainly,' and starts right up, so obliging, with this shiny grin, and ends with her arms spread and this little stamp-stamp finish—"

He bit down on his cigarette and stopped his pacing long

enough to demonstrate—both hands outflung, one foot poised to stamp. *"Just . . . because . . . it's* JUNE!" he sang, and he stamped his foot.

"I love you too," she told him.

"JUNE!" he sang.

He paused. He took the cigarette from his mouth.

"Eh?" he said.

She smiled up at him.

He tugged his beard. He shot her a sidelong glance from under his eyebrows, and then he dropped his cigarette and slowly, meditatively ground it out with his heel. When he sat on the edge of the couch, he still seemed to be thinking something over. When he bent to kiss her, he gave off a kind of shaggy warmth, like some furred animal, and he smelled of ashes and Mentholatum.

1977

1 Morgan's daughter Liz finally, finally had her baby, on the coldest night in the coldest February anyone could remember. It was Morgan who had to get up and drive her to the hospital. Then of course her husband, Chester, arrived from Tennessee, and when Liz was released from the hospital, she and Chester and the baby stayed on in her old room a few days till Liz was strong enough to travel. Meanwhile the house filled further, like something flooding upward from the basement. Amy and Jean kept stopping by with their children, and the twins drifted in from Charlottesville, and Molly and her family from New York, and by the time Kate arrived

with her boyfriend, there was nowhere to put the boyfriend but the storeroom on the third floor, underneath the eaves. This was on a weekend. They'd be gone by Monday, Morgan reminded himself. He loved them all, he was crazy about them, but life was becoming a little difficult. The daughters who hadn't got along in the past didn't get along any better now. The new baby appeared to be the colicky type. And there was never any time to see Emily.

"If we feed the children in the kitchen," Bonny said, counting on her fingers, "that makes sixteen grownups in the dining room, or fifteen if Lizzie wants a tray in bed, but then the mothers would have to keep running out to check on them, so maybe we should feed the children early. But then the children would be tearing around like wild things while we were trying to eat, and I just remembered, Liz said her old college roommate was coming at seven-thirty, so we can't eat too late, or maybe she meant she was coming for supper; do you think so? and in that case we'd be *seven*teen at table, assuming Liz does not want a tray in bed, and naturally she wouldn't if her roommate's eating downstairs, but we only have service for sixteen; so we'll have to divide it up, say you and me and Brindle and your mother in the first shift and then the girls and their husbands and . . . oh, dear, David is Jewish, I think. Is it all right I'm serving ham?"

"Who's David?" Morgan asked.

"Katie's boyfriend, Morgan. Pay attention. This is really very simple."

Then after supper one of the grandsons either broke a toe or didn't break a toe, no one could be sure, though everyone agreed that broken toes required no splints anyhow, so there wasn't much point in troubling a doctor outside office hours. Actually, Morgan would not have minded driving the boy to the hospital, which by now he could have found in his sleep. He needed air. The living room was a sea of bodies—people reading, knitting, wrestling, quarreling, playing board games, poking the fire, lolling around, yawning, discussing politics. The shades had not been drawn, and the darkness pressing in made the house seem even murkier. Louisa's black Labrador, Harry, had chewed a Jiffy bag into little gray flecks all over the carpet.

Morgan went upstairs to his bedroom, but two toddler girls were standing at the bureau trying on Bonny's lipstick. "Out! Out!" he shouted. They lifted their smeared faces to him like tiny, elderly drunks, but they didn't obey. He left, slamming the door behind him. In the hall he was hit by the lingering smell of ham, which made him feel fat. He heard the baby fussing in an edgy voice that clawed at the small of his back. "It's too much," he told this what's-his-name, this David, a thin, studious young man who was just descending the third-floor stairs with a paperback book in his hand. David was too polite to say anything, but there was something about the way he fell in with Morgan, going down the next flight of stairs, that made Morgan feel he sympathized.

Bonny was walking the baby in the entrance hall, which seemed to be the only space left. "Could you take Pammy for a while?" she asked him.

"Pammy. Ah. The baby."

He didn't want her, but Bonny looked stretched and gray with fatigue. He accepted the baby in a small, warm, wilted clump. No doubt she would spit all over the shoulder of his pinstriped, head-of-the-family suit that he always wore for these occasions. "Bonny, I think we may have carried things too far, this visit," he said.

"Now, Morgan, you always tell me that. Then the next day after they leave you wander through the house like a dog that's lost its puppies."

"Yes, but every visit there are more, you see," he said, "and they seem to hang around for a longer spell of time."

Molly came through from the kitchen, carrying a bucket. "Christopher's thrown up," she said.

"How does the world strike you so far?" Morgan asked the baby.

The doorbell rang. Bonny said, "Who can that be?"

"It must be Liz's roommate."

"Morgan, honestly. Liz's roommate is sitting in the living room."

"She is?"

"She just had supper with us, Morgan."

Morgan opened the door, one-handed. Emily stood waiting. She landed in his vision like a pale, starry flash of light. He felt everything around him lift and brighten. "Oh," he told her. She smiled at him. She was holding a package tied with pink yarn. (In some illogical way, it seemed the gift was for him. It seemed *she* was the gift.)

Then Bonny said, "Emily!" and stepped forward to kiss her. Emily looked at Morgan over Bonny's shoulder. Grave as a child, she drew away and turned to him and patted the baby's bare foot.

"She's beautiful," she said.

She was gazing into his eyes.

The baby had been cranking up to cry again, but gave a sudden hiccup and fell silent—taken aback, maybe, by the icy wind from the door, or by the touch of Emily's cold hand. "Come on inside," Bonny told Emily. "You must be frozen! Did you drive? Have you ever seen such weather?"

She led Emily into the living room. Morgan followed. He felt that Emily was the single point of stillness. Everyone milled around her while she stood upright at the center. There was something wonderfully prim about the way she offered her package to Liz, as if she weren't sure it would be accepted. But Liz was already exclaiming as she took it. (Motherhood had enlarged her, fuzzed her edges; she was a flurry of bathrobe and milky smells.) And of course she loved the lamb puppet inside. Everyone had to pass it around and try to work it. The lamb's quilted face was nuzzled to the baby's cheek. The baby started and batted the air with both fists. "Offer Emily a drink, will you?" Bonny told Morgan.

Morgan stooped to lay the baby in Louisa's lap. Louisa took her uncertainly, one gnarled hand still clutching a glass of port. "What *is* this?" she asked.

"It's a baby, Mother."

"Is it mine?"

He reconsidered, took the baby back, and gave her to Brindle. Brindle was reading a mail-order catalog and passed her on to a twin. Throughout all this the baby looked better entertained than she had the whole day.

"She's the image of Liz," Emily said. "Isn't she? She's just like her. But with Chester's eyes."

"Emily, honey, where's Leon?" Bonny asked. "And where's Gina? Didn't she want to see the baby?"

"She has a science report due Monday. She's been working on it all weekend."

Morgan imagined the hush in their apartment: the bare, clean living room, Gina concentrating on a single book.

"But Leon, at least," Bonny said. "You could have brought Leon."

"He wanted to watch this program on TV. If I waited till it was finished, the baby would have gone to bed, I figured."

Two years ago the Merediths had bought a small television set. Morgan tended to forget that. Every time Emily referred to it, he mentally blinked; he felt himself having to make some disruptive inner adjustment. He went to the sideboard and poured her a glass of sherry—the only drink she'd ever been known to ask for. When he handed it to her, she was just slipping out of her coat. "Let me hang that up," he told her.

"Oh, I'll keep it. I can only stay a minute."

She sat on the couch, talking to Bonny and Liz, and Morgan harumphed his way around the living room. He stepped over a Monopoly game, threw another log on the fire. He wound the clock on the mantel. He squatted, grunting, and picked up the discarded paper from Emily's gift and folded it carefully for future use. She must have decorated the paper herself, or bought it from Crafts Unlimited. It was patterned with a block print of little bells. He loved her old-time, small-town manners—her prompt gifts and cards and thank-you notes, her Christmas fruitcake, her unfailing observance of every official occasion. She was the most proper person he had ever met. (A while back, she had angled a night away from home—their one whole night together. They were so tired of snatched moments. She'd told Leon she was going to Virginia. She'd met Morgan at the Patrician Hotel and insisted on signing her true name in the register—her name and address and telephone number, all written with the pen held perpendicular to the page in a stiff, quaint manner that delighted him. He'd asked later, why not a false name? It wouldn't be right, she had said.)

"I parked the car at the corner," she was telling Bonny, "and just as I got out I saw this little family. A man, a woman, two children. One of the children had fallen, he was crying, and I slowed down to check on him; you know how it is when you hear a child cry. Well, it was only a scrape or something, a scabby knee. But evidently the father was blind. He didn't seem to know what had happened. He just kept saying, 'What is it, Dorothy? Dorothy, what is it? Dorothy, what's gone wrong?' and Dorothy wouldn't answer. She picked up the child that was crying and then she got the older one, really much too big a child to carry, hoisted on her other hip, and she was so swaddled around with winter coats and scarves and also she had a big purse and some huge kind of tote bag, I don't know, groceries or things; it was hard to tell by the streetlight. She was *staggering*, just tottering along. And he was still asking. 'What is it?' and feeling all around him, frantic. She said, 'Look, you wait here, I've got to go bring the car. Nicholas can't walk.' He said, '*Why* can't he walk? For God's sake, what's happened?' and she got all exasperated and said, 'Just wait, I tell you; keep calm. Stay right here and I'll be back. Jason, you weigh a ton. Hang on to Mommy, Nicholas . . .' I wanted to tell the man, 'It's a scrape. It's nothing.' I wanted to tell the woman, 'Why bring the car? Why are you doing this? Or if you do have to bring the car, why not leave the children with him, and the bags and things? He can manage those. Why wade off like that, *why?* Why make things, oh, so ingrown, so twisted?' "

"Oh, when you see how other people have such handicaps," Bonny said, "you have to thank your stars our own lives are so easy. Don't you?"

She'd missed the point. So had everyone else, Morgan supposed. They went on rattling their dice, clicking their needles. A log fell in the fire, sending out a shower of sparks. The dog stirred and half-heartedly thumped his tail. Brindle turned the pages of her catalog, with its garish, blurred illustrations. *Amazing Soap Cradle!* Morgan read. *Remarkable Perma-Tweezers! Astounding Hair Trap Saves Costly Repair Bills!* He lifted his eyes and met Emily's. She looked beautifully remote to him, so distinct from everyone else that she seemed smaller even than the children.

Then when she had to go, it was Bonny who told Morgan to walk her to the car. Operating on her own misguided version of events, Bonny said, "Now, make sure she locks her doors, Morgan. You heard what peculiar people are running around loose." Emily let Morgan help her into her coat, and she waved good night to the others and kissed Bonny on the cheek. "Come back on a weekday," Bonny said. "Have lunch with me one day while Gina's at school. It's been so long since we've had lunch! What's become of you?" Emily didn't answer that.

She and Morgan went down the front steps, out to the street. It was such a cold night that there was something flinty about the air, and Morgan's heels rang as if on metal. He was bundled into his parka, with the hood up; but Emily's coat didn't look warm and, although she wore black tights, her papery little shoes were probably no protection at all. He took her hand. She had tiny, precise knuckles and a cluster of chilly fingers. "Tomorrow's Sunday," he said. "I guess you can't get away."

"No, I guess not."

"Maybe Monday."

"Maybe."

"Come out at suppertime, to buy milk or something. I'll stay on late at the store."

"But I've done that so often."

"He hasn't said anything, has he?"

"No."

They dropped hands, separated by that "he"—a word that pointed out their furtiveness. In private, they no longer mentioned Leon. Morgan could not picture him without an inner twinge of sorrow and remorse. It seemed he liked Leon even better than before, and appreciated more fully the sober dignity of his high-cheekboned face, which was—come to think of it—admirably stoical, like an American Indian's. (Leon had a way of looking at Morgan, lately, with his long black eyes expressionless, lusterless, impassive.) But with Bonny, strangely enough, Morgan felt no guilt at all. He had sealed her off in another compartment. Coming home to her, he would be as pleased as ever by her easy chuckle and her heavy breasts and the absent-minded hugs she gave him as she slid past him in the choked and crowded corridors of their house.

He and Emily reached her car. She started into the street, to the driver's side, but he stopped her and drew her in to him. She smelled clear and fresh, like snow, and there was sherry on her breath. He kissed the curve of her jaw, just below one earlobe. "Morgan," she whispered, "someone will see." (She had an exaggerated fear of rumor; she imagined that people were more observant than they really were.) He felt he was trying to fill up on her. He kissed her mouth—a dry, sharp, wrinkled mouth, oddly touching—and unbuttoned her coat to slip his hands inside and circle her. Her body was so thin and pliant that it always seemed he was missing something, leaving a part of it behind. "Stay longer," he said in her ear.

"I can't," she said, but she held on for a moment, and then she pulled away and ran to climb into her car. The headlights lit up. The engine coughed and started. Morgan stood watching after her, pinching his lower lip between his fingers and thinking of what he should have said: Come even if it's Sunday. Promise you'll come Monday. Why don't you wear gloves? Mornings, now, when I wake up, I have this springy, hopeful feeling, and I see that everything is worth it, after all.

2 As soon as the weather thawed, Emily started jogging. It was a strange thing for her to do, Morgan thought—not really her type of activity. She bought a pair of clumsy yellow running shoes and a pedometer that she strapped to her waist with an old leather belt of Leon's. Several times, when Morgan was on his way to see her, he caught sight of her approaching at the other end of the block, wearing her unrunner-like skirt from which her legs flew out like sticks. Her yellow feet seemed the biggest part of her. She always looked as if she just *happened* to be running—as if she had a bus to catch or had suddenly remembered a pot left boiling on the stove. Maybe it was her tripping gait, which lacked seriousness. Maybe it was the flip and swing of her skirt. As she drew near, she would call out, not breaking stride, "Be with you in a minute! Once more around the block!" But when she stopped, finally, her pedometer would surprise him: four miles. Four and a half miles. Five. Always pressing her limits.

Once Morgan asked what she was running for.

"I just am," she told him.

"I mean, your heart? Your figure? Your circulation? Are you training for a marathon?"

"I'm just running," she said.

"But why push yourself?"

"I'm not pushing myself."

She was, though. After a run, there was something intense about her. She'd be glossy with sweat, strung up, a bundle of wiry muscles, vibrating. Her hair, loosened, flew out in an electric spray, each strand as crinkled as her amber-colored, crinkly hairpins. She was so different from other women that Morgan didn't know quite how to go about her. He was baffled and moved and fascinated, and he loved to slide his fingers down the two new, tight cords behind each of her knees. He couldn't imagine what it felt like to be Emily.

In the hardware store one afternoon he closed his eyes and said, "Tell me what you see. Be my seeing eye." She said, "A desk. A filing cabinet. A couch." Then she seemed to give up. He opened his eyes and found her looking helpless, wondering what he wanted of her. But that was all he wanted: her pure, plain view of things. Not that he would ever really possess it.

Morgan himself wasn't so fond of exercise. He hated exercise, to tell the truth. (Oh, to tell the truth, he was a much, much older man, and not in such very good condition.) And Leon had no interest in it either. Leon was one of those people who seem permanently athletic without effort. He was in fine shape, heavy and solid, sleekly muscled. He watched Emily's jogging distantly, with a tolerant expression on his face. "She's going about it all wrong," he told Morgan. "She's driving herself too hard."

"Ah! Didn't I say the same thing?"

"She has to be in charge so. Has to win."

They were sitting on the front stoop of the apartment building on a sunny day in March. The weather felt tentative. After this bitter, shocking winter, people seemed to view spring as a trick. They went on wearing woolen clothes, and removed them piece by piece each day as they grew warmer. Bonny still had her boxwoods shrouded in burlap. She mourned for her camellia buds, which had been fooled into emerging and would surely drop off with the next freeze. But spring continued. The camellia buds opened out triumphantly, a vivid pink with full, bloused petals. Morgan and Leon sat in their shirtsleeves, almost warm enough, too lazy to go in for their jackets, and around the corner came Emily: a little black butterfly of a person with yellow feet, far away. There was something about her running that seemed eternal. She was like the braided peasant girl in a weatherhouse, traveling forever on her appointed path, rain or shine, endearingly steadfast. Morgan felt himself grow weightless with happiness, and he expanded in the sunlight and beamed at everything with equal love: at Leon and the spindly, striving trees and Emily jogging up and away and the seagull wheeling overhead, floating through the chimneys in a languid search for the harbor.

3 Leon's father had a heart attack, and Leon drove to Richmond to see him. Morgan visited Emily that evening. In the kitchen Gina was mixing a cake for her school's bake sale. She kept coming into the living room and asking where the vanilla was, or the sifter, or prancing around Morgan and checking all his pockets for the coughdrops she was fond of. Morgan was patient with her. He held his arms out passively while she searched him. Then when she returned to the kitchen, he and Emily made casual, artificial conversation. He might have lounged on the couch beside her in the old days, not giving it a thought, but now he was careful to sit some distance from her on a straight-backed chair. He cleared his throat and said, "Bonny told me to ask if you wanted to borrow her car."

"Oh, that's very nice of her. No, thank you."

"What if he's gone a long time? You might need it."

"No."

"What if he's gone through the weekend and it interferes with a puppet show?"

"I'll cancel it."

"Or I could come in his place. Why not? I'll come as Leon."

"I'll just cancel."

They looked at each other. Emily seemed paler than usual. She kept smoothing her skirt, but when she saw him watching she stopped abruptly and folded her hands in her lap. The strain was affecting her, he supposed. She was not accustomed to deceit. Neither was he, really—not to this kind. He wished they could just tell everyone and have done with it. Leon would say, "I understand," and Morgan could move in and the four of them would be happy as larks, complete at last; they would laugh at how secretive they had been at first, how possessive, how selfish.

There was a blue tinge around Emily's eyes that gave her a raccoon look.

He stood up and said, "I have to go. Will you see me out?"

"Yes, certainly," Emily said, and she stood too, smoothing her skirt again with a nervous gesture that wasn't like her.

They went down the hall, passing the kitchen, where Emily poked her head in and said, "Gina, I'll be right back."

"Oh. Okay," Gina said. She was covered with flour and she looked harassed and distracted.

Morgan took Emily by the hand and led her out the door. But halfway down the stairs they heard footsteps coming up and he let go of her. It was Mrs. Apple in a bushy Peruvian poncho, briskly jingling her keys. "Oh! Emily. Dr. Morgan," she said. "I was just stopping in to ask about Leon's father. Is he going to be all right? Have you had any news?"

"Not so far," Emily said. "Leon said he'd phone me tonight."

"Well, I know how anxious you must be."

Morgan leaned against the banister, exasperated, waiting for this to end.

"Oh, but with modern medicine," Mrs. Apple said, "these things are nothing. A heart attack's so simple. Everything's replaceable; they'll give him a Teflon tube or a battery or something and he'll go on for years yet. Tell Leon he'll go on forever. Right, Dr. Morgan?"

"Right," said Morgan, staring at the ceiling.

If he inched his hand up the banister, he could just touch the back of Emily's skirt—a slink of cool, slippery cloth with a hint of warmth beneath it. His fingertips rested there, barely in contact. Mrs. Apple didn't notice. "If he's not home by tomorrow night," she was telling Emily, "you and Gina come for supper. Nothing fancy; you know I'm a vegetarian now . . ."

When she finally let them go, Morgan strode rudely down the stairs and out the door without saying goodbye. Emily had to run to catch up with him. "I can't abide that woman," he said.

"I thought you liked her."

"She repeats herself."

They walked fast, crossing the street and heading up the block toward Morgan's pickup. It was a cool, windy night with a white sky overhead. A few people were out on the sidewalk—teenagers hanging around a lamppost, some women on their stoops. When Morgan reached the pickup, he took hold of the door handle and said, "Let's go someplace."

"I can't."

"Just a short way. Just to be alone."

"Gina will start wondering."

He sagged against the door.

"I don't know what to do," she said.

"Do?"

He looked at her. She stood with her arms folded, gazing at some fixed point across the street. "I'm thinking of leaving," she said. "Getting out."

It must be Leon again. Morgan thought she'd stopped being bothered by all that, by whatever it was . . . he had never quite understood, although he'd tried. It seemed he kept missing some clue. Were they talking about the same marriage? Emily, what is your *problem*, exactly? he sometimes wanted to ask, but he didn't. He leaned against the pickup door and listened carefully, tilting his Panama hat forward over his eyes.

"I'm even packed," she said, "or half-packed. I've been packed for years. This morning I woke up and thought, 'Why don't I just leave, then? Wouldn't it be simpler?' These clothes are so foldable and non-crushable. They take up a single drawer and they'd fit with no trouble at all in the suitcase in the closet. I still have this cosmetic kit that I bought when I was first married. I'm set! It seems I always knew that

I might have to be. I've worked it so I could grab my bag up any time and go."

Morgan was interested. "Yes, yes," he said, nodding to himself. "I see what you mean."

Emily rattled on, like somebody clacking away in a fever. "When I jog, you know what I imagine? I imagine I'm in training for some emergency—a forced flight, a national disaster. It's comforting to know that I'm capable of running several miles. Nights, sometimes, I wake with a jolt, scared to death, heart just racing. Then I tell myself, 'Now, Emily, you can manage. You are very good at surviving. You can run five miles at a stretch, if you have to, and your suitcase can be ready in thirty seconds flat—' "

"What you need is a backpack," Morgan said. "An Army surplus backpack to leave your hands free."

Emily said, "I am seventeen days overdue."

"Seventeen days!" Morgan said.

He thought at first she was referring to some new jogging record. Then even after he understood, he seemed to have trouble absorbing it. (It was years since he and Bonny had had to concern themselves with such things.) "Think of that!" he said, stalling for time, nodding more rapidly.

"Of course, it could be a false alarm."

"Oh, yes, a false alarm."

"Will you please stop echoing?"

It hit him all at once. He straightened and yanked the truck's handle, and the door swung out, flooding Emily's face with light. She looked sleepy and creased; her eyes had adjusted to the dark. But she met his gaze firmly. "Emily," he said, "what are you telling me?"

"What do you think I'm telling you?"

He noticed that her face was pinched, as if from fear. He saw this suddenly from her viewpoint—seventeen days of waiting, not telling a soul. He shut the door again and laid an arm around her, heavily. "You should have mentioned this earlier," he said.

"I'm scared of what Leon will say."

"Yes, well . . ." He coughed. "Ah . . . will he realize? That is, will he realize that, ah, this is not his doing?"

"Of course he will," Emily said. "He does know how to count."

Morgan thought this over—all that it revealed. He patted her shoulder and said, "Well, don't worry, Emily."

"Maybe it's nerves," Emily said.

"Oh, yes. Nerves." He saw that he was echoing again and he quickly covered it up. "These things are vicious circles. What's the word I want? Self-perpetuating. The greater the delay, the more nervous you become, of course, and so the delay is even greater and you become even more—"

"I do believe in abortion," Emily said, "but I don't believe in it for me."

"Oh?" he said.

He frowned.

"Well, for who, then?" he asked.

"I mean, I don't think I could go through with the actual process, Morgan."

"Oh, yes. Well—"

"I just couldn't do it. I couldn't."

"Oh. Well, naturally. Of course not," he said. "No, naturally not."

He noticed that he was still patting her—an automatic gesture that was beginning to make his palm feel numb. "We shouldn't stay out here, Emily," he said. "You'd better go in now."

"I thought I was so careful," she told him. "I don't understand it."

Bonny used to say that—long, long ago in a younger, sunnier world. He had been through it all before. He was a grandfather several times over. He steered Emily back to her building at a halting, elderly pace. "Yes, well, yes, well," he said, filling the silence. On her front steps he thought to say, "But we could always ask a doctor. Get some tests."

"You know I can't stand doctors. I hate to just . . . hand myself over," Emily said.

"Now, now, don't upset yourself. Why, tomorrow you may find this was all a mistake—nerves or a miscalculation. You'll see."

He kissed her good night, and held the door while she slipped inside, and smiled at her through the glass. He was calm as a rock. And why shouldn't he be?

None of this was happening.

4 Now every day that passed meant another blank on the calendar, another whispered conversation on the phone or in Cullen Hardware. Leon was back from Richmond; they couldn't talk in the apartment. But Emily's sheeted eyes, when Morgan stopped in for a visit, told him all he cared to know.

A week went by, and then two weeks. "What's the matter with Emily?" Bonny asked. "Have you seen her? She never comes around any more."

Morgan thought of answering her. Just simply answering her. "Well," Bonny might say, "these things happen, I suppose." Or maybe, airily, "Oh, yes, I guessed as much." (She was his oldest friend. She had known him over thirty years.) But he said nothing—or something offhand, inconsequential; nothing that mattered.

Once he met Emily by accident in the Quick-Save Grocery. She was choosing a can of soup. Instantly, without even a greeting, they fell upon her signs and symptoms. ("I'm not the slightest bit morning-sick. And I would be, don't you think? I was terribly sick with Gina.") In the middle of the aisle Morgan set his fingertips precisely within the neckline of her leotard and gave a clinical frown into space, but her breasts were as small and tight as ever. He dismayed himself by longing, suddenly, to take her away to his faded office couch again. But he didn't suggest it. No, if this turned out to be a false alarm, he promised, they would become the brightest, gayest, most aboveboard of companions—he and Emily and Leon, racketing along in a merry threesome, and he and

Emily would not so much as hold hands except to . . . what, to help each other out of boats, through the windows of burning buildings.

He turned these thoughts over continually, plowing them under, digging them up again, but the odd part was that he still felt sublimely, serenely distant. He seemed to have grown removed from everything. Even his own house, his family, he suddenly saw from outside. Often he paused in a doorway, say the door to his room, and looked in as if he were judging someone else's life. It was not a bad place: the window open, curtains fluttering. He observed how lovely Bonny was when she fell into helpless laughter, which she was always doing. He noticed that when the house was full of women, there was a sound like water flowing in and out of the upstairs rooms. His mother and his sister spoke their chosen lines, which were as polished as the chorus of a poem. "This is the time when the artichokes begin, those spiky little leaves with a lemon-butter sauce . . ." "If Robert Roberts had not taken all my energy, all the care I ever had to give . . ." One of the twins —Susan, who had never married—was home recovering from a bout of hepatitis, and she lay peacefully in her old spool bed, knitting Morgan a beautiful long stocking cap from every color of scrap wool in the house. As for his other daughters—why, it began to seem he'd finally found a place in their eyes, basking among their clamorous children. What had been embarrassing in a father, it appeared, was lovably eccentric in a grandfather. Yes, and on second thought, even his work was not so terrible—his hardware store smelling of wood and machine oils, and Butkins perched on a stool behind the counter. Butkins! He was a skeletal, hay-colored man, with a nose so pointed that it seemed a clear drop hung perpetually at its tip. He had once been young—twenty-three when Uncle Ollie hired him. In Morgan's mind he'd stuck at that age forever after, but now Morgan took a closer look and found him nearing forty, bowed by his wife's ill health and the death of his only child. He seemed collapsed at the center, cavernous. His eyes were the palest, milkiest blue that

Morgan had ever seen, celestially mild and accepting. Morgan felt he had wasted so much time, had nearly let this man slip through his fingers unnoticed. He took to hunkering on his office steps and bemusedly smoking cigarettes while he studied Butkins at work, till Butkins grew flustered and spilled coins all over the counter as he was making change.

Emily phoned him at the hardware store. "I'm calling from home," she said. "Leon's gone out."

"How are you?" Morgan asked her.

"Oh, well."

"Are you all right?"

"Yes, but my back is starting to ache."

"Backache. Well, good! Yes, that's a good sign, I'm certain of it."

"Or else not," Emily said. "And anyhow, I may be just imagining things."

"No, no, how can you imagine a backache?"

"It's possible. There's nothing so strange about that."

"Well, what are you feeling, exactly?"

"I don't know, it may be all in my mind."

"Just tell me what you're feeling, please, Emily."

"Morgan, don't snap at me."

"Sweetheart, I wasn't snapping. Just tell me."

"You always get this . . . older tone of voice."

He lit a cigarette. "Emily," he said.

"Well, I have a dragginess in my back, you see, a really tired dragged-outness. Do you think that's hopeful? I tried to jog this morning and I couldn't do more than a block. Right now I have to go to Gina's gymnastics meet, and I was thinking, 'I'll never make it, I know I'll never make it. All I want to do is crawl into bed and sleep.' Oh, but that's a terrible sign, sleepiness. I just remembered. It's the worst sign I could have."

"Nonsense," Morgan told her. "You're feeling the strain, that's all. Why, naturally. You ought to get some rest, Emily."

"Well, maybe after Gina's meet."

"What time is that? I'll go in your place."

"Oh . . . in half an hour. But she's expecting me."

"I'll tell her you weren't feeling well and she'll have to take me instead."

"But I'm always letting her down, these days—"

"Emily, go to bed," he said. He hung up.

He told Butkins he would be out for a while. Butkins nodded and went on alphabetizing packets of flower seeds. When all this was over, Morgan decided, he was really going to devote himself to the hardware store. He'd start bringing a sandwich and staying here through lunch hour, even. He set his beret at a steeper angle and went to find his pickup.

Gina's school was in the northern part of town—St. Andrew's, a girls' school that Leon's parents had selected for her. They were paying her tuition and had the right to choose, Morgan supposed. Still, he didn't think much of St. Andrew's. He'd have preferred her to stay on at public school. He thought Leon's parents were a bad influence: last Christmas they'd bought Emily an electric mixer. If Emily didn't watch out, that apartment would be as overstuffed as anyone's. These things could creep up on you, Morgan told her.

He turned down the shady driveway of St. Andrew's and parked beside a school bus. The gym must be the building straight ahead. He recognized the hollow sound that voices take on in a gymnasium. He crossed the playground, tucking in his workshirt and combing his beard with his fingers, hoping he made a good showing. (Gina was ten years old now—the age when you had to start watching your step. Any little thing could mortify her.)

Evidently, he was late. The meet had already begun. In acres of echoing hardwood that smelled of varnish, little girls were teetering on a high chrome frame. Morgan crossed to the bleachers and settled himself on the lowest level, alongside a scattering of mothers. All the mothers wore blazers and blond, pageboy haircuts. He tried to picture Emily sitting here with them. He hunched forward in his seat and looked around for Gina. It took a moment (there were swarms of little girls in blue leotards and swarms in lavender, and he didn't even know which color was St. Andrew's), but he spotted her, finally. She was the one in blue with the cloud of curls. Her face was still round and opulent—he would know those heavy-lidded eyes anywhere, and that pale, delicate mouth—but her body had become a stick, the narrow hips pathetically high above legs so long and thin that he could see the workings of her kneecaps when she walked. She came over to him, her bare toes gripping the floor. Ordinarily she would hug him, but in front of friends she never did. "Where's Mama?" she asked him.

"She doesn't feel well."

"She never comes to anything any more," Gina said, but without much concern; her attention had already wandered elsewhere. She turned to study the girls on the other team. Then, "Morgan!" she screeched, spinning on him. "You can't smoke in here!"

She must have eyes in the back of her head. Morgan muttered, "Sorry," and replaced his cigarette in the pack.

"I could die of embarrassment," she said.

"Sorry, sweetheart."

"Are you giving me a ride home afterward?"

"I will if you like."

"That red-haired girl is Kitty Potts. I hate and despise her," Gina said. She ran off.

Morgan watched a series of girls perform slow and trembling labors on a balance beam. Periodically, one would fall off and have to climb back on. Gina, when it was her turn, fell off twice. By the time she'd finished, Morgan's muscles ached; he'd been holding his breath. He remembered that his daughter Kate had also liked gymnastics, a few years back. She'd won several ribbons. In fact, he didn't believe he'd ever seen her fall or make an error, not once in any meet that he'd attended. He might have just forgotten, of course. But he was sure that her scores had been better. Gina's was a 4.3, read off by a bored-looking woman at a microphone. Coming here today was an unnatural act, Morgan decided. He really had nothing to do with any of this—the unfamiliar gym, the blazered mothers, someone else's daughter in a leotard. He wished he could get up and go back to the hardware store.

They'd finished with the balance beam and moved in the horse for vaulting. Morgan thought vaulting was a monotonous event to watch. He tucked his boots in off the floor so the girls could run past him, one by one, for two leaps each. Their arms and legs looked stretched with concentration, and their faces were comically intense. Gina raced by with her eyes tightly focused. She sprang up and cleared the horse, but then she did something wrong. Instead of landing upright, she fell in a twisted heap on the mat.

The mothers went rigid; one laid her needlepoint aside. Morgan leaped to his feet. He was certain Gina'd broken her neck. But no, she was all right, or nearly all right—in tears, but not seriously injured. She rose holding on to one wrist. A young woman in shorts, with a whistle dangling from her neck, bent over her to ask her questions. Gina answered inaudibly, blotting her tears on her sleeve.

The woman led her up the floor again for her second try, though Gina was shaking her head and sobbing. The woman was saying something in a coaxing, reasoning voice. She smoothed Gina's hair, speaking urgently. It was barbaric. Morgan hated sports. He sat down and put an unlit cigarette in his mouth with a trembling hand.

Gina shrugged the woman away, drew herself up, and narrowed her eyes at the horse. There was still a little catch in her breath. It was the loudest sound in the gym. Everyone leaned forward. Gina set her jaw and started running. By the time she passed Morgan she was a steely, pounding blur. She cleared the horse magnificently and landed in perfect form, with her arms raised high.

Morgan jumped up and flung away his cigarette. He galloped in her footsteps all the way to the horse, and veered around it to hug her. Tears were streaming down his cheeks. "Sweetheart, you were wonderful," he said. She said, "Oh, Morgan," and giggled. (She was unscathed; she had forgotten everything.) She slipped away from him to join her teammates. Morgan returned to his seat, beaming and wiping his eyes. "Wasn't she wonderful? She was wonderful," he told the mothers. He blew his nose in his handkerchief. He felt suddenly joyous and expansive. What could he not accomplish? He was a wide, deep, powerful man, and it was time he took some action.

5 "How was the meet?" Emily asked Gina.
"It was all right."
"I'm sorry I couldn't be there. Morgan, do you want to come in?"

"Yes, thank you," Morgan said. Emily's appearance shocked him. Four days ago—the last time he'd seen her—she'd been a little drawn, yes, but now her skin had the yellow, cracked look of aged chinaware. "Emily, dear," he said. Emily slid her eyes sideways, reminding him of Gina, but he ignored her. He didn't even glance around for Leon, who might very well have returned by now. "I've come to take you to a doctor," he said.

"Is Mama really sick?" Gina asked.

"She needs a check-up. You stay here, Gina. We won't be long."

He started hunting through the closet for a sweater or a jacket, something light, but all he found was Emily's winter coat. He took it off the hanger and helped her into it. She stood docilely while he buttoned the buttons.

"It's not that cold," Gina told him.

"We have to take good care of her."

He led Emily out the door, closing it behind him. Halfway down the stairs, he heard the door swing open again. Gina hung over the banister. "Can I have that last banana?" she asked her mother.

Morgan said, "Yes. For God's sake. Anything you like." Emily was silent. Like someone truly ill, she made her way falteringly down the stairs.

In the truck she said, "Do we have an appointment?"

"We'll make one when we get there."

"Morgan, it takes weeks."

"Not today it won't," he said, pulling out of the parking space.

He drove to St. Paul Street, to Bonny's old obstetrician. He couldn't remember the number, but recalled very clearly the upholsterer's establishment next to it, and when he found a display window full of dusty velvet furniture, he stopped immediately, blocking an alley, and assisted Emily from the truck.

"How do you know this person?" Emily asked, looking around her at the gaunt, grimy buildings.

"He delivered all my daughters."

"Morgan!"

"What?"

"We can't go in there."

"Why not?" he asked.

"He knows you! I mean, we have to find someone else. We have to assume an alias or something."

Morgan took her elbow and guided her up the front steps, through the brass-trimmed door, and into a carpeted lobby. "Never mind all that," he told her, punching a button for the elevator. "This is no time to play around, Emily."

The elevator door slid open. A very old black man in a purple and gold uniform was sitting on a stool in the corner. Morgan hadn't realized that elevator men still existed. "Three," he said. He stepped in beside Emily. The silence in which they rode was dense and charged. Emily kept twisting her top button.

In the waiting room Morgan told the receptionist, "Morgan Gower. Emergency."

The receptionist looked at Emily.

"We have to see Dr. Fogarty right away," Morgan said.

"Doctor is booked solid. Would you care to make an appointment?"

"It's an emergency, I tell you."

"What seems to be the trouble?"

"I'll discuss the trouble when I see Fogarty."

"Dr. Fogarty is very busy, sir. Perhaps if you leave a number where he can call when he's through with his patients—"

Morgan stepped past her, around her desk, and through the oak door behind her. Often, biding his time in various waiting rooms, he had imagined doing this, but he had always assumed it would be necessary to wrestle the receptionist to the floor first. In fact the receptionist was a tiny, mousy girl with limp hair, and she didn't even stand up when he came through. He barreled down a short white corridor, into a room full of instruments, out again, and into another room. There an older, grayer Dr. Fogarty was seated behind a kidney-shaped desk, placing his fingertips neatly together, holding a discussion with a very young couple. The couple looked bashful and pleased. The girl was leaning forward, about to ask some earnest question. Rushed though he was, Morgan had time for a little spasm of pity. How shallow they seemed! Probably they thought this was the most significant moment in history. "Pardon me," Morgan told them. "I hate to interrupt this way."

"Mr. Gower," the doctor said, unsurprised.

"Ah! You remember me."

"How could one forget?"

"This is an emergency," Morgan said.

Dr. Fogarty let his chair rock forward at last, and parted his fingertips. "Is something wrong with Bonny?" he asked.

"No, no, it's Emily, someone else. This is Emily." He should have brought her in with him. What could he have been thinking of? He grabbed a hank of his hair. "It's terribly important. She's going to pieces, believes she's pregnant . . . Fogarty, if she's right, we need to know it now, this instant, not at two-fifteen next Tuesday or Wednesday or Friday."

"Mr. Gower, honestly," the doctor said. He sighed. "Why you have to take every stage of your life so much more to heart than ordinary people—"

Immediately, Morgan felt reassured. So this was merely a

stage, then! He turned to the couple and said, "I beg your pardon. Have I told you that? I'm sorry to seem so rude." The couple stared at him with blank, unformed faces.

"Show her into the room next door," the doctor said. "I'll be with you in a minute."

"Oh, thank you, Fogarty," Morgan said.

He felt a rush of affection for the man—his benign expression and his puffy gray mustache. It must be wonderful to view events so matter-of-factly. Maybe Morgan ought to shave his beard off and wear only a mustache. He stumbled out of the office, tentatively fingering his whiskers. He went back to the waiting room, where Emily was sitting alert, ready to fly, on a loveseat next to a pear-shaped woman in a smock. The receptionist didn't even glance at him. (Maybe this happened every day.) He beckoned to Emily, and she rose and came toward him. He led her to the room beside the doctor's office, the one that was full of equipment, and he helped her take her coat off. There was no place to hang it. He folded it into a wrinkled, oval bundle and set it on an enameled cabinet. "Didn't I tell you?" he asked Emily. "Everything will be all right. I'll take care of you, sweetheart."

Emily stood looking at him.

"Sit down," he told her. He steered her toward the examining table. She sat gingerly on the foot of it, smoothing her skirt around her.

Then Morgan started circling the room. All the instruments struck him as gruesome—tongs and pincers. What a world of *innards* women lived in! He shook his head. In one corner he found a hospital scale. The last person to stand on it had weighed a hundred and eighty-two pounds. "Mercy," he said disapprovingly. He slid the weights to the left. They felt solid and authoritative. "Ahem, young lady," he told Emily, "if you'll just hop on our scales, please . . ."

"I should have called a clinic. Family Planning or something," Emily said, as if to herself. "I meant to, every day, but I don't know, lately it seems I've got locked in place, frozen."

"Would you like a johnny coat?" Morgan asked, rooting through the cabinet. "Look here, they're pink. Just slip into our Schiaparelli johnny coat, Miss . . ."

Emily didn't respond. She was holding herself tense, with her hands clasped tightly in her lap.

Morgan went over and touched her arm. "Emily. Don't worry," he said. "This will all work out. Emily? Am I getting on your nerves? Do you want me to leave? Yes, I'll go outside and wait for you, that's a good idea . . . Emily, don't feel bad."

She still didn't answer.

He left and went to sit in the waiting room. He chose a chair in the corner, as far as possible from the pear-shaped woman. Even so, she seemed to be pressing in on him. She gave off a swelling, insistent warmth, although she pretended not to and seemed immersed in a *Baby Talk* magazine. Morgan let his head drop and covered his eyes with his fingers. Everything was a bluff. He knew the truth by now, however long it might take Fogarty to prove it scientifically. This was it. This was it.

He was done for.

The woman flipped the pages of her magazine, and car horns honked in the distance, and the telephone rang with a muted, purring sound. Morgan raised his head and stared at the oak door. He began to see the situation from another angle. An assignment had been given him. Someone's life, a small set of lives, had been placed in the palm of his hand. Maybe he would never have any more purpose than this: to accept the assignment gracefully, lovingly, and do the best he could with it.

6 On Wednesday morning, after Emily heard from the doctor, Morgan came home from work to tell Bonny. Bonny had launched one of her spring-cleaning attacks that always made the house seem untidier than before. Morgan could smell the dust flying the minute he walked in. She was

in the dining room, wearing a kerchief over her hair, washing down her ancestors' portraits with Spic and Span. Various scowling gentlemen in nineteenth-century frockcoats leaned against the chairs. Bonny was not intimidated. She scrubbed their faces with the same brisk energy she had once shown in scrubbing her children. Morgan stood in the doorway watching.

She wrung out a sponge, wiped her forehead with the back of her wrist, and then looked over at him. "Morgan? What is it?" she asked.

He said, "Emily's pregnant."

In the second it took her to absorb it, he saw he had worded it wrong. She could easily misunderstand. She might say, "Why, isn't that nice! They must be thrilled." But no, she understood, all right. Her mouth dropped open. She took on a white, opaque look. She reared back and threw the sponge at him. It skimmed his cheekbone, wet and warm and rough like something alive. Partly, he was impressed. (What a woman! Direct as some kind of electrical charge—undiffused.) But he had never been able to tolerate being hit in the face. He felt bitterly, gloriously angry, and free. He turned and walked out of the house.

At the hardware store he pushed past Butkins and went to use the phone. "Emily? Can you talk?" he asked.

"Yes. Leon's loading the car."

"Well, I told her," he said.

"What'd she say?"

"Nothing, in fact."

"Was she very angry?"

"No. Yes. I don't know," he said. "Emily, have you talked to Leon?"

"No. I'm going to."

"When?"

"Soon," she said. "Right now we've got a show at the library. I have to wait till after it's done."

"Well, I don't know why," Morgan said.

"Maybe I could tell him tonight."

"Tonight? Sweetheart, you'd better get this over with," he said.

"It's just . . . you know, just a matter of finding the proper moment."

After he had hung up, Morgan had a sudden fear that she would *never* tell Leon. He pictured having to sleep on the couch in his office forever—a man unkempt, uncared for. Like someone who had fallen between two stepping stones in a river, he'd let go of Bonny without yet being certain of Emily. He could not imagine life as a bachelor.

He sat a while drumming his fingers on his desk. He had an urge to write letters. But whom would he write to? He wondered how he could get hold of his cardboard file box. Surely Bonny wouldn't do anything rash with it, would she?—burn it? set it out for the trashmen? She knew how much it meant to him.

Finally he rose and went downstairs. Butkins was outdoors, helping a customer. In the spring they put some of their merchandise on the sidewalk—flats of seedlings, giant bags of mulch and fertilizer. Morgan peered through the window and saw Butkins tenderly fitting a marigold plant into a brown paper bag. He turned away and went into the stockroom. There were cartons of garden tools here, waiting to be unpacked. He opened one and pulled out trowels, dozens of them, which he heaped on the floor. He opened others and pulled out hedge trimmers, then cultivators, then shiny-toothed wheels for edging lawns. The stockroom became a tangle of chrome blades and painted wooden handles.

Butkins came in and said, "Um . . ."

Morgan surveyed all he had unpacked. Then he pried up another flap and reached for a pair of grass shears in a cardboard sheath.

Butkins said, "Mr. Gower, there's some things of yours on the sidewalk."

"Things?"

"It looks like . . . belongings. Clothing. Also a dog."

"How'd they get there?"

"Mrs. Gower, ah, dumped them there."

Morgan straightened up and followed Butkins through the store and out onto the sidewalk, which was a sea of hats and clothes. An elderly woman with a cane was trying on a pith helmet. Harry, who had never been much of a watchdog, was smiling at her with his tongue hanging out. He was sitting on Morgan's red-and-white-striped, 'twas-the-night-before-Christmas nightshirt. "I'm sorry, Mr. Gower, I didn't know what to do," Butkins said. "It happened so fast. She *threw* them, like. Knocked over half the seedlings."

"Yes, but why the dog?" Morgan asked.

"Pardon me?"

"The dog, the dog. It's not my dog; it's my mother's. I never even liked him. He dribbles. Why did she send me the dog?"

"Well, and there's some articles of clothing here too, you see."

"It isn't fair. I don't want a dog."

"There's hats and nightwear."

"Come back here!" Morgan told the old lady. She was making off with his pith helmet. She wore it tipped too far forward—had no idea of the proper angle. "Come back with my helmet!" he cried. She walked faster and faster, as if on little wheels. Considering her age and her cane, Morgan had to marvel.

"Shall I go after her?" Butkins asked.

"No, help me bring in the rest of the things. People will be all over them," Morgan said. Butkins stooped for an armload of clothing, but stopped when Morgan told him, "She won't even know to dampen it, I'll bet."

"Pardon?"

"You dampen the helmet in hot weather. It cools your head by the process of evaporation."

"Shall I go after her, then?"

"No, no."

"Are these boots yours too?"

"Everything," said Morgan. He scooped up an armload

of hats and followed Butkins inside. "Actually, I don't think she brought nearly my whole wardrobe, though. Where's my gnome hat? Where's my sombrero?"

"Are you and Mrs. Gower experiencing some difficulty?" Butkins said.

"Not at all. Why do you ask?" said Morgan. He went outside for another armload, chasing away two small boys who were interested in a sheepskin vest. "Come in, Harry," he told the dog. "Butkins, we'll need those cartons from the stockroom."

They made a total of six trips. Bonny had not, in fact, forgotten anything. Morgan found his file box under a cloak. He found his gnome hat and sombrero, and also a Napoleonic tricorne he'd forgotten all about. He blew the dust off and tried it on. He checked his reflection in the nickel surface of the cash register. Under the cocked brim his bearded face peered out hollowly. He was sickened. What a farce! How ridiculous! He had always, even in infancy, been a fool for hats. As a child, he'd worn firemen's helmets and Indian headdresses to bed at night. This was no better. He tore the tricorne off and flung it on the floor.

"Oh!" said Butkins. "It's an antique."

"I hate it."

"You don't want to get it dusty," Butkins said, picking it up.

"It's already dusty. You can have it."

Butkins did not seem to want it, however. He gave the hat a doubtful, troubled look, and placed it cautiously on the counter beside a flashlight display.

7 At lunchtime, when Morgan was alone in the store, he dialed the Merediths' number again. Nobody answered. They must not have returned from their puppet show. He let the phone ring on and on. Harry lay at his feet, his nose between his paws, rolling his eyes at Morgan.

When Butkins came back, Morgan decided not to go to

lunch himself. He wasn't hungry. And he didn't climb the stairs to his office, but stayed close to Butkins, drawing some kind of comfort from him, mutely watching the dull, homely transactions that took place: the purchasing of paint, nails, a screen-door hook, the return of a defective light switch. He noticed that when Butkins had no customers, he fell into a kind of trance; he gazed into space, sighing, and absently fingered an earlobe. Perhaps he was thinking of his wife. She had some slow, creeping illness; Morgan couldn't think of the name. Something to do with her muscles. She was no longer able to walk. And the child who died had been struck by a hit-and-run driver. Morgan remembered the funeral. He wondered how Butkins endured it, where he found the strength to open his eyes every morning and dress himself and force down a little food and set out for the hardware store. He must feel nothing but contempt for Morgan. But when Butkins came out of his trance and found Morgan's eyes on him, he only gave his gentle smile. "Why don't you leave?" Morgan asked. "Take the afternoon off."

"But it's not my day; it's Wednesday."

"Leave anyhow."

"Oh, I might as well stay."

It was lucky he did, as it happened. Around three o'clock Jim showed up—Amy's husband. From the focused way he strode in the door, wearing his slim gray lawyer suit, carrying his calfskin briefcase, Morgan guessed that he'd been sent by Bonny. Plainly, he knew everything. His face was pulled downward by long, severe lines. "Where can we talk?" he asked Morgan.

"Why, my office, I suppose."

"Let's go there."

Jim led the way himself. Morgan followed. He didn't so much walk as drift, dimly touching T-squares and hammers as he passed down the aisle. He wondered, idly, how Jim would handle this. What had ever prepared him for such a discussion? He trailed Jim up the stairs. Jim took a seat in Morgan's swivel chair. Morgan had to sit on the couch, like an applicant for something. (They must teach you this strategy in law school.) Morgan prinked the creases of his trousers and smiled at Jim, showing all his teeth. Jim didn't smile back.

"Well, I heard the news," he told Morgan.

"Yes, I figured you had."

"It's not clear to anyone what you plan to do next, Morgan."

"Do?"

"What steps you plan to take."

"Ah."

Jim waited. Morgan went on smiling at him.

"Morgan?"

"Well, for the moment I may have to sleep on this couch," Morgan said. "It's not the best of beds, as you see—damn buttons, tufting, whatever you want to call it—"

"I'm not inquiring about your *mattress*, Morgan. I'm asking what arrangements you contemplate."

"Arrangements."

"Have you told this other woman you're assuming responsibility?"

"She's not 'this other woman,' Jim. She's Emily. You've met Emily. And of course I'm assuming responsibility."

"Morgan, I don't like to be tactless—"

"Then don't be," Morgan said.

Jim sat back in the swivel chair, studying him. He had his briefcase set across his knees like a desk. Although he had long ago traded his crew-neck sweaters for suits, he had never lost his mannequin look. Even now that he was graying, Morgan saw, he was doing it in a mannequin's style—handsome silvery wings above his ears. Jim tapped his briefcase thoughtfully. "You realize," he told Morgan, "that you're not the first man this has happened to."

"Oh? I'm not?"

"Well, I fail to see what's so humorous, Morgan."

"No, no . . . What I mean to say is, I *am* the first man it's happened to in quite this way. Or rather, it's the first time it's happened to *me*, and to her. There's no point trying to fit us on a graph."

Jim sighed. "Let's start all over," he said.

"Certainly."

"You know, Morgan, that Bonny was pretty upset this morning when she heard the news. But it's not the end of the world, I told her. It's not what you'd break up a marriage for. Is it? Get a hold of yourself, I told her. Oh, sure, she'll take a while forgiving you. It's a shock to everybody—Amy, Jean . . . they might be hard on you at the moment . . ."

Morgan nodded, trying to look reasonable. Of course, he should have realized the girls would be involved. They were loyal to Bonny, naturally, and it must look terrible, what he'd done. Oh, he didn't blame them at all. But still he felt a little hurt, picturing Bonny surrounded by clucking daughters. How they rushed to scenes of tragedy and melodrama! He was reminded of Susan, their most difficult child, who had spent a tiresome, extended adolescence bickering with Bonny. She would drive home from college for weekends and he'd barely have unloaded the laundry from her car when she'd be storming out again. "I'll never come back here, never. I was an idiot to try." "But what happened?" he would ask, astonished. She would yank her laundry bag from his hands and flounce into her car and grind the engine. "And how did it happen so *fast?*" he would call after her departing taillights. Spontaneous combustion! Flint rocks, miraculously magnetized! They rushed to battle with such enthusiasm.

It was just as well he was done with all that. In his mind Emily shone as clear and still as a pool.

"I plan to ask Bonny for a divorce," he told Jim.

"Morgan. Christ, Morgan. Look, man . . ."

"I don't suppose you give discounts to family members, do you?"

"I don't handle divorces."

"Oh."

"And anyhow . . . Christ, Morgan, what's got into you? You're throwing everything away!"

"I've already told Emily," Morgan said, "that I'll take care of her and Gina and the baby. She could never just stay with her husband; she's said that. And she has nobody else to rely on. See, I realize I'm behaving badly, Jim, but this is one of those times when, whatever you do, it's bad from one angle and good from another. I mean, I can't be virtuous on every front in this situation. Can I?"

"Listen," Jim said. He hunched forward over his briefcase, as if about to pass on a secret. "Life is not always X-rated, Morgan."

"I beg your pardon?"

"I mean, generally it's more like . . . oh, a low R, I'd say: part bed, part grocery-shopping. You don't want to ruin everything for the sake of, ah . . ."

Morgan fished for his cigarettes. What did Jim imagine? Life with Bonny, after all, was not exactly rated G. He decided not to say that out loud. He offered Jim a cigarette. Jim, who didn't smoke, took one and waited for Morgan to strike a match. "See, what I'm getting at—" he said.

"I know what you're getting at," said Morgan, "but you miss the point. I've already made my mind up, Jim. I'm not going to change it. I have this feeling of . . . swerving, like seizing my boat and wrenching it around, steering it off course and onto a whole new, unlikely one. It's not bad! It's not a bad feeling! You aren't going to make me give it up!"

And as he spoke, he felt drunk with his own decisiveness. He could hardly wait for Jim to leave, so that he could go find Emily and settle this forever.

8 He had trouble coaxing the dog into the pickup. Harry didn't like traveling. He had to be dragged across the sidewalk with his nails scritching. But Morgan couldn't leave him behind, because Butkins had begun to sneeze. He heaved Harry into the truck, tucked his tail in, and closed the door. Then he went back to the store to tell Butkins, "I'm not sure

how long I'll be. If I'm still away by closing time, lock up, will you? And don't let anyone bother my clothes."

It was the time of afternoon when children were coming home from school—neat little grade-schoolers with satchels, junior-high boys in baggy Army jackets and girls with plastic combs sticking out of their jeans pockets. Teenagers milled at intersections, making driving difficult.

On Crosswell Street the mothers were waiting on their stoops. They shaded their eyes and discussed the weather, the Orioles, what they planned to serve for supper. A fat woman in a dress like a petticoat had opened a can of beer and was passing it around. Burnished lavender pigeons clustered at a sack of spilled popcorn.

Morgan pushed through the door of the Crafts Unlimited building and pulled Harry after him. Harry hung back, whining, but Morgan hauled him up the stairs with a length of rope he'd borrowed from the store. He knocked on the Merediths' door. Emily opened it. "Good, you're back," he said. He walked in.

"Morgan? What are you doing here?"

"I've come to get this settled." He paused in the hall and glanced around for Leon. "Where is he?"

"He's picking up Gina. It's our turn for the carpool."

"Have you told him yet?"

"No."

He turned to look at her. She was twisting her hands. "I can't," she said. "I'm scared. You don't know what a temper he has."

"Emily . . . Sit, Harry. *Sit*, dammit. Emily, what are you saying?" he asked. It cost him some effort, but he said, "Would you rather not do this at all? Rather go on the way you were, work it out somehow—the two of you? You should say so now, Emily, if that's true. Just tell me what you want of me."

"I want to be with you," she said. "I wish we could just run away."

"Ah," he said. He was immediately taken with the idea.

"Yes! Run away. No luggage, no fixed destination . . . Will Gina come willingly, do you think?"

"I don't know," she said. She swallowed. "It's telling him face to face I mind. Maybe I could go to a pay phone and call him up, tell him from a distance."

"Well, that's a thought."

"Or you could tell him."

"Me?"

"You could . . . get behind a table or something where he couldn't hit you and then break the news to him."

"I preferred the running-away plan," Morgan said.

"But taking Gina: I couldn't do that to Leon. And I'd never leave her behind."

"All right," Morgan said. "I'll tell him myself."

He assumed it was all arranged then, and went into the kitchen to sit down and wait for Leon. But Emily floated after him, still twisting her hands, and said, "Oh, no, what am I thinking of? I don't know why I'm such a coward. Of course I have to be the one to do it. Go away and come back later, Morgan."

"That's impossible," he said. "I'm lugging this dog around."

"I feel sick," she said.

"Dear heart. This is really very simple," he told her. "We're all adults. We're reasonable beings. What do you imagine will happen? Could I have some water for Harry, please?"

She took a bowl from the cupboard and filled it at the sink. She set the water in front of Harry, who started slurping it up. Then she shifted her purse from a chair and sat next to Morgan. "If we ran away, I would have to find some other kind of work," she said. "Something I couldn't be traced by. It's so easy to track down a puppet show, at any fair or church bazaar."

"Well, then. You can't run away," he said. "What would you do without your puppets?"

"I could manage fine without my puppets," she said.

"No, no . . ."

"I never planned to stick with them forever."

"Oh, of course you'll stick with them, Emily, dear."

She slumped in her chair, massaging her temples with her fingertips. Harry raised his head and shook water all over the kitchen floor. "Mind your manners," Morgan told him. He reached across the table for Emily's purse. It had an interesting weight to it. Most days, all it contained was keys and her billfold, but whenever she had a puppet show she loaded it with carefully selected equipment. You could live in the wilderness for a month off that purse, Morgan thought. He rummaged through it and came up with a ball of string, a roll of Scotch tape, her Swiss Army knife, a pair of needle-nosed pliers . . . "What's this for? And this?" he kept asking.

"I think I'm going to throw up," she said.

"What's this little Baggie full of Cheerios?"

"They're the doughnuts for Red Riding Hood's basket."

"Oh, yes. Oh, excellent."

He began to feel very happy. He piled everything back in the purse and started humming, patting his knees, looking around for something new. "How's your burner doing?" he asked.

"It's fine."

"See? I told you all it needed was unclogging."

He hummed a few more bars. Then he said, "Don't you want to know why I have this dog with me?"

She didn't seem to. He continued anyway. "Bonny brought him. Threw everything out on the sidewalk: hats, clothes, vacuum-cleaner instructions . . . and Harry. But Harry belongs to Mother. Mother's always owned a dog. This must be her tenth or twentieth. Who did she have when you first met us—Elmer? Lucille? She pays them no mind at all, never looks at them, it's me who walks them . . . but she's always had one, so she always will. That's the way they work things, back home. The extras! The stacks of unnecessary extras! This Harry, you see, is Bonny's revenge. Oh, she knew what she was doing, all right. Cluttering up my leaving, even. I'm surprised she didn't bring the cat as well."

"I always did want a dog," Emily said unexpectedly.

"Eh?"

"But I couldn't because my mother was allergic."

"Yes, that's Butkins' trouble, too. Allergic."

"Butkins?"

They heard the front door open. Emily sat up straighter. "Mama," said Gina, bouncing in, "guess what I got on my science test. Hello, Morgan, what's Harry doing here?"

"I brought him in for a drink. Well, Miss Gina," Morgan said. "What'd you get on your science test?"

"A-plus," she said. She twined an arm around him and looked down at Harry, who was scratching fleas. Leon walked in.

"Hello, Morgan," he said.

"Leon."

"Taking the afternoon off?"

"Yes, well, there's something I want to discuss with you."

"What's that?" asked Leon.

Morgan glanced over at Gina. She had dropped her arm but continued to stand there, so close that he could smell her salty, summery smell of fresh sweat and chewing gum. He scratched his head. "Leon," he said, "would you like to . . . come walk the dog with me?"

"Do what?"

"Walk the dog."

Leon looked at the dog, who grinned.

"Don't if you don't want to," Morgan said. "Do you want to?"

"All right, Morgan," Leon said calmly.

Morgan stood up, tucking in his shirt, adjusting his Panama hat. They went out of the apartment together. Just as Leon was closing the door, Gina called, "Wait!"

"What's the matter?"

"You forgot the dog."

"Oh," Morgan said. He shuffled back to the door and took Harry's rope from her.

They went down the stairs and outside. The rush-hour traffic was just beginning. Trucks rumbled past, and cars with single, determined drivers, and taxis carrying ladies submerged in packages. It took a while to cross the street. Then they started north. Leon led, with both hands loose at his sides in an easy, unquestioning way that gave Morgan a sudden pang.

"Well," Morgan said.

He waited for Harry to sniff out the proper spot in the grass. Leon straightened a sign that had pivoted on its post.

"I find myself in a little difficulty," Morgan said.

"Say it, Morgan."

"It's Emily."

They walked on. Morgan thought of the old women in the neighborhood where he had grown up—how they never announced a death straightforwardly but prepared the bereaved first, planting tiny seeds of news and allowing them to sprout on their own, no faster than the bereaved could handle. Emily's name, he hoped, might be such a seed all by itself. Certainly Leon seemed to be turning it over in his mind. They stopped and waited for a light to change, although no cars were coming.

"Emily and I . . ." Morgan said.

They crossed the street. They avoided a shattered whiskey flask.

"She's expecting a child," Morgan said.

Leon didn't slow down. Morgan cast a sideways glance at him and found his face unmoved. "You knew all along," Morgan said.

"No," said Leon. "Not about the child."

"But the rest of it, you knew."

"Yes."

"Well . . . how?"

"Osmosis, maybe," Leon said. "Something or other."

"You have to believe me," Morgan said. "I never intended any harm. I really can't explain . . . I mean, day by day, you see, it didn't seem so terrible. But I know how it must appear from outside."

"What are your plans?" Leon asked politely.

They paused, facing each other, with Harry on his haunches between them. If Leon was going to get violent, now was the time. But he didn't, of course. Morgan had never understood why Emily thought he would. She must have been mistaken, suffered one of those funny blind spots married people often have. Or maybe she was talking about an earlier Leon; that possibility occurred to him. Morgan gazed off, seeing the last of someone he'd been hearing about for years. He sighed and pulled his nose.

"Well," he said, "if you're willing, I suppose I'll move her and Gina to some other town. I don't know."

"Do you want the apartment?"

"*Your* apartment?"

"Do you want the puppets, the equipment, the job? Want me to be the one to go?"

"Oh, well, no, I couldn't ask—"

"Really, what do I need with all that? Take it," Leon said.

"Oh."

"Take it."

"Well, if you're sure," said Morgan.

Then Leon said, "Aah, God, Morgan." He spoke wearily, disgustedly, but not with any sharpness.

Even so, Morgan flinched.

When they resumed walking, it was in the other direction, homeward. They passed Eunola's Restaurant, where the three of them had so often stopped for coffee. Then they came to the laundromat where Morgan had stood, countless times, watching Leon and Emily setting out with their baby. Perhaps, he thought, this was not so much a love story as a friendship story, and he felt saddened by Leon's patient, trudging figure beside him. (Where was that thin, olive-skinned boy parting the curtains to call for a doctor? Would Emily ever again, in the future, wear that tilted look she had first tossed Morgan?)

They crossed the street and entered the building. When Morgan saw the long stairway, he believed, for a moment, that he might not make it. He was exhausted, and his chest ached. But a strange thing happened. As he climbed, it seemed his spirits climbed too. He speeded up, leaving Leon behind, taking steps two at a time. He wanted to get on with this. He wanted to begin his new life.

1978

1   Cinderella was dancing with the Prince, nestled in his brown felt arms, gliding across the walnut desk in somebody's father's study. Over her head, blue satin swoops hung from the folding wooden stage. There was a scrim at the rear that didn't entirely conceal the puppeteers, but the audience was too entranced to notice. It was a very young audience—mostly four-year-olds. The birthday child wore a gilt paper crown that resembled the Prince's.

"Mercy," Cinderella said, "it must be getting late. I'm sure it's nearly midnight."

"Midnight? So what?" the Prince asked in his gruff, rasping voice. "We'll dance till dawn. We'll dance all the next day!"

"Um, well, but you see, Your Majesty . . ."

They were stalling for time. Where was the clock? "The clock!" Emily whispered. Gina was off in a trance again, holding the cassette recorder just beyond Emily's reach and gazing dreamily at the audience. Joshua, who was supposed to be in Gina's care, was creeping under the desk. He gurgled to himself and dribbled on a nest of extension cords.

"Ding, ding!" Emily called in desperation. "Ding, ding, ding . . ."

Somewhere in there she lost count, but she trusted that the audience wouldn't catch it. She could hardly wait to whisk Cinderella off the stage so she could rescue the baby. The instant the curtain was lowered, she snatched him up. He wore only a grayish diaper. His solid little trunk, barrel-shaped, was faintly sticky, and he trailed a silvery, cool thread of spit down the back of Emily's hand.

"Gina, honey," Emily said, "I thought you were going to watch him for me. 'Oh, I can manage both,' you told me, 'mind Josh and do the props too . . .' "

Morgan, meanwhile, was digging through a pile of objects on the floor. "Fireplace, fireplace," he muttered. "What's happened to the fireplace?"

"Gina had it last."

But Gina was busy with thoughts of her own. Eleven years old, tall and secretive, languorous from half a summer of lolling about in the heat, she sat on a leather chair with her knees cocked and hummed the waltz that Cinderella had been dancing to. "Here we are," Morgan said. He straightened, puffing, and held up the cardboard fireplace. Joshua reached for it, but Morgan was too quick for him. He set the fireplace in one corner of the stage. "Now, where's the stepmother?" he asked Emily. "Where are the sisters?"

"Gina? Take Josh for me, will you?"

Gina unfolded herself with a sigh and accepted the baby. He grabbed at her shiny hair clasp. He grabbed at Morgan's sailor cap, in passing, but was borne away to the leather chair. "Tra la la," Gina sang, rocking him too hard.

Out front, the audience grew hushed and expectant. Emily slipped off Cinderella's ballgown, exposing her burlap rags. She held her up, ready to go, and smiled at Morgan. He nodded and raised the curtain.

2 "You know that Kate's home," Bonny said.
"Oh, really?" said Emily. "I hadn't heard." She switched the receiver to her other ear. She was trying to stir a stew and talk on the phone simultaneously. "Has something happened?" she asked.

Instead of answering, Bonny let out a long, thin breath. All of a sudden, this late in her life, Bonny had taken up smoking. She didn't smoke very competently and always seemed to be inhaling or exhaling at exactly the wrong moment, leaving her listeners suspended. She had also developed other new habits. She continually joined strange philosophical societies and women's groups, began unpromising jobs and then resigned almost at once, and telephoned Emily at any hour she pleased. Although she never mentioned Morgan without biting his name off, she seemed not to blame Emily at all. This was a relief, of course, but it was also a little insulting. (It implied that Emily was powerless, without a will of her own.) When Bonny paused for one of her cigarette breaths, Emily pictured the humming wires that linked them. Bonny was knotted into her line, knotted into her whole existence. Even if Emily were to hang up, Bonny's phone would still connect hers because Bonny was the one who'd placed the call.

"She has this back," Bonny said. "This sprained or twisted back, or something. The way it came about was, she and her husband were involved in a head-on collision. David walked away from it without a scratch, but Kate did something to her back."

"What happened to the other driver?" Emily asked.

"What other driver?"

"The driver of the other car."

"David was the driver of the other car."

"You mean she collided with her husband?"

"Yes, and got this injured back, this sprained or twisted back; I'm telling you," Bonny said.

"Oh, now I see."

"Well, I wanted her to come home because I can nurse her better than David could. Heaven knows I've had the practice. And besides that, I've been attending these lectures on a whole different kind of nutrition, a diet that heals any sort of ailment. It works on physical problems, mental problems, depressions, infections, tumors . . . You may not remember this, but last winter, when Molly was mugged in Buffalo while she was taking her son to the emergency room . . ."

Salting the stew, tasting it, listening with half an ear, Emily considered the Gowers' accidents: their wrecks, falls, and fires, all those events through which they slid so blithely. To Emily, who had no accidents whatsoever, their lives sounded catastrophic; but to Bonny, sheer custom must have leveled everything out. Emily tried to imagine reaching such a stage. She couldn't begin to.

Even now that Morgan's household had moved to hers, she thought—his mother and sister and dog, his hats and suits—she herself didn't seem to have been transformed in any way at all.

3   Emily took Gina shopping. Gina was going to Camp Hopalong in Virginia for the month of August, at Leon's parents' expense. It was time she learned to live away from home, they said. Emily was uneasy about it. She didn't like doing without Gina for so long, and also she was afraid that in Virginia, near Leon and his parents, Gina would somehow be stolen from her—turned against her. They would point out that Emily was immoral or deceitful or irresponsible, oh, any number of things, she just knew it; and Emily would not be there to explain herself. But she didn't tell Gina that. Instead, she said, "You're so young, you might get lonesome.

Remember how Morgan had to bring you back from Randallstown? You couldn't make it through a simple slumber party."

"Oh, Mama. That was at Kitty Potts's house and she had that group of girls that didn't like me."

"Still," Emily said.

"*Everybody* goes to camp. I'm not a baby any more."

Emily hoisted Joshua on her hip and walked Gina down Crosswell Street to Merger Street, to Poor John's Basement. Holding Camp Hopalong's checklist in her free hand, she informed the salesgirl that they needed six pairs of white shorts. Six pairs! It was lucky Leon's parents were paying for the clothes as well. Gina took a stack of shorts into a curtained booth, while Emily waited outside. (Recently, Gina'd turned modest.) The salesgirl, awkward on her platform sandals as some frail, hoofed animal, hung in the background, clutching one elbow. Joshua started fussing and leaning out of Emily's arms, but she couldn't put him down because the floor was filthy—blackened boards permanently stamped with scraps of foil and gray disks of chewing gum. Joshua grew heavier and heavier. Emily called, "Gina? Honey, hurry, please. It's nearly lunchtime."

There was no answer. She knocked on the wall near the booth and then drew the curtain aside. Gina was standing before a full-length mirror, wearing a stained T-shirt and a pair of blinding white shorts with cardboard tags dangling from a belt loop. Tears rolled down her face. She seemed to be watching them in the mirror. "Honey!" Emily said. "What's wrong?"

"I look like a freak," Gina said.

"Oh, Gina."

"I'm fat."

"Fat! You're skin and bones."

"Look: great bobbles of fat. Obese! And my knees don't match."

"That's ridiculous," Emily said. She looked to the salesgirl for help. "Isn't that ridiculous?"

The salesgirl blew a perfect pink bubble.

"I wish I were dead," Gina said.

"Honey, would you rather not go to camp?"

Gina sniffed and said, "No, I'll go."

"You don't have to, you know."

"I want to."

"They can't force you."

"I *want* to," Gina said. "I want to get out of here! And never come back. I'm sick of everything always so messy, babies and diapers and those two old ladies taking up my bedroom. You just let them move right in on me. You acted glad to have them. Nobody *else* at St. Andrew's sleeps on a fold-out bed. And that dog that snores, and Morgan's stupid tools and things anyplace I want to sit. I'm fed up with him! Does he have to wear those hats all the time? Does he have to make such a show of himself?"

"Why, Gina!" Emily said.

But later, when they'd walked home, it was to Morgan that Gina acted friendliest. At lunch she kept giggling with him, and then flashing some kind of challenge at Emily with her flat, black, unreadable eyes.

4 "I'm much more free than I used to be," Bonny said. "I mean, he used to color my world so. You know how that is?"

There was something wrong with the telephone. Other lines seemed to be spilling into it. Emily heard faint laughter and a burble of distant voices. "No," she said, worming a screwdriver out of Joshua's grasp. "No, not exactly."

"Oh, he was so tiring! Everything had to be larger than life, extravagant, grandiloquent. Take my brother, Billy. You've met Billy. He hasn't been lucky in marriage. He's had three wives. But three is not an impossible number. I mean, the way Morgan always spoke of him, you'd think Billy'd been married *dozens* of times. 'Now, who is his wife at the moment?' he'd ask. 'Do I know her name?' And somehow we all fell in with it. Even Billy, it seemed, came to believe that he'd had this great, long train of wives. He made jokes about it, acted like a drop-in guest at his own weddings. There! See? I'm talking as if he had a wedding every week."

Something was boiling over on the stove. At the kitchen table Brindle slouched in her long, white, dingy bathrobe, laying out her Tarot cards, and when she heard the hiss of steam she looked up, but she did nothing about it. Emily stepped over the dog, stretched to the end of her cord, and took the pan off the stove and set it in the sink. "Bonny, I'm cooking supper now," she said.

"He only feels he's real when he's in other people's eyes," Bonny told her. "Things have to be *viewed*. All alone in the bathroom, he's no one. That's why his family doesn't count. They tend not to see him; you know how families are. So he has to go out and find himself in someone else's line of vision. Oh, how wearing he was! I blame it on his mother. She expected so much of him—especially after his father died. 'You can be anything,' she told him. He must have misunderstood. He thought she said, 'You can be *every*thing.' "

"He's wonderful with Gina," Emily said.

"I feel sorry for you," Bonny said.

5 Trunks and dress forms, a rusty birdcage, barrels containing a gigantic cup-and-saucer collection muffled in straw, stacks of *National Geographics*, Brindle's catalogs, Louisa's autograph book, a samovar, a carton of records, a lady's bicycle, a wicker elephant. And this was only what lined the hall, which had once been as empty as a tunnel. In the living room: two sets of encyclopedias (one general, one medical), a spread-out jigsaw puzzle, Louisa's platform rocker with several yards of knitting coiled in the seat, and half a dozen runny watercolors of peaches, pears, and grapes —products of an art course Brindle had taken twenty years

ago, back when she was married to her first husband. The husband himself (pink-faced, with a windowpane of white painted on his bald skull like the shine on an apple) hung in a curly gold frame above a bookcase full of manuals.

In Gina's room there was almost no floor—just a field of bureaus and unmade beds. In Morgan's and Emily's room were more bureaus (two and a half for Morgan alone), the bed, the sewing machine, Gina's old, yellowed crib with the tattered eyelet canopy they'd brought up from the basement for Joshua, and puppets dangling from the picture rails, since there wasn't space in the closet. The closet held Morgan's clothing. There, also, no floor was evident—no air, even. Step inside and you'd be impacted in a solid, felty darkness, faintly smelling of mothballs.

Emily loved it all.

She began to understand why Morgan's daughters kept coming home when they had to convalesce from something. You could draw vitality from mere objects, evidently—from the seething souvenirs of dozens of lives raced through at full throttle. Morgan's mother and sister (both, in their ways, annoying, demanding, querulous women) troubled her not a bit, because they weren't hers. They were too foreign to be hers. Foreign: that was the word. All she touched, dusted, and edged around was part of a foreign country, mysterious and exotic. She drew in deep breaths, as if trying to taste the difference in the air. She was fascinated by her son, who did not seem really, truly her own, though she loved him immeasurably. At meals, she tended to keep silent and to watch everybody with a small, pleased smile. At night in bed, she never lost her surprise at finding herself alongside this bearded man, this completely other person. She felt drawn to him by something far outside herself—by strings that pulled her, by ropes. Waking in the dark, she rolled toward him with a kind of stunned sensation. She was conscious of their two surfaces meeting noticeably: oil and water.

But Morgan said they had to move to some place bigger—a place with more bathrooms, at least. He was sorry, he said, to be putting her through this. He knew she had never bargained on having his female relatives dumped at her door like stray cats. (Actually, they had climbed the stairs themselves, wearing gloves, but it was true that Bonny'd just dropped them off in front of the building.) He would like, he said, a house in the country—a large, bare farmhouse. However, there was the matter of money. Even keeping this apartment was difficult, nowadays. Mrs. Apple had raised the rent. She was not as friendly as she'd once been, Emily thought. And Morgan had lost his job. Emily felt that this was spitefulness on Bonny's part. Why should Morgan's private arrangements affect his work at Cullen Hardware? But Morgan said that was Uncle Ollie's doing, not Bonny's. In fact he said, Uncle Ollie had seemed to leap at the opportunity— had rushed to the store as soon as he heard the news and flung Morgan's wardrobe onto the sidewalk, the selfsame wardrobe Bonny had flung there earlier. (People were so eager to get rid of his *clothes*, Morgan mourned.) It so happened that Morgan was out, at the time. He returned to find Uncle Ollie planted in front of the store, rising from a billow of hats. "Is it true what they tell me?" "Yes." "Then you're fired." If he had said, "No," Morgan claimed, Uncle Ollie would no doubt have been disappointed. He must have been waiting all along for such a chance.

Now Morgan had no steady employment, although a couple of times a week he clerked at the plumbing-supply store down the street. Emily tried to make more and more puppets, faster and faster, working late at night while Josh was asleep. Whenever Morgan saw her bent over her sewing machine, he apologized. He said, "You look like someone in an ad for unions." What he didn't understand was that Emily felt happier now than she'd ever felt before. She rattled inside this new life like . . . well, like Morgan in one of his hats, she supposed. But he went on apologizing. He couldn't believe she didn't mind.

When the time arrived for Leon to drive to Baltimore and pick up Gina, Emily cleaned the apartment so he wouldn't imagine she had let things go. But she didn't try to straighten the clutter, or get Brindle out of her bathrobe. And she didn't hide Morgan's collection of outdated Esso maps or his latest woodworking project—a formless bundle of two-by-fours leaning in a corner of the bathroom.

It was a Saturday he was coming. Saturday morning she got up early, not that she had any choice: Joshua woke her. She took him out to the kitchen and fed him, balancing his warm, damp weight in her lap. He waved his fists and pedaled with his feet as soon as he saw his cereal. His four lower teeth, as crisp as grains of rice, clicked against the spoon. He was a beautiful baby—dark and creamy-skinned, like Gina, but easier than she had been. Leon had never met him.

Gina came in, wearing her new white shorts and a Camp Hopalong T-shirt. "How come you're up so early?" Emily asked her.

"Brindle's snoring."

"Don't you want to save your new clothes till later in the day? You'll get them dirty before Daddy sees them."

"He said he was starting out at crack of dawn."

"Oh."

Emily looked at the kitchen clock. She wiped Joshua's mouth with a corner of his bib, scooped him up, and carried him off to his bath.

When she brought him back to the bedroom, dripping wet, Morgan was standing in front of a bureau threading a belt through his jeans. He was humming a polka. Then he stopped. Emily looked up from toweling the baby and found Morgan watching her in the mirror, his eyes darkened and sobered by a black felt cowboy hat. "What's wrong?" she asked him.

"Should I go?"

"Go where?"

"When he comes, I mean. Do you want me to leave you two alone?"

"No. Please. I need you to stay," she said.

Morgan saw Bonny all the time. Any dull moment Bonny

had, it seemed, she would come unload something new on them—some belonging of Brindle's or Louisa's, some piece of furniture she'd suddenly decided was really more Morgan's than hers. But Emily hadn't seen Leon since the day he moved out. Even at Christmas she'd just put Gina on a Greyhound bus.

Morgan came over to stand opposite her. Lately, he had started wearing rimless, octagonal spectacles—real ones, not mere window glass. They gave him an expression of kindness and patience. He said, "I'll do whatever you want, Emily."

"I have to have you here. I can't go through it without you."

"All right."

His calm unnerved her.

"Not that this means anything to me," she said. "His coming: I don't care."

"No."

"It couldn't matter less."

"I understand."

He went back to the bureau and slipped his cigarettes into his pocket. On the bed Joshua flapped his arms and suddenly crowed.

Louisa and Brindle were having breakfast in the kitchen while Emily did the dishes. Louisa chewed her toast in a mincing way. Brindle sat with her chin in her fist and stirred her coffee aimlessly. "Last night I dreamed of Horace," she told Emily. Horace was her first husband. "He said, 'Brindle, what'd you do with my socks?' I felt terrible. It seems I'd thrown them out. I said, 'Oh, why, Horace, they're right where they belong. Just use your eyes,' I said. Then, while he was looking again, I went running to the garbage cans and dug through everything, hunting."

"I dreamed of chili," Louisa said. "My, Morgan used to love chili. He was one of those boys that, you know, likes to hang over pots in the kitchen. Always took an interest in what I cooked. Many's the time he asked me exactly what I'd put in something. 'Why do you brown the onions first?' Or, 'Which

is better in spaghetti—tomato sauce or tomato paste?'
'Neither one,' I'd tell him, 'you cook down your own to-
matoes, from scratch.' Well, that's another story. Chili is what
he loved best. But nowadays, I don't know, I make this extra-
special effort to talk about food with him the way he used
to enjoy so much and it seems he doesn't take the same interest. Hardly bothers to answer. Hardly even listens, it sometimes seems to me. But of course I may be wrong."

The doorbell rang. Emily turned from the sink and looked
at Brindle.

"Who could that be?" Brindle asked her.

"I don't know."

"Maybe it's Leon."

"But this is so early," Emily said.

"Well, for heaven's sake, go see. You always act so
wooden," Brindle said.

Emily wiped her hands and went to the door. Leon stood
there in a new gray suit. He looked more polished than she'd
remembered—his hair cut very close to his head, his skin
dark and sleek—and he'd grown an oversized, droopy mustache. Emily had seen so many of those mustaches, exactly
the same shape, on young men with briefcases, lawyers,
executives. She could almost believe it was a borrowed mustache, pasted on. "Leon?" she said.

"Hello, Emily."

She took a step back. (She hadn't had time to get into her
shoes yet.)

"Is Gina ready?" he asked her.

"Yes, I think so."

Then Morgan appeared, swinging Joshua in the air, saying,
"Ups-a-daisy . . ." He stopped and said, "Why, Leon."

"Hello, Morgan."

"Won't you come in?"

"I can't stay," Leon said, but he stepped inside. Emily shut
the door behind him. After a moment's hesitation, Leon followed Morgan down the hall to the living room.

Emily wished Morgan would take his spectacles off. Wearing them, he looked humble and domesticated. He held the baby slung over his shoulder and padded around the room, arranging seats. "Here, I'll just move these, find someplace for this knitting . . . Well, ah, shall I call Gina?"

"If you will, please."

Morgan gave Emily a look she couldn't read and left, still carrying Josh.

"So!" Leon said.

"How are you, Leon?" Emily asked him.

"I'm fine."

"You look well."

"You do too."

There was a pause.

"You know I'm taking courses at the college," Leon said.

"Oh, really?"

"Yes, when I get my degree, I'm enrolling in this training program at Dad's bank. It's interesting work, when you see it up close. You'd think it would be dull, but it's really very interesting."

"That's nice," Emily said.

"So I'd like to keep Gina year-round."

"You *what?*"

"Now, Emily, don't be hasty. Think this over. I've got a good apartment, stable life, schools nearby. I promise she could visit you any time she liked; I swear it. Emily, you have your son now. You have another child."

"Gina stays with me," Emily said. Her teeth were chattering.

"What kind of set-up is this for her?"

"It's a fine set-up."

Louisa appeared in the door, navigating the floorboards as if they lay under a foot of water. She made her way to Leon and said, "You're sitting in my chair."

"Oh, sorry," Leon said.

He stood up. Emily said, "Um, do you remember Leon, Mother Gower?"

"Yes, perfectly," she said.

Leon moved to the sofa next to Emily. He smelled of after-shave—not his own smell at all. Louisa arranged herself in her rocker and spread her skirt all around her.

Then Brindle entered with a large, cracked mug of coffee. She sat on the end of the sofa nearest Leon. "So what have *you* been up to?" she asked him.

"I'm planning to enroll in this training program at the bank."

"Oh, yes. Training program. Well, things have been in a fine pickle here, I can tell you."

"Brindle—" Emily said.

But Louisa suddenly interrupted. "And where's your pretty wife?" she asked Leon.

"Excuse me?"

"Where's that girl that used to bring me fruitcake?"

Leon looked at Emily.

"I'll go check on Gina," Emily said.

Even the flow of her skirt, as she walked out, seemed strained.

She found Gina and Morgan standing together among the unmade beds, fiddling with Gina's camp flashlight. "Naturally it doesn't work," Morgan was saying. He tipped the batteries into the palm of his hand. "You've filled it wrong."

"How could I have filled it wrong? I used what they said to use, D size."

"Yes, but the poles are not reversed, Gina."

"What poles?"

"You know that batteries are polarized," he said.

Gina said, "No . . . but I have to leave now, Morgan." She was jittery and restless, twisting a piece of hair, glancing toward the hall. Joshua had worked his way to a bureau and was tugging a satin strap from a drawer. Morgan noticed none of this. He was busy with the flashlight.

"Observe," he said, holding up a battery. "A plus sign on the positive end. A minus sign on the negative end."

Emily felt wrenched by his elderly, instructive tone of voice. She came over to him and kissed his cheek. "Never mind that," she told him. "We're making Leon wait. Gina, run say hello to Daddy. We'll fix your flashlight."

Gina left—released, like something snapped from a rubber band. Morgan shook his head and dropped the batteries in place. "Eleven years old and doesn't know batteries are polarized," he said. "How will she manage in the modern world?"

"Morgan," she said, just above a whisper. "Leon wants to keep her."

"Keep her? Hand me that cap, please."

"You don't think he can make us give her up or anything, do you? In some court of law?"

"Nonsense," Morgan said, screwing the flashlight shut.

"Morgan, I don't understand how he and I switched sides here," Emily said. "He used to claim I tied him down. Now all at once he's going to work in a bank, and I lead an unstable life, he says."

"How can you have a more stable life than ours?" Morgan asked her. He dropped the flashlight into Gina's trunk, closed the lid, and snapped the locks down.

But in the living room it seemed that everyone was conspiring to seem as unstable as possible. Gina was sitting on Leon's knee, which she had not done in years. She looked awkward and precarious. Louisa was knitting her eternal scarf. The dog was asking to go out: he paced up and down in front of Leon, his toenails clicking on the floor. And Brindle had somehow worked around to her favorite subject: Horace. "I never thought we had much in common because he was a gardening man, always messing in his garden. He owned the rowhouse next to ours when I was just a girl. We only had a little puddle of a yard, but he had a corner lot, with roses and azaleas out back and some of those tiny fruit trees that you flatten to a wall—tortured, I always said. I never liked that kind of tree. And a real little fountain with a statue of a goddess. Well, not real, exactly; just plaster or something, but still. He came out every morning and watered his flowers, pruned his shrubs if the merest sprig was out of place. I laughed at him for that. Then he brought me fresh-picked roses with the dew and the aphids still on them and I would say, 'Oh, thanks,' hardly caring, but if he didn't come I started noticing. What doesn't leave an empty space, if you're used to it and it goes? I think he was lonesome. He said I put him in mind of his plaster goddess, but that just made me laugh more. One of her bosoms was hanging out and she didn't have a nipple. And he was an *old* fellow, really, or seemed old then, these knotted white legs in gardening shorts . . . but when he came calling he wore trousers, and a white shirt with one of those collars that spread wide, like wings. Oh, I sincerely miss him still," she said, "and I suppose I always will. Now it's me that's bringing roses, when I go to visit his grave."

"Everything's packed," Emily told Leon.

"Good."

He set Gina aside and stood up.

"What's funniest," said Brindle, rising also, "is I'm older now than Horace was when he started courting me. Can you believe it?"

Leon gave Emily a long, stern look. It was plain what he was saying: Call this a fit life for a child? As if she understood, Louisa lifted her chin and fixed him with a glare.

"Usually," she told him, "I would be in a much more elegant place, I want you to know."

Then Brindle wheeled on her and said, "Oh, Mother, hush. Wouldn't every one of us? Be quiet."

Still Emily wouldn't answer what Leon was asking her.

Leon and Morgan together carried the trunk through the hall. Harry led the way, in a joyful rush, and Gina followed with her sleeping bag. Emily had Joshua astride her hip. Already, so soon after his bath, he had a used look. Emily pressed her cheek to him and drew in his smell of milk and urine and baby powder. She trailed the others down the stairs.

"I brought my father's Buick because I knew we'd need the luggage space," Leon was telling Morgan. "But maybe still

I'll have to get a rope from somewhere. I'm not so sure the lid will close."

"You want to keep a rope in your car at all times," Morgan said. "Or better yet, one of those nylon-coated cords with hooks at either end. Simply go to any discount camping store, you see . . ."

Leon set down his end of the trunk and rummaged through his pockets for the keys. The sun gave his hair a hard blue shine, like bits of coal. Emily studied him from the doorway. The odd thing was that although she no longer loved him, she had the feeling this was only another step in their marriage: his opening his father's Buick, Morgan helping him load the trunk in, Gina tossing her sleeping bag alongside. They were linked, in some ways, forever. He turned back to her and held out a hand. It was probably the first time in her life that she had shaken hands with him.

"Emily," he said, "think about my suggestion."

"I can't," she said. She lifted the baby's weight. Barefoot, with one hip slung out, she felt countrified and disadvantaged.

"Just think about it. Promise."

Instead of answering, she went over to the car and bent to kiss Gina through the window. "Honey, be careful," she said. "Have a good time. Call me if you're homesick; please call."

"I will."

"Come back," she said.

"I *will*, Mama."

Emily stepped away from the car, and stood in the crook of Morgan's arm, smiling hard and holding Josh very close.

6   "I've decided to become a writer," Bonny said. "I've always had a bent in that direction. I'm writing a short story composed entirely of thirty years' worth of check stubs and budget-book entries."

"What kind of story would that make?" Emily wondered.

She sat down in the nearest kitchen chair, holding the receiver to her ear.

"You'd be surprised at how a plot emerges. I mean, checks to the diaper service, then to the nursery schools, then to the grade schools . . . but it's sad to see things were so cheap once. It seems pathetic that I spent ten dollars and sixteen cents on groceries for the second week of August nineteen fifty-one. Did Morgan see my personal?"

"What personal?" Emily asked.

(Of course he'd seen it.)

"My personal in the classified section. Don't tell me he doesn't read the papers any more."

"Oh, did you put a personal in?"

"It said, MORGAN G.: *All is known*. Didn't he see it?"

"Morgan can't be bothered reading every notice in the paper."

"I thought that would really get him," Bonny said. "How he would hate for all to be known!"

She was right. He'd hated it. He'd said, 'What does this mean? Of course I realize it must be Bonny's doing, but . . . do you think it might be someone else? No, of course it's Bonny. What does she mean, all is known? *What's* known? What is she talking about?"

"He likes to think he's going through life as a stranger," Bonny said.

Emily said, "I believe I hear the baby crying."

"Sometimes," Bonny said, "I wonder if there's even any point in blaming him. It's the way he *is*, right? It's in his genes, or . . . None of his family has ever seemed quite normal to me. I didn't know his father, of course, but what kind of man must he have been? Killing himself for no good reason. And his grandfather . . . and his great-great-uncle! Has he told you the story of his great-great-uncle? Uncle Owen, the black sheep. What would it take to be the black sheep of that family? You wonder. No one ever says, if they know. This was when the family was still in Wales. Uncle Owen was such an embarrassment, they sent him off to America. Sort of a . . . remittance man, is that what they call them?"

"I'd better hang up," Emily said.

"When they sailed into New York Harbor, Uncle Owen was so excited he started dancing all over the deck," Bonny said. "The sight of the Statue of Liberty drove him wild. He started jumping up and down too close to the railing. Then he fell overboard and drowned." She started laughing. "Do you believe it? This is a documented fact! It really happened!"

"Bonny, I have to go now."

"Drowned!" said Bonny. "What a man!" And she went on laughing and laughing, no doubt shaking her head and wiping her eyes, for as long as Emily stood listening.

7 One night in August the doorbell rang with a stutter—two quick burrs before it fell silent. Morgan had gone out shopping. Emily thought he might be the one at the door, maybe too burdened to manage his key. But when she answered, she found a young, pale, fat boy, sweating heavily, teetering on dainty feet and holding a bouquet of red carnations. He said, "Mrs. Meredith?"

"Yes."

"Will the dog bite?"

She didn't want to say he wouldn't, though it should have been obvious. Harry sat beside her, no more interested than was polite, slapping his tail against the floor with a rubbery sound.

"Well, fella. Down, fella," the boy said, advancing. Emily stepped back. "You don't know me," he told her. "My name is Durwood Linthicum from Tindell, Maryland."

The shine on his forehead gave him a desperate, determined look. She thought he couldn't be more than eighteen. She wondered if the flowers were for her. But then he said, "I brought these to give your husband."

"My husband?"

"Mr. Meredith," he said, pressing farther inward. She took another step back and bumped into a china barrel. "My father was Reverend R. Jonas Linthicum," he said. "He's passed now. Passed in June."

"Oh, I'm sorry to hear that," she said. "Mr. Linthicum, my husband isn't here just now—"

"I see the name don't strike a chord," he said.

"Um . . ."

"Never mind, your husband will know it."

"Well, but, um . . ."

"My father and Mr. Meredith used to correspond. Or at least, my father corresponded. My father ran the Holy Word Entertainment Troupe."

"Oh, yes," Emily said.

"You've heard of it."

"I remember your father wanted us to come . . . give Bible shows, wasn't it?"

"Now you got it."

"Well, you see, Mr. Linthicum—"

"Durwood."

"See, Durwood . . ."

Behind him, the door opened wider and Morgan stepped in, carrying a twenty-five-pound keg of powdered skim milk with a water stain at one edge. "Mr. Meredith!" said Durwood. "These are for you."

"Eh?" said Morgan. He set down the keg and took the carnations. He was wearing his tropical outfit—white Panama hat and white suit. Next to all that white, the carnations were startling, too bright to be real, like a liquor ad in an expensive magazine. Morgan buried his beard in them and took a long, thoughtful sniff.

"I been wanting to meet you since I was thirteen, fourteen years of age," Durwood said. "Any time we came near Baltimore, I begged and pestered my father to let me see one of your shows. Durwood Linthicum," he said, producing the name with a flair. He held out a large, soft hand. Emerald and ruby (or colored glass) rings were embedded in his fingers. "I know *you* know me, all those letters you received."

"Ah. Linthicum," said Morgan. He shook the hand, looking past Durwood to Emily.

"Holy Word Entertainment Troupe," Emily said.

"*Oh*, yes."

"Not to speak ill of the dead," said Durwood, "but my father didn't always have such very good business sense. Like, he saw one of your shows and thought right much of it, saw those articles about you in the papers, but all he thought was, 'That fellow could put on some fine, fine Bible stories. Daniel in the lions' den and Ruth and Naomi.' Right? Why, *I* knew that you would say no! You do other things besides, you do 'Red Riding Hood' and 'Beauty and the Beast.' *I'm* aware of that!"

Morgan stroked his beard.

"Could we maybe take a seat?" Durwood asked. "I got something to lay out before you."

"Why, surely," said Morgan.

He went down the hall to the living room, and Durwood followed. Emily came last, unwillingly. Some moment had slipped past her, here. She'd intended to clear all this up, but now it seemed too late.

In the living room Louisa was rocking and knitting. She glanced at Durwood and cast her yarn busily over her needle. "Mother," Morgan said, "this is Durwood Linthicum."

"It's a pleasure," said Durwood. He sat down on the couch and leaned toward her, lacing his fingers in front of him. "Ma'am, I guess you know what kind of son you got here."

Louisa looked over at Morgan, her shaggy black eyebrows like two sharp roofs.

"I been telling my father for years," Durwood said. " 'Daddy, you take that fellow however you can obtain him. We want to branch out, anyhow; nobody cares for this Bible stuff these days. With all our connections—schools, clubs, churches—we got a sure thing!' I said. 'We got everything we need!' There's this other group I like too—the Glass

Accordion. I'm just crazy for their music. But he said no, we're only booking gospel music here. Wouldn't give them the time of day. Wouldn't even come hear them. Well, that's another story. I plan to pay them a visit right after I leave you folks. But it's you I feel this special interest in. Mr. Meredith, sir, you are near about my idol! I been following all the news of you. I think you're wonderful!"

"Why, thank you," said Morgan, smelling his carnations.

"Only, it's funny: you don't much look like your photos."

"I grew a beard, you see."

"Yes, a beard will do it, I guess." Durwood looked over at Emily. He said, "But I hope it don't mean you've . . . gone hippie, or some such."

"No, no," Morgan said.

"Well, good! Well, good! Because, now, maybe me and my father didn't always see eye to eye on every little thing, but, you know, I still want a Christian outfit, still want a fine, upstanding group we wouldn't be ashamed to take to a school auditorium . . ." He trailed off, suddenly frowning. He said, "I surely hope those Glass Accordion folks are not on drugs. Do you think?"

"Oh, no, no, I shouldn't imagine they are," Morgan said soothingly.

"You're going to like it in Tindell, Mr. Meredith."

"Tindell?"

"Well, you wouldn't want to keep on living in Baltimore, would you? We got connections all over the state of Maryland, and clear through southern Pennsylvania."

Louisa said, "I've been to Tindell."

"Well, there now!" said Durwood.

"Hated the place."

"Hated *Tindell?*"

"Didn't seem truly populated."

"Well, I don't know how you can say that."

"Empty as a graveyard. Stores all closed."

"You must have gone on a Sunday."

"It *was* a Sunday," she said. "Sunday, March sixth, nineteen twenty-one. Morgan had not been born yet."

"Who's Morgan?"

"Him," she said, jabbing her chin at Morgan.

"It's a family nickname," Morgan said. "A sign of affection. Emily, could you show Mother off to bed now?"

"Bed?" said his mother. "It's not even nine o'clock yet."

"Well, you've had a hard day. Emily?"

Emily rose and went over to his mother. She set a hand under her wiry arm and helped her gently to her feet. "What's got into him?" Louisa said. "Don't forget my knitting, Emily."

"I have it."

She led the old woman down the hall and into her room. Brindle was already there, writing in her diary. She looked up and said, "Bedtime already?"

"Morgan has a guest."

Louisa said, "I wish we were back at Bonny's house. A person had breathing room at Bonny's house. Here I'm shunted around like an extra piece of furniture."

"I'm sorry, Mother Gower," Emily said. She went to the closet for Louisa's nightgown, which hung on a hook. Brindle's and Louisa's silky dresses packed the rod. At the far end were Gina's things: two school jumpers, two white blouses, and a blue quilted bathrobe. It made Emily sad to see them. She removed the nightgown from its hook and closed the door. "Can you help her with her buttons?" she asked Brindle. "I'd better get back to the living room."

But when she left, she didn't go to the living room after all. She stood in the hall a moment, listening to Durwood's breathy voice—Mr. Meredith this, Mr. Meredith that. "Used to be I didn't even *like* a puppet show, never liked that Punch-and-Judy stuff, but your puppets, Mr. Meredith, they're another matter altogether."

She crossed the hall and went into her own room. First she closed the door partway, so that only a thin crack of light showed, and then she changed into her nightgown and slipped between the sheets. Across from her, Joshua stirred in his crib and gave a snuffling sigh. The window was open and she heard all the sounds of summer—a police siren, someone whistling "Clementine," music from a passing radio. Durwood said, "Think how it'd free you! Think on it, Mr. Meredith. We do the booking; we do the billing, let you attend to more essential things. Why, we even got Master Charge. Got BankAmericard. Got NAC, I tell you."

There was something about a sound heard from a lying-down position: it was smaller, but clearer. She even heard Morgan's match strike when he lit a cigarette. She smelled his sharp smoke. She was reminded of houses she had visited as a child—the rough, ragged smoke of hand-rolled cigarettes and the smells of fried fatback and kerosene in the Shufords' and Biddixes' kitchens, where she had been ill at ease, an outsider. Shrinking inwardly, as her family would have expected her to, she had waited barely within the door for some schoolmate to snatch up a spelling book and a couple of cold biscuits for lunch. But she had longed, all those years, to step farther into those kitchens and to have them open up to her. She smiled now, in the dark, and fell asleep listening to Morgan's rumbling answers.

Then the apartment was suddenly still and Morgan was in the bedroom. He stood in the light from the hall, gazing into the mirror above one bureau. His Panama hat was still on his head. He took off his glasses and rubbed the bridge of his nose. He emptied his pockets of change, a crackling pack of Camels, and something that rolled a short distance and fell to the floor. He stooped for it, grunting. She said, "Morgan?"

"Yes, sweetie."

"Has he gone?"

"Yes."

"All this 'Mr. Meredith' business," she said. "Why didn't you tell him?"

"Oh, well, if it makes him happy . . ."

He came to sit on the edge of the bed. He bent over to kiss her (still in his hat, which seemed about to topple onto her), but just then, slow, unsteady footsteps started across the hall. He straightened up. There was a tiny knock.

In the lighted doorway Louisa stood silhouetted. Her long white nightgown outlined two stick legs. "Morgan?" she said.

"Yes, Mother."

"I fear I may have trouble sleeping."

"Jesus, Mother, you've barely got to bed yet."

"Morgan, what was the name of the man we used to see so much of?"

"What man, Mother?"

"He was always around. He lived in our house. Morgan, what was his name?"

"Mother! Christ! Go to bed! Get out of here!"

"Oh, excuse me," she said.

She wandered away again. They heard her in the living room—first in one part, then in another, as if she were walking without purpose. The springs in the sofa creaked, directly behind their heads.

"You shouldn't be so rude to her," Emily told Morgan.

"No," he said. He sighed.

"Shouting like that! What's wrong with you?"

"I can't help it. She never sleeps. She's down to three hours a night."

"But that's the way old people *are*, Morgan."

"We don't have any chance to be alone," he said. "Mother, Brindle, the baby . . . it's like a transplant. I transplanted all the mess from home. It's like some crazy practical joke. Isn't it? Why, I even have a teenaged daughter again! Or near teenaged; nowadays they're adolescents earlier, it seems to me . . ."

"I don't mind it," Emily said. "I kind of enjoy it."

"That's easy for you to say," he told her. "It's not your

problem, really. You stay unencumbered no matter what, like those people who can eat and eat and not gain weight. You're still in your same wrap skirt. Same leotard."

Little did he know now many replacement leotards she had had to buy over the years. Evidently, he imagined they lasted forever. She smoothed his hair off his forehead. "You'll feel better when we move," she told him. "Naturally it's difficult, six people in two bedrooms."

"Ah! And what will we use for money, for this move?"

"I'll find some other places to sell my puppets. I don't think Mrs. Apple pays me enough. And I'll start making more of them. And Brindle—why can't Brindle work?"

"What doing? Pumping gas?"

"There must be something."

"Emily, hasn't it occurred to you that Brindle's not all that well balanced?"

"Oh, I wouldn't say—"

"We're living in a house of lunatics."

She was silent. It was as if he'd twisted some screw on a telescope.

"Anyway," he said, more gently, "she has to help out with Mother. She may be a total loss other ways, but at least she saves you some of that—Mother's little mental lapses and her meals and pills."

He nudged her over on the bed and lay down next to her, fully dressed, with his head propped against the wall. "What we want to do," he said, "is desert."

"Do what?"

"Just ditch them all," he said, "and go. We want a place that's smaller, not bigger."

"Oh, Morgan, talk sense," she said.

"Sweetheart, you know that Gina would be bettter off with Leon."

She sat up sharply. "That's not true!" she said.

"What kind of life is this for her? Strange ladies in her bedroom . . . You mark my words. After that luxury camp, after she's visited Leon a couple of days and gone out sailing with Grandpa Meredith and shopping for clothes with Grandma, she's going to call and ask to stay. You want to bet? She's at that age now; she disapproves of irregularity. She'll like Leon's apartment swimming pool and tennis courts and whatever else. He may even have a sauna bath! Ever thought of that?"

"I can't do without Gina, Morgan."

"And the others," he said. "Mother and Brindle. You think Bonny wouldn't take them back? If we walked out of here and left them, Brindle would be on the phone to Bonny before we hit the pavement. 'Bonny, dear, they've left us!' " Morgan said in a high, gleeful voice. " 'Goody, now we can get back to color TV and civilization!' And Bonny would say, 'Oh, God, I suppose it's up to me now,' and here she'd come, rolling her eyes and clucking, but secretly, you know that she'd be pleased. She likes a lot of tumult. A lot of feathers flying in her nest. I'd ask her for a divorce again and this time she'd agree to it. No, I can't do that, I don't want her knowing where we are. I don't want her driving after us with hats and dogs and relatives. I'll bring one suit, one hat, and you and Josh. We'll just clear out—pull up our tent and go."

"Yes? Where to?" Emily asked. She was lying flat again, with her eyes closed. There was no point taking him seriously.

"Tindell, Maryland," he told her. "Join up with that fellow Durwood."

"It was Leon he was asking for."

"*I* am Leon, for all he knows."

"Oh, Morgan, really."

He was silent. He seemed to be thinking. Finally he said, "Isn't it funny? I've never changed my name. The most I've done is reverse it. My name has been the one last thing I've hung on to."

She opened her eyes. She said, "I mean this, Morgan. I do not intend to leave Gina."

"Oh, all right, all right."

"I absolutely mean that."

"I was only talking," he said.

Then he rose and went to the closet, and she heard his Panama hat settle among the other hats with a dim, soft, whiskery sound.

8   "It's all very easy for you," Bonny said, "because Morgan's in a position of certainty by now. You know what I mean? He's . . . solidified. You inherited him when he was old and certain. You have never got lost in a car together and yelled at each other over a map; he will always seem in charge, to you."

Emily stood in pitch dark, lifting first one foot and then the other from the cool, slick kitchen floor. She said, "Bonny, why do you keep calling?"

"Hmm?"

"This is just not natural. Why are we always on the phone this way?"

Bonny let out a whoosh of smoke. She said, "Well, I'm worried about his eyes."

"His eyes?"

"I'm reading this book. This book by some Japanese expert. Everything's in the eyes, it says. If you can see a rim of white below someone's iris, you can be sure that person's in trouble. Physically, emotionally . . . and you know Morgan's eyes. That's not just a *rim* of white, it's an ocean! His lower lids sag like hammocks. I don't think he's eating right. He needs more vegetables."

"I feed him plenty of vegetables."

"You know he has a sweet tooth. And he drinks so much coffee, chock-full of sugar. Deadly! Refined white sugar, processed sugar. It's a wonder he's lasted as long as he has. Oh, Emily! He should be eating alfalfa sprouts and fresh strawberries, organically grown."

"There's nothing wrong with Morgan's diet."

"He should cut down on red meats and saturated fats!"

"I have to hang up now, Bonny."

"If he were properly fed," said Bonny, "don't you think he'd act different? I mean, basically he's a good man, Emily. Basically he's warm-hearted and open. Openness is his problem, in fact. Oh, Emily, if I had him back, don't you think I would feed him better now?"

9 Emily felt her way down the dark hall, stubbing her toe against the wicker elephant. She arrived in the bedroom and found Morgan wide awake, propped against the wall, silently smoking a cigarette. He didn't say anything. She got into bed beside him, smoothed her pillow, and lay down. The telephone rang in the kitchen.

"Don't answer," Morgan said.

"What if it's someone else?"

"It's not."

"What if it's Gina? An emergency?"

"It won't be. Let it ring."

"You can't say that for sure."

"I'm almost sure."

At this hour, in this mood, "almost" seemed good enough. She took the chance. She didn't get up. There was something restful about simply giving in, finally—abdicating, allowing someone else to lead her. The phone rang on and on, first insistent, then resigned, faint and forlorn, rhyming with itself, like the chorus of a song.

1979

1 He was standing in Larrabee's Drugstore, waiting for his change. He'd bought a pack of Camels, a box of cough-drops, and a *Tindell Weekly Gazette*. The saleslady rang up his purchases, but then fell into conversation with another customer. It surely was cold, she agreed. It was much too cold to be March. Her cat wouldn't leave the stove and her dog was having to wear his little red plaid coat. She kept Morgan's change in her cupped hand, jingling it absently. Morgan stood waiting—an anonymous, bearded, bespectacled man of no interest to her. Finally he gave up and opened out his paper. He liked the *Gazette* very much, although it didn't carry Ann Landers. He scanned the personals. *I will not be responsible, I will not be responsible . . .*

In the Lost and Found he learned that someone had lost a rubber plant. The things that some people mislaid! The carelessness of their lives! A complete set of Revereware cooking pots had been found in the middle of North Deale Road. A charm bracelet in the high-school parking lot.

Now for the obituaries. Mary Lucas, Long-Time Tindell Resident. Also Pearl Joe Pascal, and Morgan Gower, and . . .

MORGAN GOWER, HARDWARE STORE MANAGER

Morgan Gower, 53, who maintained a home at the Tindell Acres Trailer Park, died yesterday after a lengthy illness.

Mr. Gower had served as manager of the downtown branch of Cullen Hardware, in Baltimore.

He is survived by . . .

He raised his head and looked around him. The drugstore was of old, dark wood, its shelves sparsely stocked. In some spots there was only one of an item—one box of Sweet 'n Low packets, its corners dented; one tube of Prell shampoo with a sticky green cap. It was definitely a real place. It smelled of damp cardboard. The saleslady was ancient, her skin so wrinkled that it seemed quilted, and her glasses hung on a chain around her neck.

. . . is survived by his wife, the former Bonny Jean Cullen; seven daughters, Amy G. Murphy, of Baltimore; Jean G. Hanley, also of Baltimore; Susan Gower, of Charlottesville, Virginia . . .

"Sir," the saleslady said, holding out his change.

He closed the newspaper and pocketed the money.

Outside, a cold, damp wind hit him. It was Sunday morning. The streets were empty and the sidewalks seemed wider and whiter than usual. All the other stores were closed—the little dimestore, the grocery store, the barbershop. He walked past them slowly. His pickup was parked in front of the

Hollywood Stars Beautician. The red plywood box constructed over its truckbed (MEREDITH PUPPET CO. arching across each side) creaked in the wind. Morgan climbed into the cab. He opened his pack of cigarettes and lit one. Coughing his habitual, hacking cough, he spread out the paper again.

> . . . Carol G. Haines, also of Charlottesville; Elizabeth G. Wing, of Nashville, Tennessee . . .

He set it down and started the engine.

Fool paper; fool backwoods editors. Even they, you'd think would have the common sense, the decency, to check a thing like that before they printed it. Where were their standards? You call that journalism?

He drove up Main Street, puffing rapidly on his cigarette. At Main and Howell the traffic light was red. He braked, and glanced sideways at the paper.

> . . . Molly G. Abbott, of Buffalo, New York; Kathleen G. Brustein, of Chicago . . .

Someone behind him honked, and he started off again. He veered from Howell into an alley, a moonscape of bleached, stubbled clay with a few empty beer bottles tossed in the weeds, and from there to the state highway. Up ahead lay the trailer park. A flaking metal sign spelled out TINDELL ACRES MONTHLY RATES J. PROUTT PROPRIETOR. He turned left on the gravel road and passed the office—a streamlined aluminum trailer whose cinderblock steps and flowerboxes attempted to give it a rooted look. *Also his mother, Louisa Brindle Gower,* a persistent voice continued in his mind; *a sister, Brindle G. T. Roberts, and eleven grandchildren.* Behind the office, a dozen smaller trailers sat at haphazard angles to one another. They might have been tossed there by a fractious child, along with the items of scrap all around them—discarded butane tanks, a rust-stained mattress, a collapsed sofa with a sapling growing up between two of its cushions. Morgan drove past an old woman in a man's tweed overcoat. He parked in front of a small green trailer and got out. The woman turned to look after him, brushing wisps of gray hair from her eyes. It was obvious she planned to start a conversation. Morgan would not admit she was there. He rushed toward the trailer, keeping his head ducked. His mouth felt too large. He had, he observed detachedly, all the physical symptoms of . . . shame; yes, that was it. How peculiar. He felt insufficiently shielded by his cap, which was trim, narrowly visored, of no particular character. He turned up the collar of his jacket before he fumbled at the door.

"Cold enough for you?" the woman called in a thin, carrying voice.

He bowed lower over the lock.

"Yoo-hoo! Mr. Meredith!"

Services will be private.

Emily was cooking breakfast. He smelled bacon, a special Sunday treat. Josh was toddling through the living room in a pair of sodden corduroy overalls with one strap trailing. Morgan scooped him into his arms and Josh chuckled.

"Did you get the paper?" Emily asked.

He set Joshua down again. "No," he said.

He had left it in the truck. He would dispose of it later on.

There was no reason to feel so embarrassed. Bonny was the one who ought to feel embarrassed. (For it was Bonny who had done it, he assumed. Of course it was. Wasn't it?) What a silly reaction to have! He considered himself with a remote, bemused curiosity. Even his posture seemed furtive—the way he walked the length of the trailer with as little noise as possible, stooped, head ducked, as if trying not to disturb the air. He went from the living room (one couch beneath a small, louvered window) through the narrow aisle between a table and the counter that was their kitchen. Sidling past Emily, he kissed the back of her neck. She had a ripple of bones down her nape that reminded him of the scalloped spines of some seashells.

He continued into the bedroom, with its single built-in bureau and bed. A Port-a-Crib took all the remaining space.

To reach the little curtained closet in one corner, he had to clamber across the bed. He took his cap off and set it on the shelf next to Emily's suitcase. He took his jacket off and hung it on a hanger. He had bought the jacket last November at a place called Frugal Fred's. Having left his extra clothes behind when he fled Baltimore, he had found himself with nothing warm enough to get him through the winter, and he'd paid five dollars for this heavy blue jacket that must once have been part of an Air Force uniform, although it was bland and dull now, undecorated. All the insignia seemed to have been removed, leaving empty stitches on the sleeves and across one pocket. He supposed that was some sort of regulation. They wouldn't want anyone impersonating an officer, naturally. Yes, it was only sensible. But sometimes he liked to imagine that the insignia had been *ripped* away. He pictured a scene in a field—the ranks of men standing at attention, the bugle call, the drums, Morgan stepping smartly forward, his commanding officer stripping him of his stripes in a single dramatic gesture. Whenever he thought of this, he walked straighter in his jacket and took on an impassive expression: the look of a man who had willfully, recklessly directed his life on a collision course toward ruin. However, he knew it was a jacket that no one would glance at twice. And his cap was what they called a Greek sailor cap, but not really Greek-looking, not seaworthy-looking; everybody wore them nowadays, even teenaged girls at the local high school, tilting the visors over their jumbles of curls.

He washed his hands in the tiny bathroom and returned to the kitchen. Emily was dishing out breakfast. He sat down at the table and watched her lay two strips of bacon on his plate. "Come eat, Josh," she called.

Josh was running a tin trolley car along the edge of the couch. He brought the trolley to the table with him, swaggering along in his rocking-horse gait, studiously silent. (He was the quietest, most accepting child Morgan had ever known.) In his layers of shirts and sweaters he seemed to be having trouble bending his chunky arms. Emily picked him up and set him in his chair. "What's that?" he asked, pointing to his cup.

"It's orange juice, Josh."

Josh took a bite from a strip of bacon, fed another bite to the front window of his trolley car.

"Did you mail my letter?" Emily asked Morgan, sitting down across from him.

"What letter?"

"My letter to Gina, Morgan."

"Oh, yes," Morgan said. "I took it to that box in front of the Post Office."

"It'll reach Richmond by Tuesday, then," Emily said.

"Well, or Wednesday."

"If she writes me back the same day, I might get a letter on Friday."

"Mm."

"She hardly ever writes the same day, though."

"No."

"I wish she were a better letter-writer."

He said nothing. She looked up at him.

"Is something wrong?" she asked.

"Wrong?"

"You seem different."

"I'm fine," he said.

She went back to buttering her toast. Her hands were white with cold, the nails bluish. The curve of her lashes cast faint shadows on her cheeks. It struck him how unchanged she was. Year after year, while everyone around her grew older, Emily kept her young, pale, unlined face, and her light-colored eyes gave her a look of perpetual innocence. She wore the same clothes. Her hair was the same style, piled in braids on top of her head with a few stray tendrils corkscrewing at her neck to give her a hint of some secret looseness—always possible, never realized—that could stir him still.

Well, he would go to the editors. Of course he would. He'd go storming in with the paper. "See here, what's the meaning of this? Don't you people ever check your facts? *Morgan Gower, Hardware Store Manager!* Where's your sense of responsibility? *I* am Morgan Gower. Here I stand before you."

But they would say, "Aren't you that fellow Meredith? One that works for young Durwood?"

In fact, he had no case.

2 Emily zipped Josh into his jacket for a walk, but Morgan decided not to go with them. "Don't you feel well?" she asked him.

"I'm fine, I tell you."

"Did you pick up those coughdrops?"

"Yes, yes, somewhere here . . ."

He slapped his pockets and beamed at her, intending reassurance. She went on frowning. "Don't forget we have that show tonight," she told him.

"No, I haven't forgotten."

After they left, he watched them through the living-room window—Emily a fragile little thread of a person, Josh in his fat red jacket trudging along beside her. They were heading north, across a field, toward the scrubby pine woods that ran along the highway. The field was so lumpy and rutted that sometimes Joshua stumbled, but Emily had hold of his hand. Morgan could imagine her tight, steady grip—the steely cords in her wrist, like piano wire.

He turned away from the window a fraction of a second before the phone rang, as if he'd been expecting it. Maybe he just wouldn't answer. It was sure to be someone pushing in, someone who'd found him out: "So! I hear you died." But, of course, no one had any way of knowing. He made himself go into the bedroom, where the phone sat on the bureau. It rang six times before he reached it. He lifted the receiver, took a breath, and said, "Hello."

"Is that you, Sam?" a man asked.

"Yes."

"It is?"

"Yes."

"You don't sound like yourself."

"I've got a cold," Morgan said.

Morgan grinned into the mirror.

"Well, I guess you heard what happened to Lady."

Then a strange thing happened. It felt as if the floor just skated a few feet away from him. Not that he lost his balance; he stood as firm as ever, and his head was perfectly clear. But there was some optical illusion. His surroundings appeared to glide past him. He might have been riding one of those conveyor belts that carry passengers into airport terminals. Come to think of it, he had felt this way once before in an airport near Los Angeles. He'd gone to fetch Susan—it must have been four or five years ago; she'd had some kind of crack-up over a broken love affair—and after flying all one day he'd landed but gone on flying, it felt like. Or everything had flown around him, as if he'd been traveling so long, such a distance, that a sudden stop was impossible. He blinked, and reached out for the bureau.

"Sam?" the man asked.

"I'm not Sam. Please. You have the wrong number."

He hung up. He looked around the trailer, and found it stable again.

Then he took his cap and jacket from the closet and put them on, and he wrote a note to Emily: *Gone on an errand. Back soon.* He let himself out the door and crossed the yard to his truck and climbed in.

It was a forty-five-minute drive to Baltimore, and all through it he talked steadily underneath his breath. "Silly damn Bonny," he muttered, "damn meddler; stupid, interfering meddler, thinks she's so—" He glanced in the rearview mirror and swung out to pass a van. "Sitting there rubbing her hands together, laughing at me; thinks she got *to* me somehow. Ha, that's how much she knows, yes . . ."

He wondered how she'd found out what town he lived in. He had never told her. He considered the possibility that she

had put the item in every paper in the state of Maryland—
every paper in the country, even. Lord, all across the con-
tinent, for anyone to see. He pictured her telephoning hundreds and thousands of editors, rushing into their offices,
trailing balls of Kleenex and rough drafts on the backs of
cash-register tapes—a woman with her accelerator stuck. She
had always lived a headlong kind of life. Any mental image
he had of her (he thought, honking at a wandering sports
car) showed her breathless, with her hair in her eyes and her
blouse untucked. Look how she'd thrown his clothes out,
and his mother and his sister and the dog! Cursing to himself, slamming on his brakes, he forgot that she had thrown
them out at different times. He imagined that she'd dumped
them all at once. He seemed to remember Brindle and Louisa,
deposited in front of the hardware store, waiting on little
camp stools till he could collect them. Or, why camp stools,
even? Lying on their backs, like overturned beetles, in an
ocean of discarded costumes. He recalled that Bonny often
seemed to be held together by safety pins. Safety pins connected a slip strap to her slip, a buttonhole to the thready
place where a button should have been, and her watch to its
black ribbon band. And the watch was almost never wound.
And the gaps in her hems were repaired with Scotch tape that
rustled when she walked; no, when she ran; no, when she
galloped by. She had never been known to just walk.

This used to be all farmland, but now each town was
linked to the others by a frayed strand of filling stations and
shopping malls. Morgan sped along. The superstructure on
his truckbed moaned. The padlock on its rear door clanked
whenever he slowed down.

"Thinks she's so clever, thinks I care. Thinks it matters
what fool thing she does to me."

He entered the outskirts of Baltimore. They'd put up more
apartment buildings. You couldn't turn your back, it
seemed. At a traffic light a boy braked beside him in a long,
finned Dodge that must have been twenty years old. All the
windows were closed, but the music on his radio was so loud

that it sailed out anyhow—the "Steadily Depressing, Low-Down, Mind-Messing, Working at the Carwash Blues." In spite of himself, Morgan beat time on the steering wheel.

At least there was a little sun here—a pale, weak, late-winter sun lighting white steeples and empty sidewalks. He drove north on Charles, passing a stream of small shops and then the University, deserted-looking, its buildings clean and precisely placed like something built of toy blocks. He turned into a corridor of large houses, cafés, apartment buildings, and parked on Bonny's street but some distance from her house, so she wouldn't easily see the truck from her windows. Then he got out and lit a cigarette and started waiting.

It was cold, even in the sunlight. He raised his collar around his ears. He saw the newspaper on Bonny's front walk. Ten-something in the morning and she hadn't brought it in yet; typical. A cardinal was sitting in the dogwood tree, a drop of red in a net of black branches. Morgan wondered if it could be one of those who'd hatched in that nest in the mock-orange bush a few years back. He felt some proprietary interest. All one summer he'd chased the cat away; the parent birds would alert him, fluttering and giving their anxious chirps that sounded like the clink of loose change in a pocket. But didn't cardinals migrate? His cigarette tasted like burning trash. He ground it out.

Then here came Billy's wife, Priscilla, tapping up the walk in her spiffy white coat, carrying her basket-shaped purse that was sure to have a whale carved on its lid. She disappeared into the house. (She had to step right over the paper.) She was extraneous, no one he ever gave much thought to; he dismissed her instantly. He leaned forward and watched the door open again. Out popped a boy. His grandson? Todd? If so, he'd grown. He was carrying a yellow skateboard, and when he reached the street he just skated away—here one second, gone the next, for Morgan didn't watch after him. He was centered on that door still.

A long time went by. He leaned against the hood of the truck and listened to the engine ticking as it cooled.

The door first darkened, drawing inward, and then vanished altogether. Bonny stepped out on the stoop. Beneath her matted brown cardigan she wore something peasantish, unbecoming—a gauzy, full blouse, and a gathered skirt that made her look fat. Morgan assumed she was heading for the paper, but she ignored it as the others had and continued down the walk. Morgan slid around behind the truck. She didn't even look in his direction. She turned west, bustling along. He saw something flash in her hand—her red billfold, no doubt overstuffed as always with credit cards, outdated photos, and wrinkled little wads of money.

For a while he followed, keeping well back. He knew where she was going, of course. On a Sunday morning, with Priscilla there, and Todd, and who knew how many other people, she'd be off to the bakery for cinnamon rolls. But he followed anyway, and fixed his eyes on her. She'd let her hair grow, he noticed—a mistake. The puffy little clump at the back of her neck had turned into a sort of oval, with tattered ends.

What was going on in that head?

This was why he'd come: to find out. He'd driven here without wondering what for, and was confronted with it now so abruptly that he stopped short. All he wanted to ask was, why had she *done* it?

Was some meaning implied?

Did she imagine . . . ?

No, surely not.

Did she imagine he really had passed away?

"Passed away" was all he was up to just now. "Died" would stick in his throat. No, he couldn't ask that.

He continued to stand there while Bonny went on racing toward the bakery.

Then he turned and went back to the house. He circled around it. (The front door opened to the center hall, where anyone might see him enter.) He walked to the side, toward the screen porch, reached through a rip in the screen and raised the rusty hook and let himself in. The moldy smell of

the wicker furniture—like mice, like cheap magazines—reminded him of summer. He tried the knob of the glass-paned
door that led to the living room. It was unlocked. (He'd
warned them a thousand times.) Soundlessly, he slipped in.

The room was empty. Last night's Parcheesi game lay
scrambled in front of the cold gray fireplace. A cup was making a ring on the coffee table. He crossed to the hall. From
the kitchen Priscilla called, "Bonny? Back so soon?"

He darted toward the stairs, keeping to carpets, where his
footsteps would be softest. He mounted the stairs so swiftly
that he scared himself—the blurred speed of his climb was
too hushed, too spooky. In the upstairs hall his heel clicked
once on the floorboards by accident. He ducked into the bedroom and clapped a palm to his pounding chest.

No one came.

Her bed was unmade and her nightgown was a spill of
soiled ivory nylon across the rug. All the bureau drawers were
open. So was the closet. He tiptoed to the closet. How unlike
itself it seemed: so much space. You couldn't say it was bare,
exactly (those clothes of hers she never would give up, skirts
with the hemlines altered a dozen different times, Ship 'n Shore
blouses from the fifties with their dinky Peter Pan collars),
but certainly it was emptier than it used to be. The shelf
where he'd kept his hats now held a typewriter case, a hair-
dryer, and a shoebox. He opened the shoebox and found a
pair of shoes, the chunky kind so out of date they were coming back into fashion.

He opened the drawer in her nightstand and found a tube
of hand cream and a book of Emily Dickinson's poems.

He opened the drawer in *his* nightstand (once upon a time)
and found a coupon for instant coffee, a light-up ballpoint
pen, and a tiny leather notebook with *Night Thoughts* written
in gilt across the cover. Aha! But the only night thoughts
she'd had were:

> *Woolite*
> *Roland Park Florist*
> *Todd's birthday?*

Something clamped his wrist—a claw. He dropped the book. "Sir," said Louisa.

"Mother?"

"I've forgotten the number for the police."

"Mother," he said, "I've only come to . . . pick up a few belongings."

"Is it 222–3333? Or 333–2222."

She still had hold of his wrist. He couldn't believe how strong she was. When he tried to squirm away, she tightened her fingers. He could have struggled harder, but he was afraid of hurting her. There was something brittle and crackling about the feel of her. He said, "Mother dear, please let go."

"Don't call *me* Mother, you scruffy-looking, hairy person."

"Oh," he said. "You really don't know me."

"Would I be likely to?" she asked him.

She wore her Sunday black, although she never attended church—a draped and fluted black dress with a cameo at the throat. On her feet were blue terrycloth scuffs from which her curved, opaque toenails emerged—more claws. She encaged his wrist in a ring of bone.

"I said to the lady downstairs," she said, " 'There's burglars on the second floor.' She said, 'It's only those squirrels again.' I told her, 'This time it's burglars.' "

"Look. Ask Brindle if you don't believe me," said Morgan.

"Brindle?" She considered. "Brindle," she said.

"Your daughter. My sister."

"She told me it was squirrels," Louisa said. "At night she asks, 'What's that skittering? What's that scuttling? Is it burglars?' I say, 'It's squirrels.' Now I say, 'Hear that burglar on the second floor?' She says, 'It's only squirrels, Mother. Didn't you always tell me that? They're hiding their acorns in the rafters in the attic.' "

"Oh? You have rodents?" Morgan asked.

"No, squirrels. Or *some*thing up there, snickering around . . ."

"You want to be careful," Morgan told her. "It could very

well be bats. The last thing you need is a rabid bat. What you ought to do, you see, is simply take a piece of screening—"

His mother said, "Morgan?"

"Yes."

"Is that you?"

"Yes," he said.

"Oh, hello, dear," she said serenely. She let go of his wrist, and kissed him.

"It's good to see you, Mother," he said.

Then Bonny said, from the doorway, "Get out."

"Why, Bonny!" said Morgan.

"Out."

She was carrying her sack from the bakery, and gave off the mingled smells of cinnamon and fresh air. Her eyes had darkened alarmingly. Yes, she meant business, all right. He knew the signs. He edged away from his mother. (But there was only one door, and Bonny blocked it.)

"I was just leaving, Bonny," he said. "I only came to ask you something."

"I won't answer," she said. "Now go."

"Bonny—"

"Go, Morgan."

"Bonny, why'd you put that piece in the paper?"

"What piece?"

"That . . . item. What you call . . . obituary."

"Oh," she said. There was a sudden little twist to her mouth that he remembered well—a wry look, something between amusement and regret. "Oh, *that*," she said.

"What made you do it?"

She thought it over.

His mother said, "I'm certain it's not bats, because I hear their little feet."

"To tell the truth," Bonny said, "I'd forgotten all about it. Oh, dear. I really should have canceled it; I meant to all along; it was only one of those impulses that just hit sometimes—"

"I can't figure out how you knew where I lived," Morgan said.

"I called Leon in Richmond and asked," she said. "I guessed you'd tell Leon at least, because of Gina."

"But what was the point, Bonny? An *obituary*, for God's sake."

"Or do bats have feet too?" said his mother.

"It was meant to be an announcement," Bonny said.

"What kind of announcement?"

She colored slightly. She touched the dent at the base of her throat. "Well, I'm seeing someone else now," she said. "Another man."

"Ah," he said.

"A history professor."

"That explains printing my obituary?"

"Yes."

Well, yes.

He took pity on her then—her pink cheeks, and the clumsy, prideful, downward look she wore. "All right," he said. "That's all I had to ask. I'll be going now."

She drew back to let him pass. Already she'd collected herself—lifted and straightened. He stepped into the hall. Then he said, "But, ah, God, Bonny, you don't know how it felt! Really, such an . . . embarrassment, an item like that in a public place, all on account of some whim you get, some half-cocked notion!"

The twist in her mouth returned, and deepened. No doubt she found this hilarious.

"It's probably not even legal," he said.

He started coughing. He searched his pockets for his handkerchief.

"Do you want a Kleenex?" she asked. "What's the matter with you, Morgan? You don't look well."

"I could probably have you arrested," he told her. He found his handkerchief and pressed it to his mouth.

"Let's not talk about what we could arrest each other for," Bonny said.

So he went down the stairs at last, not even saying good-bye to his mother or giving her a final glance. Bonny followed. He heard the rustle of her bakery sack close behind his ear—an irritating sound. An irritating woman. And this banister was sticky to the touch, downright dirty. And you could break your neck on the rug in the entrance hall.

At the door, when his thoughts were flowing toward the pickup truck (get gas, check tires) and the journey home, Bonny suddenly seemed to have all the time in the world. She brushed a piece of hair off her forehead and said, "His name is Arthur Amherst."

"Eh?"

"This man I'm seeing. Arthur Amherst."

"Good, Bonny, good."

"He's very steady and solid."

"I'm glad to hear it," he said, jingling his keys in his pocket.

"You think that means he's dull, I suppose."

"I know it doesn't mean that," he said.

He pulled out his keys then, and turned to leave, but was struck by something and turned back. "Listen," he said. "Those really may be bats, you know."

"What?"

"Those creatures Mother's hearing in the attic."

"Oh, well, they're not harming anybody."

"How can you be sure of that? You ought to do something about it. Don't put it off; they could chew through the wiring."

"*Bats?*" she asked.

"Or whatever," he said.

He hesitated, and then touched his cap in a salute and left.

Now there was church traffic, old men in felt hats driving carloads of tinkly old ladies, sidewalks ringing with the clop of high heels. He traveled downtown in a suspended state of mind, shaking off the annoyances of the morning. He traveled farther and farther, not out of the city but deeper into it. It wouldn't hurt to take a look at Cullen Hardware. There was always the possibility that Butkins would be there, even on a Sunday, maybe sorting stock or just standing idly, dimly, at the window as he sometimes did.

But the hardware store was gone. There was only a blank
space between the rug store and Grimaldi Brothers Realty—
not even a hole, just a vacant lot. Weeds grew on it, even. The
wastepaper crumpled in its hillocks had already begun to
yellow and dissolve. A billboard on the rear of the lot read:
AT THIS LOCATION, NIFF DEVELOPMENT CORP. WILL BE CON-
STRUCTING A . . .

He considered a minute, settled his glasses higher on his
nose, and drove on. But what about Butkins? Where was
Butkins? He turned left. He cut over to Crosswell Street.
Crafts Unlimited was still there, closed for Sunday but thriv-
ing, obviously. The ranks of pottery jars in its window gave
it an archeological look. The third-floor windows above it
were as dark and plain as ever. He half believed that if he
were to climb the stairs, he'd find Emily and Leon Meredith
still leading their pure, vagabond lives, like two children in
a fairytale.

3   "I'm certain I can fit into it," the second stepsister said.
    "It's only that I've been shopping all day and my feet
are a little swollen."

"Madam. Please," the Prince said in his exhausted voice.

"Well, maybe I could cut off my toes."

"What about you, young lady?" asked the Prince. He was
looking at Cinderella, who peeked out from the rear of the
stage. Dressed in burlap, shy and fragile, she inched forward
and approached the Prince. He knelt at her feet with the little
glass slipper, or it may have been a shimmer of cellophane.
All at once her burlap dress was mysteriously cloaked in a
billow of icy blue satin. "Sweetheart!" the Prince cried, and
the children drew their breaths in. They were young enough
still. Their expressions were dazzled and blissful, and even
after the house lights came on they continued sitting in their
chairs and gazing at the stage, open-mouthed.

It was the Emancipation Baptist Church's Building Fund
Weekend. There'd been two puppet shows on Saturday, and

this evening's was the last one. Then Morgan and Emily could pack up their props and leave the church's Sunday School hall, which had the biting, minty smell of kindergarten paste. They could say goodbye, at least temporarily, to the Glass Accordion and the Six Singing Simonsons and Boffo the Magician. Emily set the puppets one by one in their liquor carton. Joshua staggered down the aisle with one of Boffo's great brass rings. Morgan folded the wooden stage, lifted it onto his shoulder with a grunt, and carried it out the side entrance.

It was a pale, misty night. The sidewalk gleamed under the streetlights. Morgan loaded the stage into the back of the pickup and slammed the door shut. Then he stood looking around him, breathing in the soft, damp air. A family passed —cranky children, kept awake past their bedtime, wheedling at their mother's edges. A boy and girl were kissing near a bus stop. On the corner was a mailbox, which reminded Morgan of his letter to Bonny. He'd carried it with him all evening; he might as well get it sent off. He took it from the pocket of his Air Force jacket and started across the street. (. . . *simply strew a handful of mothballs*, the letter whispered, *a. along the attic floor beams; b. in the closets beneath the eaves* . . .)

His boots made a gritty sound that he liked. Cars hissed past him, their headlights haloed. He flattened the envelope, whose corners had started curling. *But if it's bats . . .* he should have said. He'd forgotten to mention bats. *You don't want to close all the openings till you're certain the bats are* . . . and he also should have said, *Remember that Mother's vitamins are tax-deductible*, and *Don't rush into anything with this professor fellow*, and *Just loving him is not all it takes, you know.* He should have added, *I used to think it was enough that I was loving; yes, I used to think, at least I am a sweet and loving man, but now I see that it matters also who you love, and what your reasons are. Oh, Bonny, you can go so wrong . . .*

He stood at the mailbox, shaking his head, stunned. It took

an auto horn to bring him to his senses, and he had the feeling
that this wasn't the first time it had honked. A woman leaned
out of a Chevrolet, her hair a bobbled mass of curlers. "Well?
Will they or won't they?" she asked him.

"I beg your pardon?"

"Will my letters get there by Tuesday, I said, or will they
drag their feet and loiter like the last ones did? You folks are
always saying next-day-delivery-this, next-day-delivery-that;
then it's me that gets stuck with the finance charges when you
drag into BankAmericard with my credit payment two, three,
four days late . . ."

She was waving a pack of letters out the window. Morgan
tipped his visored cap and took them from her. "Absolutely,"
he said. "It was Robinson who was doing all that and now
they've let him go. From here on out, you can trust the U.S.
Mail, ma'am."

"I bet," she said.

She rolled up her window and screeched off.

Morgan dropped Bonny's letter in the slot. Then he went
through what he'd been handed by the woman. Patti Jo's Dress
Shop, LeBolt Appliances . . . he dropped them in too. Clarion
Power and Light. He dropped that in. The rest were personal,
addressed in a lacy, slanted script to a woman in Essex, a
woman in Anneslie, and a married couple in Madison, Wis-
consin. He would mail them too, but first he might just take a
little glance inside. He started walking back toward the
church, coughing dryly, tapping the envelopes against the
palm of his hand. They were crisp and thick, weighted with
secrets. They whispered *spent Monday letting that dress out
some* and *labor pains so bad she like to died* and *least you
could have done is have the decency to tell me.* Up ahead,
Emily stood at the curb beside a cardboard carton. Josh rode
astride her hip. For some reason Morgan felt suddenly
light-hearted. He started walking faster. He started smiling.
By the time he reached Emily, he was humming. Everything
he looked at seemed luminous and beautiful, and rich with
possibilities.

Anne Tyler was born in Minneapolis, Minnesota, in 1941 but grew up in Raleigh, North Carolina, and considers herself a Southerner. She was graduated at nineteen from Duke University, where she twice won the Anne Flexner Award for creative writing, and became a member of Phi Beta Kappa. She has done graduate work in Russian studies at Columbia University and worked for a year as the Russian bibliographer at the Duke University Library. This is Miss Tyler's seventh novel, and her stories have appeared in such magazines as *The New Yorker, The Saturday Evening Post, Redbook, McCall's, Harper's, The Southern Review,* and *Quest.* She is married to a psychiatrist, Taghi Modarressi, and she and her husband now live in Baltimore, Maryland, with their two daughters.

A NOTE ON THE TYPE

The text of this book was set on the Linotype in Janson, a recutting made direct from type cast from matrices long thought to have been made by the Dutchman Anton Janson, who was a practicing type founder in Leipzig during the years 1668–87. However, it has been conclusively demonstrated that these types are actually the work of Nicholas Kis (1650–1702), a Hungarian, who most probably learned his trade from the master Dutch type founder Dirk Voskens. The type is an excellent example of the influential and sturdy Dutch types that prevailed in England up to the time William Caslon developed his own incomparable designs from them.

Composed by Fuller Typesetting
Lancaster, Pennsylvania

Printed and bound by The Haddon Craftsmen, Inc.
Scranton, Pennsylvania

Typography and binding design by
Dorothy Schmiderer